THE DOOM BRIGADE

by Margaret Weis and Tracy Hickman

CHRONICLES

Dragons of Autumn Twilight

Dragons of Winter Night

Dragons of Spring Dawning

LEGENDS

Time of the Twins

War of the Twins

Test of the Twins

THE SECOND GENERATION

DRAGONS OF SUMMER FLAME

by Margaret Weis and Don Perrin

THE DOOM BRIGADE

THE DOOM BRIGADE

by Margaret Weis and Don Perrin

Dedicated proudly to the Canadian Corps
of Land Electrical & Mechanical Engineers

First Printing: October 1996
Printed in the United States of America.
Library of Congress Catalog Card Number: 95-62257

9 8 7 6 5 4 3 2 1

8380XXX1501

ISBN: 0-7869-0526-3

TSR, Inc.
201 Sheridan Springs Rd.
Lake Geneva WI 53147
U.S.A.

TSR Ltd.
120 Church End, Cherry Hinton
Cambridge CB1 3LB
United Kingdom

Chapter One

"Stand to!"

Kang was on his feet, his clawed hands groping through the darkness of his cabin for his armor before he was fully awake or cognizant of what was going on.

"Blasted elves! Damn pointy-ears. Why in the Abyss can't they let a fella get some sleep?"

He found his breastplate, wrestled with it briefly, and finally managed to sling one strap over his scaled arm. The other strap remained elusive, and Kang, cursing it soundly, ignored it. Clasping the breastplate to his chest with his arm, he searched for the door, and stumbled into a chair.

A trumpet sounded the alarm off-key. More shouts came from outside, answered by hoarse yells of defiance. Kang gave the chair a kick that slivered it and once again tried to find the door.

"Foppy elves," he muttered again, but that didn't seem quite right.

A sober part of him, a part of him that had not been drinking dwarf spirits last night—a party-pooping, stern task-master, who generally hovered near Kang's shoulder, watching the other parts of him enjoying themselves with a disapproving glower—nagged at him again.

Something about dwarves. Not elves.

Kang flung open the door to his cabin. The breathlessly hot morning air hit him a good sock in the face. The sky was gray with the dawning rays of the sun, though that light had not yet penetrated to the cabins and huts sheltered beneath the pine trees. Kang blinked, shook his head muzzily, tried to disperse the dwarf spirits fouling his brain. Reaching out, he collared the first draconian who came into sight.

"What the hell's going on?" Kang bellowed. "Is it the Golden General?"

The draconian stared, lost in such amazement that he forgot to salute. "Golden General? Begging your pardon, sir, but we haven't fought the Golden General in twenty-five years! It's them pesky dwarves, sir. On a raiding party. I expect they're after the sheep, sir."

Kang let his breastplate slip down over his chest while he considered this extraordinary news. Dwarves. Sheep. Raiding party. The part of him that knew what was going on was really incensed. If he could only—

"Good morning, sir!" came a damnably cheery voice.

Water, icy water, splashed into Kang's face.

He gave a roar and emerged, scales clicking with the shock, but now relatively sober and aware of what was happening.

"Let me help you with that, sir," said the same cheery voice.

Slith, Kang's second-in-command, had hold of the breastplate and was looping the strap around his commander's arm, buckling it securely beneath Kang's left wing.

"Dwarves again, huh?" Kang said.

Draconians were dashing past, pulling on armor and hoisting weapons and heading to their assigned defense posts around the walled village. A sheep, separated from the herd and bleating in panicked terror, trotted past.

"Yes, sir. They're hitting us from the north."

Kang ran for the northern side of the wall—a wall in which he took inordinate pride. Made of stone that had been blasted by magic from the side of Mount Celebund, the wall had been built by Kang's troops—the former First Dragonarmy Engineering Brigade. The wall

2

surrounded the draconians' village, kept the marauding dwarves out and the sheep in. At least, that's how it was supposed to work.

Somehow or other, the sheep kept disappearing. When that happened, Kang could often smell the savory scent of roast mutton, born on the night breeze, wafting from the direction of the hill dwarf settlement on the opposite side of the valley.

Reaching the wall, Kang clambered up the stairs, his clawed feet scrabbling on the stone, and took his place on the battlements. It was that smudgy time of morning, not dark, not light. Kang spotted the hill dwarves running across the open ground, heading for the north face of the village wall, but it was difficult to count their numbers in the half-light. The lead runners carried ladders and ropes, ready to scale the walls. The draconians manned the walls, swords and clubs drawn, waiting to knock some hill dwarf heads.

"You know my orders!" Kang shouted, drawing his sword. "Flat of the blades only! Make sure any magic you Bozaks use is harmless, just enough to throw a scare into them."

The draconians around Kang all "Yes, sirred," but it seemed to him that their voices were distinctly lacking in enthusiasm. The dwarves had reached the bottom of the wall and were flinging up their grappling hooks and hoisting their ladders. Kang was leaning over the wall, preparing to fend off a ladder, when he was distracted from the coming battle by the sound of a commotion much farther down the wall to his right.

Thinking that this frontal assault might have been meant as a distraction and that the first wave was already over the walls, Kang left Slith in command and dashed in the new direction. He found Gloth, one of his troop commanders, shouting in loud, angry tones.

A draconian was holding a crossbow, aiming it, ready to fire it at the dwarves.

"What in the Dark Queen's name do you think you're doing, soldier?" Gloth was yelling. "Put that bow down! You know the commander's orders."

"I know 'em, but I don't like 'em!" the draconian snarled sullenly, keeping hold of the crossbow.

Kang could have charged in, thrown his weight around, brought the situation under control. He restrained himself, however, waited to see how his troop commander handled the situation.

"You don't like them, sir!" Gloth repeated.

From the north came shouts and howls and yells. The draconians, armed with sticks, were shoving the ladders, filled with dwarves, away from the walls. Gloth eyed the mutinous soldier grimly, and Kang waited tensely for his troop commander to lose control and start bashing heads together. That's what Gloth would have done in the old days.

But the draconian officer was evidently developing subtlety.

"Look, Rorc, you know we can't use crossbows, and you know why we can't use them. Do I have to go over this again?" Gloth raised his hand, pointed. "Now, take that dwarf right there, for instance. Sure, he's an ugly bastard, what with all that hair on his face and that pot-belly and those little stubby legs. But maybe, just maybe, Rorc, that there dwarf is the very dwarf—maybe the only dwarf—who knows the recipe for dwarf spirits. You shoot him, Rorc, and, yes, you send another god-cursed dwarf back to Reorx, but what happens the next time we raid their village? We find a sign on the distillery saying 'Owner deceased. Out of business.' And where does that leave us, Rorc?"

Rorc glowered but did not respond.

"I'll tell you where that leaves us," Gloth continued solemnly. "Thirsty, that's what. So you just put down that bow and pick up your club like a good draco, and I won't say nothing about this breach of orders to the commander."

Rorc hesitated, but finally threw down the crossbow. Picking up his club, he leaned over the wall, prepared to beat off the assault. Gloth grabbed the crossbow and marched off with it. Kang beat a hasty retreat to his command post.

It was a shame he'd have to pretend he hadn't seen any of this. He would have liked to have given Gloth well-deserved praise for his deft handling of what could have turned into an ugly situation.

Kang couldn't really blame the soldier. It was frustrating as hell having to put up with these annoying dwarven raids, when back in the old days the draconians would have just swooped down on the dwarves, killed them, and leveled their little village.

But the old days were gone, as Kang was constantly working to make his draconians understand.

Returning to his position, Kang surveyed the field of battle. The dwarven ladder bearers had planted their ladders, the dwarves were climbing up them. The draconians successfully pushed away four of the ladders over, but several dwarves scrambled over the remaining two ladders, clubs and fists swinging.

The dwarves were a tough target for the draconians to hit. Standing about four and a half feet tall, the dwarves ducked under the legs of the seven-foot tall draconians, whose clubs and sword blades generally whistled right over the dwarves' heads.

Kang spotted six dwarves, who darted and weaved and jumped, eluding all attempts by the draconians to stop them. The dwarves leapt off the wall and disappeared inside the draconian village.

Kang swore.

"Damn! Slith, take the First Squadron and go after them. We've only got ten head of sheep left. I can't afford to lose any of them. Go!"

"First Troop, follow me!" Slith yelled over the din.

The draconians had pushed off the remaining two ladders, but the dwarves on the outside were keeping up a steady assault, hurling rocks and mud. The draconian next to Kang slumped to his knees, then pitched face first into the dirt. Kang rolled the draconian over to find him still breathing but with a large bump rising on his forehead. A clay brick, cracked in half, lay next to him. Kang left the unconscious soldier and descended the battlements. He went to find the Support Troop.

The draconians had maintained their military ranks and organization over the years, though there had really been no need for them to do so. They had long ago left the army. But the discipline of the military unit worked well in times of emergency, such as this. Everyone knew what to do and who to follow.

The Support Troop supplied the rest of the brigade (now only two hundred draconians strong), providing food, clothing, armor, weapons, and tools. During the raids, the Support Troop served as the reserve army. Rog, the commander in charge of Support, saluted as Kang approached.

"We're ready when you are, sir!" Rog announced.

"Good! Let's go!" Kang responded and set the example by sheathing his sword.

With a yell, the forty draconians, each armed with a club and a shield, broke into a jog, heading for the gate. The draconians manning the gate saw the Support Troop coming, flung wide the wooden doors.

On the other side of the gate, the dwarves, seeing their chance, made a rush on the opened portal. Kang and his Support Troop charged through the gate. Swinging clubs and fists, they surged headlong into the attacking dwarves.

The battle was brief. Several dwarves fell, their heads cracked by club or fist. Lightning crackled, a few Bozaks were using their magic. Mindful of their commander's order, they made certain that all it did was singe a few beards and set one dwarf's pants ablaze. After five of their number had either fallen or were smoldering, the hill dwarves withdrew, pulling back their forces into the sparse woods surrounding the village. The occasional projectile weapon whistled through the air or, in some instances, plopped.

Kang was just turning to assess the situation when he was struck on the snout by a rotten egg. The eggshell broke, the stinking yolk dribbled into his mouth and down his jaws. His stomach heaved at the foul smell and worse taste. He gagged and retched. He would have almost preferred an arrow in the gut.

Wiping the putrid missile from his face, Kang called for his forces to retreat. He heard his command, given in draconian, repeated in dwarven, shouted by the commander of the hill dwarves. The dwarves ran off, leaving their wounded on the field. Their wives would be around to collect them in the morning.

The draconians on the wall let out a victory yell. Once again they had pushed back the dwarves. Kang shook his head glumly. Six dwarves had made it through, however. He could only imagine what mischief they'd managed to do before being cornered. Kang ordered his men inside, and the gates closed.

Slith was waiting for him.

"Well?" Kang asked. "Did you catch them?"

Slith saluted. "Sir, we clobbered two of them, but at least four got away, and four of the sheep are missing."

Kang kicked the dirt with a clawed foot, sending up a cloud of dust in his frustration. "Damn! And nobody saw a thing? What did the sheep do, sprout wings and fly off with the dwarves on their backs?"

Slith could only shrug. "Sorry, sir. It was all pretty confused . . ."

"Yes, yes, I know." Kang sucked in a breath, tried to calm himself. "Hand me a rag to clean this filth off, will you? Deal with the wounded, then assemble the troops in one hour in the compound. I want to talk to them before it gets too hot."

Slith laid a conciliatory claw on Kang's scaled arm. "The boys are having a rough time of it now, sir. But we're still all behind you. Every one of us."

Kang nodded wordlessly, and Slith went off to carry out his orders. He and his soldiers hauled the unconscious dwarves outside the gate and left them there. By the next day, they would be gone. They would either wake up and stumble home, or their families would haul them off the following day.

Either way, they would be safe in bed by sundown.

"Damn crazy way to run a war, if you ask me," one draconian was overheard to say to another, as they hauled a potbellied, black-bearded dwarf out the front gate.

Yes, Kang thought to himself. It was a damn crazy way to run a war.

Chapter Two

Kang had his reasons for this damn crazy way to fight a war. Reasons he'd shared with the men under him time and again. They just needed another reminder.

The draconians descending the wall shuffled into the compound, forming orderly ranks. Soon, all the draconians in Kang's command were standing in four rows. Kang took his place before them. Slith gave the order, and the draconians snapped to attention.

The morning sun, a fiery red eyeball that looked the way Kang's eyes felt this morning, peered into the compound. The red light glinted on the scales of the draconians, scales reflecting the type of dragon from which each was so hideously descended. Sunlight gleamed in the brassy tinted scales of the Baaz. Slith, one of the Sivaks, glittered silver. Stepping from the shadow of the command hut into the bright compound, Kang's own scales glinted with burnished bronze. He was a Bozak, one the few Bozaks in the troop and, for all he knew, perhaps one of the few Bozaks left in the world.

"Lizard men" was the term the humans used to derisively refer to draconians—an insult that never failed to make Kang's scales twitch. His troops bore no more resemblance to lizards than humans did to . . . well . . . monkeys, for example. The draconians were much closer akin to their parents, dragons.

The shortest draconian stands six feet tall, Kang himself was seven feet in height. They walk upright on powerful haunches, their clawed feet needing no shoes or boots. Their clawed hands are adept at wielding the weapons of war. All draconians except the Auraks (who don't get along well with their fellow draconians and therefore tend to be loners) have wings. These wings allow them to glide short distances or float through the air. The Sivaks can actually fly. Draconians' eyes gleam red, their long snouts are filled with sharp fangs.

Draconians are intelligent, much more intelligent than goblins. This created a problem during the war, for many of the draconians proved to be far more intelligent than the humans who led them. Bozaks, like Kang, have an inborn talent for magic, similar to that possessed by their doomed parents. And though the draconians had been brought into the world with only one objective—to destroy any force that opposed them—the longer they remained in the world, the greater their need to be part of the world.

Kang took a moment to regard his troops with pride, a pride that, these days, seemed always to be mingled with sorrow. Once there had been six rows of draconian solders lined up before their commander. Now they were down to four. Every time he gave this speech, there were fewer to hear him.

He glanced over at Gloth, standing with the Support Troop in the rear. And there was the soldier who had disobeyed orders and picked up the crossbow.

Kang lifted his voice. "You fought well today, men! Once again, we forced the enemy to retreat, while suffering no significant casualties." He made no mention of the lost sheep. "It has come to my attention, however, that some of you are dissatisfied with the way I've been running things around here. We're not in the army anymore. But we all agreed that our only hope for survival was to maintain our discipline. You chose me to be your commander, a responsibility I take seriously. Under my leadership, we've held on here for twenty-five years. Life hasn't been easy, but then life for us has never been easy.

"Yet, we managed to build this." Kang gestured to the neat rows of cabins made of pine logs that stood inside the compound. "This village of ours is the first settlement ever constructed by our people."

The first, said a voice inside Kang. And the last.

"I want to remind you," he continued, his voice quiet, "of the reasons why we left the army. Why we came here."

The troops stood still, not a scale clicked, no link of armor jingled.

"We, the First Dragonarmy Engineers, have a proud history of service in the War of the Lance. We were commended for our meritorious actions by Lord Ariakus himself. We remained loyal to our Dark Queen, even during that terrible time in Neraka, when our leaders forgot their noble mission and instead turned on each other."

Kang paused a moment to relive history. "Think back on that time, men, and learn from it. Our armies had succeeded, by a stroke of luck, in capturing the so-called Golden General, the elf female who was leading the troops of the so-called Forces of Good. And what did our commanders do with her? Instead of just slitting her throat, as would have been the most sensible course of action, they put her on display for the Dark Queen's pleasure. As even a kender could have foreseen, a group of her motley friends, led by a bastard half-elf, turned up to rescue her. In the fight for the Crown of Power, Lord Ariakus managed to get himself skewered. Some bloke with a green jewel in his chest impaled himself on a rock and the Temple collapsed, bringing Her Dark Majesty's ambitions down with it.

"You all remember that time," Kang said, his voice hardening. "We were ordered by our human commanders to fight to the death, while they escaped! Many of our kind died that day. We chose not to obey. Some of us had foreseen this terrible end. As far as we were concerned, these human commanders had forfeited, by their stupidity and greed, their right to lead us. We marched off, leaving the war to those who had bungled it. You elected me leader and, under my leadership, we headed south, looking for a place to hide, a place to live.

"Evil turns in upon itself, or so the god-cursed Knights of Solamnia say. But that is not true of the First Engineers." Kang spoke with growing pride. "We fought as a cohesive unit for years. We were disciplined soldiers, accustomed to obeying orders. And we had a new ambition, one that was born in the smoke and flame of battle. We were sick of killing, sick of slaughter, sick of wanton destruction. We felt the urge to build, to settle, to leave something of ourselves behind on this world. Something lasting and permanent.

"You recall that time. How we were pursued by the knights. We

11

headed for the Kharolis mountains—long a haven for exiles and out-casts. We reached it, finally, and found ourselves in the lands controlled by the dwarven kingdom of Thorbardin. The Knights of Solamnia weren't about to get themselves killed for what was now a dwarven cause. They left us for the dwarves to handle, and went back to celebrating their glorious victory.

"It might have gone badly for us, but our numbers were relatively few. We posed no threat to the heavily fortified underground kingdom of Thorbardin, and so the Thorbardin dwarves saw no reason to risk their lives chasing us down.

"We made camp in this valley, nestled in the foothills between Mount Celebund and Mount Dashinak. Our first objective—we built the wall. Our camp turned into a fortification. The fortification became a village."

Kang sighed deeply. "We have just one problem. We draconians are not farmers. Nothing we plant ever grows. No seed we sow ever bears fruit."

He did not speak the rest, they all knew it. The futile attempts to make anything grow in the barren ground was a cruel metaphor of their own lives. They were born of magic. No female draconians existed. Their race would be the first and the last to feel Krynn's sun warm their scales.

"We would have perished of starvation long ago," Kang admitted, "if it weren't for the hill dwarves."

The hill dwarves' village was located on the opposite face of the valley, on the side of Mount Celebund. During the winter, when game was scarce and the draconians were facing starvation, they did what was necessary for survival. They raided their neighbor's larder.

"You remember those first raids," Kang said grimly. "Bloody affairs for both sides. The dwarves suffered the most. With our experience and sheer size, we overpowered even the best dwarven warriors. Still, we were the ones at the disadvantage. When one of our warriors falls, he falls for good. There will be no replacements—ever."

Before the War of the Lance, the evil clerics of Takhisis had developed the arcane art of perverting good dragon eggs, changing the unborn baby dragon into a host of monstrous beings. Using various magicks and sorceries, the evil cleric Wyrllish, the black-robed mage Dracart, and the ancient red dragon Harkiel the Bender, produced the warrior race which the armies of Takhisis sorely needed—the draconians.

The dragon-spawned draconians proved to be so powerful in their strength, intelligence and cunning, that their creators feared them. Lord Ariakus decided that the commanders could control the draconians only if they could control their numbers. He and the other Dragon Highlords forbade the making of females. The draconians could never breed. The Highlords' elite shock troops had finite numbers. Presumably, when the battle was over and the Dark Queen victorious, she would no longer need the draconians. And by that time, most of them would be dead.

"I watched our people die off in battle with the dwarves," Kang said, "and I knew that, over time, we would be a people no longer. We would cease to exist. Of course, we could have wiped out the hill dwarves, but then what? Who would tend the fields of wheat? Who would raise the sheep? Who would"—Kang ran his tongue over his fangs—"distill that concoction of the gods known as dwarf spirits? We'd starve to death! What's worse, we'd die of thirst!

"The other troop commanders and I came up with a possible solution. On our next raid, I ordered all weapons left behind. You know what happened. We grabbed the same number of loaves of bread, snatched up the same amount of chickens, and—most important—we made off with the same quantity of dwarf spirits as the first raid, but our losses were considerably less.

"We fought our way in and out using fists and tails and a little magic. No one died on either side. There were bruises all around and broken bones, but they healed. And, I am pleased to note, when the hill dwarves raided us a month later, they carried no weapons. Thus a tradition was born. It has become an unspoken covenant between the two settlements.

"I know it's frustrating," Kang admitted. "I know that you'd like nothing better than to rip off a dwarf's head and stuff it down his throat. I feel the same way. But we can't give them the satisfaction.

"Understood? Then, dismissed."

"Three cheers for the commander!" Slith yelled.

The troops cheered, heartily enough. They respected and admired their leader. Kang had worked hard to gain their respect, but now he was wondering if he'd truly earned it. Oh, sure, it had been a good speech, but when all was said and done, what victory had the draconians really won? Living behind a wall, fighting constantly to survive, and for what?

All they lived for was to get drunk every night and tell the same blasted war stories over and over and over.

Why do we even bother? Kang wondered morosely.

He traipsed back alone to his cabin to indulge himself in his hangover.

An hour later, Slith knocked on Kang's door.

Kang's quarters were built into the main administration building in the center of the village. Slith's quarters were on the other side of the same building. The armory and tool shed were located in back.

Kang's quarters consisted of a large meeting room, with a small bedroom off to the side. It was not luxurious, but it was comfortable. An oil lamp—of dwarven make—rested on a bare table. Kang sat in his chair, facing the door. A mug of dwarven ale was ready for Slith. Kang had poured one for himself.

"That was a good speech today, sir," Slith said on entering.

Kang nodded. He wasn't in the mood for talk. Fortunately, he knew Slith would be.

"You're right, you know, sir. Our lives are pretty good at that. The dwarves raid us, take a few sheep and what weapons they can lay their hands on, and then we go and do the same to them, swiping spirits and ale, tools and bread. Every time they raid us, we pound 'em, push 'em back, and I come in here for ale. Believe it or not, sir, I find some comfort in that. I know what to expect out of life."

Kang gave a glum shrug. "You're right, I suppose. Still, I keep thinking there should be more to it than this."

"You're a dragon-spawned soldier," Slith said, nodding wisely. "You yearn for the battlefield. You yearn to command troops in a life-or-death struggle, a struggle for glory."

Kang took a sip of his ale, pondered this. "No, I don't think so. I don't feel like I'm accomplishing anything. None of us knows how long we're going to live, but it won't be forever. What will remain after we're gone? Nothing. We're the last of our race."

Slith laughed. "Sir, you can be the most depressing bastard I've ever met! What does it matter what happens after we die? We won't be around to know the difference!"

"I'll drink to that!" Kang said moodily, and took a long pull on his ale.

Slith waited a few moments to see if his commander was going to cheer up, but Kang remained stubbornly immersed in gloom. He stared into his ale, and watched the flies buzz around the rag on which he'd wiped the rotten egg.

"See you for dinner, sir," Slith said, and left his commander to his black mood.

Kang put away his armor and harness. By force of habit, he cleaned his already clean sword before resheathing it and hung the belt on a hook near the door.

He went to bed, to rest through the heat of the day, the heat that was so very unusual for midsummer in the mountains. He did not sleep, but lay, eyes open, staring at the ceiling.

Slith had a point.

"What does it matter after we die?" Kang asked the buzzing flies. "What indeed?"

Chapter Three

The four dwarves ran along a hunting trail that zig-zagged through the tinder-dry meadow grass. Though it was early morning still, the sun beat on their iron helms like Reorx's hammer. Three were wearing leather armor and heavy boots and sweating profusely. The fourth was clad in a belted tunic, breeches and soft cloth slippers, known disparagingly among the dwarves as "kender shoes," because, supposedly, they permitted the wearer to move as stealthily as a kender. This fourth dwarf was relatively cool and quite comfortable.

The dwarves had done well for themselves on the raid that morning. One held a small lamb over his neck, grasping it by its legs. Two carried a large crate between them. The fourth dwarf carried nothing, which also accounted for the fact that he was enjoying the walk.

One of the dwarves hefting the heavy, rattling crate noticed this singularity. Huffing and puffing from the heat and his exertion, the dwarf complained.

"Hey, Selquist, what are we? Your pack horses? Come here and give us a hand."

"Now, Auger," replied the dwarf, fixing his companion with a stern eye, "you know that I have a bad back."

'I know you can crawl through windows without any trouble," Auger grumbled. "And you can move pretty fast when you have to, like when that draconian came at us with the club. I never see you hobbling around or crippled up."

"That's because I take care of myself," said Selquist.

"He does that, all right," grumbled another of the dwarves to his companion.

Any well-traveled person on Ansalon could have told at a glance that these were hill dwarves, as opposed to their cousins the mountain dwarves. At least, the traveled person could have said that about three of the dwarves. They had nondescript brown hair, light brown skin and the ruddy cheeks that come of being raised from childhood up on the healthful properties of nut-ale.

The fourth dwarf, whose name was Selquist (his mother, something of a romantic, had named him after an elven hero in a popular bard's tale; no one is quite certain why), might have given the traveler pause. He appeared to fit into no specific category. His clothes were similar to those of his fellows, a shade less tidy, perhaps.

He wore a ring, rather battered, of a metal that he claimed was silver. This dwarf—youngish, considered lean among his stout fellows—also said the ring was magic. No one had ever witnessed any evidence of this, although all would admit that Selquist was quite good at performing at least one trick: making other people's personal possessions disappear.

"Besides, Mortar, my friend," Selquist added, "I, too, am carrying something—a most valuable treasure. If my hands aren't free, how will I defend it in case we're attacked?"

"Oh, yeah?" Mortar demanded. "What?"

Selquist exhibited with pride an amulet he wore around his neck.

"Big deal," said Pestle, Mortar's brother. "A penny on a chain. Probably worth less than a penny. Bet it's fool's gold, like those gully dwarves tried to palm off on us in Pax Tharkas."

"It is not!" Selquist returned indignantly.

Just to make certain, when the others weren't looking, he slowed his running long enough to take a good look at it.

The amulet was made of metal, but it wasn't a coin, at least not like any coin Selquist had seen, and he'd seen quite a few in his lifetime. It was shaped like a pentagram. Each point of the pentagram had a dragon's head inside it. The five-headed dragon identified it as a relic of the Dark Queen, making it worth quite a bit to those who traded in souvenirs from the War of the Lance. He had found the amulet while rummaging around in a draconian's footlocker.

"In fact," he said to himself, "it would be worth a whole lot more if it turned out to be magic!"

At that, a rather unpleasant thought occurred to Selquist. Hastily, he snatched off the amulet and thrust it in the money pouch hanging from his belt.

"The last thing I need is to be cursed by the Dark Queen for appropriating her jewelry," he muttered. Increasing his speed, he hurried after his companions. "I'll pass that along as an extra benefit to the buyer."

The four crossed over a low ridge and were at last able to slow their pace. It was unlikely the draconians would have chased them in this heat, but the dwarves were not taking chances. They could now see the smoke of the village cooking fires. They could hear the cheers of the people, welcoming the warriors home.

The main body of raiders had already returned, battered and bruised, but in good spirits. The entire population of the village of Celebundin was gathered at the meeting hall to greet the returning heroes.

These four, who lagged behind, were missing the celebration, but that didn't bother them. They wouldn't have been included anyway. In fact, there were those in the village who would have celebrated if these four hadn't come back.

Selquist and his party deliberately avoided the crowd, heading for Selquist's house, which was located on the outskirts of the village. Selquist unlocked the three locks on the door—he was of a suspicious nature—and entered. His three assistants clomped in behind him and dumped the crate on the floor. He shut the door, struck a match to light an oil lamp.

Auger set down the lamb and stood gazing at it hungrily. Bleating plaintively, the lamb piddled on the floor.

"Oh, thanks, Auger! Thanks loads!" Selquist glared around. "Just what we need to improve the decor around here, the pungent smell of lamb piss. Why in the name of Reorx did you bring that beast inside the house? Take it out and put it in the pen, then get something to clean that up. You two, open the crate, and let's see what we have."

"Steel coins," said Pestle hopefully.

"Jewels," said his brother Mortar, working on the lock.

The lock gave with a snap.

"Shovels," said Selquist, peering down. "Also picks and a saw. Come now," he added, when he saw the brothers scowl in disappointment. "You didn't really expect we'd find a king's ransom stashed in a draconian shed? Those scaly louts wouldn't be hanging around this god-forsaken valley if they had money. Heck no. They'd be whooping it up in Sanction."

"What are they doing here, if comes to that?" Pestle demanded. He was in a bad mood.

"I know," said Mortar, looking very solemn. "They've come here to die."

"Balderdash!" Selquist glanced around to make certain they were alone. He lowered his voice. "I'll tell you why they're here. They're on a mission from the Dark Queen."

"Truly?" Pestle asked, awed.

"Of course." Selquist straightened, scratching reflectively at his scraggly beard, which had once been likened by his own mother to a growth of fungus on a rock. "What other possible reason could there be?"

"Mine," said Mortar stubbornly.

But the other two laughed at him derisively and began hauling tools out of the crate. The tools were not of draconian make or design, which meant that they had been originally stolen from the dwarven village. Selquist and his friends had simply stolen them back, a proceeding that was not unusual. After twenty-some years of raiding, most objects belonging to the dwarves and the draconians had changed hands more often than gifts at a kender wedding.

"Not bad," Pestle said to his brother. "We can sell these for ten steel. They're Thorbardin-made and good quality."

Very little was manufactured in Celebundin. The town had a forge and a competent smith, but he made tools for building, not digging or fighting. Most of the dwarves' weapons were either purchased, bartered, or stolen from their richer, safer, and bitterly resented cousins, the dwarves of the mighty underground fastness of Thorbardin.

"We can either sell them to the Thane or we can sell them to travelers on the road north. What do you think?" Selquist asked.

Mortar gave the matter serious consideration. "Who is going to buy shovels and picks and a saw while they're on the way to Solace? A roving band of goblin road workers? No, it'll have to be the Thane."

Mortar always had a good sense for the market. Selquist agreed. Pestle raised an objection.

"Someone's bound to recognize these and claim them. Then the thane will make us give them back."

At the sound of the dreadful word "give" the dwarves shuddered. The brothers looked to Selquist, who was the acknowledged brains of the group.

"I've got it!" he said, after a moment's thoughtful pause. "We'll take that little pissy lamb and make a present of it to the High Thane's daughter. We'll look like heroes! After that, if there's any dispute, the High Thane will be bound to side with us."

Pestle and Mortar considered this option and pronounced it feasible. Auger, who had just come back inside, glared at them, narrow-eyed.

"What'd you say you were going to with the lamb?"

Selquist told him the plan, adding modestly. "It was my idea."

Auger muttered something beneath his breath.

"What did you say?" Selquist asked. "It sounded like 'lamb chops.' "

"It was lamb chops! You're giving our supper away to the High Thane's little brat!"

"You should think less of your stomach," Selquist said in moral tones. "And more of the Cause. We need all the money we can raise for our little expedition."

Selquist quenched the light and walked majestically out the door, accompanied by Pestle and Mortar. Auger trailed behind, carrying the lamb.

Auger knew all about the Cause.

The only Cause Selquist ever promoted was Selquist.

Chapter Four

The Hall of the Thanes was located in the center of Celebundin and sounded a lot grander than it was really was. The main roads of the town ran from the meeting hall to the edge of town like the spokes on a wheel. Ring roads connected the spoke roads, and the dwarves' dwellings were built in between. The town had no wall, but every building was made of stone, each constructed like a small fort.

The hill dwarves of Celebundin didn't like being cooped up inside a wall. Walls reminded them of their Thorbardin cousins. Reminded the hill dwarves of the terrible days after the Cataclysm, when the mountain dwarves had shut the gates of the walls of Thorbardin in the faces of their beloved cousins, leaving the hill dwarves out in the wilderness to starve.

Today, the Hall of the Thanes—in reality, a blockhouse about the size of four dwarf houses put together—was filled with dwarves, standing room only. Selquist, his friends, and the lamb squeezed their way through the entrance in the back and pushed and shoved their way forward.

"Excuse me, pardon me, mind my foot!" Selquist prodded and poked the dwarves blocking his path. When they saw who it was, his fellow dwarves made sour grimaces, as if they'd mistakenly taken a big gulp of green beer.

"Who is it? What's going on?" the High Thane inquired mildly. He was a kindly dwarf, a baker by trade, who took a hopeful view of the future and, in consequence, always looked vaguely disappointed.

"It's Selquist, the Expediter!" someone said, sneering.

The High Thane's face took on a pained expression. He had once been hopeful about Selquist, but that hope had been dashed about a hundred years previous.

"Selquist," he said, "whatever it is you're selling, we're not interested. We did quite well for ourselves tonight."

The High Thane indicated the pile before him: six bags of flour, a sack of bread, an ox-plow, and fourteen empty dwarf spirit kegs. To the side, near the exit, two full-grown sheep stood, eyeing the crowd with trepidation

"Congratulations," Selquist said. Turning around, he snagged Anvil, who had become mired in the crowd, and extricated him. "Since I see so much wealth here, I guess you won't be interested in the little gift I was bringing. I had heard," Selquist added in a flight of inspiration, "that it was your dear daughter Sugarpie's Day of Life-gift."

The other dwarves standing around looked stricken, all of them thinking in panic that they'd missed the High Thane's daughter's Life-gift Day and wondering how they could make up for the oversight.

Selquist presented Anvil, who presented the lamb.

The High Thane blinked. Behind him, a chubby youngster, who had been raised on her father's baked goods and who resembled nothing so much as a puff pastry, made animate, lurched forward, hands outstretched.

"Baa-baa. Me want!"

"But, Precious," admonished the High Thane, eyeing Selquist with a certain amount of suspicion borne of long acquaintance, "it isn't your Life-gift Day. Your Day was two months ago."

The dwarves standing around Selquist started to breathe freely again.

Sugarpie glowered and stomped her small foot. "It is my Day. Me want baa-baa!"

Her face crumpled. Two tears—squeezed out with much effort—trickled down the fat cheeks. She flung herself on the floor, and those dwarves standing in the neighborhood stepped backed up a pace or two. Sugarpie's temper tantrums were known and respected for miles.

"Don't disappoint the dear child," Selquist said kindly. Bending down, he gave her a pat on the head and whispered encouragement. "More tears, kid. More tears."

Standing beside the High Thane, his wife—a formidable woman with impressive side-whiskers—shook those side-whiskers reproachfully at her husband. He quailed beneath them.

"Thank you, Selquist. We'll . . . uh . . . take the lamb."

The High Thane accepted the animal, transferring it to his daughter, who flung her arms around the creature in a hug that nearly choked it.

Anvil, watching, licked his lips and thought regretfully of mint jelly.

Task completed, Selquist bowed to the High Thane, then made his way back through the crowd, aiming for the huge keg of nut-ale, which occupied a prominent place in one corner of the Hall. Before he reached it, however, a hand caught hold of the collar of his tunic, giving it an expert twist. Selquist was suddenly nose to nose with the grizzled, gray-haired, fierce war chief of the settlement.

"Contrary to your opinion, Master Selquist"—the war chief was red with fury—"we do not run the raids on the draconian camp for the benefit of you and your thieving scamps! It's us who take the risks, and, by Reorx, I'm getting sick and tired of seeing your skinny butt disappear through a crack in the wall when my brave lads are getting their brains knocked out!"

"No great loss there," Selquist muttered.

"What was the that?" The war chief dragged Selquist closer.

"I said, 'you're the boss, Moorbrain.' " Selquist squirmed, trying to free himself.

"It's Moorthane!" the war chief thundered. "My name is Moorthane!" He gave Selquist a shake. "Whatever you took, you bring to the High Thane to be distributed to those dwarves who are most needy."

"Fine, Moorbrain," said Selquist politely. "You go to that dear, sweet little child and tell her that you're taking her wee lamby away."

The war chief paled. Draconians with six-foot, saw-toothed, poisoned-edged swords were nothing compared to Sugarpie.

"Just heed my warning, you Daergar whelp," Moorthane growled, emphasizing his words with an extra twist on the collar, which left

25

Selquist momentarily speechless. "I don't ever want to see you on a raid again. If I do, I'll bring a motion to have you Cast Out!"

The threat was a terrible one. A dwarf who is "Cast Out" is forever banished from his home and his clan. He becomes an exile, a wanderer over the face of the land. A Cast Out may be taken in by another clan in some other part of Ansalon, but he will have no voting rights within the clan, will be viewed as essentially living on its charity.

Moorthane dropped Selquist to the floor. Rounding on his hobnailed heel, the war chief stalked off.

Selquist smiled at those dwarves standing nearby, who had been watching with stern approval. He straightened and smoothed his maltreated tunic. "Nice weather we're having," he said. "A bit hot, and I suppose we could use some rain, but otherwise great for outdoor activities."

The other dwarves, glowering, turned their backs. He heard the word "Daergar" repeated among them, but that was an old story, one in which he'd lost interest a long time ago. This threat to have him Cast Out. That was new. Admittedly Moorbrain was mostly blubber and bluster. A motion to have Selquist Cast Out of his clan would require a unanimous vote of all the dwarven heads of household—an unlikely occurence, though few of them numbered Selquist as a friend or even someone to whom they might stop to give a drink of water if he were dying of thirst in the desert.

Selquist looked in vain for his companions. Upon the arrival of the war chief, the three had blended in with the crowd, leaving their leader to his fate.

Selquist poured himself a large mug of nut-ale from the huge keg in the back and settled down to put Moorbrain out of his mind and enjoy himself. The meeting droned on for another hour, as the dwarves discussed how the booty should be divided and how they were going to defend the village from the inevitable return raid of the draconians.

Certain that the war chief was fully occupied with matters of state, Selquist's three companions emerged from the thickest part of the crowd and came to join him.

"Did I hear Moorthane right?" Mortar demanded, aghast. "Did he threaten to have you Cast Out?"

"Bah!" Selquist brushed it aside. "He can try, but he'll never get the votes. My mother will stick up for me, for one."

The other three eyed him glumly.

"Oh, sure she would!" Selquist protested.

"Speaking of your mother, he called you a Daergar," said Auger in low voice. "Doesn't that bother you?"

"No," Selquist said lightly. "Why should it? It's true. Half-true, at any rate. I'm half-Daergar. And I'm proud of my heritage. Ask anyone. They'll tell you that the Daergar are the most feared of all the dwarves, noted across Ansalon for being powerful warriors."

The Daergar—or dark dwarves—were also noted for being murderers and thieves, but Selquist's companions wisely refrained from pointing this out.

No one knew much about Selquist's father, including his mother. Having imbibed a large quantity of dwarf-spirits during a Forge-day celebration, she had danced off drunkenly into the woods by herself. She had returned several days later with the incoherent tale of having partied with wood sprites. A search of the vicinity by her father turned up bootprints that were larger and heavier than those generally left by wood sprites, plus a knife and a quiver of arrows of Daergar make and design. When, several months later, the dwarf maid gave birth to a child, it was noted that he was also of Daergar make and design. Since the baby was half-Niedar, the clan accepted him, but they made it clear that they didn't have to like it.

They'd gone on making that clear for the next hundred years of Selquist's life. And now Moorthane was threatening to have him Cast Out. Oh, well. Selquist hadn't planned on hanging around this backwater settlement much longer anyway.

Under cover of the hubbub in the Hall, the four dwarves stood close together, while Selquist issued orders.

"Mortar, the High Thane likes you, plus you're his fourth cousin twice removed on his grand-uncle's side. You go to the High Thane's bakery tomorrow and sell him the tools."

Mortar nodded. He was the only one of the four whom the High Thane even remotely trusted.

"Don't take any trades," Selquist cautioned. "We want steel, not day-old bread. And we don't—"

They were interrupted by the breakup of the meeting. The warriors headed for the keg of nut-ale, filling their mugs and then lacing them with dwarf-spirits. The warriors would spend the rest of the day bragging about their exploits during the raid. Four of the women marched off, going to collect their husbands, who had been left behind at the draconian settlement. Two well-armed warriors went with the women to ensure their safety, more from the occasional savage animal in the area than from the draconians.

Selquist turned to find the High Thane standing behind him. "So, Selquist," said the High Thane, stroking his beard, which was perpetually streaked with flour, "what prompted you to such a display of generosity tonight? I trust," he added hopefully, but without much confidence, "that this means you are planning to forge a new hammer, as the saying goes."

Selquist smiled. "I am merely fulfilling my moral obligation to the community, High Thane, as would any other productive member of this clan."

"I wish I could believe that, Selquist." The High Thane gave a pious sigh. "You're half-Neidar, after all. But I can't forget that your other half is Daergar."

Selquist's smile broadened. "Something I'm never allowed to forget myself," he said pleasantly. "Permit me this gesture tonight, O High Thane, and perhaps return the favor sometime. I do hope your daughter enjoys the lamb."

"I know I would have," Auger muttered. "Roasted."

Selquist trod on his friend's foot to silence him. "Could I offer you a mug of nut-ale, Respected High Thane?"

Selquist drank a mug of ale with the Thane, just to be companionable, but as soon as politely possible, he ditched the old fart and, rounding up his friends with a glance, left the Hall.

* * * * *

The Celebundin dwarves belonged to the Neidar Clan of dwarves. After the Dwarfgate War—a war brought on by the refusal of the Hilar dwarves to assist their kinsmen following the Cataclysm—the Niedar dwarves were forever barred from the hallowed halls of Thorbardin. The Neidar seat on the Council of Thanes within Thorbardin now stands empty.

All that was ancient history. Various parties, attempting to foster peace among the inhabitants of Ansalon, have suggested that the mountain dwarves, if properly approached, would graciously allow their kinsmen to return to the mountain. The hill dwarves have always replied that they would rather be strapped to a gnomish device without benefit of earplugs than come crawling back to the ancestral home. Neider pride had never recovered from the insult and most likely never would.

As for the Daergar, they had split off from the main clans in

Thorbardin following an unsuccessful attempt to seize control from the Hilar. Delving even deeper into the labyrinthine caves of Thorbardin, the souls of the Daergar grew dark as their surroundings. The Daergar ruler is always the most powerful of the warriors of the clan and keeps his rule by staying alive. Daergar are excellent thieves and are known throughout dwarfdom as the most dexterous and dishonest of all dwarves, traits that Selquist had inherited.

From an early age, he had shown a talent for what the kender term "borrowing." Unlike a kender, Selquist knew full well how he came by his acquisitions and what to do with them once acquired.

Selquist and Auger bid good-night to the brothers Anvil and Mortar and walked back to their own house. The two lived together as young bachelors, not yet having settled on wives. Auger fell in love about once a week, but when the word "marriage" was mentioned, he broke out in hives. Selquist had no time for dallying with the opposite sex. He had plans to make, profit to generate. This night, he was working on one of his best.

Arriving at home, he unlocked the three locks, entered, lit the lamp, and settled down to work. This meant that he lounged in the best chair, while Auger sat at the desk and wrote down Selquist's orders.

"We'll need food to last us until we reach the Daergar clan homes. After that, we can scrounge," Selquist dictated.

Auger copied this in a small bound book. Auger's mother, one of the Thane's scribes, had taught her son to read and write, skills Selquist found to be highly useful. Selquist could read, if he had to, but why bother when there was someone else to do it for you? He had never learned to write. He had better things to do with his hands, such as picking locks or pockets.

"We leave a week from tomorrow night," Selquist continued. He liked to have his plans in writing. Not that he ever forgot what he was doing, but it was pleasant to sit by the fire on winter evenings and hear Auger read the tale of their adventures together. "It will be quiet— there's no raid planned—and there will be two full moons, making it easy to travel. We can cross Mount Celebund and be halfway to the South Gate by morning. The next day, we'll complete the journey and enter Thorbardin."

Auger copied this down.

Selquist yawned, stretched, and stood up. "Time for bed, Auger. We'll continue tomorrow."

"Uh, Selquist." Reading back over his notes, Auger discovered a serious flaw in the plan. "How are we going to get into Thorbardin? I thought that the Hilar wouldn't let us Neidar inside."

Selquist patted his friend on the back. "You leave that to me. I have a way in."

"Selquist," said Auger, after a moment's hesitation, "aren't you worried about being Cast Out? I can't think of anything more terrible."

Selquist's heart did give a little flutter and an uncomfortable thump at the thought. He could not let his friend see him afraid, however.

"On the contrary," Selquist said lightly. "I'd welcome it. You don't think I plan to spend the rest of my life in this sleepy old village, do you? Why, they'd be doing me a favor. I'd go off and become a hero like that other dwarf who was Cast Out of his clan. What was his name? . . ."

"Flint Fireforge," said Auger, impressed. "You'd help save the world like Flint Fireforge did during the War of the Lance?"

"I might not save the world," Selquist conceded. "But at least I could rescue a few valuables. Now get some sleep. We did a lot of work today."

Auger did as he was told. But he paused on the way to his bedroom, sniffed the air. "I smell roast lamb," he said wistfully.

"Get over it," Selquist advised.

On his way to bed, he put his hand into his pocket and felt the medallion, which he'd thrust in there, then forgotten. He pulled it out regarded it with a certain amount of unease.

No one had ever threatened to have him Cast Out before now. Perhaps the Dark Queen . . .

"Oh, don't be silly!" Selquist admonished himself and thrust the medallion back into his pocket.

It had to be worth at least five steel, easy.

Chapter Five

Eight days after the dwarven raid on the draconian village, Kang entered the command post's conference room. The six officers of his brigade were inside, ready and waiting.

These included the First, Second, and Support Squadron commanders, as well as his chief engineer, chief supply officer, and Slith, his second. They sat around a central table—a large table, made of wood, finely crafted and polished—a prize stolen early on from the dwarves. It had taken quite a bit of skill and muscle to haul the table through the valley, but the draconians had accomplished it. They had been young back then.

Now, just looking at the massive table made Kang's back ache.

"Good morning, gentlemen. Thank you for coming. As you know, we're on the verge of a crisis situation. Our supply of dwarf spirits is running low. By the quartermaster's calculation, we have only enough for tomorrow's ration. It's time we paid the dwarves a visit. I've been talking with the chief engineer, and tonight appears to be an ideal night for our raid on Celebundin. I'll let the chief engineer elaborate."

Fulkth, the chief engineer, spoke up. "Sir, we're expecting two full moons tonight. That will make it easier for us to navigate. We haven't had an opportunity like this for the past three years."

"That was the time we stole their ox-cart and loaded it with so much ale and dwarf spirits that we almost didn't make it back home," Slith recalled. "We cleaned 'em right out! Remember the party afterward? Dark Queen alive, but that was something special!"

The other draconians began to jabber. Kang rapped his knuckles on the table, reminded them of their duty. They fell silent, gave him their full attention.

"We have work to do," he told them sternly. "If we reminisce all day, we'll be here until nightfall and miss the raid. Does anyone have any problems with going tonight?"

No one did. All of them were grinning eagerly at the prospect.

"Very well, then. We'll get down to the specifics. The First Squadron has gone on the last two raids—"

"Damned right, sir! We're the best at it!" Gloth said, poking the leader of Second Squadron, who looked glum, in the ribs.

"Yes, as I was saying"—Kang glowered at them, bringing them once again to order—"I think that the Second Squadron should take the lead in this raid. First Squadron will be held in reserve, ready to respond if something goes wrong."

Now it was Gloth's turn to look dejected. He scraped his claws across the wood, bringing a sharp reprimand from Slith.

"Look at the marks you've made! Keep doing that and we won't have any table left!"

"Sorry, sir," Gloth muttered.

Kang continued. "This time we'll take our own wagon. We'll stash it behind the stand of trees to the south of Celebundin. Yethik, can you have your supply boys ready to move before sundown?"

Yethik nodded. He was the chief supply officer, and his job was to quartermaster all of the goods and keep the food stored. He was in charge of the wagons and the oxen needed to pull them.

"Right, then," Kang said. "Be ready in eight hours. Second Squadron will move out one hour after sundown, and the First will move out half an hour after them. Support Squadron will man the battlements for the duration. That is all."

The officers stood, saluted, and marched out of the room, hastening to their other duties besides raiding.

First Squadron provided the maintenance of the village, from the upkeep of buildings to the sweeping of the dirt streets. Second Squadron was responsible for the meat—all livestock, including chickens and sheep. The draconians' creators had certainly never intended them for shepherds, but Kang's troop had proved fairly good at it. Support Squadron was responsible for farming; a disheartening task, one no one liked. But grain was necessary to keep the livestock fed, and bread was needed to supplement their meager diet of meat. All agreed, though, that it was a lot easier to steal food than to grow it.

The rest of the draconians were organized into a Headquarters Troop. These included Kang and Slith, all of the specialists such as Fulkth, Yethik and his supply soldiers, and a section of Baaz who were trained as cartographers.

Kang marched down the hallway back to his own quarters. He was in a good mood today. He always enjoyed this time, just before a raid. It took him back to the old days—back when being a soldier meant something, back when he could feel proud to command combat troops.

Certainly he was proud of the accomplishments he and his draconians had achieved in their village, but it wasn't the same. Being able to feed his draconians another day didn't offer the same thrill as charging headlong into a pack of elves, slicing their pointy-eared heads from their skinny little shoulders. If it weren't for the dwarves, the draconians would have had no excitement at all.

In fact, Kang was forced to grudgingly admit, if it weren't for the dwarves, the draconians could not have survived this long. Not only did the dwarves provide much-needed food, they served as an outlet for the draconians' inborn aggression. The potent drink known as dwarf spirits, which was said to be made from some sort of fermented fungus, brightened—at least temporarily—the bleakness and emptiness of the draconians' daily lives. If it weren't for the dwarves, the draconians would have torn each other apart years ago.

Kang was feeling almost brotherly toward his bewhiskered adversaries.

Opening the footlocker at the end of his bed, he took out his battle harness, checked all of the buckles and straps. Next, he drew his sword from its sheath and examined the blade. No rust was ever allowed to taint the blade, but a few dents had pocked its cutting edge years ago.

Each dent represented an enemy's head. Kang smiled, remembering each well-fought contest with pleasure and pride. He ran a finger over the edge, then drew a whetstone from a storage box in the locker and began to sharpen the blade.

The draconians always went into the raids hoping for the best but prepared for the worst. They fought with wooden practice swords, but they carried steel. If the raid ever turned ugly, they would have to escape fighting.

Kang returned the whetstone to the locker and put on his harness. He strapped the sword's sheath to the harness and inserted the sword into the sheath. Weapons ready, he removed a felt bag from the locker and carefully poured out its contents on the floor. These included a candle, a small pot of a gray powder, and a holy symbol of the Dark Queen.

Except the holy symbol wasn't there.

Kang scratched his head. He turned the bag inside out. No symbol. Lifting the bag to his nose, he sniffed. His snout wrinkled.

Dwarf. Some dwarf had been inside his footlocker, had stolen his holy symbol!

Kang growled. He might have known. His friendly feelings toward them vanished. Confound those hairy little bastards anyway! His sole comfort was the thought of what Takhisis would do to the wretched thief who had dared lay hands on her icon.

Kang stomped about, fuming and kicking things for a bit. He needed that holy symbol. How could he approach his Queen without it? His rampage carried him to the stand on which he kept his armor. He paused.

There, on his breastplate, was a medallion with the Queen's symbol, the five-headed dragon. The medallion wasn't holy. It marked his rank as commander. It hadn't been blessed by the dark clerics, as had his other symbol. One might say, though, that it had been consecrated in another manner. It had, on many occasions, been splashed by the blood of Her Dark Majesty's enemies.

Kang pried the symbol off the breastplate, spent a few moments polishing it, then carried it over to his makeshift altar. He lit the candle and chanted a prayer to the Queen to gain her attention. Next, he sprinkled a pinch of the gray powder over the fire. The flame flared. Blue sparkles burst in front of Kang, dazzling his eyes. He continued to intone the holy prayers. Lifting the medallion in his hands, he imagined the wings of the Many-Colored Dragon bearing him off into dark realms. . . .

A bang at the door and Slith's voice yelling for him jolted Kang from his hypnotic state

"What? Is it time already?" Kang yelled. The candle had burned down a good two inches.

Slith spoke through the door. He knew better than to burst in on his commander's visits with their Queen. "Sir, the regiment is ready for your inspection. At your leisure, sir!"

Kang grunted in satisfaction. The past eight days had been mind-numbingly dull, the routine the same every day. See to the cracks in the wall, see to the sheep, see to the few plants struggling for life in their garden—plants which Kang was more than half-convinced were weeds anyway. Maintain training, maintain discipline, settle quarrels over the dwarf spirit rations. And then, at night, get good and drunk.

But today Kang felt alive again. He carefully snuffed out the candle, took a moment to thoughtfully regard his new holy symbol. It appeared to have pleased Takhisis, to judge by the euphoric feeling that now filled him. Gratified, he placed the medallion back on his breastplate. He started, by habit, to put the bag with the powder back in the footlocker. He stopped, glowering, and searched his room for a better hiding place. A loose floorboard provided the answer.

Kang lifted the board, scraped a hole in the dirt below, and dropped the pouch into the hole. Replacing the board, he stood and rubbed his knee joints, stiff from crouching for so long. He took mental stock of his magical spells. They were as he had requested, all ready for his use.

"All right, Slith, let's go look over the troops!" Kang said, opening the door.

Slith grinned, saluted, added an enthusiastic, "Yes, sir!"

Kang wasn't the only draconian who enjoyed these raids.

The two officers marched out in front of the headquarters building to find the entire regiment formed into ranks, awaiting inspection.

The three squadron commanders came to attention and brought their commands to attention. The Headquarters Troop stood to the right of the line, indicating seniority. They, too, came to attention.

"Two hundred ready for inspection. Only sentries and three lame are not present, sir," Slith announced.

Kang nodded. The same three had been in their makeshift hospital for over a year now, having been injured when a beam fell from an unfinished roof. All suffered back injuries. The lame draconians did leatherwork, repaired torn straps on the armor and tooled new belts, sword sheaths and such. The work gave them something to do to make them feel useful, occupied their time. Kang visited them often to keep up their spirits, but still the crippled draconians tended to be low and depressed.

In the old days, the three would have been dispatched, thrown off a cliff or slung into a river, where their bodies could do no damage to anyone. Draconians are blessed—or cursed, depending on how one viewed it—with the ability to wreak havoc on an enemy even after death. When Kang himself died, his bones would explode, killing anyone in the immediate vicinity. Baaz corpses turned to stone, encasing any weapon used to attack them and thereby rendering an enemy weaponless. A Sivak changed shape when he died, assuming the form of the person who killed him, making it appear that the slayer was the victim. Many an enemy army, seeing the field littered with what they mistakenly believed were their own dead, had fled the battle.

When the three crippled draconians had learned the serious extent of their injuries, they had expected to be killed. Kang had decreed otherwise. He'd granted them life. He always wondered, seeing them sitting on wooden stools, looking longingly out on the parade ground where they'd never march again, if he'd done them any great favor.

"Sir . . ." Slith gave Kang a gentle nudge.

Kang shook the unpleasant thoughts from his head. This was a day of battle. His good mood returned.

Kang and Slith toured the ranks, inspecting every draconian. Each stood at attention, each wore the same harness and the same sword as Kang. The Second Squadron also carried short steel bars on their back braces, used when lifting bridge sections, indicating that they were bridge builders.

The bars were useless here, but they were always worn, because they were a mark of honor and brought back memories of better, more glorious times. The sight always heightened Kang's good humor. This regiment had been his first combat command, under Lord Ariakus, years ago. He recalled the time his draconians had built a bridge over a raging river, working on it while under attack from elves and silver dragons. The bridge had been a marvel. As it turned out, the bridge was never used. The entire army had retreated, instead of advancing over it. Still, Kang had been proud of his accomplishment and that of his men.

He stopped in front of the commander of the Second Squadron, a Bozak.

"Ready for action today, Irlih'k?" Kang asked, his voice booming through the compound.

"Yes, sir!" The Bozak saluted.

Kang had given the Bozak the title Irlih'k, Bridge Master, the title Kang himself had held when he had commanded the squadron.

Of course, the title was all for show. They weren't likely to be building bridges for an army any time soon. But Kang insisted that they maintain the skills which had once earned them acclaim. Every few months, he divided the squadron into teams and had them build bridges across a dry gorge which ran near their village. The team whose bridge was completed first and could bear the weight of the entire regiment was awarded an extra ration of dwarf spirits.

Kang and Slith finished inspection with the Support Squadron, and then the commanders marched back in front of the regiment.

Kang faced forward. "You look as fine today as you did the day I took command! Well done. Tonight's raid should be a good one. With luck, we'll drink a toast to the dwarves tonight before we go to bed! Drink a toast to them with their own blood!"

A cheer went up from the entire regiment. Of course, they wouldn't really be drinking dwarf blood, not like the old days. But dwarf spirits amounted to the same thing and were much more palatable.

"Brigade! Officers, fall out. Second-in-commands, prepare for battle!"

The officers saluted. Kang returned the salute. Excitement surged through the draconians. It was an hour before sundown.

Yethik saluted. "Sir, my boys are ready to head out with the wagon and ox team. Are you going to send an escort with us?"

"Have Gloth provide you with a section of troops," Kang said. "Keep yourselves under cover. If the dwarves spot you, they'll know we're going to raid. For once, I'd like to take them by surprise."

Yethik dashed off to find Gloth and start the wagons rolling. Kang turned to his second-in-command.

"Well, Slith, I think this raid will be a good one. I have the feeling that tonight the Dark Queen is taking a special interest in us."

Slith laughed and rubbed his clawed hands together. "The men haven't been this keyed up for a while, that's for sure."

"Which is one reason I want you up front with Irlih'k and the Second Squadron," Kang said. "I don't want anyone getting over-zealous and cutting off a head when bashing will do. We've got a good thing going here with the dwarves. We don't want to spoil it."

"Don't worry, sir. If there's a whip to crack, I'll do the cracking!"

Slith's long tongue rolled out of his mouth. He sucked it back in with a slurp. Not only was the Sivak quite skilled at enforcing discipline, he thoroughly enjoyed his work.

"Wait until an hour after dark," Kang continued, "and then move out with the Second Squadron. I'll bring up the First Squadron and get into position with the wagon. If you run into trouble, have Irlih'k fire off a light spell. We'll come running."

Slith saluted and went off to find an unfortunate trooper to yell at until it was time to go.

Chapter Six

The two moons were just cresting Mount Celebund when Pestle and Mortar, packs strapped on their backs, knocked on Selquist's door. The two entered immediately, not waiting for an answer. If they waited for an answer, Selquist would know that it wasn't either of his two compatriots and would hide all of the incriminating evidence.

The evidence tonight was a map on the table and two more packs, filled with supplies and ready for travel.

"Did anybody see you?" Selquist asked.

"If they did, no one gave a damn," Pestle responded in hurt tones. "They're all hepped up over something. Moorthane is running around like his beard was on fire. I asked what was going on, but he just glared at me and told me to get lost."

"Draconian raid," Selquist said knowingly, with a glance out the window. "Two full moons makes it the perfect time for a raid, and the perfect time for us to sneak out. It's what's known as a diversion.

Moorthane will be so busy wonking dracos, he'll never miss us."

This statement did not bring the whoops and cheers of joy Selquist expected. Instead, his companions appeared considerably alarmed.

"Wonking dracos! What's gonna stop the draconians from wonking us?" Auger demanded.

"They're after ale and dwarf spirits," Selquist said. "We won't be carrying any ale or dwarf spirits, so they won't be interested in us."

"We won't?" Mortar clung affectionately to an ale skin, hanging from his belt.

"We won't," Selquist said sternly. "This is a dangerous mission, and we go into it with clear heads. Well, at least as clear as some of us can manage," he added, rolling his eyes and jerking a thumb at Auger, who was generally acknowledged to have all the sense of a leaky water bucket.

The announcement of the dry expedition came as a shock to Mortar, who maintained that he couldn't stay regular if he didn't get his nut-ale once a day.

"Look, Mortar, we'll only be out in the wilderness for two nights," said Selquist, trying to lighten the dwarf's dark expression. "After that, we'll be inside Thorbardin, and I know for a fact that they have lots of ale in Thorbardin. Now, come take a look at the map."

Selquist traced their route. "Celebundin's here, where I've drawn this circle. Tonight we cross it and sleep in the valley. We'll hike over mounts Bletheron and Prenechial tomorrow during the day. Tomorrow night, we'll camp on the far side of Mount Prenechial, and the next day we traverse the Helefundis Ridge."

"When do we go inside Thorbardin?" Mortar asked.

"How do we go inside Thorbardin?" wondered his brother.

"Right here." Selquist put a finger on the map. "There's an air hole from an old mine shaft. It's hidden, but I know where it is. We go down the air hole and into the mine. After that, it's a simple task of walking through the mine, and we pop out the other end into Thorbardin."

"Go down an old mine shaft!" Auger was nervous. "Do you mean underground?"

"That's generally where mine shafts lead, yes," Selquist said.

"I've never been underground," Auger returned, round-eyed. "I'll bet it's dark," he added in low, unhappy tones.

"You'll like it," said Selquist, slapping him on the back. "You're returning to your roots. It's what dwarves were born to do: rappelling down steep cliffs, crawling on all fours on a tiny ledge over a bottomless pit, clinging like a fly to the wall with a seventy-foot drop onto jagged rocks, nary a hand or foothold in sight. By Reorx," Selquist said, drawing in a deep breath, "I can't wait!"

"I can," Auger muttered. He looked at Selquist suspiciously. "What's 'rappelling?' "

Selquist was not quite certain, having heard the word used once by the war chief. He made a hasty guess. "Rappel—a large, cave-dwelling bird. With a forty-foot wing span."

"No, I don't think so," Mortar said thoughtfully. "Rappel is the act or method of descending down a mountainside by means of a belayed rope—"

"Oh, what do you know?" Selquist snapped. "Speaking of rope, I have all the climbing gear we'll need. Rope enough to tie ourselves to each other. The pass over Mount Prenechial is a bit treacherous. We don't want to lose anybody."

Auger looked highly alarmed. "First rappels with forty-foot wing spans and now treacherous passes. I don't think I like this much."

"The descent down the air hole is chock full of big rocks and crags," Selquist said soothingly. "It's easy to climb. Now, if there are no more questions, let's—"

"What about the rappels?" Auger wondered.

"What about them?" Selquist said, sighing. He was beginning to lose patience.

"If they're birds that big, what do they eat?"

"How in the name of Reorx do I know what rappels eat?" Selquist shouted. "What difference does it make anyway?"

"It might make a big difference, if they eat dwarf," Auger pointed out.

"They don't, all right? Rappels are known to be vegetarians. Now, can we get on with this!"

Selquist rolled his eyes, thrust the map into his belt. The other dwarves hefted their packs. Mortar took a long pull on his ale skin, then corked it and left it, with a sad good-bye, on Selquist's kitchen table.

"Say, Selquist," Pestle asked, as they started out the door, "how do you know about this hidden mine shaft?"

Selquist shrugged. "Do you remember last summer when I was gone for a week?"

Auger nodded. "You said you were out hunting rabbits."

"I wasn't hunting rabbits. I was hunting for this air hole. I bought the information off a Hilar miner, and it cost me dearly, I can tell you. I went to see if my investment had paid off. I found the air hole, climbed down it, crawled through a mine shaft and"—Selquist snapped his fingers—"there I was! Smack in the middle of downtown Thorbardin."

The other three regarded Selquist with admiration.

"You never said a word!" Pestle remarked.

"Not even to us," Mortar put in.

"These things have to be kept secret," Selquist replied with becoming modesty. "Otherwise we'd have the whole village tumbling down that air hole. Now, we've wasted enough time. Let's go."

Selquist made certain, before he left, that all three locks were locked. Most dwarven dwelling places didn't even have one lock on their doors (unless they lived in a town populated by kender). Selquist was proof of the old dwarven adage that it takes a thief to suspect a thief.

The three hurried down the main road to the east. No one was walking about the streets, no lights shone in the windows. The women and children were locked up safe in their houses, their menfolk were gathered in the center of town, ready to defend their village from the draconians. It was, as Selquist had anticipated, a perfect night to sneak out of town, avoiding annoying questions about where they were going and why.

Nearing the end of the street, Selquist called a halt. "Hold on. Let me check to see if they've posted a sentry." He crept forward, keeping to the shadows. He passed the last house on the road and turned along the fence-line. A few moments later, he returned.

"Yes, confound it. There's two sentries sitting on the far end of the fence. Gilbert's one of them, so I'm not too worried. He makes Auger here look intelligent."

"Gee, thanks, Selquist," Auger said, flushing with pleasure.

Selquist grunted. "We could try another way, but we've lost enough time as it is. The dracos are bound to hit soon. We'll chance it. Keep low, and keep quiet."

The three dwarves followed Selquist to the left. Crouching down, they crawled through a small apple orchard across from the last house. The shadows from the gnarled branches kept the four concealed. They were coming out the far side, when a voice caused them to all stop in their tracks.

"Hullo," called out Gilbert nervously. He slid off the fence post. His hand fumbled for the axe at his belt.

"I see you. Who . . . who's there?"

"May Reorx fry his head!" Selquist cursed. He stood up, gave a casual wave. "Oh, is that you, Gilbert?"

"Yes, it's me," Gilbert said, suspicious. "Who are you?"

"Selquist, you ninny. You know Auger, Mortar, and Pestle."

"Sure. Hi, guys." Gilbert waved.

"Hi, Gilbert," the four said solemnly, waving back.

"What are you doing out there?" Gilbert asked.

"Picnic," said Selquist.

"In the dark?" Gilbert was doubtful.

"Best time," Selquist said. "No flies."

Gilbert thought this over. "Yes, but the draconians are coming."

"We brought enough food for everyone. Well, got to be going. See you, Gilbert."

"Yeah, see you, Gilbert." The others waved good-bye and trotted off after their leader.

"Have a nice time," Gilbert said and went back to sitting on the fence.

Chapter Seven

The draconians loped across the valley, the entire troop running in formation, taking the pace at an easy jog so as not to be worn out by the time they reached the dwarven village. When the line of trees marking the village came into sight, the Second Squadron, led by Irlih'k, advanced. As second-in-command, Slith had been assigned to accompany the Second Squadron. Sneaky, devious, cunning, the Sivak was adept at worming his way out of tight situations. If the Second Squadron got themselves into trouble, Slith was the one who would get them out.

The draconians advanced slowly and silently across the open plain leading to the tree line at the east edge of the town. Slith suddenly flopped onto his belly, flattened himself on the ground.

"Down!" he ordered in a harsh whisper, motioning with his hand.

The squadron that was spread out behind him immediately crouched down on their haunches, folded their wings into their bodies and went immobile as boulders. No one moved. No one spoke.

Cautiously, Slith raised his head. At first, he'd thought he was hearing things, but then the voice, speaking dwarven, which had first caught the draconian's attention, spoke again.

"Oh, is that you, Gilbert?"

"Yes, it's me," another dwarf answered. "Who are you?"

"Selquist, you ninny. You know Auger, Mortar, and Pestle."

The dwarves continued talking. Slith squirmed around on his belly. Spotting Irlih'k, Slith made a gesture with his clawed hand, motioned the squadron leader forward.

Crawling on his belly, pulling himself forward by digging his claws into the dirt and propelling himself from behind with his powerful legs and tail, Irlih'k slithered up to join the Sivak.

"Picnic," one of the dwarves was saying.

"This is damn odd," Slith whispered. "What do you think these fool dwarves are doing, roaming around out here at this time of night?"

Irlih'k shook his head. "Looks to me like they're leaving town. They're all wearing packs. Do you think they saw us?"

"I don't know," Slith said, worried. "I don't think so. They would have raised the alarm by now."

The draconians hunkered down, waited in tense silence.

The four dwarves never looked in the draconians' direction. Waving to the sentry on the fence, the four disappeared into the night.

"You know," said Slith, "I think those sneaky little bastards might be going to raid us!"

"Huh?" Irlih'k blinked. "Four of them?"

"Sure. The dwarves can see the two moons as well as we can. What if they think that we'll think it's a good night for a raid? Thinking that we won't be there because we'll be here, the dwarves pull a fast one and decide to go there because they know we're not."

"You lost me," said Irlih'k.

"Never mind. I'll take four of your boys and follow them. You carry on with the raid."

Irlih'k crept back to the squadron. Four draconians leapt up, ran forward to join Slith.

"Come with me," Slith whispered to his command. "The first draco that makes a sound feels my knife in his ribs. Understood?"

The four nodded. Not having heard the whispered conversation between their commanders, not having seen the dwarves, the four had no idea what was going on. They were trained to obey without question, however, and—having known Slith from long experience—they knew he did nothing without having a damn good reason.

Slith and his troops slunk through the darkness, following the direction the dwarves had taken, heading north.

A yell rose up behind them, a dwarven yell. Slith paused, glanced back. The draconians had been spotted. He could hear the sounds of bells ringing in the dwarven village, voices shouting orders, both in dwarven and draconian.

"Good luck, commander," he said softly and continued on his way.

As he trailed the dwarves, Slith pondered what they might be up to. It was obvious now that they weren't heading for the draconian village.

"Why would these four pick this night to skedaddle out of town? Scared? Cowards?" Slith shook his head. "No, dwarves are loud and obnoxious, hairy and bad-tempered. But one thing you can say for them is that they never run away from a fight.

"In fact," Slith reflected, "it's a pleasure to have dwarves as an enemy. They're not like humans, who think that the whole purpose of a battle is just to kill or get killed. And dwarves aren't like elves, thank the Dark Queen, who always have to talk about killing before they get down to it and waste time with their parleys and messengers running back and forth until a fellow is ready to slit his throat just from sheer boredom.

"Dwarves know that nothing stirs the blood and gets the old heart going like a good fight. With a cracked head and a bloody nose, a dwarf can go to bed at night feeling that he's done a decent day's work. So these four aren't running away from a fight.

"I've got it!" Slith said to himself. "They're not trying to slip away from us! They're trying to slip away from the other dwarves! Now, isn't that interesting? I wonder why?"

He could not only see the dwarves quite well in the moonlight, he could smell them as well. He and the draconians kept on the trail. The dwarves continued heading north. They could hear the sounds of battle as well as the draconians, yet the dwarves didn't look back, didn't appear to be the least bit interested. The draconians kept their distance and continued to follow. They moved through the night, the draconians silent and cautious, the dwarves pushing their pace.

Behind them all, the sounds of battle grew louder.

Chapter Eight

Kang crept forward through the underbrush. The trees were spread apart, and the bushes and vines had grown thick among them. Behind him, the seventy draconians of the Second Squadron followed. The two moons, red and silver, were like mismatched eyes, taking over duties from the single-eyed sun, as if two eyes were needed to keep watch at night. The moons, red Lunitari and silver Solinari, were sacred to the two gods of magic. Lunitari was a neutral god, taking no sides in the wars on Krynn. Solinari was dedicated to the cause of Paladine, his father, worshiped by the cursed Solamnic Knights.

Kang enjoyed the irony of knowing that the bright light of these two moons was shining down on the path of their enemies. The moon Kang knew and he alone could see, the black moon Nuitari, gave no light at all. The son of the Dark Queen shed his unseen blessing on Kang's magical powers.

Kang motioned for Gloth, lurking in the brush behind him, to come alongside. "We'll wait in the clearing up ahead. Find Yethik and bring him to me. He should already be in hiding with his wagon."

South of the village was a grove of trees. Yethik had orders to drive the wagon into that grove and wait for the draconians to launch their offensive. When the distillery was secure, Yethik would drive the wagon inside, ready to load up the kegs of dwarf spirits.

Gloth grunted a grumpy, "Yes, sir." He was still mad about being forced to wait in reserve.

Kang crept out into the grassy area, watched as his troops flowed past, a river of dark, winged shapes in the moonlight. Each draconian took up a defensive position on the far edge of the clearing. Only a thin line of trees separated the clearing from the plain beyond. Less than a thousand feet across the plain stood the dwarven village of Celebundin.

The draconians were disciplined, silent. No unnecessary chatter— Slith would see to that. Their armor was wrapped and muffled. Gloth returned with Yethik.

"No problems getting into the woods, sir. There were two dwarves on sentry duty—I guess they've figured out by now that those woods are a good hiding place. But they'd taken a jug of nut-ale with them to keep them company. By the time we arrived, they were snoring loud enough to saw the trees down. We had the dwarves tied up before they woke up!"

Kang chuckled. He had suspected that the dwarves would post a watch tonight—they knew the phases of the moon as well as the draconians did. It was good to be one up on the dwarves. It boded well for the raid.

He waited, tense and nervous, for the Second Squadron to launch the assault. It seemed to him that they were past their time, and he was beginning to worry, when the three officers spotted movement to their right.

"Here they come!" Gloth said excitedly.

The draconians, armor shining red in Lunitari's light, were sweeping across the plain. Suddenly, the advancing draconians of the Second Squadron came to a halt, dropped down into the dry grass.

Gloth sucked in a breath between his teeth. "By our Queen, what the devil are they doing, sir? Stopping like that right out in the open!"

Kang shook his head. "Beats me. Look! There go some of them now."

A group of five draconians leapt to their feet and ran off to the north, heading away from the village. Kang thought he recognized Slith in the lead. Within moments, they were out of sight. Kang was baffled.

Gloth was hissing like a boiling kettle. "Sir, please let me go in! The Second Squadron's botched this raid already! I could—"

He was interrupted by a rustling sound. Kang looked back to see the Second Squadron on the move again. They closed within five hundred feet of the village before a yell went out from the closest watchtower.

"Go! Go! Go!" Kang urged them on, though they were too far away to hear him.

Irlih'k, the commander of the Second Squadron, shouted his battle cry, and it was echoed by the entire squadron. They charged.

Unfortunately, the dwarves were waiting for them. Now Kang knew why his men had stopped. Fifty dwarves poured out of the village, trying to intercept the draconians before they reached their objective.

Gloth was jumping up and down in excitement.

Yethik jerked a claw in Gloth's direction. "Commander Kang, you might as well send in the First Squadron. Gloth'll blow out a row of scales if you don't and it looks like the Second could use the help."

The Second Squadron hit the dwarves full force. The sounds of thumping and whacking, yells, cries, and curses in two languages were audible. The dwarves were taking the worst of it, but the draconians were stopped cold, at least for the moment.

Gloth quivered like an arrow stuck in a tree trunk. Kang considered Yethik's advice. It was important to overwhelm the dwarves before they could muster an effective defense.

"All right, go," Kang said.

Gloth lashed his tail in pleasure. "Up, boys! We're on! Let's go!"

The First Squadron rose out of the brush. Cheering, they ran forward, yelling their battle cry.

Even from this distance, Kang could see that the dwarves were startled. More than a few paused, peering around, trying to determine the location of this new threat. Irlih'k's draconians took advantage of the dwarves' distraction and pushed ahead. But it was a reduced force. Fewer than forty draconians from the Second Squadron were on the move. The rest were either fighting or lying on the ground, knocked out of the action.

"Sure you don't want us to join them up there, sir?" Yethik asked, obviously eager to enter the fray.

"No, we can sit this one out. If they get in trouble, I'll do my bit. It's good for them to work on their own once in a while. Builds character."

Yethik looked startled, glanced at Kang to see if he was in his right senses. Kang grinned. Yethik, realizing it was a joke, grinned back.

But not for long. The night sky over Celebundin grew suddenly, unusually, magically bright.

Kang recognized a Bozak light spell.

"Damn!" was all he said. He was up and away, heading for the dwarven village, his clawed feet tearing up the dry grass in the parched fields.

He reached the village only to find the streets deserted. He slowed, caught up on his breathing, and wondered where the hell his army had gone. A dark shape, wings extended, jumped out of a nearby tree, landed on the ground near Kang.

"Gloth sent me to find you, sir."

"What's going on?" Kang demanded. "Where is everyone?"

"The dwarves are holed up in the distillery storage shed, sir. The Second Squadron has surrounded the shed. The First Squadron's holding the road to the center of town, where a large group of dwarves are assembling, sir."

"Well, what's the hold-up? Tell the Second Squadron to storm the damn shed!"

"There's a problem, sir." The Baaz was apologetic. "The dwarves have locked the doors to the shed and are threatening to dump their brew before they'll hand it over to us, sir."

"By the Dark Queen's heart!" Kang swore, shocked. "Are they serious?"

"We have to assume that they are, sir." The draconian looked worried, as well he might.

Kang raced off to assess the situation. When he arrived, the draconians were hissing and howling and clashing their swords against their breastplates. At the dire threat to dump the spirits, the draconians were near to forgetting their orders against bloodshed.

"What's the meaning of this?" Kang's voice boomed in anger. "You're draconian soldiers, by god, not a pack of dim-witted goblins! Put those swords away!"

"But, sir!" Gloth came bounding up, red eyes blazing. "Sir, they say they're going to dump it!"

"That's right!" came a gruff voice from the window of the storage shed. "Come any closer, and we pop the stoppers! We've taken an oath. I'm Vellmer, chief brew master, and long as there's whiskers on my chin, I'll never again hand over my best brew to you, lizard-bastards!"

"I think you're bluffing!" Kang shouted back in dwarven. He'd picked up quite a bit of the dwarven language during the past twenty-five years. "Men, go ahead."

The draconians surged forward.

"Oh, yeah! Is this bluffing?"

A dwarf rolling a barrel appeared on the roof. Silhouetted in Solinari's silver light, he raised an ax and let it fall, staving in the sides of the barrel. Liquid gurgled out, splatted on the ground. The draconians gasped and came to a standstill. A sigh like a gust of wind swept through their ranks.

"You've got to stop this, sir!" Gloth cried in agony.

"I will," said Kang. "Stand back."

Lifting his hands, he formed the prescribed circles and slashes in the air and mumbled arcane words. Gloth looked expectant, waiting for something spectacular, perhaps a red dragon to arrive and fly off with the dwarves.

Nothing happened. No dragon. Nothing.

"Sir, your spell must have fizzled," Gloth said, disappointed, but respectful.

"Wait," Kang counseled.

A sudden flurry of activity could be heard inside the shed. A moment later, the doors flew open. The dwarves burst out, running as fast as they could from the building. They were gasping and choking, had their noses and mouths covered with handkerchiefs. Several lurched to a halt, doubled over, and began to vomit.

"Let 'em go, men," Kang ordered. "They're not important. You know what is."

The draconians were already on the move. Ignoring the desperately sick dwarves, the draconians charged inside the shed to restopper the kegs and claim their prize. But the first draconians who dashed in dashed out again almost as fast as had the dwarves.

"Phew! That smell's vile!" Gloth snorted and snuffled.

"Give it a minute," Kang said.

The smell was already beginning to dissipate from the warehouse. Kang coughed and took a few steps upwind.

"What do you call that spell, sir?" Gloth was impressed.

"Stinking Cloud," said Kang, letting the words roll off his tongue.

Though he was skilled with a blade and enjoyed the organized, disorganized, brutal confusion of bone-crunching melees, Kang experienced a deep satisfaction when using his magic. He had once thought that he liked magic for the power it gave him over others. But lately he'd come to discount that reason. As a commander, he held life and death power over all his troops, with or without magic. His magic allowed him to create—even if it was nothing more than a horrendous smell. And creating was far more satisfying to him now than destroying.

"What does that remind me of?" Gloth muttered, frowning, trying to recall. "I know I've smelled that before. Cow dung mingled with puke and sour apples . . . Wait! I almost have it . . ."

"Remember that crazy minotaur officer we worked for, toward the end of the War of the Lance?" Kang asked, rocking back on his heels, allowing himself to rest, momentarily, on his large tail. "The one who did his best to try to get us all killed? The one who came to such an unfortunate and propitious end? The one who got drunk on hard cider . . ."

"That's it!" Gloth shouted.

The draconians advanced once more on the deserted shed. Kang went with them, holding his breath as he entered. The smell was fading, but he guessed it would be days before anyone was able to spend much time in this building.

The draconians worked swiftly, no one wanting to stay in the vicinity any longer than necessary. Only one of the huge kegs had been destroyed, and that was the one the dwarves had hauled up to the roof. The rest were safe and sound and still stoppered. The draconians grabbed the kegs, lifted the large heavy wooden barrels up onto their shoulders, and ran for the outskirts of town where Yethik's wagon waited.

"Here they come!" A shout rose from the commander of First Squadron, who was holding the road.

Kang dashed out of the warehouse.

"Right, men! Grab what you can and get going!" Kang yelled.

An avalanche of angry dwarves crashed into the front ranks of the First Squadron and rolled right over the draconians. Though the draconians were taller and outweighed the dwarves, the dwarves were closer to the ground and, with their lower center of gravity and compact build, smashed into the draconians' legs with the force of boulders bounding down a mountainside. They beat on the draconians with fists and clubs, brooms and ax-handles. And more dwarves were coming around from the side streets. The draconians fell back fighting, retreating as fast as they could, taking what they could.

As soon as Kang saw the Second Squadron draconians reach the safety of the trees, he ordered the First Squadron to run for it.

"Protect the brew!" Kang yelled.

Grabbing their wounded, flinging them over their shoulders or dragging them by the heels, the draconians hurried back to the wagons. A few dwarves—the infuriated Brew Master Vellmer among them—seemed inclined to give chase, but a grizzled old straight-backed graybeard, whom Kang recognized as the dwarves' war chief, took command of the situation and called a halt at the tree line.

Undoubtedly aware that more draconians were lying in ambush among the trees, the war chief decided to cut his losses. The dwarves had driven off the invaders. The war chief wouldn't push his luck. By his orders, two dwarves put a hammerlock on the cursing brew master and dragged him away, kicking and vowing to see all draconians roasting in Reorx's kitchen.

Kang, dashing out of town, gave the war chief a salute. The war chief returned the salute with an obscene gesture and thus ended another raid.

Back at the wagon, Kang took charge.

"Right, good haul, boys! Let's get this loot back home."

Watching the wagon roll out, Kang realized someone was missing. He motioned Irlih'k over. "Where in the Abyss is Slith? I didn't see him the whole battle."

Irlih'k shrugged. "We were closing in on the town when we spotted a group of four dwarves leaving it. We thought they'd spotted us."

"Ah, so that's why you called a halt there at the beginning. I wondered what was going on."

"That was it, sir. The four dwarves just kept on going though. Slith thought that the dwarves were up to no good, maybe pulling a sneak raid on our village. He ordered a section to follow him, and they went after them."

"Only four?"

Kang shook his head. It just didn't seem logical. Then he recalled the incident with his foot locker and the stolen holy symbol. He had a sudden vision of dwarves rooting through all the draconian's possessions, like a pack of dirty little kender. A shiver of disgust ran from his tail up his spine to his snout. He was glad Slith had taken the initiative, gone after the rotten thieves.

Dwarves turned to evil. It was a sad state of affairs. Apparently, you couldn't trust anybody these days, Kang mused as he ran alongside the wagon and wondered what the world was coming to.

Chapter Nine

Slith and his draconians trailed the dwarves far into the night. There was really no need to follow them. The dwarves weren't setting out to raid the draconian village. But Slith was now intensely curious.

In addition, the Sivak was an opportunist, and this had all the earmarks of a "for profit" deal. Dwarves didn't generally put this much effort into a venture unless they expected to gain something from it.

The mountaintops were starting to redden with the first rays of the sun. The dwarves had reached a pass between the mountains. The leader—a scrawny looking dwarf with a scroungy beard—ordered a halt. As if they didn't have a care in the world, the dwarves pulled out food from their packs and sat down to breakfast.

Slith and the draconians hid in the bushes and watched.

Slith listened to the dwarves' conversation, but he wasn't much good at languages, and he could only make out about half of what the dwarves were saying. What he could understand only increased his desire to find out where they were going. He had caught the dwarven word for "loot," repeated several times.

If this had been a party of humans, they would have curled up in their blankets and taken a rest now. Dwarves had greater endurance and stamina, and Slith wasn't surprised to see them brush the crumbs out of their beards and prepare to move on. Removing ropes from their packs, they tied the ropes around their waists and then attached themselves to each other. This done, they started negotiating the narrow pass.

The dwarves moved out of Slith's sight.

Slith motioned. Corporal Vruss crawled over.

"Yes, sir?"

"I want you and the rest to go back and report to Commander Kang. Tell him I'll be away a few days," Slith ordered.

Vruss protested. "Sir, we can't leave you out here alone!"

Slith snorted. "What do you take me for? A namby-pamby elf-maid? I can take care of myself. I can shadow these dwarves faster and quieter on my own. Now, go and report to Kang."

Vruss nodded and backed out of the bushes. He motioned for the rest to follow. Within minutes, they were out of sight, heading back south.

The pass over Mount Celebund was easy for Slith, with his clawed feet and hands, to traverse. In places where the path proved too treacherous to negotiate, the Sivak used his wings, flew over the rough spots. The greatest difficulty he encountered was keeping behind the dwarves, not passing them up. His quarry was easy to follow.

Dwarves are not noted for their stealthy ways and make more noise trying to be quiet than a brigade of Solamnic Knights makes while on parade. These dwarves had no idea they were being tracked, and they clumped and shouted and swore and rattled all the way down the mountain.

Descending into the valley between Mount Celebund and Mount Bletheron, Slith passed from daybreak back into night. The sun was obscured by the high valley walls, and the valley was shadowy and cool until nearly a third of the way into the morning. But all that would change soon. Just as the sun glared over the rocks and flooded the valley with light, Slith slid into a crevice. The dwarves—not a thousand yards ahead of Slith—stretched and stopped and looked around, appreciating the warmth.

Slith could again overhear scraps of the conversation, tried very hard to puzzle out what they were saying. He wished Kang were here. The Bozak had an excellent facility for other races' palaver.

Slith recognized the dwarven word for "sun," and he knew "mountain dwarf" and thought he heard "hate" but that was about it.

Then the wind changed direction, and Slith couldn't make out any more. Whatever they were discussing, it hadn't sounded important. He'd heard nothing more about loot. After a brief rest and a mouthful of water, the dwarves reshouldered their packs and continued north, across the valley.

It was well past noon sun when the dwarves began the crossing between Mount Bletheron and Mount Prenechial. Again, Slith stopped to let the dwarves move on ahead. He was, by now, extremely hungry. He hadn't brought along any provisions, not having expected to be gone this long. A stream bubbled from the rocks. As soon as the dwarves were out of sight, Slith bent down and took a long drink, hoping the water in his stomach would ease the hunger pangs.

He spent a moment watching for fish, but none swam into view, and he couldn't wait all morning to try to catch one.

Trying not to think about food, Slith crossed the second pass a half hour later. The trail, which skirted the right of Mount Prenechial, was carved into the side of the mountain. A huge rock face of solid granite was on his left, to the right, a cliff drop of fifty feet or more. The pass was only wide enough for one person to traverse. Slith had to move carefully, afraid of dislodging a rock and giving himself away.

He saw the dwarves only once. They were well ahead, still tied together with ropes.

Night came before Slith was ready for it. Watching his footing, he had not been paying attention to the position of the sun, and when it vanished behind the mountain peak, the valley was plunged into deep shadows. He had been only a few thousand feet from the end of the pass, or so he had judged by glimpses of a meadow beyond. But, in the darkness, he had to slow down or risk losing his footing. He considered taking to the air, but he might fly past the dwarves in the darkness, and they were certain to hear the sound of flapping wings.

At last his feet touched cool grass, not hard rock. He was about to heave a sigh of relief, when he rounded a boulder, and instead of releasing his breath, he sucked it back between his teeth.

A cooking fire burned not ten yards ahead. The four dwarves were making camp, roasting a couple of rabbits that they'd managed to snare and spreading out their bedrolls. If one of them had glanced his direction, they would have seen him. None of them did look his way, though. Slowly, carefully, Slith backed into the shadows.

The dwarves chattered among themselves; Slith understood about one word in twenty.

"Slipped . . . fell."

"Helefundis Ridge . . . wind. Danger."

More talk, then, "Mine shaft" and "Thorbardin" and "tomorrow."

Loot. Thorbardin. So that was the plan.

Slith hunched down in the shadows. Smelling the rabbit roasting, watching the dwarves eat it, watching them slurp up the juice and savor each bite was the worst torture the draconian had ever had to endure, and he'd once been captured by elves.

Two hours later, the dwarves went to bed. Soon, their snores reverberated off the mountain side.

Slith pondered what to do. He needed food now, and he would need rest later. He was alone in enemy territory, and, despite his glib words to Vruss, Slith was well aware of the danger. Not from these dwarves, but patrols had been known to emerge from Thorbardin. Ogres, too, lived in these mountains. Though they had all fought as allies during the last war, the ogres had no love for draconians. Ogres had no love for anybody, except, maybe, other ogres.

At least now Slith knew the answer to his questions. His curiosity was satisfied. As for opportunity, even though he'd come out of this trip empty-handed, the information he'd gained might prove valuable later.

When Slith started picturing the scroungy bearded, scrawny dwarf slow-roasting over an open fire, the draconian turned and headed for home.

Chapter Ten

The four dwarves were up and moving before dawn. The difficult, treacherous part of the journey was behind them. They came across a well-traveled path, probably used by Thorbardin hunting parties, which led down the mountainside.

The going was easy, no need to be roped together. Mortar, who had persistently and annoyingly claimed that he had the strangest feeling they were being followed, announced that this morning the feeling had passed. If it wasn't for the intense heat of the day, heat that made it seem as if they were walking through an oven, not a canyon, the dwarves would have actually enjoyed this part of the journey.

At length, Selquist, who was in the lead, climbed atop a large, flat outcropping of rock. He motioned the others to join him. They clumped up after him.

"What?" asked Auger.

"The fabled gates of Thorbardin," Selquist said, pointing. "Southgate, to be precise."

"Where?" Pestle asked.

"There. Right in front of your nose."

"I don't see anything except a mountain," Auger complained.

"Well, there's a gate there. Trust me."

"What does it look like?"

"Like a gate," Selquist snapped. "Well, you've seen it. Let's get going." He started to leave the outcrop. The other three stood there, staring.

"The great Southgate is, in actuality, part of the face of the mountain," Mortar explained learnedly. "It is a gigantic stone plug operated by water wheels that, when in place, is undetectable from the side of the mountain itself."

"I'd really like to see that!" Auger said eagerly.

"So would I!" echoed Pestle.

"Well, you can't," Selquist stated. "Sorry, but we're not going in that way. Follow me."

Jumping down from the outcropping, he left the path and struck out in an entirely new direction. The three dwarves traipsed after him, their enthusiasm for this journey considerably heightened. None of the three had ever seen Thorbardin before. It was the food of legend and lore, most of it dished out with a bitter sauce. Now it was reality, and nothing in the legends had prepared the dwarves for anything so grand or spectacular as a gate that took up the side of an entire mountain. They could only imagine the wonders inside the mountain.

"Whole cities, bigger than Palanthas, are built right inside." Mortar continued with his lecture. "And there's the Life-tree of Hylar. A gigantic stalactite that has twenty-eight levels that house the central city of Thorbardin. You can reach the Life-tree by traveling in boats drawn by cables—"

"Oh, give it a rest, will you," Selquist said irritably, wondering why he'd brought along such a know-it-all. "It's a hole in the ground. That's all Thorbardin is and ever will be. Quit jabbering, and come along."

"I met a Thorbardin dwarf once," Auger said with quiet pride.

"Really? What are they like?" Mortar was interested.

"He thought his beard was longer than anyone else's," Auger replied. "He kept calling me 'woodsy' and claimed that he couldn't understand anything I said, when I was speaking dwarf just as good as him."

"He," Mortar corrected.

"I said it was a he. I never a met a female."

"No, the correct grammatical expression is, 'as good as he.' "

"He who?" Auger was completely baffled.

"Never mind!" Selquist shouted.

The other three fell silent. They continued walking and shortly came to a dead end. A rock wall, lined with bushes whose long, spiky limbs were covered with very nasty-looking thorns, blocked their way.

"This is it," Selquist announced, looking extremely pleased with himself.

"What?" asked Auger.

"Another gate?" Pestle gazed at the rock face with wide eyes, as if he expected it to split wide open any second.

"The air hole," Selquist said. "Through there. Behind those bushes."

The dwarves eyed the thorny bushes, and the enthusiasm they'd experienced for this project died immediately.

"Why does it have to be there?" Auger complained.

"Where else would it be?" Selquist demanded.

"Someplace easier to get to. Those thorns look sharp."

"They are sharp. Good thing, too. Why do you think this air hole has been so well-hidden for so long? If the Thorbardin dwarves knew this was here, they would have plugged it up like they did all the others." Selquist was defensive.

"Maybe they didn't plug it up because they figured no one'd be stupid enough to try to walk head first into a thorn bush," Mortar said in an undertone to his brother.

Selquist heard the remark but pretended he didn't. He had now definitely made up his mind. Next time, Mortar was staying home.

Pestle pulled out his axe, prepared to do battle. Selquist stopped him.

"Nope. No chopping. We have to leave this the way we found it, or the Hilar will know we've been here."

"Then how the bloody hell do you expect us to get through that?" Pestle growled.

"I did it," Selquist said coldly. "You just have to take a little care and not mind a few scratches."

Selquist put on a pair of heavy gloves, placed his foot firmly on the lowest branch of the thorn bush to hold it down, used his right hand to lift up another branch and started through. A thorn scraped across his face, but he wisely kept his "ouch" quiet, not to demoralize the troops. He moved ahead another step, trampling down more branches

63

with his feet, pulling apart other tangled branches with his gloved hands. He could see the air hole, in plain sight now, just a few feet away.

"Follow me," he ordered.

"I'm really getting tired of hearing him say that," Pestle complained to his brother.

"See there. Nothing to it." Selquist turned to his fellows, who had been doing a lot of screeching and cursing.

Now he saw why. Selquist, with his scraggly beard and wispy hair, had made it through the bushes with relative ease. His companions had long, full beards and thick curly hair, which was now snagged and thoroughly tangled in the long thorns. It appeared, from the looks of things, that they were going to be snagged there forever, unless rescued.

"Can't you three do anything right?" Selquist asked irritably.

Three pairs of eyes glared at him from faces that were covered with blood. Three sets of teeth gnashed at him, and three sets of mouths said not very nice things about his mother.

Heaving a long-suffering sigh, Selquist drew his knife and waded back among the thorns.

"I thought you said we shouldn't cut them," Pestle reminded him.

"I'm not," Selquist said coolly and instead proceeded to cut Pestle's beard.

'Hey! No! Don't!" Pestle protested vehemently. A dwarf's beard is his pride, his joy. A dwarf would as soon consider cutting off certain other essential parts of himself as he would cutting off his beard.

"Fine, then!" Selquist said. "Stay here. Wait for the rappels to come eat you."

Pestle subsided and permitted Selquist to cut him free. When he was finally out of the bushes and saw hanks of his brown hair clinging forlornly to the thorns, he was forced to cover his eyes and hide his tears.

Selquist worked on the other two, and finally the rest of the dwarves, shorn and scratched, hot and sweaty, and in no very good humor, stood outside the air hole.

"Come on, men." Selquist waved his hand. "Follow—"

Pestle grabbed hold of Selquist's shoulder, spun him around. "If you say 'follow me' once more, it'll be the last thing you ever say."

Selquist, indignant, brushed off Pestle's hand. "I will lead the way," he said stiffly. "You can come or not, as you choose. But may I remind you all that there is more cold ale down there than there is up here."

"He's got a point," Mortar admitted. The tussle with the thorn bush had left him extremely thirsty.

Selquist entered the air hole, with the others right behind. The air hole was actually a shaft bored into the side of the mountain. It was designed not only to provide air and light to those working below, but it was also intended to be used as an escape route during a cave-in. Hand and foot holds were carved into the side of the smooth rock face of the shaft, as well as grapples on which to hang ropes. Selquist tied the end of his rope to the grapple, and the dwarves swung and climbed down the shaft, keeping a watchful eye out for rappels. The temperature inside the mountain was much cooler than on its sun-baked surface.

They'd gone about two hundred feet when the air shaft ended. It opened up—so Selquist said—into a tunnel below. The other dwarves had to take his word for it. The air shaft had provided some light at the beginning, but that was gone now, leaving the dwarves in the dark. All they could see with their night vision was each other, the warm bodies glowing faintly red.

"I can't feel the floor!" Auger said. He was sitting on a narrow ledge, his feet dangling.

"The rope won't reach any farther," Pestle reported.

"Doesn't matter," Selquist replied. "We'll jump for it."

"How far?" Mortar asked worriedly.

"Not far."

Selquist recalled, with a shiver, the first time he'd made this journey. Having reached this point, he had been forced to make a leap of faith, as it were, into the darkness. He had brought a lantern, but its light didn't reach far. The map had shown the air shaft opening into a tunnel. Selquist could only trust that the mapmaker was reliable and that the tunnel floor hadn't given way during the small quakes that occasionally rattled the dishes of Thorbardin.

Selquist was not the dwarf to let a paltry emotion like fear come between him and profit, but he had spent several uncomfortable moments huddled here at the end of the air shaft, trying to gather up the courage to make the drop. He'd done it, of course, and found that it was only about six feet down to the tunnel floor. Now, confident, he dangled from the last hand hold and, letting go, landed lightly on the floor below.

Pestle remained in the air shaft, peering down at his leader.

"Hold on! I'll light a lantern so that you can see where you're going," Selquist said, afraid that Pestle would land right on top of him.

Selquist removed his pack and felt around for the lantern and the flint. A few quick sparks and the lantern was burning. The others came tumbling down out of the air shaft. Picking themselves up, dusting themselves off, they gazed around with interest. All of them were in a much better mood. Though they would have been slow-roasted before admitting it, the Niedar had the pleasant feeling, deep inside, of coming home at last.

"Where do we go from here?" Auger asked eagerly.

Selquist was about to say "Follow me." Swallowing it, he said instead, "Step this way, gentlemen."

The tunnel was six feet in diameter, with a pair of iron rails built into the floor. The walls, once smooth, were cracked here and there, but such was the skill of the dwarven engineers who had first designed these tunnels that the delvings had withstood even the devastating quakes of the Cataclysm without collapsing.

"What are these things used for?" Pestle asked.

Arms flailing, he was trying to walk on one of the rails and meeting with little success. Dwarves are not noted for their agility.

Selquist, in a good mood now that they had reached their destination, waved a hand and said magnanimously, "I know, of course, but perhaps Mortar here would like to explain."

Mortar told them how the rails were used by the dwarves to haul the carts loaded with gold and silver and iron ore through the tunnels. The dwarves passed one of the carts, rusted and broken, sitting on a siding.

"What are you stopping for?" Selquist asked, turning to find that his friends had deserted him and were all gathered around the rail cart.

"Maybe there's some gold left," Auger said.

Selquist had been about to complain over the delay, but, at this, he realized that he had always longed to see the inside of one of these contraptions. He hastened back over, carrying the lantern.

The sides of the cart were as high as the dwarves were tall and rusted. They couldn't see the interior. Pestle suggested climbing in with the lantern and investigating further.

"Are you kidding?" Mortar scoffed. "The Thorbardin dwarves would have picked this clean long ago. I can't imagine why they left the cart here, in fact. It looks perfectly good to me."

"Wait!" Auger said, leaning close and staring intently at the sides of the cart. "There's writing here."

He brushed off a couple of centuries of dust with the sleeve of his shirt. The others gathered around to see.

"What does it say, Auger?"

"Yeah, what does it say?"

Auger read slowly and haltingly. " 'Here lies a . . . a coward. Let . . . otters'—no, that must be others—'Let others see his fate and beware.' It's dated about the time of the Dwarfgate wars."

"I don't like the sound of this," Pestle said.

But the dwarves were now curious. Standing on tiptoe, the dwarves poked their noses over the side of the cart. Auger promptly shrieked, a shriek that echoed eerily through the tunnels.

Selquist poked him hard in the ribs. "Shut up, you idiot! We're getting close to the populated areas! Good grief, you sound like a human who sees a spider. It's just a corpse."

"It startled me, that's all," Auger said defensively.

Drawn by a morbid fascination, they all looked back inside the cart. The corpse was that of a dwarven male, wearing an iron helm and rusted chain mail. The head had been cleanly severed from the neck.

Subdued, the four dwarves left the cart and its grisly occupant with a mumbled apology for disturbing his rest, adding the fervent prayer that he not return the favor and disturb theirs.

"Welcome to Thorbardin," Mortar said grimly.

They continued on down the tunnel.

Chapter Eleven

After two more hours of walking, enlivened by the occasional tumble over the iron rails in the floor, the four dwarves reached the end of the mine shaft. Selquist flashed the lantern light all around. They were inside a large cavern. The light would not penetrate the darkness far enough to illuminate the ceiling. They could see the light shining on the iron rails, however, and those ran straight into a solid rock wall.

The three dwarves looked at Selquist, who answered hastily, "This isn't what it looks like."

"A dead end?" Pestle growled.

"Yes. I mean, no, it isn't. As for this wall"—Selquist tapped on it—"it was added at a later date, built right over the rails. I must admit that when I first came upon this obstacle, I was more than a little disappointed. However, by means of superior reasoning, I deduced that—"

"Of course!" Mortar interrupted. "I know where we are! Yes! This must have been the very same tunnel used by the Thane of the Neidar to lead his people in their futile attempt to break into Thorbardin, after the Hylar had refused them admittance following the Cataclysm."

"How do you know that?" Pestle asked, shushing Selquist, who was trying to say something. "There's lots of tunnels and shafts down here."

"Yes, but according to legend the Thane and his clan crossed Helefundis Ridge. The same ridge we just crossed. And there was that dead fellow back there and the words were written in the old language. This is a place of great historical significance," Mortar added, solemnly and reverently removing his iron helm. "Hundreds of dwarves fought and died here."

"Wonderful story," Selquist snapped. "We'll erect a monument. Now, as I was saying, by means of superior reasoning, I deduced that there must be—"

"That would explain why the Council of Thanes had this area walled up," Pestle remarked. "This area was a reminder of a dark time in Thorbardin history. They wanted it to disappear. Out of sight, out of mind, as the specter says."

Selquist made another try. "I'm sure that's exactly what the Council of Thanes was thinking, Pestle, and thank you for sharing that. Now, as I was saying, I thought at first I was trapped down here, until I came to the conclusion—the rather brilliant conclusion that—"

"So," said Auger, pondering this out slowly, "if this entrance to Thorbardin is walled up, how do we get through?"

"I'm trying to tell you!" Selquist shouted, forgetting his own admonition to be quiet.

Pestle reminded him.

Selquist seethed silently.

While he was seething, Mortar said, "You know, the dwarves must have had a forge down here. How else would they have repaired the rails?"

"You're right!" Pestle said eagerly. "And if they had a forge, they would have needed pipes to vent the heat. Which means that the pipes would lead . . . right back outside." His eagerness faded. "We don't want to go back outside."

"Not necessarily!" Mortar picked up the thread of his brother's thought and ran with it. "Venting the heat outside would be wasteful. But if you ran the pipes into Thorbardin, you could use the heat from the forge to—Selquist, why are you banging your head against the wall?"

"Never mind," Selquist said bitterly. He really had to put together a new team. "Just stop your yammering and come with me."

Selquist turned to his right and stalked off. Raising his lantern, he flashed it over one of the largest forges the dwarves had ever seen. Huge cauldrons, suspended on enormous chains, hung over gigantic fire pits. An underground stream fed into a dwarf-made lake used to cool the molten iron.

A few broken tools lay scattered about the floor, but the thrifty dwarves had long ago carried off anything useful before walling up this area.

The dwarves stared in awed silence, picturing the hundreds of dwarves sweating and toiling in the light of the roaring forge fires, hearing the ringing blows of hammer on iron, the sizzle of the hot ore plunging into the water, the steam rising up like wraiths out of the turgid water.

Pestle walked over, picked up a pair of broken tongs, and ran his hand over it lovingly. Selquist was half-Daergar and half-Neidar. Pestle was suspected of being at least half-Hylar, or mountain dwarf. He was fascinated with forging. He had once been apprenticed to the village blacksmith, but the disappearance of several steel coins from the smith's money box led to heated words and Pestle's eventual dismissal. Pestle's ambition was to acquire money enough to open his own smithy.

Selquist flashed his lantern overhead, illuminating the remnants of a system of large iron pipes that would vent the heat from the forge, carry the heat to the inhabited portions of Thorbardin. The iron had long since rusted and corroded, leaving scraps of pipe strewn across the tops of the forges.

Selquist climbed up onto one of the enormous stone hearths, set his lantern down. From there, he grabbed onto a dangling chain and shinnied up it until he was opposite the hole. It was about as wide as he was tall. With the agility of a spider (which Selquist's detractors said he rather resembled), the scrawny dwarf swung from the chain into the hole and disappeared.

The three dwarves waiting below were startled, but before they could say anything, Selquist reappeared, grinning and waving. "Come on!"

His companions, who weighed considerably more and who were not built for leaping blithely from chains into holes, glanced at each other dubiously. Auger shook his head.

"I'll help you!" Selquist said.

"What about the lantern?" Mortar asked.

"Douse it and leave it there. We'll need it on the way back."

The dwarves clambered up onto the hearth and climbed the chain, Pestle in the lead. Selquist held out his hands. Pestle swung over to the hole. Selquist grabbed the dwarf, helped him down off the chain without mishap. The other two made it with only minor difficulties—such as Auger swinging himself into the wall instead of the hole—but eventually all four dwarves were crouched, safe and sound, inside the hole. Selquist took the lead.

The opening narrowed considerably, forcing the dwarves to drop to their hands and knees and crawl. It ran horizontally for twenty feet, then turned to the right and extended on for another twenty feet. By this time, they could all see light at the end of the pipe, beyond an iron grating.

Once they reached the grating, Selquist cautioned his friends to silence and peered out to see if anyone was in the tunnels underneath.

The tunnels were empty. Swiftly, Selquist removed several bolts from the grating—he'd had the foresight to loosen these bolts on his previous trip—and swung the grating open.

"Hurry!" he whispered. "And keep quiet!"

Selquist held the grate while the other three exited. They tumbled out onto the floor of a torch-lit corridor. Unlike the abandoned shafts through which they had been walking, the corridor had every sign of being well-traveled. It was clean, well-lit, and they could hear voices, very faint and far away.

They looked up at Selquist, who was still in the pipe.

"People live here?" Pestle gulped.

"Of course, people live here," Selquist returned. "It's difficult to steal from people if there aren't any people to steal from! Now, shut up and take these."

Selquist handed down several objects wrapped in cloth, which he'd left inside the pipe on his previous visit.

"What are they? Burglar tools?" Pestle asked Mortar.

"No," said Mortar, on the receiving end. "They're brooms."

"Brooms!" The three glowered up at Selquist.

"I'll explain in a minute."

Letting the grating fall, Selquist squeezed out and dropped to the floor himself. Grinning in triumph, he turned to his companions.

"Gentlemen," he said. "As our friend Mortar has already said once today, welcome to Thorbardin."

The three did not share his glee. They were staring at him and at each other in dismay. All were covered, from beard to boots, in greasy black soot.

Mortar tried in vain to wipe off the soot, succeeded only in smearing it across his face.

"We can't go waltzing around Thorbardin looking like this!" he spluttered. "They'll think we're . . . we're gully dwarves or something and slap us in jail for sure!"

"Nonsense," Selquist said. "And don't wipe that off. It's the ideal disguise. I used it myself with much success on my last trip here. Here, each of you take a broom. Now, if anyone asks, we're chimney sweeps!"

The eyes of the three soot-covered dwarves widened. They continued to gaze at Selquist, but now it was with admiration. This was why he was their leader.

They shouldered their brooms and marched off down the corridor. Rounding that corridor, they stepped out onto a balcony overlooking Thorbardin.

Each halted, awe-struck. The view was magnificent.

The entire nation of Thorbardin is housed inside the Kharolis mountains. Here are seven major cities, three farming warrens, two governmental areas, a fortress at Northgate and Southgate, and the City of the Dead. From their vantage point, the dwarves could see only a small portion of the vast delvings, but what they saw was enough to stop their breath.

Their village of Celebundin, of which they were rightly proud, could have been dropped intact into this vast hall and made hardly a splotch at the bottom.

Far off, in the distance, they could see the famed Life Tree of the Hylar, the enormous stalactite that was a self-contained, heavily fortified city. Its many stone turrets and towers, stairs and walkways housed everything from important government offices and private residences to gardens and shops.

If an enemy did manage to break through the stone gates of the mountain, the dwarves could withdraw into the Life Tree and hold out against a besieging army for—by some estimates—a hundred years.

By that time most besieging armies would have lost interest.

Three of the dwarves stepped up to the railing of the balcony and looked down.

Auger stayed behind, his back firmly against solid rock. He got dizzy just climbing a tree. When the others leaned over the balcony to take a look below, Auger shut his eyes and grabbed hold of a piece of the wall.

"That's the Seventh Road down there." Selquist pointed out the sights. "We're just north of the West Guardian Hall, which enters the Valley of the Thanes. We'll go north along this road, then skirt around the West Warrens. Then, we head straight for Theiwar territory. Once there, we can relax."

At this, even Auger's eyes opened.

"Theiwar!" Mortar repeated. "You didn't say anything about the Theiwar!"

"They're bad dwarves," Pestle said.

"We're bad dwarves," Selquist pointed out.

"It's not the same," Pestle muttered.

"They're vampires," Auger said in a low voice. "They drink blood, and they hang from the roofs of their caves by their feet, and if the sunlight hits them they vanish in a puff of green smoke."

"Where do you come up with this stuff?" Selquist glared at him.

"My Nana told me," Auger replied.

"Mortar, explain," Selquist said.

Mortar explained that the Theiwar, through years of living underground had indeed formed an aversion to sunlight but that this did not make them vampires. And though generally conceded to harbor dark and twisted ambitions of dominating all the other races of dwarves and therefore shunned by all other races of dwarves, the Theiwar did not eat dwarven babies, as was popularly maintained.

And, yes, they were the only race of dwarves with any interest whatsoever in practicing magic but, though this showed them lacking in common sense, it did not necessarily make them bad people.

While Mortar was thus learnedly discoursing, Selquist herded his team over to a staircase, which was cut out of the rock wall and zigzagged down the side of the cliff.

"I can't!" Auger gasped, clinging to the wall. The tallest tree in the forests in their valley would look like a sprig from this far above.

"Who ever heard of a second-story man afraid of heights?" Selquist demanded.

"I'm more a cellar man, myself," Auger said, quavering.

"Shut your eyes and hold onto my hand," Selquist said finally. "We'll guide you down. That's the Seventh Road down there."

Dwarves always take a no-nonsense approach to names (with the exception of Selquist's mother), and the road was known as the Seventh Road because it was the seventh road leading out from Northgate, where began the First Road.

Slowly, with Auger painfully clutching their hands, the dwarves made their descent.

Chapter Twelve

The four traveled north along the Seventh Road. No one stopped them or even paid much attention to them. Most of the Hylar they passed seemed unaware of their very existence, although several matronly dwarves did cross the street, gathering up their skirts to avoid brushing against the filthy sweeps. One wedding party actually halted long enough for the bride to shake hands with Selquist, it being well-known that shaking hands with a sweep brings luck.

They were just dragging Auger away from ogling the bride, when, rounding a bend, they were accosted by four unusually tall dwarves wearing highly ornamented breastplates and huge battle-axes at their belts.

Auger knew immediately that they'd been apprehended. Giving a whimper, he started to sink to his knees, intending to throw himself on the mercy of the court.

"What's that idiot doing!" Selquist hissed. "Mortar, pick him up! Pestle, bring him in here!"

Mortar propped Auger up from behind. Pestle pulled from the front. Selquist herded his companions into a convenient doorway.

A wooden handcart adorned with a coat of arms rolled past, pulled by two shabby dwarves. Two more dwarves, rather more rotund than their fellows and much better dressed, walked along on either side of the cart. The well-dressed dwarves—both of whom were wearing massive golden chains around their necks—smoothed their glossy beards and talked in loud boisterous tones to each other.

The armed guards gave the four chimney sweeps suspicious looks and rattled their axes but passed by without accosting them.

"It's nothing. Probably the tax collectors," Selquist whispered hurriedly. "They're not after us."

The cart, heavily laden with bulging sacks, rolled by.

"I bet that's full of gold and steel!" Pestle said wistfully.

Selquist gave the air an investigatory sniff, his nose twitched. "Gold, I think. Some steel mixed in, maybe a couple of bars of silver. They wanted nothing to do with us, that's for sure. Still, this is just a sample of the wealth we'll find. Where we're going, there'll be riches for us all. Stick with me, and someday you, too, Auger, will wear a gold chain around your neck."

"Either that or a noose," Pestle said gloomily to Mortar. The sight of the battle-axes had shaken his nerves.

The hill dwarves continued on, thankful that Selquist knew where he was going. (At least, they hoped Selquist knew where he was going.) Unable to see the sun, they had lost all sense of time and place, wandering around inside the mountain. Mortar guessed by the growling of his stomach that it was well after the dinner hour.

"Where's the ale you promised?" he grumbled to Selquist. "And food?"

"Soon, soon," Selquist said. "Keep moving. We have to be there by night."

"It's always night down here," Auger said, but no one paid any attention.

The Seventh Road ended at a building. Here they ran across the wooden cart again. The contents were being unloaded into a larger cart, drawn by what appeared to be some sort of giant badger. The well-dressed dwarves stood slightly apart from the working dwarves, still chatting casually, though neither of them took their eyes from the tax money.

"Circle around it," Selquist said.

The four scooted around the outside of a series of tunnels which Selquist said were called the West Warrens. They came upon the Second Road, which was, according to Selquist, one of two roads leading from the North Gate to the Theiwar city of Themadlin. As one might imagine, this road was not heavily traveled, except, perhaps, by rats.

The four entered a part of Thorbardin far different from the parts through which they had recently traveled. The passageway was poorly lit, littered with refuse, and foul smelling. Enormous cracks gaped at their feet. These cracks appeared to have been caused by quakes, but they had not been repaired, and might have been left to slow down any threatening force. Crude wooden bridges spanned the chasms, planks that could be taken up swiftly in a defensive situation.

Auger shook and shivered while crossing these planks, and it was several long hours after they first entered Thorbardin before they finally reached the outskirts of the Theiwar city.

The Theiwar dwelt on several levels, burrowing downward deep into the mountains' roots. This area—the bottom floor for the Hylar—was the top floor of the Theiwar settlements.

The Theiwar had built no walls; there were no guard houses or barracks marking the entrance to their territory. But there were guards. Four dwarves, each with a battle-axe at the ready, stood blocking the road.

The dwarves were dressed in clothes that appeared to be cast-offs; the breeches and tunics were mismatched and tattered. Their hair was uncombed and matted, their beards were greasy and contained remnants of past meals. One of the dwarves was missing an eye. The eyelid covering the empty socket had been sewn shut. Yellow puss dribbled from beneath the wrinkled eyelid, ran down the dwarf's chin, making tracks into his beard. The axes the Theiwar carried were top notch—well made, the blades sharp and gleaming in the light of many torches.

Auger, Pestle, and Mortar bunched together and wished they hadn't come.

Selquist greeted the Theiwar with a nonchalant, "Good-evening, sirs," and continued on.

"That's far enough," said the lead Theiwar—the one missing an eye. "What brings you swells to the city of Themadlin? Out slumming?"

"Relax, Theiwar cousin. We are not Hylar." Selquist stepped forward.

He rubbed some of the dirt from his face, so that the Theiwar could get a good look at him. Even though they were travel worn and blackened with soot, he and his companions still presented a distinct contrast to the Theiwar, who both looked and smelled as if their last baths had been taken about the time of the Dwarfgate wars.

"We are Daewar, come to learn from Chronix. I am his apprentice. My name is Selquist."

The four armed Theiwar discussed the matter in low tones. When their conversation ended, the one-eyed dwarf walked closer and thrust his face into Selquist's.

"You're Daewar, all right, or I've never smelled Daewar before. Which I have. I hate the smell of Daewar." He fingered his axe.

"We're not Daewar!" Auger protested, despite Selquist's attempt to warn his friend off with an alarmed look and a jerk of the head. "We're Neidar."

"Oh, yeah?" The Theiwar clomped over, twisted his head to regard Auger with the one good eye. "Well, ain't that too bad. 'Cause while I don't like Daewar none, I got a healthy respect for 'em." The glaring eye came closer and so did the axe blade. "I got no respect at all for Neidar pukes. I'd just as soon crack open a Neidar's skull as look him in the face."

Auger shrank back between his comrades, who were attempting to crawl into the rock wall behind them.

Selquist, with a sigh, strode forward. He slapped the Theiwar on the back.

"By Reorx, man, don't you know a joke when you hear one? Auger's such a comedian. Neidar! Ha, ha! That's a good one! Why look at these dirty rascals. Do they look like Neidar to you?"

"They look more like gully dwarves than anything," the Theiwar said.

"And what would Neidar be doing in Thorbardin? How would they get in? Unless you think the Hylar opened the Great Gate for us." Selquist laughed loudly at the thought. His companions, with some prompting, laughed—a little sickly, but it was laughter.

"Or maybe we crawled through a crack in the mountain!" Selquist laughed harder.

His companions fell silent, glared at him.

The Theiwar scratched his head with the blade of his axe. "I guess maybe you're right."

Losing interest in the other three, much to their vast relief, the one-eyed Theiwar turned back to Selquist.

"You've been here before, ain't you?"

Selquist nodded. "As I said, I am Chronix's apprentice. He's teaching me the fine art of acquistions. He will vouch for me and my party. Now, if you'll just direct me to his dwelling—"

"You ain't goin' nowhere, Daewar cousin." The Theiwar gave the term a most uncousinly emphasis. "You're gonna wait right here. Chronix can claim you if he wants. I ain't gonna let four Daewar loose in Themadlin. Wait in there."

He pointed to a mean-looking hovel that the four at first took for a refuse dump but which turned out to be the local tavern. Selquist and his friends shuffled inside, slipping in spilled ale and treading on broken crockery. The Theiwar guard sent a runner after Chronix and then clomped inside to keep his one good eye on the visitors.

The four, conscious of the scrutiny, sat down at the only table they could find that was actually standing upright and tried to look nonchalant. A fire sputtered in the fireplace, belching out more smoke than heat. Several huge kegs, with spigots attached, looked as if they were holding up the wall at the back.

A slatternly barmaid slouched over to the table. She had black hair, brown eyes, and the longest, curliest side-whiskers any of them had ever seen. Auger was smitten.

"What'cha want?" she growled.

"Ale," said Selquist promptly. "Four mugs."

The others regarded him with horror.

"I promised you ale, Mortar," Selquist said virtuously, "and ale you shall have. We want to keep you regular, you know."

Mortar groaned and closed his eyes. He had visions of being a good deal more regular than was good for a fellow.

The ale turned out to be surprisingly potable, as even Mortar—who was a connoisseur—admitted. It was dark and foaming, with a smoky quality that spoke of oak kegs stored in cool, deep caverns. Once the dwarves fished out the small black-winged objects floating dead on the surface, they enjoyed the ale considerably.

They waited for nearly half an hour. Finally the runner returned, accompanied by another dwarf trotting along at his side. This Theiwar was short, even for a dwarf. He came only to Selquist's shoulder. Bounding over to the table, breathless from the exertion—for he was forced to run where others walked—the dwarf gave Selquist a good, hard look, sniffed at him, then nodded.

"Yes, that's him. I never saw the other three, but I'll take responsibility for them."

"All right. Off with you," the leader snarled. He gave them one last baleful glance from his good eye and stalked back to his post.

Chronix stood regarding each of them in silence. The dwarves grew nervous beneath his intense gaze.

Finally, Selquist said, "As you requested, Chronix, I brought along my friends."

Chronix broke into a gap-toothed grin. "Good," he said, rubbing dirty, pudgy hands together. "For this job, that's very good indeed."

Chapter Thirteen

It had been a good party. A helluva good party. Kang couldn't recall a better party, but then he couldn't recall his own name at the moment. The raid on the dwarven village had netted the draconians five kegs of ale and three barrels of dwarf spirits. During the days and nights that followed—and Kang wasn't sure how many of those there had been—he had drunk his full share.

Staggering through the door of his quarters, he saw six beds in front of him. Something in his dwarf-spirit fuzzed brain told him that he only owned one bed. The other five were not really there. But he had no idea which bed was which.

Choosing one, he headed for it, flopped down on it.

He missed, landed snout-first on the floor, hard.

It didn't matter. Before he hit, he was asleep.

A thunderous boom roused him from his stupor. He had been dreaming about a battle with the Knights of Solamnia, dreaming that a gnomish device had exploded in the midst of the conflict, wrecking havoc on friend and foe alike.

Groping for a blanket, Kang dragged it over his head, to protect himself from the flying shrapnel and tried to go back to sleep.

The thunderous boom came again. Kang pulled off the blanket, listened. There was something familiar about that boom. Something he knew he should recognize. It was . . . It was . . .

A knock on his door.

Kang groaned. "Go away!"

Instead, the knock was repeated. That meant that it was the duty sentry, and the fact that he had knocked twice meant that it was important—really important. The last piece of business Kang had conducted, before settling down to some serious guzzling, had been to make certain the sentries were set, the long and short range patrols were assigned. Isolated in a hostile environment, the draconians could not afford to let down their guard. A share of the take was set aside for those on duty, who would have their chance to celebrate on their return. It must be one of those patrols reporting now.

Kang groaned again, lifted his head, which seemed to have grown in size since their last meeting. "I'm asleep. What d'ya want?"

The knock was repeated a third time. This was an emergency.

Kang knew better than to try to stand up. He rolled over, faced the door. "Come in!" he yelled.

The door opened, letting in a full blast of blaring sunlight. Kang peered painfully through the glare.

A Baaz by the name of Clotdoth stood in the doorway. He saluted. "Sir, I didn't want to wake you, but the—"

"Just say what you've got to say, and then leave me the hell alone," Kang snarled.

Before the Baaz could answer, a Bozak pushed through the door. His name was Stemhmph, and he was the reconnaissance officer.

Startled, Kang sat upright on the floor. He instantly regretted his hasty move. The floor heaved and buckled, as did Kang's stomach.

"I'm sorry to bother you, sir, but it's urgent." Stemhmph reported. "My patrol came in early by three days. They reported seeing a dragon flying across the Plains of Dust. I thought you'd want to know right away."

Kang's brain fought its way through the fumes of the dwarf spirits. The word "dragon" aided in the mental battle, and in a relatively few minutes, Kang was on his feet and about as sober as could be expected. More sober than he wanted.

"Was the dragon flying north, in this direction? What kind was it?"

Stemhmph shook his head. "It was flying across the Plains, sir, heading west. As to what kind it was, the patrol leader couldn't tell. It was silhouetted against the sun. He thinks it was a red dragon, by its size. And he reported that he did not sense the normal 'dragon dread' that we used to feel whenever any of Paladine's cursed wyrms came near us."

Kang's head had won the battle but lost the war. His brain felt too big for his skull, which throbbed and ached.

"One of our Queen's dragons? Flying in broad daylight? Something's up," he muttered, adding, "Have the duty officer call Officer's Call at mid-morning. I'd tell you to double the guard on the walls, but I don't think you'll find anybody sober enough to climb up there. Good work, Stemhmph. Now let me go back to sleep."

The draconian saluted and shut the door behind him very, very gently.

*　*　*　*　*

Two days later, the effects of the dwarf spirits had been wrung out of Kang's body by a long and arduous march through the mountains, down to the Plains of Dust. Locating an outcropping of rock, cooled by the shade of a gigantic pine tree, he sat down to watch.

In the rocks and trees behind him crouched a troop of draconians from First Squadron, combat equipped. Back at the village, the entire regiment was at battle readiness. The draconians had no idea what had brought their dragon cousins and allies back out into a world they had lost, a world now ruled by Paladine's dragons, but they guessed it might be war.

The last time Kang had seen a red dragon was at Neraka, at the end of the War of the Lance. That had been over twenty years ago.

He waited patiently, squinting into the waves of heat that roiled off the desert sands below. At first, all he saw was a buzzard wheeling in the cloudless sky. Then, as his eyes became more and more accustomed to the bright light, he was aware of something flying the skies over the Plains of Dust. He couldn't tell what it was, but it was large. Two specks, moving steadily and rapidly forward, heading toward his position.

The buzzard ceased its circling, and flapped down with a contented croak in the rocks below.

"This is it," Kang said to himself.

Rising to his feet, he turned around, looked behind him, searching for a glint of armor, a shining scale, anything that might have given away the fact that there was a squadron of draconians hidden among the rocks. He saw nothing and smiled. His men were good. Damn good. It was a shame that they might all be dead in the next ten minutes.

Turning, Kang left his rock, scrabbled down the hillside. He passed the buzzard, feasting on a dead deer, and walked out into the burning hot sand of the Plains of Dust. He waited.

The two dots drew rapidly nearer, near enough for Kang to get a good look at them.

Two red dragons and, on their back, two dragon riders. They had been flying from west to east when, suddenly, the dragons veered from their path. They had spotted Kang.

The dragons spiraled downward, their wings extended, riding on the thermals rising from the desert floor. The sun glistened on their red scales. Massive, enormous, over forty-eight feet in length from their fanged mouths to their lashing tails, the red dragons were not as graceful as most of the others of their kind. But, like all dragons, they possessed a horrific, awful type of beauty.

And, like all dragons, even those who worshipped her Dark Majesty, the reds loathed the perverted spawn of the eggs of their cousins. The reds would not dare admit it, nor would the blacks, nor the whites, nor any of the other colors of dragons serving She of Many Colors and of None. Red dragons and draconians were allies, ostensibly. But Kang knew well that the glittering eye of a red never fell on him but that it was filled with hatred born of deep-rooted fear. What had happened to one clutch of dragon eggs could happen to another.

The two red dragons landed fifty feet in front of Kang. They were male and female, probably a mated pair, and they regarded him with sneering disdain. Their riders wore full dragon armor, a type Kang had never before seen—black metal with red facings, adorned with emblems of death.

One of the riders remained mounted, on the alert. The other rider dismounted and began to walk toward Kang. The rider was helmed, wore a sword. Kang could not see the face.

"Come no closer," Kang warned.

The dragon rider halted, pulled off her helmet. Hair as red as the fiery sun was pulled back, away from her face, fell in a long braid over her black armor. She might have been attractive for a human. Kang couldn't tell. Some draconians, having no females of their own, lusted after human females. Kang didn't happen to be one of them.

He stood in silence, leaving it to the rider to speak.

"Tell me, draconian," she said in a clear voice that echoed among the rocks, "why do I find dragonspawn a day and a half's march from Thorbardin, twenty-five years after your kind was, to all intents, exterminated?"

Kang made a mental check of his magical spells, catalogued them. They had seemed powerful to him, when he'd received them as a gift from his Queen. Now—recalling the immense magical power of the red dragons—his little spells were puny, worth less than the sand on his clawed feet.

"We are here because we survived," Kang answered. "Now, tell me why I find two dragon riders mounted on red dragons who, if they are caught out in the open by Paladine's gold dragons, will most surely be exterminated?"

The rider gazed at him steadily. "I am Talon Leader Huzzud, Knight of the Lily, as is my companion. We are the scouts for the Fifth Army of Conquest, led by Lord Ariakan, ruler of Ansalon."

Kang's wings fanned him, cooled him. Standing under the beating sun, he had to fight off a tendency to drowsiness. "Ariakan?" He repeated the name. "Any relation to Ariakus, the long-dead former ruler of Ansalon?"

The woman frowned at his sarcasm. "Lord Ariakan is his son," she said coldly. "And I would take care with my tongue, draconian, lest you want me to cut it out. You will speak of my lord with respect."

"If and when he earns it," Kang growled. "I am Kang, commander of the First Dragonarmy Engineer Regiment. You call yourself a Knight of the Lily. Is that anything like a Solamnic Knight of the Rose?"

He expected this question to be answered with a foul oath and spitting denial. Instead, to his astonishment, the woman nodded gravely, solemnly. "We are equal in rank and in honor," she said, "though not in our beliefs."

Noting Kang's mouth part, his tongue flick in derision, she gave a slight smile. "Times have changed, draconian. Those of us who serve the Dark Queen have learned our lesson. A hard one, I must admit. We Knights of Takhisis are pledged body and soul to Her Majesty, to our duty as soldiers, and"—she paused for effect—"to honor, and to each other.

"We are bound to sacrifice everything for Our Queen's great Cause. Not only our lives, which are hers to do with as she sees fit, but our ambition, our desires, our own selfish goals. All are subsumed in her greater glory. Our duty lies in serving her to the best of our abilities."

Kang was impressed. He'd never heard any servant of the Dark Queen speak like this. Generally her greater glory came second to greed, lust, ambition, and self-aggrandizement. If what this knight said held true—and, admittedly, talk was cheap—than this Ariakan might be a commander Kang could respect.

"So, draconian, I take it that you are the lone survivor of this Engineer Regiment. It is a wonder you have survived all by yourself, so near the dwarven homelands."

"Not quite alone, Sir Knight," Kang said, with a grin.

A wave of his hand brought movement among the rocks. The draconians rose to their feet. The rider, startled, took two steps backward. Behind her, the red dragons lifted their wings, thrashed their tails, and dug their feet into the sand.

"This is the Second Troop of the First Squadron. I have over two hundred engineers in my command," Kang said with pride. "We live in a walled city in the mountains. If this Lord Ariakan is looking for soldiers, I would be pleased to speak to one of his commanders."

The rider hesitated for a moment, staring at the draconians scattered about the hill above her. "The army is three days' march behind us. We intend to camp in these very foothills. If you will tell me where your village is located, I will send a messenger . . ."

"That won't be necessary," Kang said. "I'll be waiting."

The knight didn't like that, but she apparently understood Kang's reluctance to reveal the location of his headquarters—even to those who were ostensibly allies. On more than one occasion, allies had very nearly gotten him killed.

She gave a cool nod, turned smartly on the heel of her boot, and left him. After a few moments speaking to her wingmate, she mounted her dragon and gave a yank on the reins. The red female glared balefully at Kang, then propelled herself off the ground with powerful hind legs, claws digging great holes in the sand. Spreading her enormous red wings, the dragon lifted up into the air. Notoriously bad-tempered, the red female snorted a gout of flame in Kang's general direction before flying off.

Kang was careful to take no offense; the dragon's rider spoke a sharp word of reprimand. She lifted her hand to Kang in salute. The rider's wingmate joined her in the air. The dragons flew off across the desert, dwindling in the distance until they vanished from sight.

"The Dark Queen is once again on the move. This could be good," Kang said to himself, his sun-drowsed blood now pumping hot with excitement. "This could be good! This could be very good indeed."

Chapter Fourteen

The hill dwarves did not see the dragons, knew nothing of the fact that an army of those whom the rest of the world was calling dark knights was marching across the Plains of Dust. The dwarves of Celebundin sent out patrols, but those patrols never bothered patrolling the Plains of Dust. No one was out there except the barbarian humans known as the Plainsmen, and they kept to themselves, had as few dealings with other races as possible, which was good, in the minds of the hill dwarves. Everyone knew the barbarians were crazed. They'd have to be, to live voluntarily in the desert.

The hill dwarves did not like the desert. They did not like the heat, the glaring sun, the vast open spaces without cover. Born to burrowing and delving, born to cool underground caverns or heavily wooded forests, the hill dwarves could not conceive of any sane being setting foot on the burning sands.

Selquist and his companions might have seen the dragons and the army of knights on their return trip from Thorbardin, but they chose to take a westerly route back around the mountain. Loaded down with loot, they opted for the easiest paths possible. They reached Celebundin without seeing anything more threatening than glimpsing an ogre from a distance. The dwarves had rapidly increased that distance, and they arrived back at the outskirts of the village with nothing worse than sore feet and shoulders that ached from carrying their heavy packs.

They waited in the woods for nightfall, in order to sneak undetected back into the dwarven village. It would never do for the High Thane to discover they'd been out on a private raid. He'd make them do something dreadful with the loot—like share it. Utilizing the same apple orchard they'd used to effect their escape, the dwarves crept past the slumbering sentry and made their way safely and unobserved back to Selquist's house.

He unlocked the three locks, grateful to see that no dishonest person had been tampering with them in his absence, and the four tromped inside.

Once there, safe and sound and away from Theiwar and Niedar and corpses in carts and tax collectors, the four dwarves all breathed a heart-felt sigh of relief. Even Selquist announced that it was good to be home. With that, he dumped the contents of his sack out onto the large central table.

"Incredible!" he said. "Absolutely incredible."

The other three had to admit he was right.

The take consisted of two silver ale mugs, a pair of bone candlesticks adorned with semiprecious stones, a half-dozen rings whose value was not immediately obvious but were hopefully worth something, and—Pestle's favorite—a silver hair comb adorned with an amulet carved in the shape of a skull. The skull's eye sockets glowed red in the dark. Pestle was convinced it was magic.

"Of course, it's magic," Selquist maintained knowledgeably. "It'll fetch a fine price at this mage-ware shop I know in Palanthas. It's run by a woman named Jenna who isn't at all particular about how a fellow comes by his wares. Here now, don't be messing with that, Pestle. Put it back. You might say the wrong word and turn yourself into a human or something worse. An elf maybe."

Hastily, Pestle let the skull drop back onto the table. He continued to gaze at it, fascinated.

"I just can't figure out what makes the eyes glow like that!"

Auger removed a large, tattered, and dirty leather-bound book from his backpack and thumped it onto the table. "I don't know what you made me carry this all the way back for. It's heavy, and it smells funny."

"Mildew," said Mortar, eyeing the book.

Selquist picked up the book, ran his hand over the torn binding lovingly.

"This is more valuable than everything on that table combined. More valuable than everything in the Thane's warehouse. In my long and not inglorious career, this is the most valuable object I've ever stol—um . . . acquired."

"Is it magic?" Pestle regarded the book with more interest, though he was disappointed that it didn't glow.

"No, it's not magic," Auger said scornfully. "Not unless I can suddenly read magic, which, thank Reorx, I can't. It's written in our language, though some of the words are spelled funny. And, from the looks of it, the book's a record of some Daewar raiding party from about thirty years ago. It might be of some value historically."

Mortar gazed at Selquist in puzzlement. "Since when do you go in for history?"

"Since it stands to turn a handsome profit," Selquist replied, with a wink. "I've said it before and I'll say it again, you three have no imaginations. None whatsoever. If it wasn't for me, you'd all be picking potatoes in the High Thane's garden."

The three looked at the old book and tried to imagine something valuable about it. They failed.

"Where'd you find it?" Mortar asked, hoping to come up with a clue.

Selquist lowered his voice, leaned forward, and said softly, "From a chest under old Chronix's bed. A locked chest. So it must be valuable."

He stood back and allowed the others to regard him with astonished admiration.

"You . . . you stole that book from . . . from Chronix!" Mortar was the only one able to talk. Auger and Pestle were rendered speechless.

"Of course," Selquist said, modestly.

"But, he's your teacher! Won't he be mad?"

"Why should he? It's a compliment to him, really." Selquist shrugged. "He taught me well."

"But what could be valuable about a book about a Daewar raid? Unless it's got jewels hidden inside it somewhere," Auger argued.

"A raiding party means treasure. Treasure that has to be stashed away. Hidden. A book about the raiding party means—"

"—that it might tell where the treasure's hidden!" Pestle shouted.

"Very good," Selquist said, patting Pestle's head in approval. "Keep your voice down."

"But"—Mortar was thinking again, a habit Selquist found annoying—"if this book does tell where the treasure is stashed, then Chronix must have already found it."

"Not so," Selquist replied. "Chronix can't read."

"But he could have had someone to read to him."

"Maybe he doesn't trust anyone else. Maybe he doesn't know anyone who can read," Selquist returned. "Look at it this way. If he'd already found the treasure, he wouldn't still be keeping the book under lock and key, now would he?"

Mortar frowned. "Well, yes, but—"

"No more buts!" Selquist said, irritated. "I don't have all the answers now, but I will have in just a few days. Just as soon as Auger and I read this book.

"While we're doing that," he continued, "you and Pestle will take this load to Pax Tharkas and sell it there. Just be careful traveling the road. There's a lot of thieves running about these days."

"True enough," Pestle said and shook his head over the degeneracy of the times. "It'll take three days to reach Pax Tharkas and three days to return. Give us a day to sell the stuff."

"Not in the marketplace," Selquist cautioned. "Someone from Thorbardin might recognize some of these things."

"I may not have an imagination, but I'm smarter than that," Pestle said stiffly. "I'll go see my kender friend Rhanga Changehands. He'll take this stuff and give us a good price."

"A kender?" Selquist was skeptical. "Since when are they in the buying end of the thieving business?"

"He's been in business a long time. He's smarter than most kender. I think he must be part human."

"That's not saying much," Selquist grumbled. "Very well, if that's the best you can manage. But don't come back with less than twenty steel. And make sure the kender gives you a receipt."

Pestle and Mortar repacked all the items.

"See you in a week," Mortar said. "Good luck with the book."

* * * * *

Selquist and Auger slept late, thankful to be in their own beds once again. Once Selquist was up and moving, he woke Auger, started him on the book, and then fixed breakfast.

The book was more than two inches thick, with heavy parchment pages. Some of the pages were loose and hung out of the binding. The cover was made of limp brown leather, which was worn and starting to peel off in places. No title or marking adorned it. The writing was scratchy and barely legible.

Handing Auger a plate of eggs and a rasher of bacon, Selquist sat down. "All right. What have we got? Read it aloud. No, not with your mouth full! You're spitting egg all over the table."

Auger gulped down his meal, started with the opening page.

" 'First Day: Halfest, our commander, orders us to hurry up with gathering the provisions. He says that we must leave today, or abandon the quest. He hit Grumold with the whip when Grumold sat down to rest. We hurry.

" 'Later: Grumold is now our commander. He killed Halfest, but says we still have to hurry. Grumold now has the whip. We obey.' " Auger looked up at Selquist. "Nice bunch, these Daewar."

"I'm sure Grumold had his reasons," Selquist said stiffly. "Keep reading."

Auger settled back and read. Selquist sat in his comfortable chair and listened. Toward evening, when Auger's voice appeared about to give out, Selquist kept him supplied with nut-ale, which was known to have a coating effect on the throat.

The book was written, so they discovered, by a Daewar scribe who was in the service of the Daewar Thane at that time. The scribe had been sent along on the quest by the Thane to keep a record of the expedition. Not for posterity, apparently, but because the Thane didn't trust the expedition's leaders.

The first day's reading followed the Daewar from their home in Thorbardin out into the wilderness. The Daewar marched for days, their scribe writing down such notable events as a knife fight over the remains of the evening's rabbit stew, during which three Daewar were incapacitated and had to be left behind.

The only treasure taken thus far was the theft of a fresh-baked pie from a window of a farmer's cottage.

By that point, Selquist had fallen asleep in his chair. Waking suddenly from a bad dream in which Chronix was chasing him with a knife in one hand and a hot apple pie in the other, Selquist discovered that Auger was also asleep, his head on the book.

The two gave up and went to bed.

*   *   *   *   *

The second day of reading took the Daewar expeditionary force through some unnamed mountains, over an unnamed wasteland, where two more Daewar succumbed to thirst, an affliction with which Auger could sympathize. Toward lunchtime, he complained of a sore throat and, indeed, he could barely croak out the words. Selquist brought more ale and this time laced it with dwarf spirits for both of them. He felt in need of a restorative tonic.

"I can't believe this!" Selquist said during a pause in the reading while Auger soothed his vocal cords. "Where's the loot? Where's the treasure? Why the devil are they trekking through some godforsaken desert when they could just have easily stolen something closer to home? I don't think much of this Grumold as a leader."

"Should I quit reading?" Auger asked hopefully.

"No, we'll give it until tonight. Keep going."

Auger sighed and read on. " '. . . the approaches through the Doom Range were covered by regiments of draconian warriors—' "

"Stop!" Selquist shouted, and jumped out of his chair. He ran over to a large wooden chest, fastened with three locks. Unlocking the chest, he rummaged about for a moment. Auger, thankful for the respite, took another pull on his ale.

Selquist removed a map case, opened it, and drew out the map. Mumbling "Doom Range" to himself, he spread the map out on the table. He pointed his finger.

"Does that say what I think it says?"

Auger looked. "If you think it says 'Doom Range,' you're right."

"I knew it! The Doom Range. Those are the mountains just south of Neraka. Neraka! That's where they're going. This could be something, after all. The Dragon Highlords stored all their booty there, or so I've heard." Selquist rubbed his hands together. "This could be big! Very big! Keep reading!"

Fortified by the ale and buoyed in spirit, Auger continued where he had left off. His monotone droned on into the small hours of the morning, but other than a barroom brawl in Sanction, the scribe recorded nothing of any interest.

"Damn. I was hoping for more." Selquist sighed.

Auger yawned. He was half-drunk, bleary-eyed and barely able to speak. "The rest of the book is in real bad shape. It looks like someone dropped it in a fire."

He pointed to the next page, which was partially burned, the writing illegible.

"I wonder who the idiot was who tried to burn up my book," Selquist said indignantly. "Probably that louse, Grumold. I hope his Thane sacks him."

A snore was the only comment. Auger had fallen forward onto his forehead, sound asleep. Selquist shook him.

Auger never moved.

"All right." Selquist sighed. "I get the hint. Go to bed. We'll start again in the morning."

*   *   *   *   *

But by next morning, Auger had lost his voice completely. Selquist was forced to go hunting down the village cleric, who recited a healing prayer to Reorx, recommended a honey-mustard poultice for the chest, and charged Selquist the exorbitant sum of sixpence for her services.

The honey and the mustard cost another tenpence and by the time Selquist returned from the market, he'd forgotten whether the poultice was to be applied externally or taken internally. Just to be safe, he did both. By nightfall, Auger could talk, though he was now attracting flies.

" 'Day eighty-one: We've been underground for four days now. The quakes caused the walls of our cavern to cave in, but the stone held the roof in place. Vissik and Grevik are leading the digging, but with the loss of Romas and Uluth, who were buried under the rubble, we are sorely undermanned. The—' "

Auger stopped.

"The what?" Selquist said.

"I can't make it out. I think . . ." Auger pointed to the page. "I think that's blood!"

"Great! Not only does this idiot drop my book in the fire, he bleeds on it, too!"

Auger turned to the next page, which was torn, but readable.

" '. . . black-robed mages. We found two alive under all the rocks. We dug them out, then killed them. They did not try to cast spells. We continue to dig into the chamber, and have found what Grumold believes is the north wall. He says that according to the map, we should find a huge oak case that stands taller than a human and which contains many magical items and money and jewels. We are concentrating here in hope . . . ' "

"Yes, yes!" Selquist sat forward eagerly. "Good old Grumold! He's getting close! What does it say next."

"I don't know." Auger shook his head. "More blood."

Selquist consigned Grumold to the Abyss.

*   *   *   *   *

The next day, Selquist fed Auger more honey-mustard and slathered the concoction on the dwarf's chest, ignoring his protests and the fact that Auger's skin was starting to peel off. Selquist handed his friend the book.

Auger groaned, but Selquist was merciless. "Read."

Auger read. " ' . . . finally broke into the storage antechamber. The damage is not as bad here. The south wall held. The spellbooks were still in place on the shelf. We took them and several weapons that we believe are magical, plus some other stuff.' "

"Stuff! What stuff?" Selquist was excited.

"He doesn't say. He just says, 'We're all going to be rich. Richer than the Thane. Richer than all the thanes in all of Thorbardin.' "

Auger and Selquist stared at each other. Selquist, grinning widely, jumped up from the table and did a little dance around the living room.

Auger no longer needed any urging to keep reading. He read so fast now that Selquist could barely understand him. " 'We have filled nearly all of our packs with steel and jewels.' "

"Yes! Yes!" Selquist sang and danced.

" 'Some think that this is enough and that we should leave. But Grumold has commanded that we continue digging. He says that he feels great magical power coming from this room.' "

"Dear old Grumold! A true leader of men!" Selquist relapsed back into his chair, breathless but happy. "What did they find? Go on! Go on!"

" 'Later that day: Grumold was right! Just after midday break, Kuvoss discovered a dragon egg in a container under a wall support. What a find! It is still intact, and it is worth more than all of the other items combined!' "

Selquist looked stricken. "That's it? That's the big treasure?"

Auger glanced down the page. "Yeah, it looks that way."

"Dragon eggs." Selquist was gloomy. "Maybe they were worth something twenty-five years ago, but the bottom's dropped out of that market. Dragons are laying eggs all over the place now. Besides, any egg that's been sitting around for twenty-five years . . ." He wrinkled his nose, shook his head. "Grumold, that ninny! No foresight."

"You want to hear the rest?"

"I suppose," Selquist said glumly.

" 'Later: We have found nine more eggs. They are all unbroken and in good condition. But, unfortunately, they're not worth as much as we had first hoped.' "

"Hah!" Selquist said in gloomy satisfaction. "Grumold must have taken a look at the futures' market."

" 'Vissik found some writing on one of the storage cases. Noorhas translated them, as best he can, for they are written in Common. These eggs purportedly contain female draconians, which were never permitted to hatch. Still, the outer appearance of the eggs has been unchanged. Grumold says we could still sell them as regular dragon eggs—let the buyer beware!' "

"Grumold turns out to be smarter than I gave him credit for," Selquist admitted. "Keep reading. Maybe it says how much money they got for the eggs."

Auger read on, but the rest of the book was nothing more than the story of the Daewar's journey home, made interesting by accounts of fights breaking out over the treasure, fights which resulted in the deaths of several more Daewar. By the time the book ended, only Grumold and the scribe were left alive.

The next to the last entry read: " 'Grumold and I hid the treasure in a very cunning hiding place that no one will ever find.' "

The last entry went as follows, " 'Grumold was executed today on the Thane's orders for trying to keep the treasure all for himself. He did not know that I was writing this journal, or I am certain he would have never left me alive. I have been handsomely rewarded by the Thane. The map to the treasure trove is in this book, which I will soon hand over to the Thane.' "

"Let me look! Let me look!" Feverishly, Selquist grabbed the book from Auger and turned to the final page.

It was dirty, crumpled, and blank.

"Damn! Maybe the map's in the front."

"It's not," Auger said, but Selquist had to see for himself.

He saw. Nothing.

Selquist sank down in his chair and stared at nothing. "No map," he said. "No map."

Reaching his hand into his pocket, he pulled out the medallion of the Dark Queen. "I should have sent this off with Mortar. He wouldn't get near the price I could for it, of course, but about now I'd exchange it for a kender farthing."

He paused, let the ideas connect in his head. "Kender farthing. Nonexistant. Invisible. That's it!" he cried. "Invisible ink."

Selquist held the book to the sunlight streaming in through an upper window. He examined every page in the light, but, again, nothing. He tossed the book back onto the table in disgust.

"There must be a map," Auger said stubbornly.

"Maybe not," Selquist said. "Maybe that's why that wretch Chronix never used the book. He didn't have the map. I never did trust him." He threw the medallion down on top of the book. "As for that bauble, tomorrow night, I'm burying the damn thing. I'm obviously cursed."

"But the scribe said that the map was in the book."

"Another dwarf whose obviously not to be trusted," Selquist said dourly. "Look how he betrayed poor Grumold. 'The map is in the book. The map is in the book.'" He suddenly sprang to his feet with a wild, "Ah, ha!"

"What?" Auger cried, alarmed.

"Dear, sweet scribe. Blessed beautiful scribe! How could I ever doubt you?"

Selquist pulled a knife out of his boot. Sliding the blade inside the front cover, he slit the binding open and turned the leather back.

"The map is in the book," Selquist said, and triumphantly held up a folded piece of parchment.

Carefully, his hands trembling with excitement, he unfolded the paper, spread it out on the table.

It was indeed a map, indicating a maze of tunnels and passageways. The map was obviously drawn by dwarves, for it was extremely detailed, thoughtfully marking traps, how to spring them, and the angle of descent of various passageways.

Selquist studied the map carefully, then suddenly let out a cry. "I know where this is!"

"You do?" Auger rubbed his bleary eyes.

"Yes! Look, here's Southgate down here and Northgate up here. The chamber where the map starts is to the left. It can't be far from the air shaft I found." Selquist picked up the Dark Queen's medallion, gave it a reverent kiss. "Your Majesty, blessed Majesty! You've done something for me at last!"

Carefully, Selquist packed up the map and placed it inside the bone map case. He stowed the case back in the chest and locked the three locks. He put the medallion in his pocket. Then he sat back on his heels and heaved a sigh of blissful contentment.

"We're going to get rich from this one, aren't we, Selquist?" Auger asked.

"Yes," Selquist agreed, his voice choked with emotion. "Very rich indeed."

Chapter Fifteen

The draconians, bivouacked in the hills, spent the next two days watching the army of Lord Ariakan cross the Plains of Dust and establish a camp in the mountains.

The draconians were excited at the prospect of once more going to battle, and, though Kang did his best to rein in their enthusiasm, he had to admit that he shared their feelings. To serve under a commander who would respect them for their unique abilities, to have the chance to do what they were trained to do, which was to build, design, and man everything from bridges to trebuchets, assault towers to siege engines. The chance to be useful, as opposed to stagnating in their village, pickling their brains in dwarf spirits.

The moment the flags of the command tent were raised, Kang left his outlook position in the hills. Taking two Baaz with him to serve as honor guard, he marched down to meet with the commander of the Army of Takhisis.

In the old days, the campsite would have been a scene of confusion, with the commanders of individual regiments arguing over who had the best position and trying to cheat each other out of supplies. Brawling, drunkenness, camp followers getting in the way, their children under foot—the bad memories flooded back. If he saw any of that, Kang resolved to himself, he was turning around, taking his men, and marching back home.

He was pleasantly surprised. Not only surprised, but impressed. Damned impressed.

The soldiers moved about the camp site in orderly fashion, performing their allotted tasks with quiet efficiency. Orders were obeyed without question, without the need for whip-cracking, bullying superiors.

Kang stopped a knight clad in a black surcoat, adorned by the symbol of the flower known on Ansalon as the death-lily.

"Pardon, Sir Knight," Kang said, "but could you direct me to the location of the command tent?"

The draconian knew well enough were the tent stood. He'd spent the morning watching them erect it. Still, he wanted to see the knight's reaction.

The knight's gaze swept over the draconian, taking in Kang's armor—which he had polished until it outshone the sun—his harness with its indicators of rank, and the golden mallet that indicated his status as an engineer.

Kang tensed, expecting the sneer of derision or—worse—the patronizing smirk usually worn by humans when they spoke to draconians.

The knight, however, saluted and said, with marked respect, "Sir, the command tent is in that direction, about twenty-five paces. You can see the flag from here, sir. If the commander wishes, I will accompany him."

"Thank you, Sir Knight," Kang said, returning the salute. "I see the flag. I will not take you from your duties."

The knight saluted once more, and walked off.

Kang felt a warm glow suffuse his body. He'd once heard a poet speak of this feeling as love.

The command tent had been set up on a large flat rock shelf. Kang approved the site. During the hottest part of the day, the tent would be shielded from the sun by the shadow of the mountains. The tent was large, made of black and red panels sewn together. Two flags flew above it, the first one black, decorated with the black lily of violent death, its severed stem entwined around a bloody axe. Beneath that flew the flag denoting a lord commander, further adorned with a white skull. Standing outside the tent were two huge carved statues, resembling humans, but too tall for humans and grotesquely painted a garish color of blue.

Kang was wondering why these statues were present, assumed that they must be some form of new icon dedicated to Her Dark Majesty when, to his paralyzing astonishment, one of the statues moved. Eyes, swathed in a mask of blue, greasy paint, focused on Kang. A hand as big as Kang's hand—counting the claws—tightened around the hilt of a sword so enormous that most humans probably could not even lift it.

Kang came to a halt. The two Baaz behind him nearly bumped into him. He stared at the human, who stared back at him, and it was obvious that this was the first time either race had encountered the other. The human's blue-painted lips curled in a snarl. He let out a grunt, and drew a good six inches of steel from the outlandishly decorated scabbard.

A knight inside the tent came out to see what was going on. Spotting Kang, the knight said something to the human in a strange and uncouth language. The human grunted again and sheathed the sword blade. The eyes, however, did not leave Kang.

The draconian's eyes did not leave the human.

"Wait for me here," Kang ordered the Baaz. "And get your tongues back in your mouths," he added irritably.

The knight walked over to Kang and saluted. "This way, Commander. We've been expecting you."

He led the way into the tent. The senior officer sat at a small field desk with a leather writing surface. He wore the same black surcoat, this one decorated with a skull. Inside the tent was cooler than outside, but not by much. The heat was oppressive. The canvas flaps hung straight, no breeze stirred. The officer but did not appear to suffer in the heat, however. He was flanked by two more of the savage-looking humans. These guards wore two swords each and were clad from head to toe in heavy chain mail that must have weighed more than they did. They were not even sweating.

The general finished whatever it was he was writing, then rose to his feet.

"I present Robert Sykes, Lord of the Skull," announced the knight who served as the general's aide.

Sykes regarded Kang with frank curiosity. "Greetings, Commander—"

"Kang, sir," Kang said. "Of the First Dragonarmy Engineers."

"Indeed." The lord knight smiled slightly. "Not much remains of the First Dragonarmy anymore, Commander."

"We do, sir," Kang said proudly.

"So I am told." Sykes was in his middle years with dark hair and, in startling contrast, white, bristling eyebrows. His beard was short and neatly trimmed, streaked with gray and white strands. His gaze was cool, appraising, and saw more of others than he permitted to be seen of himself.

Turning to his aide, he said, "Have the First Wing assemble, ready for inspection."

The knight saluted and left. Sykes turned back to Kang.

"You have two hundred draconians under your command, Commander Kang," Sykes said. "Is that right?"

"Yes, sir. And I have to say, my lord, that I am very impressed by what I've seen here today. The armies of the Queen have improved a great deal since the War of the Lance, apparently."

Sykes smiled. "I was a company commander in the Second Dragonarmy during the War of the Lance. I have to agree with you, Commander Kang. The soldiers under such leaders as Dragon Highlord Verminaard were very much like their superiors—little more than thieves and butchers. I have always been inclined to include draconians among that number. I'm therefore afraid, Commander, that I have no need of your services."

Kang crossed his arms across his chest, and extended his wings. He was large for a Bozak, making him equal in height to the tallest of the blue-painted savage bodyguards.

"Some draconians, maybe, sir, but not those under my command. We would not have survived this long if we had been, my lord. I have two hundred draconians, all well-trained. We are engineers. We think on our feet, we keep armies on the move, and deny the same to our enemy."

The lord knight's smile broadened at Kang's boasting, but the draconian had the feeling that Sykes was impressed. He took care not to show it, however. He raised one of the white eyebrows.

"You must have been in Neraka, Commander Kang. To have survived that battle and to have escaped alive . . . Well, it could be said that you were deserters."

Kang did not flinch or lower his gaze. "Sir, it could be said that any of the Dark Queen's army who survived the War of the Lance were deserters."

Sykes stiffened at this. His face paled with anger and for a moment Kang thought he'd gone too far. Then, the lord knight relaxed, shook his head ruefully.

"You're right, Commander. More than one of us laid down our arms in disgust and walked away from the fight, rather than face the humility of surrendering to the elven whore who called herself the Golden General. Why give our lives for a cause that even our own commanders refused to support? But all that's changed now," Sykes said, speaking softly, more to himself than to Kang. "All that's changed."

He was silent a moment, gazing out his tent in a reverie Kang was careful not to interrupt. The two were still standing in silence when the aide returned.

"First Wing assembled, my lord."

"Thank you, Talon Leader." Sykes turned to Kang. "Come with me, Commander. Let me show you the new army of Lord Ariakan."

The two exited the tent, closely followed by the two blue-painted bodyguards. Lined up in front was an entire squadron of mounted cavalry, lances held in the upright position. They wore black armor, their horses were all black. The knights came to attention when the lord knight appeared.

"As a young man, Lord Ariakan was a prisoner of the Solamnic knights for many years after the war," Sykes explained to Kang. "They treated him well, for they admired his courage and his skill. He, in turn, came to admire them."

Kang blinked. This was new, indeed!

"He learned from them, as well," Sykes continued. "Learned much that he put to good use when he was finally able to escape. The Oath and the Measure, that we once used to sneer at, kept the Solamnic Knights a cohesive unit, even through those years preceding the war when they were reviled by the populace. Lord Ariakan instituted the Code for our forces. The Code and the Vision guide our conduct on and off the battlefield. With this Code and the Vision, we will bring peace and order to this chaotic world."

None of the knights moved a muscle in the saddle. They kept their horses under strict control, as well. Knight and horse might have been carved of obsidian.

"Tell me the Code, my lord," Kang said.

"The Code is different for each of the three orders of knighthood. The Code for the Knights of the Lily is 'Independence breeds chaos. Submit and be strong.' The Code for the Knights of the Skull is, 'Death is patient. It flows both from without and from within. Be vigilant in all and skeptical of all.' And for the Knights of the Thorn, who are wielders of magic, the Code reads, 'One who follows the heart finds it will bleed. Feel nothing but victory.' "

"And the Vision, my lord?" Kang asked. He approved highly of all three.

"The Vision comes to each of us from our Queen," Sykes said. "It is given to each, suited to each. From this, we know our direction. From this, we find our inspiration."

Kang drew his sword from its scabbard, drew it slowly and deliberately. The two bodyguards had their hands on their hilts, were watching him warily. Reversing the sword, Kang held it out to Sykes, hilt first.

"My lord, it has been many years since my troops have served our Queen. Still, fighting is what we were bred for, what we are best at. Our engineering skills may prove of value to your army. I offer you the First Regiment of Draconian Engineers, to serve as engineers for your army. I believe it to be the Queen's will."

The lord knight accepted the sword. "I accept your offer, Commander Kang. There is a great deal that you draconians can do for me. When can you be ready to move?"

"In four days I can meet you at the first mountain pass into Thorbardin. I assume that's where you're headed? To take the dwarven stronghold?"

The Lord Knight gave away nothing. "Let's say only that you and your regiment should meet us at the first pass leading into Thorbardin."

Kang saluted. "I understand, my lord. We will be there."

"I look forward to it," said the lord knight. He handed Kang's sword to his aide, who returned it, with ceremony, to Kang. The lord knight strode forward to inspect his command.

Kang was dismissed.

He left with the sights and sounds of armored knights wheeling in perfect formation. The familiar sights and sounds of an army.

He felt blessed as one who has come home after a long, long absence.

Chapter Sixteen

The march back to Mount Dashinak was a long one for the draconians. A long march and silent, except for the slap and scrabble of their clawed feet, the gentle fanning of their wings, to dissipate the intense heat. Kang had never experienced a hotter, dryer summer. He couldn't remember the last time it had rained. Even the dwarves, better farmers than the draconians, were watching their crops wither and die. The winter could be desperate for both races living in the valley.

"But then," Kang said to himself, "we won't be living in the valley any longer. Perhaps we'll be stationed in a nice cushy city like Palanthas. Or maybe even the High Clerist's Tower. Lots to eat and drink then."

His pleasant daydreams carried him along at a good clip for at least five miles before nagging doubt caused his feet to slow their marching pace.

"I'm giving up twenty-five years of toil, of hard work. In a way, I'm

107

giving up twenty-five years of battle—the battle we fought to survive. And now, maybe I'm ordering everyone off to march to his death. But," he argued with himself, "like I told the commander, war is what we were bred for. We are soldiers. We were born soldiers. Glory will be ours in battle. This army of knights cannot lose. This time, we will be on the winning side!

"And some of us will die," he admitted. "Maybe all of us, and our race will be gone. But then," he added, remembering Slith's words, "we won't be around to notice. So it won't matter anyway."

Still, he couldn't help feeling sad and depressed at the thought. His pace lagged.

One of the subcommanders came up behind, brushed Kang's wing tip, to draw his attention.

Kang looked up to discover that most of the troop had come to a straggling halt, were staring at him in concern. He had not yet told them of his decision, and he'd ordered the two Baaz to keep their mouths shut. He had no intention of letting anyone know anything until he'd absolutely made up his mind.

"Excuse me, sir," said the subcommander, "but if you're tired, we can rest up ahead. There's a place—"

"Tired!" Kang roared, rounding on the unfortunate draco with a snap of his jaws. "What do you mean tired? We've got a war to fight! Double-time, and smartly now!"

The subcommander hastily retreated back among his comrades. Kang broke into a run. He'd show them who was tired! He began to sing a rousing marching song, and after that he started a draconian war chant. It was at that moment that he realized his mind was made up.

Kang made certain that the draconians ran all the way home. And he himself led them.

The entire regiment was lined up on the walls, waiting for Kang's return. All were turned out in full battle gear. Kang marched his troop into the walled village, brought them to a halt in the center square.

"Bugler, call Assembly!" he ordered.

The notes rang out, echoed back from the mountains.

Having anticipated the command, most of the regiment's members were already in the square, forming up in troops under squadrons. Within moments, the troops were ready for inspection. Kang had never seen them move so fast. He grinned. They were as excited as he was.

And there was Slith, standing at attention.

What with the party, the reports of the dragons, and discovering the army of Lord Ariakan, Kang had completely forgotten that his second-in-command had gone off on an expedition of his own.

"Regiment! Atten-tion!" the regiment's second yelled.

Feet pounded on the packed dirt. Kang marched up to Slith, and accepted the salute. In a low tone, he said, "Glad to see you back! After this, I want you to tell me where the hell you've been!"

"Very good, sir," was all Slith said. But he winked.

Kang ordered the regiment to stand at ease. No sense in taxing their strength in this heat. Fortunately evening's shadows were beginning to fall, though they seemed to do little to lower the temperature. At least it was cooler here in the mountains that it had been on the Plains of Dust.

"Draconians of the First Regiment of Engineers! Battle calls us. We are going back to being soldiers! Lord Knight Sykes of the Fifth Army of Conquest has requested that we join him in the conquest of Ansalon!"

There was stunned silence. The draconians who had accompanied Kang had all seen the army, but they had no idea they'd been invited to join. Those left behind had been expecting to be attacked by dragons. Now all had just learned that they were being called to once more wage war on the peoples of Ansalon.

Slith started a cheer. The others picked it up, and soon their voices combined in a shout that boomed through the mountains like thunder. The dwarves must have heard it clear across the valley.

"We have made a good life here on the slopes of Mount Dashinak, but it is not a soldier's life," Kang continued, when the cheering finally ceased. "We were born for one purpose, and one purpose only—to follow the will of the Dark Queen and aid her in the conquest of this world. This we are called upon to do. We must heed the call."

No cheer went up this time. This was a solemn moment, almost reverent.

"Squadron commanders, have your troops ready to march in two days. Officers' conference will be at 0700 hours. Slith, dismiss the regiment."

Slith jumped to attention, called the regiment to attention, saluted Kang, and sang out, "Regiment dismissed!"

The draconians did not leave the parade ground, but immediately clumped together, wings flapping, teeth snapping, voices hissing. Someone rolled out the keg of dwarf spirits. They cheered Kang, as he passed, and called out an invitation to join them. He shook his head and headed for his own quarters. He was suddenly very tired.

Events had taken a most unexpected turn. He didn't quite know what to think of it all.

Kang dropped his field gear on the floor, letting it lay where it fell. He flopped down on his bed and stared at the ceiling.

"Have I done the right thing?" he asked himself again. "Is this what my soldiers want? I am their commander and must look out for them. I must think on their behalf. Still, for the past twenty-five years, we have not been soldiers. We have been settlers in an unforgiving and barren land. And we've survived. Not only that, but we've made this land our home—"

His thoughts were interrupted by a knock at the door.

"Slith here, sir."

"Come in."

Slith entered, saluted, and closed the door. He had been thoughtful enough to bring along a jug. "I thought congratulations were in order. You must have impressed the hell out of that commander. What does he call himself? A lord knight? What is he, some renegade Solamnic cast-off? Are you sure we want to be part of this, sir?"

Kang stood up, clomped over to the table. "Pour yourself a drink, and me one too while you're at it." He took a long pull on the spirits, paused a moment to wait for the explosion in his brain to fade away and the fire to die out in his stomach. That done, he continued.

"We're soldiers, Slith, you and me. We know how to fight, and we know how to lead warriors. You said it yourself. The yearning. The yearning to fight, and fight for the Queen. It's why we're here."

Slith sat down, leaned back in the chair. His tail curled around to his side, covered his feet. "I know. Still, you remember what happened last time. I doubt our Queen had much to do with that last war. But then, I don't know. She never spoke to me."

Kang stared into the dark, potent spirits. "She's spoken to me," he said quietly. Every time he asked for his magic, he heard her voice. Suddenly, he slammed his fist on the table. "This time we won't fail! I'm convinced of it, Slith. You should see this army! Disciplined, well-trained, devoted to her Cause and to each other. Honor. Slith, they spoke of honor! Can you believe it? This army had a whole different feel to it. They're out to win, not just kill for the sake of killing, like the last time."

"Speaking of killing, sir. We're all still alive here, after twenty-five years, and that counts for something."

"Alive, yes, but we're not living. In fact, if you come to think about it, we're all just waiting to die. We have a chance now to at least make our deaths mean something."

"You're in a cheery mood tonight, sir. Take another drink." Slith obeyed his own command.

Kang laughed, though he only sipped at his spirits. He couldn't let himself get drunk. Not tonight. He had work to do. He pushed the jug to the end of the table, out of reach.

"Now tell me, old friend, where did you sneak off to during the raid? The corporal you sent back said something about you chasing after some dwarven thieves?"

"I saw a group of four dwarves sneak out of Celebundin the night of the raid. They were using the confusion of the raid to cover their movements. You might say that we aided in their getaway."

Kang tried to appear interested, but it was hard work. A week ago, he would have found this fascinating information. Now, the dwarves mattered little to him.

Slith continued. "I followed them for two days. They headed north through the mountain pass. They crossed two more mountains, then went over the Helefundis Ridge. I had to stop at that point for fear that they'd see me. But I found out where they were headed."

"Where?" Kang asked, because it was expected of him, not because he cared.

"Thorbardin."

Kang was suddenly very interested. He was certain that Thorbardin was the objective of the knights.

"Thorbardin? Hill dwarves? They wouldn't find a very big welcome there."

"They weren't looking for a welcome. From what I overheard and what I managed to piece together, these four are light-fingered as kender. They weren't going to Thorbardin for a family reunion. Unless I miss my guess, they were going to relieve their rich cousins of some of their jewels and steel. I think the dwarves have played us for suckers. Here we've been raiding their distilleries when we should have been raiding their treasure room!"

Kang shrugged. "Damn. I wish we'd known about this earlier. But it won't make any difference now. We're off to war, and we'll be leaving the dwarves behind. Still, it's good to know that there's a back way into Thorbardin. The lord knight might be very interested in that piece of intelligence."

"Here's to glory, sir."

"To glory, Slith!"

The two draconians raised their flagons and drank.

"Two days, Slith. Have the men ready."

Slith finished his drink in one last gulp. "Two days. Hard to believe we're leaving this place after so many years. Yes, sir. The regiment will be ready. Two days."

*   *   *   *   *

The two days went by in a blur of activity. Kang gave orders, supervised the loading of the wagons, made certain the provisions were readied. He had to deal with innumerable crises, some minor, one major. The major crisis occurred when the three disabled draconians—hearing that their fellows were marching off to war and assuming that they would be left behind to starve—tried to kill themselves by mixing the ground-up petals of the death lily with their nut-ale. They were discovered in time to prevent the deed.

Kang spoke to them, showed them their names on the roster, and promised that not only would they march with the draconian regiment, but that they would have their share of duties to perform. He put them in charge of inventorying the supplies and the weapons, determining what they should take and what they should leave behind. This freed up three able-bodied draconians for other duties, so that what Kang had done proved worthwhile. Still, it was just one more distraction.

"Perhaps it's just as well I don't have time to think about this too much," he was reflecting over a delayed dinner, when a knock sounded on his door.

It was at least the one hundredth knock in the space of an hour. Kang sighed. "Yes, what is it? I'm eating! Or trying to."

"Excuse me, sir, but we've got a report from one of the scouts. I think you should it hear it, sir."

"Of course I should hear it," Kang grumbled. He shoved aside his plate. "Send him in."

The scout, a Baaz, shuffled inside, bobbing his head and darting quick glances about. He'd never been in his commander's quarters before.

"What is it? And be quick," Kang growled.

The Baaz ducked his head again. "Yes, sir. Some dwarves have been watching us, sir. We spotted 'em yesterday. They're up a tree in that copse about a mile away. We didn't report it, because they weren't doing anything except just sitting in the tree. But they were back today, and our lieutenant wants to know what to do. Do we haul 'em down, sir? Or let 'em be?"

"Let them be," said Kang with a smile. "They're only trying to figure out what we're up to. Probably quaking in their boots, afraid we're getting ready to launch a major assault on them."

"Aren't we, sir? I mean, wouldn't it be a good idea. Suppose they tell someone we're leaving."

Kang had considered just such a course of action. A dwarven village burned and a wagon load of dwarven heads would be a fine present for their new commander. And it would insure the dwarves' silence.

But Kang had already rejected the idea, if for no other reason than the mug of dwarf spirits next to his plate. He owed the dwarves a debt; they had provided food, drink, and an odd sort of companionship over the years. If the Knights of Takhisis could talk of honor and speak with respect of their enemies, then, by the Dark Lady, so could Kang.

"Who are they going to tell?" Kang shook his head. "The nearest Solamnic Knight's probably a hundred miles away, and the dwarves don't have much use for them anyhow. And by the time the dwarves realize we're gone for good, they won't care where we went."

He laughed. "We grab the glory, they grab this town. Good for them. They'll at least get most of their belongings back!"

The draconians marched on the second day, just as Slith had promised. They were six hours behind schedule, but they were ready to go. The regiment assembled in the village square for the last time.

Kang stood in front of them. "Life has been good, these past years," he said simply. "But it's going to be better. Today, once again, we march for the glory of the Queen!"

With that, he turned, strode to the front of the column, and led the way out of the gate, out of the wall, which his men had built, the one thing they had built that might actually outlast them.

The only thing.

He did not look back.

Chapter Seventeen

The draconian squadrons marched as single units. All were in full fighting gear, all their provisions and engineering tools and equipment were loaded onto the wagons. Each draconian wore a small pack on his back, containing any personal objects that he had acquired over the years of living on the side of Mount Dashinak. That wasn't a lot. Most of what they owned, they left for the dwarves.

More out of curiosity than because he feared any trouble from the dwarves, Kang had left Slith behind with a scouting party to see what the dwarves were up to. The party caught up with the main body late that night.

"Well, what happened?" Kang asked.

"As soon as we marched out," Slith reported, "one of the dwarves in the tree shinnied down and ran like his pants were on fire back to the village to report. Horns blew and bells rang. The whole damn village turned out to drive off the assault."

115

Slith grinned. "They waited and waited, the sun beating down on them, and, of course, we never showed up. That war chief of theirs finally gathered together a group and they marched over to the village.

"They met up with the three dwarves still sitting in the tree, who reported that we were nowhere in sight. The war chief took a squad with him and marched up to the gates, which were standing wide open. You should have seen those dwarves, clutching their battle-axes, ready for us to leap out and massacre them! When the war chief finally got up nerve enough to walk inside the gate, the wind blew it and those hinges creaked, made a squealing sound. The old dwarf jumped so high it was a wonder he didn't bump his head on Lunitari!"

Kang laughed appreciatively. "What'd they do then?"

"Marched off," Slith said. "Went back to their village. We watched, but they didn't send out any runners or messengers."

"Good. Excellent. Well done, Slith."

The Sivak nodded and returned to take his place in line.

Kang's spirits, which had been extremely low when he left the village, soared, now that he was on the road. He was marching at the head of a regiment of well-trained soldiers, some of the best in the business, off to join a mighty army of conquest. He'd made the right decision. He was sure of it.

They crossed the mountain pass over Mount Dashinak, traversed the Forthin Ridge, and camped in the valley beyond.

Slith was also in a good mood. The draconians hadn't made a forced march like this in years. They were out of shape and out of practice, tripping over their own tails, complaining about the heat and sore feet. More than a few keeled over from a combination of unaccustomed exercise and an overabundance of dwarf spirits.

Slith ranged up and down the line, his baton tickling stragglers, keeping them moving, and answering all complaints with a whack to the head. Those who fell were tossed into the wagons. No one envied them the ride. Slith prowled around the wagons, gleefully waiting for them to come to their senses.

The journey was difficult, especially with the wagons, which had to be pushed and pulled and hauled over the rocky terrain. And then the trail ended at the edge of a cliff. The only way to reach their destination was straight down.

The drop was easy enough for the winged draconians, but both wagons had to be lowered down the side of the mountain on ropes. This task took up an entire afternoon, and everyone was worn out by the end of it.

Kang allowed them only a brief rest, however. Wrestling with the wagons had put them behind schedule and he did not want to start off on the wrong foot with Lord Knight Sykes by showing up late.

The second day, the draconians reached the mountain pass where they were to meet up with Lord Knight Sykes and his army. They were right on time.

No army in sight.

Kang and Slith led the column over the last rise and were the first to notice that they were alone up here.

"Where the hell is everyone?" Slith demanded. "I knew it—"

"Hush," Kang warned. "Keep moving. We're not as alone as we thought we were."

He pointed forward. A single knight, clad in black armor, stood up from a rock, and motioned for the draconians to approach. As the knight removed her helm, red hair flowed behind her, her own personal banner.

Kang recognized her, Talon Leader Huzzud.

"Greetings, Commander," she called.

Kang saluted. "Where is your army, Talon Leader? I was told to meet Lord Knight Sykes here on this day."

"We came upon a patrol of mountain dwarves the day you left. We believe that we killed all of them, but, on the off-chance that one might have escaped to spread the warning, the lord knight determined that he had to move fast, hoping to invade Thorbardin before the dwarves could close the gates leading into the mountain. He force-marched the army through here a day and a half ago. I'm to lead you to the encampment."

Kang had once seen the formidable gates of Thorbardin, gates that could be closed flush with the mountain wall. Attacking those gates would be tantamount to attacking the mountain itself and probably just as successful. No wonder the lord knight had been in such haste.

The draconians had taken the opportunity of the halt to snatch a bit of rest. They were lying in what shade they could find, drinking sparingly from their water skins. Kang gave the signal to Slith, who ordered every man back on his feet. Aware of the eyes of the dark knight upon them, the draconians made haste to form into their lines, stood rigidly at attention.

The regiment marched for the remainder of the day without pause, without complaint. Huzzud glanced back occasionally at the line. It was an impressive sight, the sun gleaming on scale and metal, the air stirred by the cooling breeze of the draconians' wings. Only when the sun was setting behind the mountain did Kang call a halt for a brief rest.

"We could camp here tonight," Huzzud suggested. Her red hair was wet from perspiration, her fair skin reddened by the blazing sun. She wiped her forehead with the back of her leather-gloved hand. "The lord knight isn't expecting us before tomorrow. We have the mountain to cross, and it's difficult journeying in daylight."

Kang scratched his jaw. "How much farther?" he asked Huzzud.

She glanced at the mountains, at the sky, and said, "Ten miles."

Kang looked back down the line. His troops were tired, but not exhausted. They'd have a chance to rest tonight, be fighting fit for battle tomorrow.

"We'll carry on then, provided that's all right with you."

"Of course." Huzzud appeared pleased with his response.

A thought occurred to Kang. "Can you lead us through the pass in the dark?" he asked, concerned. "You humans cannot see well in darkness, or so I am told. No offense," he added hastily.

Huzzud smiled. "None taken. What you say is true. And," she admitted, "I've only flown over the pass by dragon, I've never walked it. But I know the way. I am trained to know the way."

Kang bowed. He had complete confidence in her. "My compliments to the trainer."

Huzzud tied back her long red hair, regarded Kang with earnest intent. "I had never met any draconians before you, Commander. I didn't expect you to be so ... well ... civilized, if you take my meaning. I thought you'd be more like goblins. Crude and not very bright. No offense," she added slyly.

Kang laughed. "None taken. Underestimating us is a mistake many humans make, mostly to their detriment."

He grew pensive. A day's marching side-by-side with someone makes them close as kin. He felt at ease with her. Perhaps that was the reason he shared thoughts with her he'd never shared with anyone else.

"We are bred of dragons, Talon Leader. Perhaps the most intelligent, the wisest beings alive on Krynn. The capacity to attain such wisdom, such knowledge is within us. If we only had time! Time to live in this world, to learn its ways, to come to know its peoples. And if we could only pass on what we learn to—"

He stopped, embarrassed. What he was saying was foolish and he knew it. He expected the talon leader to regard him with scorn, or—worse—laugh at him.

To his astonishment, she was gazing at him with serious attention. "Don't mind me," Kang added, waving a clawed hand. "I've been in the sun too long. Heat and dwarf spirits always make me say crazy things."

"It's not crazy," she protested. "What you are talking about is interesting. I never looked at it quite that way."

"No, it isn't, though you're kind to say so." Kang changed the subject abruptly. "My men are rested now. If you're ready, we should be moving out."

She agreed and, after drinking a few sips of water, they marched on. Neither she nor Kang spoke again during the long march, except to consult now and again on direction. But she looked at him a good deal, and her expression was thoughtful. He had definitely risen in her estimation.

An hour later, they came upon the road leading north, a road that was relatively new, as Kang—regarding it with an engineer's eye—could tell. Trees had been recently cut and cleared, the marks of pick and hammer were still visible upon the rocks.

"When did they build this?" Kang asked. "And who built it?"

"The dwarves. Can't you tell their work? But it was a project begun by all three races: dwarves, humans, and elves. They were supposed to have signed a great treaty that would have allied all their kingdoms, opened up all their territories to trading, one with the other. They were going to build roads like this one to link Solamnia with Thorbardin, Thorbardin with Qualinesti. Thus, if any one of them was attacked, the others could send armies in defense."

"It seems a wise plan," Kang said, worried. "And it will make our task more difficult."

"It was a wise plan. A half-breed known as Tanis Half-elven and his wife Laurana, the one they used to call the Golden General, came up with it. But, no need to fear. The three races are their own worse enemies."

In the light of waning Solinari, Kang saw a fall of rock that had not been cleared from the road, ditches that were left unfilled. "I see what you mean. This road is broken."

"Like their treaty," said Huzzud with a wry grin. "It never even made it to parchment, or so I've heard. The elves are going back to their old isolationist ways. They have insulted the dwarves, who blame it all on the humans, who, in their turn, are offended by the exclusionist attitude of elves. One won't lift a finger to help the other. No, Commander, our task is going to be easy. Very easy indeed."

An hour's march up the road, they were stopped by two soldiers, who stood blocking their way. Kang heard rustling in the brush on either side of the road, guessed that there must be at least fifty arrows, aimed right at him and his men.

Torches flared.

"Halt! Send forth one and be recognized!" the soldier yelled.

Kang ordered his men to halt. He and Huzzud walked forward.

"I am Talon Leader Huzzud," she said. "This is Commander Kang and the First Regiment, Draconians."

The soldier saluted. "Yes, ma'am. We weren't looking for you until morning, Commander. Please accompany me."

The two officers followed the sentry along the road. Although he had not been told to bring his command with him, Kang wasn't about to leave his troops standing in the road after their long march. He signaled to Slith, who started everyone moving again.

The sentry turned, frowning, and appeared about to protest.

Kang extended his wings, lashed his tail slowly, back and forth, and stared, hard and cold, at the sentry in the torch light.

Whatever the sentry had been going to say was left unsaid. The man turned hastily on his heel and continued down the road.

Kang heard smothered laughter. Huzzud, marching beside him, said nothing. But she was grinning broadly.

They passed through two more checkpoints, then finally left the road and entered a grassy field to the side. Picket fires and cooking fires glowed like stars fallen to the ground in the surrounding fields.

"Slith!" Kang yelled out.

Slith trotted forward, saluted.

"Have the men set up right here. Same drill—no slacking off. I want a defensive ditch dug and sentries posted before anyone goes to sleep. Got it?"

Slith saluted, then turned and issued orders in a rapid-fire staccato. The draconians fell out of formation and set to work, each performing his assigned task efficiently and with a minimum of confusion and noise.

Huzzud spent a few moments watching, then turned to Kang. "I must return to my talon this night, but I will be back in the morning to escort you to the lord knight's command tent. I'll meet you here at sunup."

Kang agreed, saluted. "Until tomorrow, Talon Leader."

Huzzud returned the salute. "Until tomorrow, Commander."

The officer walked away into the night. Kang turned to see his soldiers working with speed and efficiency. He smiled, his scales clicked together with pleasant anticipation.

"Until tomorrow!"

Chapter Eighteen

A week had passed since Pestle and Mortar had left the dwarven village. The week had been eventful for Selquist—he had discovered the location of a vast treasure horde. It had been eventful for the dwarves of Celebundin, who discovered the draconians had, to all appearances, abandoned their homes of twenty-five years. It had been eventful for the draconians, who had marched out to join up with Lord Ariakan's army. The week for Pestle and Mortar had been a bust.

Upon arriving at Pax Tharkas, they found that city, which had, after the war, been about equally populated by humans and elves, along with a smattering of other races, to be half-deserted. The elven contingent had packed up and moved out, according to reports, most of them gone to join with a rebel elf named Porthios. The human population was in an uproar over reports that the High Clerist Tower had fallen to an army of dark knights and that the city of Palanthas was in the hands of some evil lord known as Ariakan.

Rumor had it that Pax Tharkas itself was soon to come under attack. The gates of the fortress which had once housed the infamous Dragon Highlord Verminaard were shut, the walls manned. The guards had not wanted to allow Pestle and Mortar inside. When the dwarves hotly insisted, the guards marched them to the gatehouse and put them through a rigorous interrogation to make certain they weren't dark knights in disguise.

Conscious of the stolen booty in their packs, the two dwarves were considerably alarmed by these proceedings. They quaked in their boots when the guards searched their packs, certain that they would be tossed in the Pax Tharkas jail.

"It'll probably be filled with kender!" Pestle groaned.

"They always are," Mortar agreed gloomily.

If the guards had found weapons in the packs, the dwarves would have most certainly been spending the night in prison, clutching their belongings and kicking any kender who ventured too close. As it was, finding only a few mundane household items, which Mortar claimed he was here to sell to raise money for homeless orphans, the guards let them pass. They did, as an afterthought, confiscate the skull with the glowing red eyes.

"Our most valuable item." Pestle sighed. The two were walking as fast as they could away from the guard tower.

"Selquist isn't going to be happy about this," Mortar noted.

They made their way through the city, which was preparing to be besieged. Homeowners were boarding up windows. Men were filling barrels with water, to put out fires. The city guard drilled in the streets. Women and children were heading for the hills.

The marketplace was empty.

The dwarves looked at each other and at their bags of loot and dismally shook their heads. Selecting a stall, they set out their wares, but the few people who passed merely glanced at the items and hurried on. The dwarves waited all day and sold nothing.

"Well, maybe it'll be better tomorrow," Pestle said. They packed up, found a cheap inn, and spent the night battling the fleas in the mattress.

The next morning, sore and itchy, they went back to the market. They stayed until noon and had one visitor, a gully dwarf, who tried to sell them some dead rats on a string.

"Well, there's always Rhanga," Mortar said.

"He won't give us much, but anything's better than nothing," Pestle agreed.

Packing up their loot, they trudged off to the kender's house.

They had no difficulty finding it, though they hadn't visited in a year or so. It was the only house on the block with a bright purple door, glaring yellow walls and stunning emerald green curtains. Wincing, the dwarves knocked at the door, doing their best to shade their eyes.

The door popped open. A kender female greeted them.

"Why, hello? My goodness. You're dwarves, aren't you?" the kender said.

"Yes," said Pestle, keeping tight hold of his pack. "We're—"

"Hey, everyone!" The kender turned around. "Come here and look! Dwarves!"

A whole passle of kender came to the door, another group gathered at the window. They jabbered and chattered.

"You're right. It is dwarves."

"What kind of dwarves? Gully dwarves?"

"Are you gully dwarves?"

"We're not gully dwarves!" Mortar shouted, above the hubbub. "We're Neidar."

"I don't need her. Do you need her?" one of the kender asked.

This produced gales of laughter, though Mortar couldn't see anything at all funny. But then kender never needed a reason to laugh, one attribute which drove other more sane and sober races to distraction. The kender poured out into the street to get a better look at their visitors. Mortar grit his teeth, held his pack to his chest, and carried on as best he could, while fending off curious hands.

"I'm looking for . . . Put that back! I said I'm here to see . . . That's mine, confound you! No, don't tug on that! I say I'm here to see Rhanga!" he roared.

"Rhanga?"

"Rhanga. Did he say Rhanga?"

"I think he said Rhonda. Do you know Rhonda?"

"Maybe that's who he needs. He said he needed her."

"Do you need someone named Rhonda?"

"We don't know anyone named Rhonda, but if you want us to ask around—"

"Rhanga!" Pestle yelled. "We want to see Rhanga Changehands!"

"Ah!" sang out the kender all at once. "Rhanga Changehands!"

"He doesn't live here anymore," added one.

"Not live here." Mortar was astounded. "Where did he go?"

"Out," said one.

"Yes, he stepped out to borrow some sugar."

"When will he be back?" Pestle asked.

"Couldn't say." The kender shook their top-knotted heads.

"Before nightfall, surely," Mortar continued. He was beginning to feel desperate.

"Maybe. Maybe not."

"Well, surely it can't take long to borrow a cup of sugar. When did he leave?" Pestle joined the fray.

The kender put their heads together. "Last month?"

"No, two months ago at least."

"I think it was last year sometime. He wasn't here for my Day of Life-gift."

"You weren't here for your Day of Life-gift!"

Mortar gave his own beard a sharp yank. The pain brought tears to his eyes, but it also restored his sanity, which he felt slowly slipping away. He caught hold of Pestle and the two began to retreat back down the street, keeping their eyes fixed on the kender at all times.

"Uh, thanks. We'll just be leaving now."

The kender surrounded them, reaching out for them.

"Don't go!"

"Not so soon!"

"Can't you stay for tea?"

"What's in the bag? Can I see?"

"Do you want me to go look for Rhonda?"

"What shall I tell her, when I see her?"

"Come on, Niedar! Stay for tea! Stay for tea!"

The kender crowded around, chanting and grabbing at the dwarves.

"Let go of that! Put that back! Don't unbuckle that strap. Now look, you've cut a hole in it. That's my pouch!" The dwarves slapped roving hands and shoved curious kender heads out of their packs, but they were slowly being overwhelmed and ultimate defeat appeared imminent. Already, one kender was pretending to drink out of one of the silver ale mugs, while two more kender were having a mock sword fight with the bone candlesticks.

"What do we do?" Pestle gasped, prying a kender hand out of one of his pockets.

"Stay for tea! Stay for tea!" Several kender were dancing around the dwarves in a circle.

"Run for it!" Mortar cried. He was engaged in a desperate tug-of-war with a kender over the second silver ale mug.

"What about the loot?" Pestle shouted, making a vain attempt to recover the candlesticks.

"The loot's lost. We have to save ourselves!"

"Selquist'll be furious!"

"Hang Selquist!" Mortar said viciously. Plunging forward, he broke through the circle, sending kender tumbling and laughing in all directions.

Pestle was right behind him. They didn't dare take time even to close their packs, which bounced and jounced on their backs. Whatever they had managed to save spilled out behind them, as they could tell by the chorus of "oohs" and "aahs" from the kender.

"Are they coming after us?" Mortar asked fearfully.

Glancing back over his shoulders as he ran, Pestle saw the kender on their hands and knees in the street, searching for dropped treasure.

"No!" he breathed thankfully. "We're safe."

"We won't be safe until we're out of Pax Tharkas," said Mortar.

As if to emphasize his words, they heard a shrill voice call after them, "Hey, about Rhonda—"

The dwarves increased their pace.

* * * * *

The two dwarves, in a glum mood, traipsed back to the front gate. They hoped to leave quickly, but they had almost as much trouble leaving as they had entering.

"You're crazy, going back out there," said one of the guards.

"Why?" Mortar asked. "What's out there?"

"Haven't you heard? Knights of Takhisis, they call themselves. Dark knights. They're working for Queen Takhisis. You better stay here, where it's safe."

Mortar and Pestle looked at each and rolled their eyes. Dark knights! Humans were so gullible.

"Thanks, but we've got to get home."

"Yeah, well, warn your people. War's coming."

"We will. Thanks."

The dwarves left Pax Tharkas. The gate door slammed shut behind them. They heard the bolt slide into place.

Dispirited, overheated, empty handed, the dwarves plodded gloomily down the road. They were far poorer after leaving Pax Tharkas than when they'd arrived, which hadn't been the plan.

Selquist was, indeed, going to be furious. Especially when he heard that they'd lost their loot to a pack of ravening kender.

"They would have ripped off our clothes!" Pestle said defensively.

"Right. Tell that to Selquist," Mortar responded.

The dwarves walked until they were tired, then camped for the night. They didn't take any precautions. Dark knights! What would the humans dream up next?

The evening passed peacefully. It wasn't until about noon the next day that both dwarves began to grown uneasy.

"You know," said Mortar, "this road is usually well traveled. It's the main thoroughfare between here and points north. And we haven't seen a soul since we left Pax Tharkas."

"It's the heat," said Pestle, though he kept glancing around nervously. "Everyone's staying home because of the heat."

"You're probably right," Mortar agreed, but he didn't sound convinced.

They traveled on, but now they kept to the side of the road and the shadows of the trees. Suddenly Mortar jumped and swung around, staring behind him.

"What?" Pestle snatched his ax out of its harness. "What do you see?"

"Nothing," said Mortar. He also had his axe in his hand. "But I feel like I'm being watched."

"Me, too." Pestle peered into the shadows. "Maybe we should go back to Pax Tharkas."

"We've come too far. We should just keep going."

"All right. But I think we should leave the road. We're too exposed. Let's move into the woods."

The two took a step toward the trees.

They were stopped by a twanging sound, and two arrows thudded into the ground, one in front of each dwarf.

"Move and you die," came a voice, a human voice, speaking dwarven. He spoke it badly, but the two weren't about to correct his pronunciation.

An archer, dressed in black leather armor adorned with a hideously grinning skull, emerged from the woods. He had lowered his bow, but the dwarves could hear movement in the woods and guessed that others' arrows were still aimed in their direction.

"Do you understand Common?" the archer asked.

Both dwarves nodded.

"Throw your axes down in the dirt in front of you, then put your hands on your heads."

"Are you going to rob us?" Pestle asked.

"If you are," Mortar said, "I feel it only fair that we warn you—you're wasting your time. We don't have anything of value."

"We are not thieves," the archer said, his lip curling in scorn. "It is you who have broken the law. We are placing you under arrest."

Mortar sighed in relief. He thought he knew where he stood. "Look, we were never anywhere near Thorbardin. Ask anyone. On the night in question, we were home sound asleep—"

The archer raised his bow. The arrow pointed straight at Mortar's heart. "I said, drop the axes."

Mortar dropped the axe. Pestle did likewise.

Nine more archers, clad in black leather identical to the first, stepped out of the woods. They kept the dwarves covered. The first archer bent to retrieve their weapons. While the dwarves stood with their hands on their heads, the archer ran his hands over them, removed two knives from their belts and two more that they had stashed in the tops of their boots.

The archer swung the axes, sent them spinning into the woods. "Tie their hands," he ordered his comrades. He turned back to the dwarves. "This road is closed by order of Lord Knight Sykes, Commander of the Second Army in the service of Queen Takhisis. Failure to comply will result in arrest. If you're on this road, you must be spies. We're taking you back for interrogation."

The two dwarves glanced at each other in despair.

"I guess those humans knew what they were talking about," Pestle said sadly.

"We're done for," Mortar muttered.

"Shut up! No talking." The knight emphasized his words with an impersonal blow to the side of Pestle's head.

The archer retrieved his arrows, cleaned them off, and put them back in his sheaf. Two of the knights tied the dwarves' hands behind their backs.

"Move along now."

The leader shoved Pestle down the road. Mortar stumbled along behind his brother. The rest of the knights followed.

"All in all," Pestle said, his head throbbing from the blow, "I would have rather have had tea with the kender."

Mortar had to think about this a moment but, after looking at the grim, stern, and pitiless faces of the knights, the dwarf was forced, miserably, to agree.

Chapter Nineteen

By the time the sun rose in the morning, the draconians had dug a defensive ditch around the perimeter of their camp, constructing bunkers at each corner. The entrance was guarded by two more bunkers. Inside, the tents were arranged in neat rows, according to squadron. The large tent in the middle was the command tent, where Kang slept.

He awoke to the smell of roasted meat. The march had given him a voracious appetite. Last night, he had foregone dinner, spent some quiet time in communing with his Queen. She had, as was customary, awarded him his magic, though she had seemed a bit distracted. Probably due to the war effort. He donned his leather harness, but left the armor behind. Strapping on his sword, he went outside.

Slith stood by the fire pit, gnawing on a half-eaten bone. When he saw Kang approach, the Sivak gave the cook a nudge.

"Hurry up there, trooper. The commander's coming."

A haunch of venison on a spit was roasting over the fire. The Baaz cut off a hunk of meat and handed it to Kang. The juices bubbled beneath blackened skin.

"Morning to you, sir!" Slith said. He saluted with the bone.

"Good morning, Slith." Kang devoured the meat. "Excellent! Where did this come from?"

Slith smiled. "Compliments of Lord Knight Sykes. Welcoming us to the neighborhood. Eat up, commander. There's more where that came from. You know, I'm beginning to like this guy Sykes after all."

Kang carved off another hunk for himself. He and Slith moved away from the cook, to have a private talk. Kang knew his second well. Slith had probably been up for hours already, or maybe had not even gone to sleep. Slith could not rest until he'd nosed around, ferreted out the latest camp gossip, learned all he could about the situation.

Like following those four dwarves, just to see what they were up to. Kang had always said that Slith was more curious than any kender and that this curiosity would probably land him in a whole mess of trouble one day. Until then, it came in very handy.

"So, what's up?" Kang asked, chewing.

Slith pointed down the road on which they'd marched. "Lord Knight Sykes has his headquarters in the mayor's house in the center of that village. It's known as Mish-ka, dedicated to the good goddess." Slith sneered and both draconians spit on the ground.

"The army moved in three days ago," Slith continued. "The knights killed anyone who offered resistance. Most didn't. The town is under iron control."

Kang squinted, peered down the road. "I don't see any smoke. They're not razing the place?"

"Nope. No massacres of the civilian population. No torturings, public floggings, or property confiscations." Slith grinned. That was a polite term for looting.

"I'll be damned." Kang grinned back. "You mean that they're actually going to concentrate on fighting a war for a change?"

"Get this." Slith leaned near. "It seems that the town has a Temple for the worshippers of Mishakal."

Again, both draconians spit on the ground.

"Well, the first thing Sykes does is visit that temple. He didn't go inside, of course, but he stood outside it, admired it, and asked to see the priest. The priest comes out and he's about dead from fear. He begs Sykes to spare the temple, saying that there's a bunch of sick people inside. What do you think happens, commander?"

"Sykes cuts off the priest's head, marches inside the temple, kills the wounded and then burns the temple to the ground."

"No, sir!" Slith slapped his thigh with his hand. "Sykes says that he holds all the gods sacred. Their dwelling places are sacred and that, so long as the priest and his followers obey the law as set down by the knights, he will personally guarantee their safety."

"Times have certainly changed." Kang marveled.

"Of course," Slith added, with a wink, "the knights have a list of laws as long as my tail. Curfews. Everyone has to have papers proving who they are. No one leaves town without the word from Sykes himself. No one enters town without being questioned. Civilians are not permitted to own or carry weapons. All magical items must be turned over to Sykes's wizards, the Gray Knights. No brawling, no gambling, no public drunkenness."

Slith nudged Kang in the ribs. "That goes for soldiers, too, sir."

Kang grunted. "I guess we'll have to watch our step. Where'd you put that keg of dwarf spirits?"

"In my tent, sir. Under the bed."

"Good man. Any word on Thorbar—"

Slith looked over Kang's shoulder, straightened, performed a salute. "Talon Leader Huzzud, sir," he announced.

Kang turned, pleased to see the talon leader.

"Good morning, Sir Knight!" Kang said. "Have you had breakfast?"

"Good morning, Commander. Yes, thank you. You're to report to headquarters this morning. If you're ready, I can show you the way."

"Right," Kang said. "Let's go."

The two left the camp, headed toward the village. The two regiments of troops they passed on the way into the village were well entrenched, with defensive ditches dug in a square, hastily constructed wooden guard towers at the corners. Archers were posted in each. The two units faced each other across the road. The troops' demeanor, from what Kang could see, was highly professional. He felt a qualm of guilt about the dwarf spirits.

Sykes had turned the mayor's house into a command post. He was taking no chances from the civilian populace. Huzzud and Kang had to pass through two sets of sentries before they were allowed to enter. Once inside, joining the other officers, they were taken to what must have once been an elegantly appointed banquet room. The table was now being used to display a large map. Huzzud introduced Kang to an officer, who was seated at a desk, adding up a series of numeric columns in a leather-bound book.

"Commander Kang, this is Quadron Leader Leader Mumul, the logistics commander for the Second Army. Quadron Leader, this is Commander Kang of the Draconian Regiment of Engineers." Huzzud saluted, then left.

Mumul looked up from his numbers. "Please sit down, Commander Kang. I want to discuss with you what your role will be within the Second Army."

"Yes, Quadron Leader." Kang could barely contain his excitement. Arranging his tail, he sat down in the chair, which had not been designed for draconians. It was damnably uncomfortable, pinched his wings if he folded them in and poked them if he unfurled them. The discomfort was a small price to pay.

"Could I ask a question before we start, Quadron Leader?"

"Certainly, Commander."

"What's the status of the attack on Thorbardin? As I understand it, the lord knight force-marched his men to get here, and now, instead of attacking, you're just sitting."

The quadron leader shrugged. "We were too late. The dwarves had been warned. They've sealed up the mountain."

"Are you going to besiege them, sir?"

"No. There's no time for that. The damn dwarves could hold out for a year against us. It would be a futile waste of manpower. We'll let them sit, holed up in their mountain, if that's what they want. Meanwhile, we'll seize control of all the roads leading into and out of Thorbardin. We have time. Someday, they'll have to come out."

Kang was impressed. It was a simple, but good, strategy.

"And now, Commander, what is the strength of your command?" The quadron leader flipped over a new page, prepared to record the information.

Kang responded. The quadron leader asked question after question, wanting to know the size, composition, training, equipment, and disposition of the draconian regiment. Kang was pleased with the interest the officer was showing in assessing the regiment. The knight recorded the answers in a table in his book. At last, he laid down his quill pen and sat back in his chair.

"Thank you, Commander. The first thing I want you to do this morning is haul all that bridge-building equipment you brought us over to Third Talon."

Kang felt a twinge in the vicinity of his shoulder blades, a painful twinge that had nothing to do with the chair. "Yes, sir," he said. "Do they need a bridge constructed, sir?"

"No, Commander. They're my engineering unit. They can use the materials and tools you brought. You can leave the wagons with Third Talon. You won't be needing them."

"Ah, I understand, sir. You want us to build siege engines. Catapults, trebuchets, we've built them all. Why, once, during the War of the Lance, we built a catapult big enough to fling a minotaur—"

Kang stopped. He didn't like the way the quadron leader was smiling—patient, patronizing.

"Third Talon is quite expert at building and manning siege engines, Commander."

"Sir," Kang began, drawing in a deep breath to try to ease the knot of disappointment that was slowly tightening his stomach, "we are all well-trained engineers. Probably the best you'll ever find. Plus, we have experience in battle. Did your Third Talon ever build a bridge with silver dragons flying overhead, filling you with dragonfear, while the elves on the other side of the bank are trying to fill you full of arrows?"

The commander just sat there, smiling.

"Look, sir," Kang said, "come visit our encampment. See how we're dug in. We only moved in ten hours ago, and yet we've already got the place defensible!"

For the first time, the quadron leader showed some interest. "Very good, Commander! Very good indeed!"

Kang was puzzled. "What do you mean, sir?"

"Damn good diggers!" Mumul said, thumping the table in his enthusiasm. "I'm glad to hear that you're good diggers."

"I beg your pardon, sir."

"You draconians. Damn good diggers. Since we can't take out the dwarves, this army has been ordered to move up and conquer the elves in Qualinesti. We already have plenty of engineers, but we can always use good diggers! I'll assign you to the Army Commissary officer, Talon Leader Stonchwald."

Kang's jaw dropped, his tongue lolled. He sucked it back in with an irritated snap of his jaws. "Sir, Commissary? We aren't cooks, we're engineers!"

The quadron leader had picked up his quill, was returning to his work. "Yes, very good, Commander Kang. The Commissary

Command is also responsible for troop hygiene. Please report to Talon Leader Stonchwald after we've arrived at our base camp in the southern region of Qualinesti. Until then, try to stay out of the way of troop movements. It's hard enough keeping this army on the move without your regiment clogging the works. We'll be marching first thing in the morning. Have your men—make that draconians"—he said, this with a slight curl of the lip—"ready to go. That will be all, Commander.

"Oh, and, by the way," quadron leader added, as an afterthought, "you can each keep a short sword for your own defense, but turn in the rest of your weapons. They'll be needed for the front-line troops. Dismissed."

Kang stood up, started to salute, decided the hell with it.

Latrine duty. The quadron leader had called it by some fancy name, "troop hygiene," but Kang knew what that meant.

Kang looked for Huzzud on his way out. He didn't see her and, on second thought, was glad that he didn't. He knew she would sympathize, but he couldn't face the shame of telling her his assignment. He marched back to his camp alone. His anger grew stronger with every step, his feet pounding it into the ground, like a hammer pounding molten steel.

By the time he'd reached camp, he had worked himself into a tail-lashing, wing-flapping fury. His troops, recognizing the symptoms, fell over one another to get out of his way. Ignoring them all, he stomped over to the command tent.

"Slith!" Kang's yell resounded across the entire camp.

Slith had been in Yethick's tent. At the sound of his commander's bellow, he realized something was amiss. He ran out, saw the other draconians muttering to each other, their expressions grim, unhappy. Dashing over to the command tent, Slith flung back the tent flap.

"What's wrong, sir?" he asked. "What's happened? Are the dwarves attacking?"

Kang started to tell him, but words were inadequate. His temper blew. Jumping to his feet, he picked up a camp chair, smashed it over a table. The chair slivered. Kang smote the table with his fist, chopped it in two. He was going after the tent post next, when Slith collared him.

"Sir, I wouldn't hit that, if I were you! You'll bring the tent down around our ears."

"Good! Fine!" Kang yelled. "We can always dig our way out! That's what we're good for! Diggers! Good diggers! Damn these bastards to the Abyss and back again!"

Slith's wings drooped. He stared at his commander, incredulous. "Did you say 'dig,' sir?"

Kang gnashed his teeth. Since he couldn't knock down the tent post, he proceeded to dismember the table, pulling off its legs and smashing them on the ground.

"Dig as in . . . latrines, sir?" Slith asked.

Kang's fury had spent itself, a cyclone blowing itself out. He was suddenly very tired. He sank down on his bunk. "We've been assigned to the Commissary Command to dig latrines and cooking pits," he said angrily. "They have humans for the real combat engineering. They don't need us. In fact, we're probably freeing up some of these blue-painted savages of theirs so that they can be useful somewhere else!"

Slith sat down next to his commander. He looked as dejected as Kang felt. "Latrine duty. I'll be twice-damned. What are we going to do, sir?"

Kang shook his head. "I don't know. I really don't know this time. Call a command staff meeting for an hour from now. Inform all of the senior officers what's going on. We'll talk about it then."

* * * * *

An hour later, all of the draconian squadron commanders and specialist officers sat in borrowed chairs around the empty space in the command tent where the table had been. Its remnants, along with those of the chairs, were piled up in a heap outside the tent, a mute testimony to the commander's foul mood.

Kang opened the meeting. "As you have already heard, gentlemen, we have been assigned to latrine duty. You know as well as I do that we'll have the makings of a revolt in our ranks if we have to dig latrines again."

Every draconian present hissed and muttered his agreement.

Kang continued. "We didn't join this army to dig holes for the humans to crap in. I can't believe that this is how Her Majesty intends us to serve her. The question is, what do we do? I'm open to suggestions."

Fulkth, the chief engineering officer spoke first. "Maybe they'll give us line infantry duty?"

Kang snorted. "I forgot to mention that we're to turn in our weapons."

He waited until the howls of outrage died down, then proceeded.

"They don't trust us. That much is obvious."

Slith had been sitting silent, in deep thought, his claws drumming on the side of the chair. Kang did not disturb him. When his second was ready to talk, he'd talk.

Kang was relating everything the quadron leader had said, when Slith suddenly interrupted. "What exactly did you say when you volunteered our services to this Lord Knight Sykes, sir?"

Kang had to think about that one. "I believe I said that I offered the regiment to serve in the Second Army, and he accepted. Why?"

Slith's eyes glistened. "I know you, sir. You're proud of us. Are you sure you didn't say something about serving as engineers?"

"I think I did. No, I'm sure I did," Kang said, recalling his talk with the lord knight. "I said that we'd serve as engineers to this army."

Slith leaned forward. "Then that's it, sir. We're not being employed as engineers, therefore the terms of the agreement are canceled. We don't have to stay."

Yethick nodded approvingly. "They don't want us here. That much is obvious. I say we leave."

Kang looked at all of them. This was now deadly serious. He lowered his voice. "You realize that Sykes will consider this desertion. Or maybe worse. He might think we're spies. We know too much about his movements, his strength, his plans. If we leave and they catch us, they'll kill us."

Slith shrugged, grinned. "We've out-fought Solamnic knights, sir. I don't see why we can't take on the other side, if we have to. But they won't fight, sir. I doubt if they'd even come after us. They've got elvish fish to fry. And if they did come after us, well, personally, I'd rather die with a sword in my gut, sir, than dig latrines again. I say we go back to Mount Dashinak."

Kang considered. He hated the thought of deserting—again. He imagined what Huzzud would think, that he'd run because of cowardice. She wouldn't understand and there was no way he could explain. But did it matter what she thought? What any human thought? So long as he and his men and his Queen knew the real reason they were leaving, what the humans thought about it wasn't worth spit.

"Very well, gentlemen," Kang said. "It's decided. Tomorrow, the army of dark knights marches for Qualinesti, only we won't be here to march with them. We move out tonight, when Solinari is low, and we march until we drop, or we get back home to Mount Dashinak, whichever comes first. We'll take a circuitous route, to throw them off.

We leave nothing behind, not our tools, not our weapons. Load up the wagons again."

"What if someone asks what we're doing, sir?" Fulkth wondered.

"They won't. They'll think we're operating under special orders. Remember, the army's moving out tomorrow morning. There'll be people coming and going all night. No one'll notice us. Yethik, send out foraging parties to replenish our food and water. Slith, seal off the entrance to our camp. Bring any human visitors to me. I doubt we'll get any, but you never know. Fulkth, have a march order ready for last light. All right, let's move."

The officers returned to their duties.

Alone, Kang walked over to his bed and sat down, stared at the dirt floor. He was still staring at it when a shadow darkened the open tent flap. Kang looked up.

Slith stood there. Next to him was Talon Leader Huzzud.

"Official visitor," Slith announced.

Kang rose to his feet. Huzzud stepped inside the tent, glanced around. She must have seen the remains of the table and the broken chairs being hauled away outside.

Huzzud hesitated, then, straightening her shoulders, she spoke the speech she'd come to deliver. "No work is menial in the eyes of our Queen, Commander. Everything we do, we do for her glory."

"I see you wielding a sword, Talon Leader," Kang said dryly. "Not a shovel."

The Talon Leader opened her mouth, then shut it again. Turning on her heel, she left.

Kang sighed and went back to his cot.

"I just hope we're doing the right thing."

He closed his eyes, and lay back on the bunk. He didn't sleep, but lay there thinking.

He lay there for a very long time.

Chapter Twenty

The dark knights forced their dwarven captives along at a quick pace, shoving them from behind when they lagged, and emphasizing haste with a few lashes across the shoulder blades. The knights spoke to each other in the human tongue, either thinking that the dwarves couldn't understand or not caring much if they did. Both dwarves did speak human, however. They'd found it helpful in selling their wares.

The knights were a long-range patrol, apparently. They spoke about returning to the main body of some army, which was headquartered in a village somewhere up ahead. A human settlement called Mish-ka. The dwarves looked at each other. They knew of that village. The knights mentioned preparing for battle against the Qualinesti, wondered when the army was going to attack.

Mortar breathed a gentle sigh of relief. This army was much too close to his home for his liking. The dwarf was thankful these dark knights were going to go beat up on somebody else.

Pestle must have been thinking along the same lines. At one point, when the knights halted to give themselves and their captives time to catch their breaths, Pestle leaned over to his brother and whispered, "Do you know where we are? We're really close to home! If we could just get these knots loose!"

"Wait till they're asleep—" Mortar began.

"No talking!" The knight lashed out with his sword, struck Mortar on the side of the head with the flat of the blade. "Shut up, or I'll gut you right here."

The knights forced their captives to their feet and marched on. It was well after darkness fell before the knights called a halt. Pestle and Mortar plunked down on the ground, glad for the rest. They did not dare talk to each other. Any attempt to communicate was met with swift punishment. They sat silent in the darkness, their fingers busy trying to unravel the knots of the leather thongs tied around their wrists.

The knights set up camp. Opening their packs, they took out food, which they shared with the dwarves, much to the dwarves' astonishment. The knights gave each dwarf a cup of water, then, once dinner was finished, one of the knights checked their bonds—fortunately, neither dwarf had managed to make much headway in loosening the thongs—then tied them to a tree by means of a rope attached to the bonds around their wrists and another tied around their ankles.

"Go to sleep," the knight ordered, speaking Common. "We'll be up before dawn."

He left to lay out his own bedroll. Two knights took the first watch, one going across the road, disappearing among the trees. The other sat down on a fallen log.

The dwarves wriggled about amid the dry leaves, made a show of trying to get comfortable. In reality, they were trying to squirm into the best position for untying the knots. Unfortunately, every time one of them moved, the leaves rustled and crackled.

The knight on watch stood up, came to glower down at them.

"Keep still!" he ordered.

The dwarves did as they were told, remained unmoving for at least an hour. The other knights had fallen asleep, were softly snoring. The knight on watch was humming a marching song to himself, keeping time by tapping out the rhythm on his knee.

Mortar scrunched over closer to his brother, moving slowly so as not to disturb the knight.

"You know," he whispered, "I've been thinking. This is all Selquist's fault."

"How do you figure that?" Pestle whispered back.

"If he hadn't made us steal all that loot and then made us go sell it, we wouldn't be here. We'd be home in our beds." Mortar sighed. His bed had never before seemed so wonderful.

"We did go along with the plan, you know," Pestle said, determined to be fair.

"Yes, but we would have never even thought up the stupid plan if it weren't for Selquist," Mortar pointed out.

"You're right there," Pestle admitted. He was quiet a moment, muttering to himself.

"What did you say?" Mortar asked.

"I was making a deal with Reorx," Pestle returned. "I promised him that if he got us out of this, I'd never steal anything again."

"That's a good idea!" Mortar regarded his brother in admiration. "I'll do the same thing."

He added his promise to that of his brother, both bargaining with the notoriously irascible and often unpredictable God of Forging, whom the dwarves worship exclusively.

The knight ceased his humming, and the dwarves had to be quiet. But by now, both had managed to work the knots into position so that their nimble fingers could yank and pry and tease the thongs apart.

The knight said something out loud and the dwarves froze, until they realized he wasn't talking to them. He was, by the sound of it, chanting a prayer to the Dark Queen.

"How you doing?" Mortar whispered.

"Almost got it." Pestle whispered back. "There. My hands are free. You?"

Mortar grunted. He was having more trouble. "They tied mine tighter," he complained.

"No talking over there," the knight said.

Mortar waited for the man to return to his prayer chants, which fortunately appeared to occupy him a good deal and to be of considerable length. Mortar tugged and pulled and suddenly, the knot came loose.

"Reorx be thanked! I got it!" he whispered.

"Good," said Pestle. "Now we wait for him to fall asleep."

"What if he doesn't?" Mortar asked.

"Pooh! He will. Humans always fall asleep on guard duty."

143

The dwarves waited confidently for another hour, then two. The human was destined to disappoint them. The knight rose, refreshed from his prayers, appearing more wide awake than ever. Worse, he started walking toward them, apparently with the idea of checking their bonds.

"Hear me, Reorx!" Mortar whispered in desperation. "Not only do I promise that I will never steal again, I'll give back everything I ever took!"

The guard halted. His head jerked around, stared toward the road He stood silent, listening, then leaned down and shook two of his comrades by the shoulder.

"Something's moving out on the road."

The other knights were wide awake, on their feet with their swords in hand, before the first had completed his sentence. Moving silently, the two knights crept about, waking the others. They grabbed their bows, nocked arrows, and took up position behind a hedgerow.

The tromp of many feet could be clearly heard, along with the jingle of armor.

"It must be part of our own army," one of the knights said softly. "Who else would be moving around this time of night?"

"We weren't informed of any troop movements," said the leader. "And they're moving away from Mish-ka, not toward it. I don't like this. You keep concealed. I'll ask to see their orders. If they give the wrong answer, fire your arrows into them."

Mortar and Pestle looked at each other. It was now or never.

The dwarves cast off the bonds around their wrists, reached down and untied the cords around their ankles. One of the knights glanced over at them, and the dwarves ceased all movement. The knight returned to watching the road.

"Now!" Pestle whispered.

The two jumped up, and began to run, heading away from the road, hoping to throw off pursuit by losing themselves in the forest.

They heard no sounds of anyone chasing them. Perhaps the knights—preoccupied with the army on the road—hadn't even missed them. The dwarves ran faster. Crashing through underbrush, they caromed off trees, tripped over fallen logs.

Mortar saw the red-glowing outline of a body loom in front of him just a fraction of a second too late to warn his brother. Strong arms grabbed hold of him, a hand clapped over his mouth. He recognized the smell, the clawed fingers, the short, stubby wings extending from the shoulders.

Draconians!

Mortar struggled and fought, kicking and biting the hand. By the sounds of thrashing and swearing, Pestle had also been captured.

"Blast! Ouch! Damn it, he bit me! Bastard knight! Hold still or I'll slit your throat."

Caught in a grip of iron, claws digging into his skin and the horrid taste of draconian flesh in his mouth, Mortar ceased his struggles. He had a few choice remarks to make to Reorx when he saw him, which was probably going to be soon.

"It's not the knights, you fool Baaz," hissed the draconian holding Mortar to a fellow draconian, the one who had grabbed Pestle. "They're dwarves! Those two the knights were holding prisoner. By our Queen, you've smelled dwarf enough the last twenty-five years. You'd think you recognize it by now. And since when did you ever see knights this short and this hairy?"

From behind them, out by the road, they heard a clear voice shout, "Halt! Advance and be recognized."

A grating draconian voice boomed, "Ho! Well met, Sir Knight. You have lonely duty this night, it seems."

"What is this?" the knight asked, sounding amazed. "An army of draconians?"

"The First Regiment of Draconian Engineers," was the proud reply.

"I must ask to see your written movement orders, Commander," the knight said. "I know of no authorized movement of troops, especially an entire regiment, down this road in the middle of the night."

"They've got archers in the trees," whispered one of the draconians. "We have to warn the commander. I don't know how we're going to talk our way out of this. I'll—" He stopped, then said, excited, "By Our Queen, these godforsaken dwarves could come in handy! Come on!"

"Yes, Subcommander Slith," the Baaz answered.

The draconians tucked the dwarves under their powerful arms and started off through the forest at a rapid pace, heading back to the road. Mortar's heart would have fallen into his boots, if it hadn't been for the fact that he was being held in a position where his boots were higher than his heart.

The draconians charged right through the ranks of the concealed archers, who had turned at the sound of the crashing and yelling. The knights held their fire, but they kept their bows raised.

"Hello, boys," Slith said loudly, giving them a salute. "Nice night for target practice, ain't it?"

Emerging from the forest, still carrying the two dwarves, the draconians marched over to a very large draconian who was standing in the middle of the road, talking to the two knights. Behind the draconian stretched a line of draconians as far as the eyes of the dwarves could see.

"You have archers hiding in the woods," the big draconian said.

"Yes, sir." The knight was grim. "Now if I could see your orders, sir—" He stopped talking. He had just noticed the two dwarves.

"You aren't by any chance missing two prisoners, are you, Sir Knight?" Slith asked.

He took a firm grip on Mortar's shirt collar, held him up for display. Mortar swung and kicked, trying to hit the draconian, but he did so more out of frustration than because he thought he might connect.

"We caught them running loose in the woods, Commander Kang," Slith continued, saluting the big draconian.

Mortar suddenly took a good look at the draconian, realized he recognized him. Twisting around in mid-air, Mortar looked at his brother, who was staring at the draconian with fearful eyes. Yes, Pestle apparently recognized the draconian, too. It was the big Bozak from the draconian village, the one the war chief said was the leader.

"We're doomed," Mortar said for a second time and went limp in the draconian's grasp. "If these knights don't kill us, the draconians will."

"Dwarven prisoners? Running about loose?" Kang was eyeing the knight, who appeared extremely discomfited. "What is the meaning of this, Sir Knight?"

"We had taken them prisoner earlier, sir. They must have managed to work the knots free. Then we heard you coming. I went to investigate, and when I turned my back on them, they took off."

"Good thing we were here to catch them again, wasn't it?" Kang said, rocking back on his heels, balancing on his tail.

"Yes, Commander," the knight said glumly, adding, "If you'll hand them over, sir, we'll see to it that they don't escape again."

Kang looked at the two dwarves. Mortar had the unhappy feeling that the draconian had recognized the dwarves, as well. The Bozak scratched his chin.

"You seem to be rather careless with your prisoners, Sir Knight. I think we'll take them in charge."

The knight was not pleased. He must have been wondering how he'd managed to lose control of this situation. "Sir, the prisoners are our responsibility. And you still haven't shown me your orders—"

The Sivak holding onto Mortar dropped the dwarf to the ground. Slith strode forward, thrust his jaw into the human's face.

"Now, listen here, Sir Knight. I want to know your name and rank immediately."

"My name is Glaf Herrik, Talon Second under—"

The Sivak gave a howl. "Talon Second! And you dare to talk sass back to a Regimental Commander. I'll have you flogged in front of Lord Knight Sykes's command tent for this. Now take your skulking, leather-creaking, prancing beauties back into the woods, and leave the real work of the war for us veterans. These prisoners are now under our jurisdiction. Carry on, Talon Second."

The knight was going to argue, but at that moment, his archers walked out of the woods, escorted by at least fifty draconians. The knight muttered several threats about reporting this to his superiors, then, with a grudging salute, he called off his men and returned to their camp.

"Company for'ard!" Slith yelled.

The draconians fell into ranks and marched off. Slith remembered at the last moment to pick up Mortar, plucking him out of the road, saving him from being trampled by the clawed feet of two hundred draconians.

Slith, with Mortar tucked under his arm again, hurried up to march at the side of his commander.

"You think they'll report this, sir?" Slith asked.

"Hell, yes," Kang said. "They've probably got a runner on his way right now. At least we know the road's not safe. They've likely got patrols up and down it. We'll put about five miles behind us, then head into the mountains. Double time march! Move! Move! Move!"

The Sivak shouted commands, and the draconians picked up the pace. Mortar craned his neck, peered under the draconian's arm, tried to see what had become of his brother. Pestle was being carried on the back of the same Baaz draconian who had captured him.

Seeing Mortar looking at him, the Baaz grinned. Wicked teeth gleamed in the lambent light of the stars. The Baaz flicked his tongue over them. "Dwarf-meat for breakfast! Yum, yum," he said.

Mortar gulped and looked hurriedly away.

"No talking in the ranks," Slith ordered. "Save your breath. You're going to need it."

The draconians maintained their breakneck pace all through the long night. Leaving the road, they ascended into the mountains. The going proved rough and difficult, but even this did not slow them by much. Their clawed feet and hands made them expert climbers; their wings saved them from what might have otherwise been nasty falls.

The dwarven prisoners proved to be the biggest hindrance. The draconians could not carry the dwarves and climb too. Mortar assured the draconians that they could leave him and his brother behind, and there would be no hard feelings, but Commander Kang said no. He ordered the dwarves roped together, put two Baaz in charge of them, and ordered the dwarves to march.

Pestle refused. He was rumpled and rattled, but defiant. He planted his feet, folded his arms across his chest and glared. "I'm not moving."

"Me neither," said Mortar.

Kang bent down to dwarf-eye level. "I can always toss you back to the knights," he said.

Pestle and Mortar looked at each other.

"We'll march," Pestle said meekly.

* * * * *

It was now midmorning. Mortar had never worked so hard in his life. He scrabbled and slipped and slid. His hands were torn and bleeding. More than once, some draconian caught him when he started to fall, saving him from tumbling off the mountain. Whenever they reached a bit of level ground, the Sivak made them run, striking their shoulders with a lash if they slowed their pace. Then it was back to climbing. Always in Mortar's mind was the unhappy thought that he was undergoing this torture only to be cooked in the end.

By the time morning came, Mortar was so exhausted and hurting that he didn't care if he was a draconian's breakfast. Just as long as he didn't have to climb or run anymore. He was trudging along, his head down, forcing his boots to move one after the other, when a hand clutched him.

"Mortar! Look!" Pestle was pointing.

Mortar gazed wearily upward. He drew in a deep breath. Mount Celebund. Only one pass stood between them and their home.

So close. And yet, so far.

"Halt!" Kang called out. "Cease march. Fifteen-minute rest."

The draconians halted, as exhausted as the dwarves. Many collapsed where they stood, lying on the rocks, panting, their tongues lolling. Others grabbed their water skins, guzzled water thirstily.

Mortar and Pestle sat down, staring wistfully, longingly at the mountain peak.

The Sivak loomed above them, blotting out the view.

"On your feet. The commander wants to see you."

"This is it," said Mortar. "Good-bye, Pestle. You've been a really good brother."

"You, too, Mortar," Pestle said, tears in his eyes.

The two embraced.

"Oh, for the love of the Dark Queen, come on!" The Sivak snarled.

The two trudged over to where the big Bozak was seated on a rock.

"I recognize you two. You're from Celebundin, aren't you?" Kang growled. The draconian was gray with fatigue.

"Maybe we are," Mortar said, determined not to cooperate. "And maybe we're not."

The Bozak smiled. "Well, if you are from Celebundin, that pass there will take you home. Good-bye and thanks."

Mortar and Pestle stood and stared so long it seemed they had turned into part of the mountain.

"Did you say good-bye?" Pestle was not certain he'd heard right.

"Do you mean we can go?" Mortar asked for clarification.

"Go! Get! Skedaddle," Kang said.

Mortar felt renewed strength. The two dashed off, fearful that the draconian might change his mind. A few yards away, though, Mortar came to halt. He looked back, his brow furrowed.

"You said thanks. Thanks for what?"

"You saved our lives back there," Kang said. "The least we can do is return the favor." He waved a clawed hand. "See you in a couple of weeks. We're almost out of dwarf spirits."

"What?" Mortar was puzzled. "Oh, I get it. You—"

Pestle grabbed his brother's arm and dragged him off.

Two hours later, they reached the highest part of the pass and looked down on their secluded valley.

"We made it!" said Mortar, drawing in a deep breath. He gazed down lovingly on Celebundin. "I swear I can smell the smoke of the cooking fires."

"It's not cooking fires!" Pestle said grimly, pointing at the other end

149

of the valley, where thick black smoke was rising into the air. "Take a look!"

"Reorx's beard!" Mortar said, alarmed. "There's going to be hell to pay! Run for it! We have to warn the Thane!"

Pestle was already running, fear lending strength to his tired legs.

Mortar was right. There would be hell to pay.

Chapter Twenty-One

There would be hell to pay, but not, Kang figured, as long as the draconians kept clear of Lord Knight Sykes. And Kang certainly had no intention of reenlisting. The knights might chase after the deserters, but why bother? Sykes had more important things to do—like conquer Ansalon.

Having determined to his own satisfaction that there would be no pursuit, Kang looked forward to returning to their walled enclave. Who knows? Now that it looked as if their village was going to be a permanent home, they might even give it a name.

The regiment had been on the move since early the night before. They had taken a short break, and were now headed home. They had been gone only six days, but it seemed like six hundred years to Kang. All he could think about was sleeping once again in his own bed—if the dwarves hadn't made off with it.

Kang grinned. Six dwarves laid end to end could fit in Kang's big bed. That was one thing he could be fairly certain they wouldn't have stolen.

Strung out single file, the draconians entered the narrow mountain pass that would take them home. Kang was in the lead. Slith remained back to see that everyone made it safely and to make certain there was no one chasing after them. He would be the last through.

Kang was the first one over the pass. He paused to look down on their village.

He couldn't see it. Couldn't see it for the smoke rising into the air.

Kang felt the blow in the pit of his stomach. The sight was so shocking, he reeled backward a step or two, almost trod on the foot of the Baaz coming up behind him. The Baaz reached out a hand to steady his commander. Shaking off the soldier's assistance, Kang let out a ferocious roar and charged down the mountain.

Kang hit the sun-burnt grass of the valley at a dead run. Draconians galloped after him.

They were too late, however. There was nothing they could do.

Kang came to halt. The others jammed up behind him. No one spoke. No one said a word. They stood and watched their village burn.

Flames had already blackened and consumed most of the central buildings. The guard towers had been toppled. The gate came crashing down in a shower of sparks. And there, swarming around the walls, torches in their hands, were the dwarves.

Kang had been angry when the knights ordered him to dig latrines. But now he felt rage, a white-hot fury that was fiercer and blazed hotter than the flames that were burning up the last twenty-five years of his life. He had been tolerant of the dwarves, and they had betrayed him. He had left them his creation, he had even taken pleasure in the thought that they could make use of it, and they had spit in his face.

It took nearly thirty minutes for the racing draconians to cross the glade and reach the burning village. Kang led the way, his sword in his hand and death spells in his mind.

They were near the outer walls before the dwarves— intent on their destruction—were aware of them. One dwarf, standing on the wall, glanced over his shoulder, saw them, and let out a yelp.

Kang lifted his hand. Lightning crackled from his fingertips. The magical bolt struck the dwarf in the chest, knocking him backward. The dwarf fell off the wall, plunged to his death in a burning shed.

Kang ran right over the wreckage of the smoldering gates. The blackened wood glowed red, burned the pads on the bottom of his bare feet, but he never noticed the pain. Blisters were nothing compared to the pain of seeing his creation go up in smoke. That pain was like a dagger, twisting in his gut.

The draconians surged after Kang, and once they were inside the walls, they spread out, searching for dwarves. There were only about fifteen or so inside the village. The others had probably made off with what they could carry, left behind enough men to torch the place. These dwarves were trapped inside the walls with nowhere to run.

Seeing their deaths loom before them, the dwarves drew their swords and grimly stood their ground wherever they happened to be. Most died without ever getting in a hit, however. The enraged draconians hacked them to pieces. Picking up the pieces, the draconians threw those into the fire.

Kang was cutting off the head of a dead dwarf, preparatory to hanging it from the charred stone wall, just about all that now remained of the draconian village. He heard a draconian shouting his name, but he ignored it. The draconian kept on shouting. Then someone grabbed hold of his arm. Annoyed at the interruption, Kang turned, his bloody sword in hand.

It took a moment for the red mist to clear from his eyes. When it did, he saw Slith.

"Sir!" Slith's voice was hoarse from the smoke and from yelling. "Sir! For the love of the Queen, listen to me, sir!"

Kang lowered his sword.

"Sir," Slith said, coughing. "We've got to get the troops under control! They're preparing to march on Celebundin. If they rush off now, without any discipline or orders, they'll all get slaughtered!"

Kang stared at Slith. He knew his second was talking to him. He knew Slith was saying something important, but Kang couldn't hear a word for the blood beating in his head.

"Again," he said, his mouth dry and parched.

Slith repeated what he'd said. This time Kang was calm enough to comprehend.

"Yes. You're right. Go . . ." Kang waved a bloody hand.

Slith turned and ran, yelling orders over the crackle of the dying fires. Kang knew he should be helping, but he felt oddly lethargic. He was in one of those terrifying dreams, where you want to move, you know you have to move, but you keep standing in the same place.

For a moment, Kang didn't think Slith was going to prevail. The draconians were a mob, shouting wildly about slaughtering every dwarf in the world. But a mob is no match for an organized army and Kang guessed that the dwarves would have heard of the draconians' return and would be expecting them. And that would be the end.

Very well, then, Kang thought to himself. That's how we'll go out. He'd feel some satisfaction at least before he went to serve his Queen.

And then, the notes of the bugle rang over the din: Officer's Call. At the sound, the draconians lifted their heads, looked around, dazed. Slith had lost his voice, but apparently didn't realize it, because he was still shouting, though no one could hear him. It had been a stroke of brilliance, latching onto the bugler. A few officers came to their senses, began helping to restore order.

Slowly, the draconians shuffled into ranks, forming up on the grasslands outside their burning town. Kang would have to go speak to them. He remembered feeling this way before, as a junior officer, losing his first battle. He dreaded the meeting.

Slowly, he picked up his sword, wiped it on the body of the dead dwarf at his feet, noting, at the time, that the dwarf was wearing a uniform. Kang sheathed his weapon. He walked through the smoke-filled streets and out the blackened gates. Now he could feel the pain of his burned feet.

He arrived to find all of the officers present, and the draconian troops standing at attention. Discipline had won out over chaos. Discipline. It had kept them going this long. Her Dark Majesty willing, it would keep them going a lot longer.

Kang straightened his shoulders and marched tall.

Slith called the officers to attention as Kang approached. Slith croaked the words, "All officers present but two, sir. Gloth and Stehmph are off collecting the stragglers, as per your order."

That lie was for the benefit of the other officers. Kang had given no such order. But maintaining the unity of command was of paramount importance.

"Thank you, Slith," Kang said quietly. "I owe you one. Another one."

Slith stood at attention, pretending he hadn't heard.

"Troop leaders," Kang yelled, his own throat raw from the smoke. "Take your troops and begin putting out the fires. Yethik, I want your supply people to go through every square inch of this village and salvage anything of use. That includes nails, hinges, anything. Gloth, take a troop from the Second Squadron and set up a cordon to our north, two hundred yards out from here. I want no one in, other than returning stragglers, and I want no one out. Have your draconians gather up anything that's left of those damned dwarves and nail them to poles. Post them out here in a line. We've been too soft with these dwarves. But all that's going to change."

Slith turned to the officers. "You heard the commander! Move!"

The draconians dispersed, left to accomplish their tasks. Kang was fairly certain that they wouldn't find much to salvage, nor were they in any danger of attack. The dwarves were probably barricaded in their village, fearing the worst. What was important was that his troops were doing something constructive, working off their anger. When the two were alone, Slith turned back to Kang. Smoke wafted past them. Somewhere, a burning timber crashed to the ground.

"What do we now, sir?" Slith asked in a husky whisper, all he could manage.

Kang sighed, rubbed his hand over his chin. "I don't know. I guess we'll set up camp over to the west of the town. At least we'll be up-wind of the stench. When things cool off, maybe we'll clear away the rubble and rebuild."

Slith shook his head. "It won't be the same, sir."

"No, you're right there. It won't ever be same."

The relatively peaceful life of the past twenty-five years had gone up in a roar with the fire. Their attempts at co-existing with their neighbors had failed. That relationship had been based on a certain amount of trust, and that was now gone.

"Why did they do it, sir?" Slith was puzzled and hurt. "There was lots of value in there. They could have hauled it off, made some use of it. But they burned it! Why?"

"Hate," said Kang. "They hate us so much that they couldn't bear to have anything of us left. I thought maybe that might have changed. I don't mean that I thought they'd come to like us. I don't like dwarves. Never will. But I can tolerate them. I thought that's maybe how they felt about us. I guess not. I'll tell you this much, though, Slith." Kang's voice hardened. "Celebundin is going to pay for this."

Slith nodded in satisfaction. Turning, he ran off to join the troop heading out to their assigned picket.

It took four hours to put out the fires. Not one building was saved. Luckily, when the draconians had left to join the army, they had taken their tools, weapons and armor with them. They had their tents, and they could at least erect temporary shelters until Kang decided what to do and where to do it.

The wood smoldered and would continue to do so for several days. Kang knew he would never get the stench out of his nostrils. The draconians were black from sifting through and cleaning up the still-warm ruins. Gloth's pickets rounded up those few draconians who had gone berserk, disobeyed orders, and rushed off to slaughter dwarves. They were stopped before they reached Celebundin. All were punished severely. No army can survive when discipline falls lax and soldiers feel free to act of their own volition.

By sundown, the draconians had evacuated their old town. They began to dig breastworks around a new camp, just as they had done so many times before. The work was slow-going and half-hearted. The draconians had not slept for nearly three days. Their fury had sapped what strength they had remaining. A few fell asleep on their feet, toppled into the ditch they were digging. Even when they fell, they did not wake up. After nightfall, Kang ordered a complete standdown.

As his soldiers straggled off to their tents, Kang ordered the bugler to sound the Officer's Call again. The officers gathered around their commander.

"Tonight," Kang said, "we officers are going to keep the watch. The men are so tired that they'll fall asleep at their posts or do something stupid—like shoot an arrow in someone going to the latrine. It's up to us, as officers, to keep our heads clear. No one goes to sleep until sunup. Understood?"

"Yes, Commander." Slith answered for them.

They each went off to find a sentry post to guard.

Kang settled himself down to watch. The sky was cloudless. The stars seemed unusually bright, almost feverishly bright, as if heaven itself was restless and disturbed. Kang didn't have to worry about falling asleep. Tired as he was, his nerves were raw and twitchy. If he'd laid down, he would have stared at the tent flap all night.

As it was, he stared at the glittering stars, his thoughts darker than the night. He was beginning to doubt himself, doubt his ability to lead, to command. He thought back to when things had started to fall apart—the day he'd discovered the holy symbol missing.

And it was a damn dwarf who'd run off with it.

Every decision he'd made since that time had been the wrong one.

Perhaps he should resign, hand command over to Slith.

Gazing into the heavens, he found the constellation that was His Queen's—the five-headed dragon. Kang spoke to his Queen, not asking for magical spells, power, or glory. He begged her forgiveness. He asked her for help and guidance.

And it seemed, by the peace that filled his soul—and the idea that She gave him—that help was granted.

By morning, only half the officers on watch were still awake. The rest slumbered at their posts.

Kang never said a word.

Chapter Twenty-Two

Two days later, Kang passed the word for Slith.

The Sivak, who was still with the picket lines, entered the command tent that also doubled as Kang's living quarters. "Sir? I was told you wanted to see me."

Kang was seated at a hastily constructed table, in a rudely constructed command chair that creaked loudly whenever he moved. He had been out inspecting the newly constructed breastworks. Now, back inside, he was honing the blade of his knife. "Yes, I do. I have a job for you, my friend. One I think you'll enjoy."

Slith grinned. "Yes, sir!"

Kang's next question took the Sivak by surprise.

"What are the men thinking, Slith? You're closer to them than I am. What are they saying?"

Slith looked uncomfortable.

"Permission to speak freely, sir?"

"Since when haven't you ever spoken freely, my friend?" Kang asked wryly.

"Well"—Slith was embarrassed—"they think you've gone soft, sir. It's been two days now and instead of lopping off dwarf heads, all we've been doing is digging. We might as well have stayed with the dark knights. The men want revenge."

Kang nodded. "That's what I thought. The men want to exterminate the dwarves, wipe them out."

"Do to them what they did to us, sir."

"They didn't wipe us out," Kang said. "They burned down our village while we weren't in it."

"Yes, sir, that's true, I guess, sir." Slith looked worried. He was like the rest of them, apparently, thinking his commander was going soft. Was Kang the only one who could see past his own snout?

"What happens if we kill all the dwarves, Slith?"

"We feel a hell of lot better, sir," Slith answered, his jaw closing with a vicious snap.

Kang suppressed a smile. "And after that? After we've wallowed in bloodlust for awhile? What happens after that?"

"We have the whole valley to ourselves, sir. We can live here in peace and quiet."

"Would you like that, Slith? Peace and quiet? No raids. No midnight alarms. It might be nice at that," Kang said thoughtfully. "You could pass the time tending to your garden. Hoeing weeds, picking carrots. Maybe even raise chickens."

Slith grimaced.

"Of course," Kang continued, "you'd have to settle the fights that would break out among the troops, when the men couldn't find any other way to let off steam. Still, think of the long, peaceful nights. Very long. No dwarf spirits. No nut-ale. We could get a lot accomplished. I was thinking of starting a series of lectures—"

"All right, sir," Slith said gloomily. "You've made your point. But I got to tell you, sir. I know dwarves. And they'll think we've all gone soft if we don't at least punish 'em, and punish 'em good."

"I intend to, Slith," Kang said, tone now grim. "First, though, I want to make certain they're not planning to finish us off. They could, you know, if they attacked now in strength. We have no defenses. We're stuck out here in the open, exposed. I need to know their plans, Slith. I need to know if they're massing for an all-out assault."

"And if they are, sir?"

"Then we have to make a choice. We either leave the valley or we stay and fight."

Slith thought this over. "If we leave the valley, where would we go, sir? We've got to assume that the dark knights have every major road under their control. They'd find us for sure. I say we stay and fight."

"I agree. I'm for staying myself. And we'll put up one hell of a fight if the dwarves insist on it, but I'm hoping they won't. It's imperative that we know their plans."

"Yes, sir. And what do we do then?"

Kang paused, then said, "We fight, if they push us. If not, if they're willing to go back to the way things were before, then I'm willing to do the same. I'll arrange a parley with their High Thane. This valley's big enough for us all to live in. And we'll be gone soon enough. All they have to do is wait for us to die off."

Slith shook his head, unconvinced. But it wasn't his place to argue. "So what's the plan, sir?"

"I want you to take three other Sivaks and do some scouting. You know how to sneak into that village without being spotted."

"Yes, sir!" Slith, the shape-changer, grinned again. This was more to his liking. "It's going to mean killing, though."

"Yes, and that will show the dwarves that we don't intend to roll over and turn to stone. But we kill only soldiers. No killing of civilians, especially no women or children. The dwarves we caught torching our village were all soldiers. That was different from the raids, if you'll remember. On the raids, every dwarf who could walk came to share the fun. It makes me think this burning was strictly a military action, probably the idea of that war chief of theirs, and so it's their militia we'll target. Besides, you and the other Sivaks need to take the shape of soldier dwarves, anyway. Then you can infiltrate their ranks and find out their plans."

Slith was eager. "When do we go?"

"Tonight."

Slith saluted. "Yes, sir."

"Oh, one more thing," Kang added. "I'm going with you."

Slith stiffened. "If you don't trust me, sir—"

Kang was exasperated. "Blast it, Slith, you've known me for thirty years! You've saved my butt so many times I've lost count. Of course, I trust you. But don't you think a magic-wielding Bozak might come in handy?"

Slith relaxed. "Yes, sir. You're right, as usual, sir."

"I'll be meditating, communing with our Queen. Let me know when you're ready to leave."

Slith nodded, rose, saluted, and closed the tent flap on his way out.

*   *   *   *   *

Long after dark, the Baaz sentry on duty outside Kang's tent rapped on the tent pole. "Sir, you asked to be awakened when Subcommander Slith was ready to go."

Kang had drifted off into his trance-like sleep of spell preparation. Waking, he felt refreshed, with a whole catalog of magical spells in his mind. His Queen appeared to approve of his plan. He donned leather armor, buckled on a short sword, thrust a knife in his belt.

Slith and three other Sivaks waited for their commander by the campfire. Slith was handing out strips of red cloth to the other Sivaks. "When you change form, tie this strip around your arm. I don't want us killing each other by mistake."

Slith looked dubiously at Kang. "Sir, what are we going to do with you? You're not a shape-shifter and, begging the commander's pardon, but you'll never pass for a dwarf."

"I've got a spell that will help. I'm mainly along to make certain that we don't get into trouble bigger than we can handle."

"Sir, I've been thinking. We could take the First Squadron—"

Kang shook his head. "No. The first whiff of dwarf and they'll go on a killing spree."

"Right, sir." Slith said, resigned. "Let's go."

The five draconians left camp in the darkness. Both moons were waning, although Kang could sense the third moon, the dark moon, waxing—a good omen for the draconians. The ground they covered was familiar. They moved rapidly and silently. When they reached the woods outside the dwarven village, Kang called a halt.

"I'm going to make myself invisible. The spell doesn't last long and it's not complete. Anyone looking for me can find me. You'll need to cover for me."

Kang pointed to six heavily armed dwarves, who were patrolling the main street leading into Celebundin. "Look, they're waiting for us. Once we're in, you're on your own. Meet back at our camp. If you're not back, you're considered dead. Move out."

Kang spoke words of magic, drew an arcane symbol in the air. One of the Sivaks turned to ask the commander a question, blinked in astonishment and looked all around.

The spell was working.

Slith issued orders. "You two sneak around to the west side and try to get in there. Remember, we only kill warriors. No slicing up civilians. And you're after information, not dwarf heads."

The three Sivaks padded softly into the night. Slith and the remaining Sivak crept over to the side of the nearest building—a small thatch-roofed storage shed. Kang was right behind them, although neither of them knew it. Slith slid forward, around the side of the building.

Two of the dwarves patrolling the streets marched past the front of the shed. Slith made certain they were wearing uniforms, then he motioned his partner forward. Crossing the street, the other Sivak moved to the front of the shed. Slith crept up to the corner of his building, and waited for the dwarves to return.

Moments later, the two dwarves came back, walking their beat. As one of the dwarves crossed in front of Slith, the draconian leaped out, grabbed the dwarf, jerked his head back and slit his throat. Using his ability to assume the shape of the enemy he'd just killed, Slith transformed. It was a dwarf who dragged the body of the dead dwarf back into the shadows.

The second dwarf, hearing the scuffle, turned to see what appeared to be his partner dying at the hands of another dwarf. Before he could yell, the second Sivak leaped out and throttled him. There was a sharp crack and now there were two dead dwarves and two live dwarves who looked exactly like them.

"Dump the bodies in this storage shed."

Kang stood off to the side, waiting to cast a lightning bolt spell in case any of the guards' comrades showed up. No one appeared.

"You there, Commander?" Slith asked.

"I'm here," Kang answered.

"All set, then."

Slith the dwarf and his new dwarven buddy, each with a red rag tied around his neck, walked up the center of the street, searching for a tavern. They needed to find a place where soldiers were likely to talk freely, and there is no place like a tavern for information. They even had steel in their pockets, enough to buy a few drinks. Compliments of the dead.

Halfway to the center of the town, they came across the Market Guild Tavern, a squat, two-story building that advertised itself as a "drinking and eating establishment with rooms to let." Peering in the window, Slith saw several uniforms that matched the one he wore.

"Go on in. Find out what you can. Meet me outside in half an hour."

The dwarf started, by force of habit, to give a draconian salute. Slith smacked his arm. "You're a dwarf, now. Remember?"

Chastened, the dwarf changed the salute to a wave and entered the tavern.

Slith continued on down the street, intending to investigate the center of the village, where the meeting hall was located. It had occurred to him that he might find the war chief here. What better person to ask about dwarven military plans than the head of the militia himself?

As Slith was strolling down the street, he noticed a female dwarf heading his direction. They would have to pass each other. He steered over to the opposite side of the street, tried to look nonchalant, as if he were out for an evening stroll. It would never do to let her get close to him. He looked like a dwarf, but he still smelled like a draconian.

The female was staring at him, probably one of those who were attracted to dwarves in uniform. Slith averted his eyes, hoping she would ignore him.

It didn't work. She came right up to him.

"Don't you try to sidle past me, Harold Brickman! Don't you try to sneak off! You said you were standing guard duty tonight! That's why we couldn't go visit mother! Where've you been? In the tavern, I'll wager. Drinking with your no account friends. I can smell the spirits—" The female closed in on Slith, sniffed.

It wasn't spirits she smelled.

Chapter Twenty-Three

"Brickman, whatever have you been doing? You smell just like a frog . . ."

Her eyes widened. She stared at Slith in horror. In order for the shape-changer spell to work, the victim must be prepared to believe that the person he or she is looking at is a dwarf. Once that belief is called into doubt, for whatever reason . . .

The female screamed.

Slith turned and ran. He dashed past the tavern, where dwarves—the Sivak among them—were wandering out to see what the screaming was about. They spotted Slith racing away. The female dwarf was hysterical. She could only scream and point. The other dwarves, assuming she'd been robbed, set off in pursuit. Slith kept running. Rounding a corner, he legged it for the north end of the village.

A voice came from behind him.

"Don't worry, Slith, I've got your back covered," Kang said.

Slith had forgotten the commander was with him. He didn't look back, just kept running.

"They're gaining on us," said Kang.

"Damn rotten luck!" Slith muttered. He had dwarf legs, not his own powerful draconian legs, and he was falling behind. "You'd think our Queen could look out for us better than this!"

"Maybe she is," Kang said. "Maybe she is. Look, there's an empty house. Duck in there. We'll lie low till they've gone."

Slith changed course, ran for the house, with Kang right behind him. The house was of typical dwarven design, made of stone with wooden doors and shutters. No lights shone from the windows. It did, as Kang said, look deserted.

Slith tried the door handle. When it didn't give way immediately, he threw his shoulder against the door, forgetting, as he did so, that he had a dwarven shoulder, not a big, muscular draconian shoulder. The door didn't budge.

"Hurry up, Slith!" Kang urged.

They could hear shouts and cries coming very close.

"Damn door's got three locks!" Slith said, peering at it. "You better have a go at it, sir."

Slith couldn't see anything, but he felt something large hurtle past him. The door burst open, as if it had been hit by an enormous foot.

"You go inside! I'll never fit through the door. I'll be safe enough out here."

Slith dashed inside, hastily shut the door—with its now-broken three locks. He turned around to find that they'd made a mistake.

The house was not deserted.

Four dwarves were gathered around a table on which burned a single candle. They were all peering intently at something and arguing among themselves.

At the sight of the dwarf entering their house, one of the dwarves grabbed the something they had been staring at off the table and appeared to be trying to hide it. The other three tried very hard to look innocent.

"Uh, hullo, uh, Brickman," said one of the dwarves, a scrawny fellow with a beard like a fungus. "Out on the town without the little woman, eh? Nice of you to stop by. Next time, though, knock, will you? You've wrecked my door."

I'll be damned, thought Slith. I know this dwarf!

Kang, standing outside the house, heard the voices inside and cursed. "Damn and double damn!" This empty house had seemed the answer to his prayers. Now it did indeed look as if their Queen had forsaken them. He was going to have to find another holy medal.

If Slith could just fool them for a few moments longer . . .

The dwarves in pursuit came pounding down the street. Kang crouched down beneath a heavily curtained window, hoping to be able to hear what was going on inside the house, yet remain hidden in the shadows. His invisibility spell was due to wear off soon.

The search party straggled to a halt.

"Where'd he go?"

"Beats me."

The dwarves stood in the middle of the road, staring around. "That's Selquist's house. Maybe he saw something. We could ask."

"Naw, he's not home. Look, no lights. What'd the fellow we were chasing do, anyway?"

"I dunno. Madam Brickman was yelling, fit to be tied. Robbed her, I guess. Did you get a good look at him?"

"No, you?"

"Me neither."

"He must have left town. You want to go after him?" The dwarf did not sound enthusiastic.

"What? You heard the war chief. He said those damn dracos are probably skulking about out there, waiting to pick us off one by one. Not me. I'm not going any farther. Let's head back to the tavern. All that running made me thirsty."

After further conversation, the dwarves turned and headed back into town.

A good thing. Kang could feel the invisibility spell draining away. He could hold it for only another few minutes. At least he was near the edge of town. He could make his escape into the night. He wouldn't leave without Slith, however, and he wondered what was taking so long. He hadn't heard any shouts or cries, so he assumed that Slith hadn't been discovered.

But if so, what was he doing? Having tea?

"Damn it, Slith!" Kang muttered. "Come on!"

*   *   *   *   *

Inside the house, Slith was curious. He recognized these dwarves—

they were the four he had followed for two days, the four who had talked of sneaking into Thorbardin. He definitely remembered the skinny dwarf with the scraggly beard.

These dwarves had raided Thorbardin. They had obviously found something valuable, to judge by the fact that they were being so secretive about it.

And what was valuable to a dwarf might be of equal value to a draconian.

"Well, Brickman," said the scrawny dwarf. "Are you going to stand there all night with your eyes bugging out? What the devil do you want? If it's about that small matter of the missing pewter pot, I've already explained—"

"We were never anywhere near Thorbardin!" one of the dwarves piped up, his voice quavering. "Ouch!" he said a moment later, and rubbed his arm. "What'd you pinch me for, Selquist?"

Slith sucked a breath, blew out the candle.

Dwarves can see in the darkness as well as draconians, but these dwarves had been staring into the candlelight, and it took a moment for their eyes to adjust. Slith took advantage of that moment. Changing form, returning back to his draconian shape, he leapt for the table. He backhanded one dwarf, who was in his way, surged toward the scrawny dwarf.

The scrawny dwarf could see well enough now, and what he saw terrified him. He stood, clutching something to his chest, paralyzed with fear.

Slith reached out clawed hands, grabbed hold of whatever it was the dwarf was trying to hide.

This attempt to steal his treasure jolted the dwarf to action. He hung onto the object with a tenacity typical of a certain species of dog raised by the Solamnic knights to hunt goblins. Slith picked up not only the object but the dwarf along with it.

"Let go! Damn your hairy hide!" Slith snarled, and attempted to shake the dwarf loose.

"It's m-m-mine!" said the dwarf, his teeth rattling in his head.

Slith gave a tremendous heave, sent the dwarf flying through the air. He landed, from the sounds of it, in a cabinet filled with crockery.

Object tucked under his arm, Slith ran for the front door. Unfortunately, in his haste and excitement, he forgot that this was a house built for dwarves, forgot that he had entered as a dwarf and that he was now leaving as a seven-foot-tall draconian.

Slith bashed headlong into the doorframe.

*   *   *   *   *

Kang, standing outside, heard the yelling, the scuffle and the sound of breaking crockery. He could only assume that Slith had been discovered.

No use hiding. The commander thrust his head through the open window, in time to see his second-in-command ram his skull into the doorframe and knock himself senseless.

"Oh, for the love of—"

Kang dashed around to the front. His spell had worn off by now, but the need for concealment was gone. One of the dwarves inside was screeching like a gnome-powered doomsday device. Every dwarf within miles would be descending on them.

Slith lay on his back, his feet sticking out the door. He was holding what looked like a book in his arms.

Two of the dwarves were running toward him, large clubs in their hands.

"Save the book!" cried another dwarf from the depths of a smashed cabinet.

"Slith! Wake up!" Kang shouted.

Grabbing hold of the Sivak's feet, Kang gave a heave and pulled Slith out the door, just as the two dwarves with clubs were getting ready to finish the job on Slith's skull which the doorframe had started.

"Slith! Come on! Wake up!" Kang smacked his second a couple of times in the face.

Groggily, Slith shook his head. "What hit me?"

Kang took hold of the book, tucked it heedlessly under his arm, and helped the Sivak to stand. He paused a moment to bare his fangs and growl at the three dwarves, who were racing out of the house.

At the sight of two draconians, one of them extremely large and muscular, the three dwarves skidded to a halt, with the result that they all bunched up in the doorway.

"Let me out! Let me through!" shouted a voice from behind the three. "He's got the book!"

Slith staggered to his feet. "Ooh!" He put his hand to his forehead.

"Sorry, old friend, but we have to get moving," Kang said. "Company's coming."

"Yes, sir," Slith said, gritting his teeth.

169

The two started off down the road. From this point, they could see the woods, where they could lose themselves among the trees. Kang's concentration was divided between his own running and concern for Slith, who was weaving like a drunken goblin. Thus Kang failed to hear the footsteps behind him. Searing pain flamed along his thigh muscle, pain so severe and so sudden, so unexpected, that Kang let out a howl and dropped the book. Turning, enraged, he confronted a dwarf, holding a bloody knife in his hand.

The dwarf ignored Kang, made a dive for the book.

"Save it, sir!" Slith cried. "Don't lose it!"

Kang had no idea what was so valuable about this book, but if both Slith and the dwarf wanted it, he guessed there must be something. He caught hold of the book at the same time as the dwarf grabbed it.

There was a brief tussle. The scrawny little dwarf was stronger than he looked. A strange, unholy light flickered in the dark, frenzied eyes.

Kang tried to hold on by digging his claws into the leather cover. He pulled, the dwarf pulled. The cover ripped apart and both fell backward. The tug-of-war ended with dwarf hanging onto the book and Kang hanging onto the torn cover.

The scrawny dwarf was up and running like he'd been shot out of a catapult, the book clutched triumphantly under his arm.

"Never mind, sir," Slith said, sighing. "You tried."

Torches lit the night. Bells had begun to ring. The entire village was aroused. Kang wondered if the other two Sivaks had escaped, if they'd had any luck with the mission.

"Let's get the hell outta here," Kang said.

He was limping. Slith was wobbling, his hand pressed over his aching head. The maneuver hadn't exactly turned out as planned.

The two draconians reached the shelter of the trees safely and took time to rest and examine their wounds. The pursuing dwarves had stopped at the border of the village, unwilling to go farther. For all they knew, the woods might be full of draconians.

Slith had a bump on his head the size of the egg of a goat-sucker bird. Kang's knife-slice was deep and painful, having cut into his thigh muscle. The wound bled profusely. He wore no shirt, and he was in desperate need of a bandage. Slith offered the red rag he had worn, but it couldn't be found. It had probably popped off during his transformation from dwarf back to draconian.

"What's that you have in your hand, sir?" Slith asked.

"I don't know. Part of that blasted book, I guess." Kang looked down to find a largish piece of torn leather dangling from a claw.

"It's better than nothing. Here, let me help you, sir," Slith offered.

Kang, weak and dizzy from loss of blood, handed over the leather.

Slith was about to slap the book cover over the wound, when he noticed a square piece of white parchment, stuck to the leather.

"What's this?" he asked.

"Does it matter?" Kang demanded, suppressing a groan. "I'm bleeding to death!"

Slith carefully peeled the parchment from the leather, tucked the parchment inside his belt.

"If it was hidden in the cover, it must be valuable," he explained to Kang, who only growled at him.

"Yes, sir," Slith said.

Taking the leather, he pressed it over Kang's wound and tied the leather secure with a thong torn from his armor.

The two started out for what was left of their home.

It was going to be a long walk.

Chapter Twenty-four

Selquist returned home bruised and battered but otherwise unhurt, the precious book held fast in his arms. Rounding a corner, he saw half the population of Celebundin coming toward him.

"Drat and bother!" Selquist muttered. First draconians, now his neighbors. All he needed next was a load of kender to drop out of the sky on top of him and it would be a perfect night.

Selquist stuffed the book into his shirt. Leading the pack were the war chief and the High Thane, the latter armed with a rolling pin.

Sighting Selquist, Moorthane called a halt. He held out his arms protectively in front of the High Thane. "Watch it, Your Worship. I'll handle this. It might be one of them! Stop right there!" he bellowed at Selquist.

Selquist, heaving an exasperated sigh, stopped.

"Who is that?" Moorthane thrust a torch in Selquist's face.

"It's me, Moorbrain, Selquist," Selquist said irritably. "Mind that flame! You've come near setting my beard on fire!"

"How can I be sure it's you?" Moorthane stared hard at the dwarf.

"Stick a sword into him," said Vellmer, the brew master and one of Moorthane's lieutenants. "If he dies, then it's Selquist. If he turns into a draconian, we'll know it's not."

"Maybe someone should stick a sword in you, Vellmer," Selquist said, giving the brew master a nasty look. "I notice you have a sort of greenish cast to your skin. You wouldn't be sprouting scales, by any chance, would you?"

Vellmer's neighbors stared at him in alarm and hastily sidled out of range.

"For that matter, Moorbrain, how do I know it's you?" Selquist demanded. He sniffed. "You smell sort of fishy."

"He does, you know," said the High Thane in a low voice.

The other dwarves began to back away from the war chief.

Moorthane rounded on his troops. "I ate salted fish for dinner! Now stop it, all of you! This is exactly what those cursed lizard men want to happen. If we lose trust in each other, we might as well burn down this village just like we burned down theirs! Speaking of draconians." He turned back to Selquist. "I talked to those n'er-do-well friends of yours. They said the draconians broke into your house. Where did they go? Did you see them?"

Selquist shrugged, looked modest. "I chased them down the road. They got away, but not before I managed to knife one of them." He exhibited his bloody dagger. "That's one lizard man who'll think twice before coming back to Celebundin."

The High Thane was regarding Selquist with respect. "I've never heard of anything so brave, have you, war chief?"

Moorthane snorted, glared at Selquist suspiciously. "Since when are you the heroic type?"

"When my people are threatened," Selquist said, drawing himself up tall.

The High Thane and the other dwarves all applauded. The war chief frothed a bit at the mouth.

"I'll be going home now," Selquist added. "I'm extremely tired. Fighting draconians is wearing work, especially when I must fight them alone! Interesting how you show up after the danger is past, Moorbrain!"

Having left this verbal shaft to rankle in the war chief's bosom, Selquist bowed respectfully to the High Thane, who slapped him on the back and said he was a stout fellow. The crowd then dispersed, going off to search for more draconians, especially any who might be hiding out in the local taverns.

Selquist tromped down the road. He was upset, tired, and in a bad temper, all of which combined to cause him to abandon his native sense of caution. He did not look behind him to see if he was being followed, as was his custom. His one thought was to get home and see how badly his precious book had been damaged.

He found his house blazing with light, the other three dwarves now convinced that draconians were liable to leap out of the darkness at any moment. Selquist took a moment on entering to study the broken locks. Shaking his head sadly, he entered his house and shut the door behind him.

"Selquist!" said Pestle, round-eyed. "You're back!"

"Selquist!" Auger ran over, embraced his friend, gave him a hug. "I never thought I'd see you alive again!"

"That was incredibly brave," said Mortar, gazing at Selquist with awe. "I never saw anything so brave, you running after those draconians with only your knife to defend yourself."

"Did you kill them?" Auger asked eagerly.

"Did you get the book back?" Pestle demanded.

"Did you hear something in the garden?" Mortar said fearfully, turning toward the window.

"No and yes and no," said Selquist. "It's just the cat. For Reorx's sake, Mortar, don't you start letting your imagination run away with you like the rest of those idiots." Grumbling, he reached into his shirt, drew forth the book and placed it on the table.

He gave a start, turned pale, made a sort of gasping sound, and clutched at the edge of the table to keep from falling.

"Are you sure that's our book?" Auger asked. "It doesn't look the same."

"That's because the cover's missing," said Pestle, opening the book and turning the pages. "What's the matter, Selquist? The cover's gone, that's all. We can still go after the treasure. The rest of the book is not damaged—"

"The map!" Selquist said, or thought he said. The words came out in an inarticulate gurgle.

"What?" Auger asked Pestle.

"I'm positive I heard something in the garden," said Mortar. He started to stand up, to go over and take a look out the window, when

Selquist let out an anguished cry that halted Mortar in his tracks. Fearing the worst, Mortar whipped around, expecting armies of draconians to burst into the room.

"Where? What?" he gasped.

Selquist was not being attacked. He had picked up the book, was examining it feverishly, turning it over, upending it, shaking it.

"Nothing!"

With a heart-rending moan, he sank down into his chair and buried his head in his arms.

"Uh, oh," said Auger, understanding at last. "The map's gone."

"Is that all?" Mortar sniffed. "I thought you were being strangled at the least. As for the map, I remember it clearly. I can draw you a new one like that." He snapped his fingers.

Selquist lifted a tear-stained face. "You can?" he whispered, not daring to hope.

"And the parts I can't remember, I'm sure Pestle can fill in," Mortar added.

"You bet," Pestle stated. "I'm quite good at maps."

"You remember where the treasure is and . . . and the draconian eggs and everything?" Selquist asked feverishly. "How to get there? All the warnings for the dangerous parts?"

"There's that noise again!" Mortar stated. "I tell you, Selquist, something's out there in your garden!"

"Oh, Reorx take the blasted garden!" Selquist swore. Leaping to his feet, he lunged at Mortar, grasped him by the collar of his shirt and shook him. "Tell me you can draw me my map!"

"Well, certainly, I can draw it," Mortar said with dignity. He pried Selquist's hands loose from his shirt. "Hand me something to write on."

Selquist found a blank page—only slightly charred and blood-stained—in the Daewar book, shoved it over to Mortar. Auger ran to fetch some charcoal. Pestle brought mugs of nut-ale to aid the artistic process.

Mortar picked up the charcoal, began to draw. The other three dwarves leaned over him, breathing down his neck.

"No!" said Selquist, shoving a grubby finger in Mortar's work. "You've got that bit wrong. This fork goes off to the left."

"No, it doesn't," Mortar said irritably.

"Yes, it does. Auger, what do you say?"

"I thought this was where three roads branched off—"

"No, this is where the wall was blocked up," Pestle argued.

The arguing and the map-drawing continued.
Mortar didn't hear any more sounds from the garden.

*   *   *   *   *

Moorthane did not like Selquist. He didn't trust Selquist. Moorthane didn't like or trust Selquist's friends. Moorthane was well aware that Selquist occasionally made trips away from home, which in itself was highly suspicious. Unlike their kender cousins, who are afflicted with a disease known as Wanderlust and who generally remain in one place only until their sentence is up, dwarves do not like to travel. Dwarves are homebodies. Most are born, live, and die in the same village, probably in the same house, or one nearby.

Moorthane was himself more widely traveled than most dwarves, having once been to Pax Tharkas by accident during the War of the Lance. He had not intended to go to Pax Tharkas, but, during a battle with the troops of the Dragon Highlord Verminaard, as he was defending the village of Celebundin, a red dragon had swooped down, picked up Moorthane in its claws, flown off with him to the city, where he was interrogated by the Highlord.

The most Moorthane saw of the city was its dungeons, which are said by kender to be quite nice, but which did not appear to their best advantage at the time, being filthy, smelly and overcrowded. Moorthane had just about given up all hope of escape, when a group of mettlesome adventurers arrived and cut short Verminaard's promising career as a truly evil dictator. Pax Tharkas was freed from the control of the dragonarmies, and Moorthane was released from prison.

He walked out the cell door and did not stop walking until he arrived back in his peaceful valley, which he swore never to leave again. The sad experience further convinced him that the only people in this world who traveled were villains and miscreants.

According to Moorthane's spies, Selquist traveled. Not only did he travel, but he was gone for entire days and nights. Not only that, but he took other dwarves with him. Further, Selquist encouraged his friends to continue their wandering ways. Moorthane knew for a fact that Pestle and Mortar had been gone from home for almost a week and had only just returned.

But now, Moorthane had it all figured out. He knew where Selquist had been and what he was up to. His friends, too.

Selquist was in collusion with the draconians!

Moorthane hated draconians, hated them with a hatred of which only dwarves are capable, a hatred that can last over centuries. Insults are never forgotten among dwarves, rarely forgiven. Quarrels are handed down through the ages, passed from father to son, mother to daughter. Blood feuds are every dwarf's birthright. A brother of Moorthane's had been killed by draconians during the War of the Lance. And though it was not these particular draconians who had done the killing, Moorthane blamed the entire race.

There was only one other race Moorthane hated more than draconians, not counting kender (who didn't count, because every sane person alive on Krynn hated kender), and that was the dwarves who lived in Thorbardin. The Hylar had never done anything to Moorthane personally. He just hated them on general principles.

When the draconians had first moved into the valley, Moorthane had been incensed and had insisted on launching several raids to try to destroy them. His raids had accomplished nothing except to kill a draconian here and there, while losing five dwarves for every dead draco.

Then the draconians—for reasons unknown, but undoubtedly sinister—had ceased to fight. They had stopped killing dwarves, merely knocked them over their heads instead. The High Thane, with true short-sightedness only to be found in a dough-kneading, flour-sifting baker, had been rather charmed by this turn of events and had flatly refused to even consider Moorthane's plan to take advantage of this Reorx-sent opportunity and destroy the draconians once and for all.

It had been Moorthane's idea—and his alone—to burn the draconian village. This time, he'd gone ahead and acted on his own before presenting it the High Thane, who would have probably come up with some lame-brained scheme to move the village poor into the draconians' comfortable houses.

And where would the dwarves have been then? Eh?

Moorthane had known the draconians would come back. He just hadn't counted on them coming back quite so soon. The war chief had barely escaped with his life, having been in the woods attending to some purely personal business when the draconians came roaring down the hill. Hiking up his britches, Moorthane had sped back to the village. On the way he saw Pestle and Mortar, coming down from the hills, coming from the same the direction as the draconians.

And this night, what had Moorthane found? Selquist entertaining draconians in his very own house! Oh, sure, when questioned, his thieving friends had claimed that the draconians had burst in on them and that Selquist had valiantly driven them off. Not only that, but he'd actually chased after them and purportedly stabbed one.

A likely story.

At last, Selquist had gone too far. At last, Moorthane would have all the evidence he needed in order to bring Selquist to trial and have him Cast Out. Not even Selquist's mother would stand up for her son once she heard he was in league with the draconians.

"I've got you now, you Daergar runt," said Moorthane.

Chapter Twenty-Five

Inside Selquist's house, the dwarves completed the map.

There were parts of it on which they all agreed, there were parts on which none of them agreed, and there were parts where the vote was split, but, overall, Selquist somewhat moodily pronounced it was "as good as they were probably going to get."

"I think it's quite nice," said Anvil, admiring his brother's artistic talent. "Look how he's drawn the little eggs, just like on the original, and the little draconian females with their stubby little wings—"

"Hsst!" Selquist whispered. "Did you hear that?"

"It came from the garden," said Anvil.

"I've been trying to tell you," said Mortar, exasperated.

The rustling and thumping sound grew louder, followed by a yowl, a spitting and hissing, and a deep voice cursing.

"Help! Draconians!" Auger bawled. "Help!"

"Oh, shut up, you blithering idiot." Moorthane's head appeared, thrust through the window curtains. "It's me."

"Help! Moorbrain!" Selquist yelled, deftly snatching the map off the table and stuffing it down his pants. "Help!"

Moorthane's face reddened in anger. He shook his fist at Selquist.

Standing up, Selquist walked over to the window. "Excuse me, Moorbrain. Nasty draft in here." He slammed shut the window, missing Moorthane's head, but nearly catching his fingers.

"Do you think he heard?" Auger asked.

"He heard," Selquist said, a prey to deep gloom.

The door crashed open. Moorthane clomped inside.

"You see?" Selquist said.

Moorthane stomped over to the table, peered down at it.

The table was empty, except for some scattered pieces of charcoal and four empty mugs.

"All right." Moorthane glared around. "Where is it?"

"What? Dinner? Oh, we ate hours ago. But thanks for asking," Selquist said.

"I'm not talking about dinner," Moorthane said, with a leering grin. "I'm talking about the treasure map. I want to know a) what treasure? b) where it's located? and c) what you meant by draconian eggs? Or else"—he held up a hand to halt Selquist's undoubtedly sarcastic rejoinder—"or else I will call a town meeting and tell every dwarf in Celebundin that you've found a treasure map."

Selquist paled beneath his scroungy beard. "You wouldn't do that."

"Oh, wouldn't I?" Moorthane gloated.

"Let him," said Mortar, thinking he smelled a bluff.

"What? Are you crazy? Do you know what would happen?" Selquist demanded bitterly. "I couldn't go to the outhouse without twenty-five dwarves traipsing after me, every one of them convinced that I was going off after the treasure."

"Never a moment's peace," said Moorthane, fetching up a deep sigh. "Then, of course, there'd be those who'll figure you've already found the treasure and that you have it hidden somewhere."

"They'll ransack the house!" Selquist said, horrified. "Tear up my garden!" His voice hardened. "All right, Moorbrain, you win. But no more talk of my being Cast Out."

Moorthane glowered, hesitated.

"When I get the treasure, I'll probably move to Palanthas anyway," said Selquist carelessly. "We'll cut you in, too, of course. There's four of us, five, now, with you. Let's see, five times two is ten. Ten times ten is one hundred. We'll cut you in for one-hundredth. One-hundredth of a share to keep your mouth shut. I'm too generous, I know. But it's a fault of mine."

Moorthane wasn't all that good with fractions—something he'd never quite mastered as a lad. One hundred seemed a fine, round figure. Besides, he wasn't all that interested in gold and steel and jewels anyhow. Well, he was, but all in good time.

"What about the dragon eggs?" he asked, leaning on the table, glaring around at the other dwarves, his iron-gray beard quivering with the intensity of his hate. "I heard you say something about dragon eggs and female draconians. What was it? What have you found?"

Selquist sighed. He was extremely tired and discouraged. Tomorrow, after a night's sleep and a good breakfast, he could deal with Moorthane. Tonight, he was past caring. Then, too, he had the terrifying vision of his neighbors following him about, watching his every move. . . .

"Auger, you explain," he said wearily.

"The truth?" Auger wasn't sure what was required of him.

Selquist sighed again and nodded.

"All right. I hope you know what you're doing. This book"—Auger thumped it with his hand—"is an account of a Daewar raiding party into Neraka, back during the War of the Lance. They found all sorts of treasure which the Dragon Highlords had hoarded. Not only that, but they found some eggs that were not hatched. They were female draconians. Apparently the higher powers made the females, then decided that it might be better for all concerned if the draconians didn't breed. And so the spells to hatch the eggs were left undone."

"Thank Reorx!" Moorthane said. He eyed Selquist grimly. "Just what did you intend to do with these eggs?"

"Sell them, of course," said Selquist with a shrug. "Why? What would you do with them, Moorbrain? Make omelets?"

"Damn right, I'm going to make omelets," Moorthane said viciously. His hand clenched to a fist. He brought his fist down on the table with a blow that nearly shattered it. "I'm going to break every one of those god-cursed eggs! I'll see to it personally!"

"What? No! You can't!" Selquist stared at the man, unable to believe the stupidity. "Do you realize how much we could get, selling these eggs? Maybe not a lot on the open market," he admitted, "but the draconians would pay anything! Anything, Moorthane! With one-hundredth of a share, you'll be richer than the High Thane!"

"You grasping, covetous thief of a Daewar spawn," Moorthane snarled. "You'd sell your own father if you knew who he was. If these draconian females hatch, they'll get together with the males and make baby draconians. And the babies will grow up to be big draconians and they'll take over the world!"

"Wow!" said Selquist, round-eyed. "Is that where babies come from, Moorbrain? I never knew."

"I'm going after them," Moorthane continued. "Twenty of my finest soldiers and I are going after those eggs to destroy them! What do you say to that?"

"Good," Selquist said, nonchalantly. "We need someone to carry all the loot. Of course, you'll split your share between them, since you're bringing them with us."

"Humpf." Moorthane grunted. "Who said anything about you coming along. Hand over the map."

"It won't do you much good," Selquist said with a sweet and innocent smile. "Not unless you plan to ask the Hylar to pretty please open up their mountain and let you in. I'm the only one who knows the secret way into Thorbardin."

Moorthane's snarl slowly untwisted. Frowning, he stood snorting and muttering to himself, trying to figure some way out of this.

Selquist smoothed his shirt, hitched up his pants by the belt, surreptitiously feeling to see if the map was still there, still hidden. It was. He smiled at the discomfited Moorthane.

"Are you telling me that this treasure, these eggs are in . . . in . . . " He had difficulty speaking the detested name, finally spit it out: "Thorbardin?"

"Yes, Moorbrain. That's what I'm telling you. I know the way in. A secret way—not on the map. So I guess that unless you want to go knocking on Southgate, you better take me along with you. And my friends," he added.

"I'm not sure I can go," Mortar said suddenly. "You see, I promised Reorx that if he helped me escape from those dark knights, I would never steal again, and he helped. I mean, I guess he helped. Maybe it was him who sent the draconians—"

Selquist flashed Mortar a warning look.

Mortar said, "Oh," and shut his mouth.

Moorthane was glaring from one to the other. "So your draco buddies helped you out, did they? And, in return, you gave them the map. I see how it is. They'll be going after this, too!"

Selquist's left eyebrow twitched. He nearly said something, bit his tongue and, to cover the fact that he'd almost spoken, rubbed at his scruffy beard with such intensity it seemed he might rub it off.

"We'll just have to get there ahead of them," Moorthane was saying solemnly. "We'll leave at first light. And you"—he shook his fist at Selquist—"call me Moorthane! Moorthane! Understand?"

With that and a parting snarl, he stalked out.

"Oh, well," said Auger. "Look at it this way. We'll have help carrying all that loot back. I was wondering— Erp!"

"Oh, shut up," Selquist said and dumped a mugful of tepid ale over Auger's head.

Revealing what he thought of Auger's philosophical viewpoint, Selquist slammed down the empty mug and stalked off into his bedroom.

He returned a moment later, wearing his leather armor, his helm, and holding something in his hand. He headed for the front door, what remained of it.

"Where are you going?" the others demanded, astonished.

"Out," he growled. "Don't wait up."

The three pressed their noses to the window. The last they saw of Selquist, he was walking down to the end of the road, leaving the village.

Chapter Twenty-Six

A Baaz orderly poured foul-smelling gunk onto a cloth. "This is going to sting, sir," he warned. The last time he'd administered this remedy to his commander without adding the warning, the Baaz had spent two weeks laid up with a broken jaw.

Kang gave a curt nod, gritted his teeth, and grabbed hold of the edge of the table.

The Baaz slapped the gunk-covered cloth over the wound in Kang's thigh.

Kang howled. The table shook. His claws made scraping sounds.

"Sting, he says!" Kang gasped.

Deftly, the Baaz tied a fresh bandage around the wound. Finally he poured his wincing and swearing commander a cup of dwarf spirits from their dwindling store and made a hasty departure. Kang gulped down the bitter liquid, and for a brief moment the fire in his head successfully competed with the fire burning in his leg. At length, the pain subsided.

He looked longingly at his cot. He had been up all night and most of the morning. The walk back had been hellish. Every step he took sent slivers of agony through him. Slith had been forced to help him walk; it had taken them six hours to cross the valley.

Sleep would be wonderful, but Kang didn't have time. He had to hear Slith's report on what the other Sivaks had found out. Based on that report, he had to decide what to do. It could be the dwarves were massing for an assault tonight, although from what Kang had seen, he didn't think it likely.

"Pass the word for Sub-commander Slith," he shouted to the orderly.

Kang turned his gaze firmly away from the cot. What he should do was go out and hobble around the charred parade square, keep his leg from stiffening up past use. He had just about nerved himself for this when Slith entered the command tent.

"Feeling any better, sir?" Slith drew up another chair, sat down.

"No," Kang said bluntly. "Hell-blasted dwarves. I've a good mind to go gut the lot of 'em. How about you?"

"My head feels about the size of a minotaur's ego, but other than that, I'm all right."

"Good." Kang grunted. "What's the report? I trust the others had better luck than we did?"

"Viss didn't. He had just sat down with his drink in the tavern when the hue and cry after me went up. There was nothing he could do but run out with the others. He managed to lose himself in the crowd, and then someone yelled that they'd found the corpses, and someone else recognized him as being one of them. At that point, Viss figured he wasn't going to accomplish anything, so he beat a retreat."

"What about Glish and Roxl?"

Slith grinned. "They did better, sir. They fell in with a group of dwarves pulling watch duty on the far side of the village. The dwarves weren't expecting to be attacked from back there, and so they were keeping company with a jug of dwarf spirits. By the time Glish and Roxl showed up, the dwarves couldn't have told if they were draconians or elf maidens. Glish and Roxl sat right down and chinned with the dwarves until near sunup."

"And what did they find out?"

"Well, it seems, sir, that the one who burned down the village was the war chief, a dwarf named Moorthane. The High Thane didn't know anything about it, and he was furious when he found out. Some of the dwarves thought burning the place was a good idea, but most didn't. Most considered it a terrible waste of good lumber. Now, of course, they're all scared silly that we're going to turn around and burn down their houses."

"We might at that," said Kang, rubbing his sore leg. "Any plans to attack us?"

"This war chief is pushing for it, but the High Thane is against it. Says they'll lose too many people. So far what the High Thane says goes."

"Well, that's good news. Every day that passes, we grow stronger. We'll soon have the wall repaired and rubble cleared out. Then we can start rebuilding." Kang nodded in satisfaction. "I'm glad the night went well for some of us, at least. Remind me next inspection to single those three out for commendation."

"Yes, sir."

Instead of leaving, Slith fidgeted in his chair, glanced at his commander out of the corner of his eye.

"Well, what is it, Slith? You obviously have something else on your mind."

"I know you're tired, but do you feel like talking just a little longer, sir?" Slith asked. "I wouldn't bother you, but it's kind of important."

"Sure," said Kang. "You're saving me from a hike around the parade ground. What is it?"

Slith reached into his belt, removed the folded square of parchment and carefully spread it out on the table. "Take a look at this, sir. It was inside that book we stole from the dwarves."

Kang looked. "It's a map."

"Yes, sir," said Slith. "I don't suppose you can read the writing, can you, sir?"

Kang shook his head. "Looks like some sort of dwarven language, but I can't make it out."

"Too bad." Slith gazed down at his map with fond affection. "Look at this little drawing up here, sir. What would you say those are?"

Kang squinted, leaned down. "Eggs. Large eggs, I'd guess, since they're drawn bigger than anything else."

Slith nodded in satisfaction. "That's what I thought myself, sir. These other drawings might be draconians, sir. Guards, maybe? And these drawings here. What do you say those might be?"

Kang pointed with a claw. "Those are storage chests. Those are urns. Scroll cases, maybe, or map cases. Books, probably spellbooks, since they're each marked with a symbol for one of the three moons."

"My thoughts exactly, sir." Slith grinned.

Kang leaned back in his chair, propped his wounded leg up on a footstool in front of him. "What do you make of this map then, Slith? Obviously something. You look like the dragon that swallowed the kender."

"Yes, sir." Slith paused a moment, then said, in a low voice, "I'm thinking that our luck last night wasn't all that bad. My guess is that it's a treasure map, sir! These"—he indicated the chests and urns—"are probably filled with money and jewels. And, like you say, the books and scrolls are magical. I think this map could lead us to a valuable treasure, sir."

"What about the eggs?" Kang asked. "What have eggs got to do with treasure? Unless, of course, you're on short rations."

The draconians were themselves on short rations. The only food they had left was what they had brought back from the camp of the dark knights, and that wasn't going to last long, with two hundred mouths to feed.

"I don't know. Unless they're not eggs at all. Maybe they're—"

The Baaz sentry knocked on the tent post.

"Yes?" Kang eased his leg into a slightly more comfortable position. "What is it?"

"Something I think you should see, sir."

"Very well." Kang motioned to Slith, who grabbed up the map, folded it, and replaced it in his belt.

The Baaz entered. In his hand, he held a short-statured, squirming, scruffy figure who looked vaguely familiar.

"Eh?" Kang said in astonishment. "What's this?"

"A dwarf, sir," said the Baaz.

"I can see that," Kang returned irritably. "I mean, what's he doing here?" He stared hard at the dwarf. He'd seen that face with that wretched growth of beard somewhere before. He glanced at Slith, who was regarding the dwarf with narrow-eyed interest.

"He came walking through the picket lines as cool as a white dragon's breath, sir," the Baaz explained. "The boys nabbed him and were about to skewer him, figuring him for a spy, when he flashes a medallion and says he's got to talk to the commander quick."

"What medallion?" Kang was suspicious. He had no doubt at all that the dwarf was a spy.

The Baaz dropped the dwarf to the tent floor, cuffed him on the back of the head. "Show that medallion to the commander."

The dwarf opened a grubby palm and held out his hand. As he did so, Kang recognized him.

"You!" he roared. "You're the bastard who knifed me!"

The Baaz drew his own knife. Grabbing the dwarf by the hair, the draconian jerked his head back, ready to slit his throat at the commander's order. Kang might have given that order, but Slith halted him. The Sivak was bent over the dwarf's hand, peering at the object.

"I think you should take a look at this, sir."

Reluctantly, Kang swung his leg down from his chair, heaved himself painfully to his feet and hobbled over to see what the dwarf was holding. All this time, the dwarf had not spoken a word.

"I'll be a hobgoblin!" Kang said, startled. "It's my holy symbol! The one . . . the one that was stolen from me!" He glowered at the dwarf, switched to speaking Common. "You stole this from me! Thief! What are you doing back here with it?"

The dwarf dropped to his knees and raised his hands in a supplicating manner. "Oh, wise and most glorious leader! I admit freely that I stole this, but I didn't know I was stealing from you. Not that it matters." The dwarf bowed his head. "I admit that my actions were wrong, though the same might be said of others who steal things—books especially—that don't belong to them."

Kang snarled. The dwarf gulped and continued on. "I am happy to return this to you, Honored Sir. Very happy!" The dwarf mopped his perspiring face with the sleeve of his tunic. "I ask only one thing in return." He clasped his hands together. "Take your Queen's curse off me! Please!"

"What about pleading for your miserable life?" Kang demanded, voice grating.

The dwarf considered this, finally shook his head. "No, sir. If you don't take the curse off me, my life will be worth nothing anyway. If you'd just remove the curse, I'd be grateful. Very grateful. And I'm truly sorry I stabbed you, sir. The heat of the moment. Battle-rage. I'm sure you can understand."

Kang snatched back his holy symbol. His hand closed over it, a feeling of relief flooded through him, a blessed warmth that eased the pain of his wound.

Kang reached out his hand, took the Baaz's knife. "Thank you, soldier, but I'll gut this one myself—"

"Uh, sir, a word with you?" Slith coughed in a meaningful manner, jerked his head toward the back of the tent.

"Very well," Kang muttered, still glaring at the dwarf.

He and Slith withdrew to the shadows.

"Sir, that's the dwarf from last night. The dwarf who had the book."

"He's also the dwarf who stuck a knife in me and stole my holy symbol." Kang growled. He paused, then said, "What book?" Last night's events were a bit foggy.

"The book I handed you, sir. The book with the leather cover. You used it as a bandage. That's where the map was! Inside that book! And this was the dwarf in the house with the book. And that's the reason he stabbed you, sir."

"The book!" said Kang, remembering. "By our Queen, you're right. What of it? It's just a book."

"Sir, he wanted that book back badly enough to run after you—a draconian three times his size—and stab you from behind."

"You've got a point," Kang admitted.

"And look at the way his little beady eyes are darting around. He's searching for something, sir. What else could it be but the map? He must figure we have it. Do you know what I think, sir?"

"I'm getting there," Kang said.

"The book tells what's in that treasure room. He knows!"

Kang regarded the dwarf thoughtfully. "He's a clever little bastard. Bad as they come, too. No dwarf with a clean conscience could even touch our Queen's medallion, and he's been carrying it around like some bloody heirloom. From the looks of him, though, I'd say he'll die sooner than tell us anything about the treasure."

"That's just it," Slith said, growing more excited. "The curse, sir! He spills what he knows about the treasure, and you remove the curse."

"What curse?" Kang was puzzled. "Nobody put a curse on him. Though I wish I'd thought of it."

"It doesn't matter, sir. He thinks there's a curse on him."

"Ah." Kang said. "Perhaps you're right."

He and Slith returned to the front of the tent. The dwarf was watching them askance.

"That will be all," Kang told the Baaz, who saluted and left the tent.

"Now then." Kang fixed his reptile eye on the dwarf. "What's this about a curse?"

"You know," said the dwarf sullenly. "You cast it on me." Suddenly, he burst out, "First it's war, then it's kender in Pax Tharkas, then dark knights grabbing people off the road, then draconians in my living room and, last but not least, Moorthane under my window! Take it off me," the dwarf said through clenched teeth. "Or just kill me right here and now."

All the time he talked, his eyes were searching every part of the tent and all its contents.

"This what you're looking for?" Slith pulled out the folded map, laid it on the table.

The dwarf barely gave the square bit of parchment a glance. He shrugged. "No, I'm not looking for anything."

"He's good, this one," Kang muttered to himself. He had seen, deep down in the dwarf's dark eyes, a glimmer of fire when the map appeared.

"I'll make you a deal," Kang said. Returning to his chair, he sank into it, propped up his wounded leg on the footstool. "I'll remove the curse if you make it worth my while. We happened to find this map. It looks to us to be some sort of treasure map, but the writing is all in dwarven, which we can't read."

"Give it to me," said the dwarf, the fire burning deep within. "I'll read it for you."

"Yes, I'll bet you would. And refresh your memory of it at the same time." Kang placed his clawed hand over the map. "There must be something on that map that's worth the price of a curse-removal. What is it?"

The dwarf pursed his lips, a move that sucked in his cheeks and pulled the rest of his face into a point. He was not an attractive dwarf to begin with, and this did nothing to improve his features. He bit his lip.

Kang held up the holy symbol. Reaching out, he plucked open the dwarf's pocket. "Perhaps you'd like this back—"

"All right!" The dwarf gasped, shuddered. "Get rid of it! I'll tell you . . . one thing!" The words seemed wrenched from him. "You've looked at the map?"

"Yes."

"You know it's a map of Thorbardin."

"Oh, yes," said Kang and Slith. They exchanged glances. They'd neither of them had a clue about that.

"Well." The dwarf drew in a deep breath. His gaze went to the holy symbol one more time. His shoulders sagged in defeat. The rest of the words came out in a rush. "On that map you saw some markings that looked like eggs? Well, they are eggs. Dragon eggs. From Neraka back during the War of the Lance. Did I say dragon eggs? Make that draconian eggs. Like you gentlemen, only they're not gentlemen. If you get my meaning."

They didn't. Kang and Slith looked blank.

The dwarf was exasperated. "Look, do I have to spell it in words of one syllable for you guys? What's the opposite of gentlemen? Ladies! Right? Now you're catching on. There's ladies in those eggs, my friends. Boy, girl. Boy, girl. The patter of little clawed feet. Female draconians."

The dwarf stepped back, gave a flourish, and folded his arms across his chest, like a second-rate illusionist who has just produced a coin from up his nose.

Kang and Slith sat perfectly still, staring at the dwarf. His news knocked the breath from their bodies as surely as if he'd struck them in the solar plexus with a limb from a vallenwood.

"Females," Kang whispered. "Female draconians. That's not possible."

"Yes, it is. It's all in the book. The dark clerics and the black-robed wizards made females, so that they could perpetuate your race. But then the high muckety-mucks decided that they weren't all that sure they wanted your race perpetuated. And so they left the final spell undone."

"But we were in Neraka," Slith said, voice harsh. "We would have found them!"

"Not so," said the dwarf craftily. "Because by that time, the Daewar had stolen them and taken them back to Thorbardin. They were going to sell them, but before they could, the thieves had a bit of a falling out over how to split the treasure, with the result that it was heads that got split, not the treasure."

"You're saying . . . the eggs . . . are still there?" Kang's voice failed him before he came to the end of his sentence, but the dwarf understood.

"It's a good possibility." He shrugged. "Mind you, I can't guarantee anything. Well, how about it? That valuable enough for you?"

"Yeah. Sure." Kang felt dazed. He waved his hand over the dwarf's head three times, said something in draconian. He was never quite sure what, but it appeared to satisfy the dwarf. He straightened his shoulders, shook back his hair.

"Right! I feel like a new man." He cast a wistful glance at the folded map. "I don't suppose . . . one little peek."

Slith snarled and bared his fangs.

The dwarf nodded. "Got you. See you around." He winked and, with that, ducked out of the tent.

"Sir!" The Baaz thrust his head inside. "Do you want—"

"Let him go," Kang said, still dazed. "Escort him through the picket lines. Make certain nothing happens to him."

"Yes, sir." The Baaz was dubious, but he knew better than to question his commander's orders. Kang heard the dwarf's heavy booted footsteps recede into the distance.

"What do you think?" Kang asked Slith.

The Sivak came to his senses with a start. Hastily, hands shaking, he carefully unfolded the map. The two bent over it, gazed at it intently.

"It could be, sir," Slith said, excited. "It certainly could be. Those sketches. Look at them, sir. They're different from us. Wings are shorter and stubbier. Their hips are wider and—"

"Perhaps they were drawn by a bad artist," Kang said. He sighed. "You're seeing what you want to see, my friend."

"Maybe so, sir." Slith was stubborn. "But I say it's worth a chance. What do you say?"

Kang looked ahead into the future. A future that was suddenly no longer bleak and empty. A future that was no longer a death watch. A future that held meaning.

"Yes," he said, drawing a deep, shivering breath. "Yes, I'd say it was worth the chance!"

*   *   *   *   *

Selquist found a place in a wooded area of the valley in which to hole up, rest through the heat of the day. It would be miserable walking, and he didn't particularly want to return to Celebundin during daylight hours anyway. Making himself comfortable in a cool patch of dirt underneath a large pine tree, Selquist laid down, head on his arms, and gazed, smiling, into the tree branches.

He hadn't recovered the map, but then he hadn't really expected to. Having the map wasn't all that important now, anyway. Dwarves and draconians and the map—they were all going to the same place . . .

One goal accomplished.

The second goal—to rid himself of that accursed holy symbol of Takhisis. That was accomplished, too. Selquist wasn't superstitious, nor was he particularly religious. But when things go wrong and keep going wrong, and you have in your possession a necklace that might have been worn by her Dark Majesty, and she might have a fondness for it, and the way you came by that necklace was not exactly honest . . . well, it couldn't hurt to return it.

And finally, the third goal. To get rid of Moorthane, once and for all.

That goal was not yet accomplished, but at least Selquist was off to a good start.

Chapter Twenty-Seven

Kang and Slith spent the remainder of the day making plans. They kept the map and the news about the eggs secret, not because they didn't trust their men, but because they knew that once they told them of this unexpected hope, they would have difficulty restraining them from dashing off heedlessly and probably getting themselves killed in the process.

Their commander needed to be able to present them with a plan. And once Kang emerged from his euphoric daydreams, he realized that this was not going to be easy. In fact, he couldn't imagine anything more difficult.

"Thorbardin," he muttered. "How the devil are we going to get inside Thorbardin? You Sivaks could manage, I suppose. Knock off a dwarf or two and take their shapes. Although that didn't really work out all that well in Celebundin."

"We'll need a sizable force, sir," Slith said. "More than just four Sivaks.

For one thing, we'll have to carry those eggs out ourselves. Dragon eggs are big, and they're heavy. Not to mention we might have to fight. I don't trust that scroungy little dwarf, not for a moment. I have the feeling he's setting us up. He was all too eager to hand out this information."

"It could be a trap," Kang said.

"It probably is, sir." Slith agreed. He was silent a moment, then said, "We can abandon this, sir. If that's what you want. I'll never say a word to anyone."

Yes, Kang said to himself. That's what I should do. This is wild, impossible, dangerous, and probably all for nothing. We'll stay here, rebuild our village. Every few weeks we'll raid the dwarves. Every few weeks they'll raid us. Eventually—who knows how long?—we'll start to die off. One or two at first. Then more and more. We'll dig the graves behind the city, dig them deep, so the animals don't drag off the bodies. The last one that's left won't have a grave. There won't be anyone around to bury him.

Maybe that'll be me. Maybe I'll be the only draconian left alive. I've watched all the others die, all my friends, all my comrades, all those I've led. I'll bury them all, and there'll be only me left. Our legacy—a row of graves.

Kang looked at Slith. "All right. How the devil do we get into Thorbardin?"

Slith grinned. "I think I know a way, sir."

*   *   *   *   *

The small force of twenty-five draconians, made up of Sivaks and Bozaks, crept silently through the forest north of Celebundin. The troop had traveled far to the north of the village, then swung back down to return to the forest, hoping by this tactic to keep any dwarven scouts in the valley from running across them.

Kang glanced behind him. He could barely make out the draconians lurking in the woods and he knew where to look for them. They were wearing leather armor and, with their coloration, blended in with the browns and faded greens of the sun blistered forest. Each chose his spot, hunkered down, and did not move. They could have been boulders, scattered beneath the trees.

Satisfied, Kang turned his attention back to the house they were keeping under close scrutiny.

"They're still in there, sir," said Gloth, leader of the hand-picked squad. "I can see them moving around."

"I hope they haven't stolen a march on us," Kang said.

"I don't think so, sir," said Slith, who had the sharpest eyes of anyone in the troop. "There's four of them inside, the same who were there with the book. I recognize that scrawny dwarf with the moldy beard, and there's a chubby dwarf with him, plus the two we snatched from the dark knights."

"And you think they'll all go?"

"Positive, sir. Those are the same four that I followed the last time. They're in this together."

The fiery sun was setting, sending shadows creeping through the forest. This was a dangerous time, because the lengthening shadows often fooled the eye, making a soldier think he sees movement. All it would take to cause this mission to end in disaster was a single draconian leaping up with a yell, ready to attack something that wasn't there. The dwarves would be on the pursuit so fast they'd probably leave their beards behind.

The last rays of light gilded the crest of Mount Celebund. It was dark now in the valley, and Kang was thinking that the dwarves would be on their way soon, when Slith dug an elbow in Kang's ribs.

"Damn! Look at that, sir!"

Kang was looking. With his night vision, it was easier to see in the full darkness than it had been in the half-light of dusk.

Twenty dwarves, clad in uniform, under the direction of a commander, were marching down the street.

"They've found us!" said Gloth, reaching for his sword.

"No, wait!" Kang ordered. "Those dwarves aren't going to battle. Or at least if they are, it's not with us."

The other two now saw what their commander had first noticed. In addition to their weapons, the dwarves carried hefty packs on their backs and water skins. Several had brought along stout walking staffs.

Slith glanced at Kang. "What gives?"

Kang shook his head. "Don't know. My guess is that's their war chief, the bastard who ordered our village burned. I've seen him before, giving orders."

The leader—a large, grizzled dwarf whom Kang recognized from earlier raids—entered the house. The small troop of dwarves huddled together in the yard, keeping watch, though not for draconians. They weren't facing that direction. These dwarves were looking back toward their own village.

A few minutes later, the occupants of the house emerged, with the war chief right behind. The four also carried packs, waterskins, and weapons. Slith and Kang both spotted the scrawny dwarf, talking to the war chief.

"You were mentioning a trap, sir," Slith whispered. "Think this is it?"

Kang mused. This was completely unexpected. "No, I doubt it," he said at last. "A trap for us would have been more like two hundred dwarves, not twenty. No, I think they're facing a logistical problem, the same one we faced—how do four dwarves carry back all that loot? Not to mention the fact that these Niedar will be about as welcome in Thorbardin as we will, if they catch us."

The dwarves moved out.

"Quite the expedition, isn't it, sir?" Slith said.

"Yes," Kang agreed. "Somehow I don't imagine this is what our skinny little friend had in mind."

The dwarves swung past them, the war chief in the lead—looking very smug and triumphant. The scrawny dwarf and his three friends marched along glumly behind.

Kang glanced over his shoulder. "This is it. Gloth, prepare to move out."

Gloth crawled back into the underbrush. The draconians were also well equipped, carrying heavy packs containing food and, in addition, tools and equipment which could be used for tunneling, climbing, building. Fifty-foot rope cords looped around their bodies like sashes. All wore swords. Kang had a full complement of magical spells.

It might have been his imagination, but since he'd recovered his holy symbol, Her Dark Majesty had seemed more gracious to him. More gracious, yet he thought he detected an undercurrent of unease.

Perhaps her dark knights were running into trouble.

Gloth crawled back. "We're ready whenever you give the word, sir."

They didn't have to wait long. The dwarves exited the village, heading north. No one came out to cheer or wave or see the dwarves leave. The High Thane was not making a speech, urging his men on to glory. These twenty were sneaking out under cover of darkness. Kang could guess why. The dwarven village was still expecting to be attacked by the draconians. And here were twenty able-bodied men, who should be preparing to defend hearth and home, leaving it.

The dwarves marched straight for the Celebund pass. The night was extremely dark. It would be some time yet before Lunitari rose, and then she'd be only a thin sliver of red, like a scar. The black moon was full, though. Kang gave the dwarves a ten-minute head start.

"Move out."

Kang ordered Gloth to pass the order, which would be done by each draconian whispering the command to the next in line. "I want absolute quiet," Kang reiterated. "Anyone so much as coughs—no dwarf spirits for the next two months."

This was a terrible threat, and completely unnecessary, as Kang knew. His troops were well disciplined, well trained, and these were the best of the best. The draconians moved out of the north end of the wood, marching along after the dwarves.

Kang led the troop up the rocky entrance to the well-worn path that wound over the edge and down the side of Mount Celebund. Every time they topped a rise, he could see the line of dwarves, their bodies glowing faintly red in his sight, trailing down the mountain ahead of him.

They'd marched about six hours and had just completed the crossing of the pass, when the dwarves called a halt. They settled themselves in a glade, pulled out waterskins, and rested from their labors.

Kang stopped the troop. Slith moved forward.

"What is it, sir?" he asked.

"Down below the ground opens up. We have to cross a meadow. We should increase the distance between our two parties. At this rate, we should still reach Mount Bletheron by sunrise. Are they following the same path they took the first time?"

"Exactly, sir." Slith's tongue flicked over his teeth. "I was right. They're leading us straight to their secret entrance."

Kang's troop waited for the dwarves to move on. Half an hour later, the dwarves packed up and continued their march.

The draconians reached the approaches to Mount Bletheron as the sky began to lighten.

"We'd better stop and take cover here," Kang said. "Once it's daylight, any dwarf who so much as turns his head to look behind him will see us."

The draconians crouched behind boulders or lay down beneath bushes. Most fell asleep. Kang and Slith took turns keeping watch.

The morning passed without incident. When the sun had reached its zenith, was burning down on them as if it meant to roast each one alive, Kang decided that the dwarves had an adequate head start. He woke everyone up. After a cold meal, they were on their way again. They crossed the pass over Mount Bletheron just as the sun began to set.

Kang was beginning to worry. He had set his best trackers on the trail and they reported no sign of the dwarves. Of course, it was difficult to track anything among the rocks and boulders. One thousand dwarves could have marched through here without leaving a trace. But Kang fretted and fumed. What if Slith was wrong? What if the dwarves had struck off on another path?

Kang motioned for Slith and Gloth to move up to join him at the front of the line.

"I let them get too far ahead. We have to make up some time. The dwarves are a good half-day's march ahead of us. They didn't stop last night, so my guess is that they'll stop and rest tonight. Do you know where?"

Slith nodded. "They'll probably camp in front of the Helefundis ridge, on the other side of Mount Prenechial, just like they did when I followed them last time."

"They're going to spot us once we start to cross the ridge. We can't hide up there," said Gloth. "And we can't let them get too far ahead, or they'll sneak into Thorbardin, and we'll never find their entrance."

Kang nodded. "Don't worry about that. I have a spell in mind that will solve that problem. Our first objective is to make certain we're on the right trail!"

The troop marched on. By midnight, they had crossed Mount Prenechial, and were climbing the approach to Helefundis Ridge. Kang was picking his way through a clump of boulders, thinking that this would be a good place to camp for the night, when he nearly stepped on a slumbering dwarf.

Kang stopped so suddenly he very nearly tumbled snout first down the mountain

His first thought was: At least we've found them.

His second: the dwarves have found us.

Chapter Twenty-Eight

Moving slowly and carefully, testing his footing with every step, Kang crept backward. If he dislodged so much as a pebble, it would go bounding down the mountainside and give them away. When he was out of sight of the sleeping dwarf and within sight of his men, Kang made frantic hand signals, ordering an immediate halt.

The draconians froze where they stood, tense and wary.

While Kang listened for sounds of alarm from the dwarven encampment, he searched desperately for cover for his troop. On the other side of the path, a stand of half-dead bushes clung to the rock. He glided toward the bushes, using his wings to take the weight off his feet and reduce both the noise and the possibility that he might slip and fall. The troop was right behind him, marching in single file.

Circling the bushes, the draconians crouched and lay down on the other side.

Slith was last in line. Kang had not spoken a word, but every soldier had guessed what had happened.

"I don't think anyone heard us," Slith whispered.

Kang nodded in response. He had feared the dwarves had sent an ambush for them, but that didn't appear to be the case. He let himself breathe again.

Slith drew his sword, then lay down to hide. Kang did the same. The draconians waited. This time, no one fell asleep.

There hadn't been a cloud in the sky for months, but Kang thought that the Dark Queen might take an interest in their cause and send a storm along the next day. It would be difficult for the dwarves to discover they were being followed in a driving rain storm and the draconians could sneak close enough to see where the dwarves entered the mountain.

But if Her Dark Majesty was taking an interest, she wasn't bothering to help. Morning broke, clear and sunny. Kang swore silently to himself. A blind dwarf could see them in weather like this.

They heard sounds from the dwarven camp. Kang risked raising up, spotted two dwarves performing their morning ablutions behind a rock. Then came sounds of pot-banging and cheerful swearing. The dwarves were cooking breakfast. After that, they packed up and left.

Kang kept his men hidden, waited two hours before he permitted them to move. He ordered the troop to eat, sent out a patrol to scout.

The patrol returned with good news. "We could see them from a distance, strung out along the ridge. They should be to the other end before nightfall, sir."

"Slith, Gloth, over here." Kang spelled out his plan. "We'll cross the ridge tonight using cover of darkness. I don't think we have to worry about being seen. We're close to Thorbardin. Their secret entrance must be near, and the dwarves will probably be underground before we even reach the ridge. Once we're there, we'll wait until daylight to search for the hidden entrance. I'll ask our Queen for my spells."

All went as planned. The troop reached the ridge, never seeing a dwarf, confident that the dwarves had not seen them.

Kang made certain his men were settled, saw the watch posted. Rummaging in his pack, he drew out his newly restored holy symbol and, holding the medallion fast in his hand, he began to climb up a dry creek bed, the water having long ago vanished in the hot, brittle summer. He'd caught a glimpse of what he thought might be a cave up there—the perfect place for him to use to commune with Her Dark Majesty.

The creek bed wound around a large flat ledge that jutted out over the place where his men were resting. The going was a bit difficult here. Kang was forced to use hands, feet, tail, and wings to help him over the last little stretch. He made it and had just straightened, was wiping his hands clean, when he was suddenly aware that he wasn't alone. Someone was up here, someone was hiding in that cave.

Human, to judge by the smell. A smell that was familiar.

Kang was an easy target, standing on the ledge in full sunlight. Well, there was no help for it.

Cursing his own carelessness, he peered into the darkness of the cave.

"You can come out, Huzzad," he said quietly. "I know you're in there."

At first, he heard no sound of movement and he tensed, waiting for the arrow to come flying out of the darkness, the arrow that would end his life.

He could always shout for help. Slith and his Sivaks could fly up the mountain, whereas Kang had been forced to climb. They wouldn't arrive in time to save their commander, but they could at least exact vengeance on his slayers.

But no, Kang reasoned. This didn't make sense. If there was a squad of archers on their trail, they would have killed him long before this. Killed him and all the rest. And, now that he was closer, he only smelled one human. Huzzard was alone. Perhaps she expected the draconians to be intimidated by her authority, her rank and standing as a knight of Takhisis, maybe even the fact that she was human. Perhaps she figured they'd be so impressed that they would just meekly surrender.

Kang raised his hands, opened them. "I'm not armed. My men are asleep down below. It's just you and me, Huzzad. If you've come here to settle the score, let's settle it between the two of us."

The knight emerged from the cave.

She was clad in leather armor, not plate mail, with leather breeches. Her arms were bare. She wore no shirt, due to the heat. She was dressed for stealth, for tracking, not armored for battle. Her red hair hung in two limp braids down her back. She wore her sword, but she kept it sheathed. Her hand was on the hilt, however. Standing in the shadows of the cave, she regarded Kang with cool speculation. Then she motioned.

"Come inside, out of the sun. I'm alone," she added.

"I'm not," said Kang dryly. "I have twenty men down below. Twenty men who would like nothing better than to see those red braids of yours hanging from their belts. We're not going back, Sir Knight. There's nothing you can do or say that will make us change our minds. We're warriors. Not crap-hole diggers. And we're sure as hell not going to go back and be executed as deserters."

Huzzad tilted her head, squinted to see him. The sun was fierce, beat off the rocks. "But that's what you are, Draconian. Deserters."

"No, ma'am." Kang was emphatic. "We agreed to join up on terms that we would work as engineers. Your commander accepted our terms, then he went back on them. In a manner of speaking, you might say that the lord knight deserted us."

The corners of Huzzad's mouth twitched and then, to Kang's amazement, she began to laugh. She laughed until tears came to her eyes. She wiped her hand over her eyes, removed her hand from her sword hilt.

"I would dearly love to see my lord's face when you presented that argument, Kang." Sighing, she shook her head. "Who knows? Perhaps my lord is no longer still alive. I am not here to exact punishment on you and your men, Commander. True, I was sent to find you and I have been following you for days. If I had wanted to kill you before now, I could have done so. You admit that?"

Kang gave a brief nod, kept his eyes on her.

She seemed to find what she next had to say somewhat difficult. She ran her hand through her sweat-damp hair, stared out over the horizon. "I am ordered to tell you that your role in the Army of Takhisis has been reevaluated, Commander."

Kang grunted. "Oh, so now you have a job for us to do. A dirty one, I'll bet. Will we need shovels?"

She flushed in anger, but it was quick to pass. Her gaze came back to Kang. "Strange and terrible events are happening in this world. Events of which you know nothing, or so I'll wager. Come inside, please, Commander. We have to talk."

Kang shrugged and entered the cave. It was shallow, more a depression in the rock than a true cavern. A quick glance revealed that she was telling the truth. Huzzad was alone. Kang settled himself on the ground. Huzzad sat down on a small boulder near him.

Clasping her hands, she rested her elbows on her knees. Kang noted that the knuckles of her hands were white. Out of the glaring sun, he saw new lines of strain and tension on her face.

She had called him in here to talk, yet now she remained silent, pondering.

"You said something about your lord being dead. The elves proved tougher than you'd thought, apparently," Kang said.

"Elves!" Huzzad snorted. "Tough! Qualinesti fell to Lord Ariakan's troops before our division even arrived. For the first time in the history of Krynn, Kang, the forces of Her Dark Majesty control Ansalon. Oh, certainly, there are pockets of resistance. Thorbardin, for one. But the dwarves are bottled up inside and are no threat to us, so we're letting them be. The High Clerist's Tower is ours, as is Palanthas and all the rest of Solamnia. The cursed dragons of Paladine have been forced to flee.

"Southern and Northern Ergoth are ours; we control the high seas. Pax Tharkas has fallen, Solace is ours, even Kendermore." She grimaced. "Pity the poor knights who have duty there. Victory is ours, Kang. Victory for Her Majesty."

Kang drew in a deep breath. He had known the knights were good, but he hadn't expected anything like this. Victory, at last. The knights were the conquerors of Ansalon.

Takhisis would rule.

Then why Huzzad's white-knuckled grip? Why had she been sent by her commander to find the draconians? Why had she doubted if her commander was alive? The war was won and good as over. Kang had an alarming thought.

"Your lord doesn't intend to post us in Kendermore, does he?"

"No." Huzzad smiled, a fleeting smile. She was again quiet a moment, then said abruptly. "My lord told you of the Vision?"

Kang nodded, wondering why the sudden shift in subject.

"The Vision gives each knight a clear understanding of the goals of the knighthood," Huzzad explained. Her gaze shifted to the bright sunlight beyond the cavern. "The Vision reveals the knight's own part in Her Dark Majesty's plan. The Vision comes first at our investiture, and then many times after that, changing and flowing with the river of time."

Her gaze shifted back to Kang. A line furrowed her brow. The knuckles of her clasped hands grew even whiter, as if the skin had been peeled back, revealing bare bone.

"My lord has, these past two weeks, experienced a new and frightful Vision, Kang. And he is not the only one. The same Vision came to many of us in the knighthood."

Ah, now we're getting somewhere, Kang thought. "And what is this Vision, Sir Knight?"

"The High Clerist's Tower is under attack—"

"Solamnic knights," Kang said with an oath.

"No, not the knights. In fact"—she paused, sounding awed—"the Solamnics fight at our side! We fight against horrible creatures, demons that are not of this world. Or perhaps they are of this world, but have been held prisoner in the fathomless darkness below the Abyss, prisoner until now. Now they swarm over the walls of the High Clerist's Tower. Each person they touch becomes as nothing. Not one memory of their existence is left behind. It is said that even the dead fear these demons.

"Lord Ariakan falls, mortally wounded. The Gods are fighting in the heavens. The Gods are fighting, and they are losing." Huzzad's voice was hushed, as she spoke. Her face was pale, her eyes rapt and staring. She was seeing the Vision again in her mind. "A band of heroes rides forth to do battle with the Father of the demons. The Father of All, the Father of the Gods. Chaos. He has sent these fiends to destroy us, to obliterate our sun from the heavens, to return us to the Void of which we were made. No memory of us, of any of us, will remain."

A shiver made Kang's scales click. The draconians might well perish as a race, if their quest for the eggs failed, but at least there would be those who would remember them. Their deeds during the War of the Lance were even now being sung by bards all over Ansalon. The songs weren't particularly complimentary and mostly told of how some hero or another had bested the Dark Queen's evil minions. But at least someone would be here to remember. At least someone would be here to sing.

Kang tried to imagine Nothing. All the pain, the suffering, the love, the hatred, the laughter, the gallantry, the heroes, the ordinary, all for Nothing, reduced to Nothing.

"What happens?" Kang asked, his mouth dry.

"The heroes are defeated," Huzzad said softly. "The world falls into the hands of Chaos, and he crushes it and wipes the dust from his fingers."

Kang blinked. "So that's the end for us? What do we do? Sit here and wait to die?"

"We do not," said Huzzad sharply. She shook off the Vision, snapped back to duty. "The Vision changes as Time changes. What I have seen in the future may never come to pass. It may only partially come to pass, or it may never come to pass at all. We are instrumental in shaping the Vision. In a way, we are most honored, for we are given the opportunity to fight alongside the Gods. You are going to Thorbardin, aren't you, Commander?"

She slid that one in so swiftly that Kang was caught off guard. He recovered, shrugged, and said, "We are? That's news to me."

Smiling, Huzzad reached out and took hold of Kang's clawed hand. He stared, astonished, at the firm, thin and calloused fingers that gripped his scaley hide. It was the first time human flesh had ever voluntarily touched his. Her hand was warm, and her grasp strong.

"You were in my Vision, Kang. That is why the commander sent me to find you. I have a message to give to you. A message from Her Dark Majesty.

"She is well pleased with you, Commander Kang. You have survived in a hostile world for many years and, in all that time, you have remained loyal to her. You have shown intelligence and wisdom. Others would have killed the dwarves in your valley. But you, by permitting your enemies to live, have, in turn, lived off them. Your wisdom has been rewarded. The dwarves have stumbled across a valuable treasure, very valuable, indeed. And I do not mean steel or jewels."

Kang stared at Huzzad. His hand trembled. Huzzad could not have known about the dwarves. Kang had never told her anything about them. Certainly she could not have known about the treasure map. This message was, indeed, from the Queen. Kang bowed his head, humbled and grateful.

Huzzad's grip on his hand tightened.

"Inside a chest decorated with my symbols are ten dragon eggs: two gold, two silver, two bronze, two brass, two copper. They contain female draconians. The females are alive, or rather, they will be when the final spell is cast."

Kang's heart sank, his hopes dashed.

"And how can that spell be cast?" Kang asked bitterly. "We have no dark clerics among us, no black-robed wizards."

"You do not need them," said Huzzad calmly. "Their work has been done. You need only a wand, a very special wand."

"How will I know it?"

"The wand is made of obsidian and is as long as your forearm. The bodies of five dragons twine around it, each dragon made of precious gems. The heads of the dragons join at the top, their tails twine together at the bottom. The knowledge of how to use this wand will come to you when needed. Speak my name. That is all that is required. The wand will do the rest."

"Thank you, Sir Knight. Tell Her Majesty"—Kang was choked with emotion—"that I do not know how to thank her."

"She has a way," said Huzzad and her voice was grim. "Deep inside Thorbardin live those who will, if they are not stopped, be Krynn's doom."

"We will destroy them!" Kang vowed, clenching his fist. "If you want us to wipe out every dwarf in Thorbardin, every dwarf on Ansalon, we will do it!"

"Not dwarves, Kang," said Huzzad. "Haven't you been listening? The enemy you may be called upon to face is far more terrible than any living enemy you could possibly face on Krynn. These are the creatures of Chaos."

"What are they?" Kang asked.

Huzzad stared intently into the darkness, stared back into the Vision. At length, she shook her head. "No, I cannot tell. All I see is fire, the heroes withering and dying in the flames. I see the world itself withering and dying. I am sorry, Kang. I know nothing more. Here my Vision ends and so does my message."

"Then how do we know what we're supposed to fight?" Kang asked, frustrated. "How will we know when we meet these fiends—the Dark Queen's enemies?"

"When you see her sign. This sign"—Huzzad released Kang's hand. With her finger, she traced around the image of the five-headed dragon on his breastplate—"you will know that what you do you do for Her Dark Majesty and at her behest and with her blessing."

Huzzad rose to her feet. "That is my message, Kang. I'm sorry if it is not clearer. I hope you find the eggs. I hope your race survives."

Kang stood up. "I hope we all survive. Thank you, Sir Knight. Thank you for coming. You've brought me great hope."

The two walked to the cavern entrance and paused, loath to go out into the baking sun.

"We are near Thorbardin. The dwarves patrol this area sometime. Do you need an escort?" Kang asked. I could detail two of my men. . . ."

"No, thank you, Kang." Huzzad reached beneath her leather armor, drew out an amulet of a red dragon on a silver chain. "My mount is within call."

"Good-bye, then, Sir Knight," Kang said, adding, "Where do you go now?"

"To the High Clerist's Tower," Huzzad replied. "Who knows? Perhaps I will be among that band of heroes to make that last, fateful ride. Farewell, Commander."

"Farewell, Sir Knight," Kang said. "Glory and the Dark Queen ride with you."

Huzzad left the cavern, followed a trail that led her higher up the mountain. Kang watched her until she passed out of his line of sight. Even then, he remained at the cavern entrance for long moments, pondering what had been said, going over her words in his mind.

Kang drew out the holy symbol, held it in his palm. Then he presented the symbol to the fiery sun. It seemed to him that the symbol, tinged with a red light, was dipped in blood.

Humbly, he sank to his knees and thanked Her Dark Majesty for her favor. The dwarf had spoken truly. The eggs were draconian eggs, female draconians! At last, he and his men had a future to contemplate.

Even in his joy, Kang did not miss the cruel irony. Now that they finally had something to live for, he had just pledged their lives to fight these creatures of Chaos, whatever those might be.

Yet, if only a few of his draconians survived the battle and—Kang gloried in the thought—the young female draconians could be rescued from their egg-shell prisons, their future would be assured.

Chapter Twenty-Nine

When Kang awoke, he realized that night was falling. He was tired, but the warmth of his Queen's approval eased the weariness. In addition, she had given him the spells he had requested. It was time to be moving.

Returning to camp, he found Slith just waking up.

"Did you get any rest, sir?" Slith asked.

"Some," Kang said.

He considered telling Slith that he'd seen Huzzad, that she'd brought a message to him from the Queen. Kang rejected the idea. Slith was an excellent soldier and the best friend Kang had in the world, but Slith was cynical when it came to humans. He would immediately start to poke holes in Huzzad's story, and before long he'd have Kang doubting Huzzad, doubting the Queen, doubting himself.

No, better to keep both hope and fear locked inside.

*   *   *   *   *

The draconians were on march once the sun had fully set. This Helefundis pass was a difficult one to traverse. The draconians tied themselves together with ropes for safety. Kang ordered all of them to bind their mouths with lengths of cloth. If anyone did fall, Kang didn't want them to give away their position by screaming.

The troop spent the night crossing the pass. They reached the other side of the ridge an hour before sunup. Kang ordered a halt.

"Rest while we can. Once it's light, we'll start the search."

The sun rose, blistering the Kharolis Mountains, flooding the valleys with heat. Before them, hidden in the mountain, was the great dwarven city of Thorbardin, the gates shut against the threat of the dark knights, the mountain sealed. Thousands upon thousands of dwarves were inside there, waiting and alert for attack. And Kang and twenty draconians were going to try to sneak inside.

Kang let his imagination play with the notion of what would happen if he and his small band were discovered. There wouldn't be any graves to worry about. That much was sure.

With daylight, Gloth ordered the troop to spread out, try to find the dwarves' trail.

They hadn't been searching long before Slith yelled. "Here, sir!"

Kang hastened over to look. The grass had been beaten down, and a twig on the end of a bush had been broken.

"You and I'll follow this. The rest of you, stay here. Oh, and, Slith, leave any rope you're carrying behind."

Slith looked a bit startled at this strange request, but did as his commander ordered. He and Kang took over, following the trail, which was extremely clear. They even found bits of bread and other food tossed aside. The dwarves weren't being at all careful to conceal their tracks. Evidently they had no idea they were being followed.

"Either that or they're luring us on with bread crumbs like the witch in the kender-tale," said Slith. "She ended up cooking the children, I hear."

"We'll see who cooks whom, if that's the case," Kang growled.

They made good progress for nearly a mile, and then, unaccountably, the trail vanished. The draconians stood in front of a rock wall that was, to all appearances, solid.

"What now, sir?" Slith asked.

"I have a spell that allows me to find certain objects. I figure that if

214

the dwarves are entering the mountain, using a secret entrance, that entrance must be an old mine shaft or maybe an air hole. What else could it be?"

Slith gave the matter thought. "Right, sir."

"And, if that's the case, they'll have to use rope to lower themselves down. I'll cast a magical spell that searches for rope."

"That's ingenious, sir." Slith was impressed. "And so simple. That's why you made me leave my rope behind."

"I already know where you are," Kang said, grinning.

"What happens if they haven't used rope, sir?"

Kang grunted. "Then we have a problem. Let's just hope that's not the case."

He held a forked stick in his right hand. Speaking the words of the spell, he drew a symbol in the air with his left hand, held out the stick. He and Slith gazed at it expectantly.

The stick didn't move.

"Damn! The entrance must be here somewhere! The blasted dwarves didn't fly off. Search north for any signs," Kang said, frustrated. "I'll follow this wall south. Five hundred paces, then meet me back here."

"Well?" Kang asked, when the two met up again.

"I haven't found anything, sir. Should I call down the rest of the troop?"

"No, not with all the rope they're carrying." Kang thought the matter through. "Let's look at this logically. A mine shaft or an air hole would have to come to the surface somewhere higher than ground level. Otherwise, the mine below would flood every time it rained."

"You're right, sir. I never thought of that." Slith looked around, suddenly pointing to the west. "What about up there?"

He gestured toward a small rock butte, several hundred yards away. He and Kang hastened over, searching on the way for tracks.

"Ah, ha!" Slith pointed to a small fir seedling that had been trampled into the ground.

Kang climbed the first rock, leading up to the butte. He tried his spell again and this time the stick moved in his hand, moved so violently that he nearly dropped it. The stick pointed upward.

Excited, Kang climbed onto the next rock, only to find the way blocked by a hedge of bramble bushes. The forked stick pointed directly at the brambles.

"Look at this, sir!" Slith cried.

Reaching out, he plucked a few strands of brown hair from the brambles. "That came from a dwarf beard, or my wings don't flap. And, see, sir? There's others broken, and more hair, and here's a bit of cloth. They came this way, that's for certain."

Kang forced his way through the thorns, which had little effect on his scaled hide. Below the bramble bush, they found a large stone cover, looking like a plug in the side of the mountain.

"Let's get rid of this mess," Slith said, drawing his sword and attacking the brambles.

Kang replaced his stick on his belt. The two chopped the thorns away from the stone cover. Once clear, they each lifted one side of the stone. It came off easily.

Below them, a hole opened up, leading straight down and vanishing into darkness. Plainly visible in the sunlight were ropes, attached to grapples on the side of the wall.

"We're in!" Kang said.

Chapter Thirty

The dwarves descended the ropes leading down into the air shaft. The descent was accomplished with an immense amount of clumping, banging, swearing, and talking in what they considered loud whispers, which would have been shouts to any other race.

Leading the way down, Selquist cringed. Thorbardin was a considerable distance away, but with the noise this troop was making, he wouldn't have been surprised to find every Hylar dwarf in the place down at the bottom awaiting their arrival. The worst of it was, Moorthane and his soldier dwarves thought they were being both sneaky and stealthy.

"Try to be a little more quiet!" he ventured to call softly, when he had reached the bottom.

"What'd he say?" boomed Moorthane.

"Dunno, can't hear," came back several loud replies, along with a dropped pickax that crashed to the ground with an unholy clang and nearly took off Selquist's foot.

"Chemosh take the lot of you," Selquist muttered into his beard. "Now what's the matter?" he asked Mortar, who was next down.

The dwarf landed, shook his head. "It's not right," he said. "It's just not right."

"What isn't right?" Selquist thought something had gone wrong up top.

"I shouldn't be here," Mortar said in a low voice. "I promised Reorx I wouldn't steal anymore and—"

"Oh, for the love of—" Selquist sighed. "We've been through this, Mortar. What we're doing is not stealing. The stealing's been done for us. We're"—he searched for inspiration—"being thrifty. Making use of valuable resources which would otherwise go to waste."

Mortar hesitated, considered this new idea. "We're not receivers of stolen merchandise?"

"No, no," Selquist said soothingly. "The statute of limitations is up on this crime. The owners have collected the insurance money. They don't want any of the stuff back. It's free for the taking."

"Oh." Mortar thought this over, liked it, and waited to impart this information to his brother, who was now descending.

Selquist shook his head. As if he didn't have enough trouble, now he had to deal with a dwarf who had developed a conscience! Sometimes it didn't pay to get out of bed. Grabbing hold of Auger, who had just landed, Selquist took him in tow and hastened over to the other rope, down which the soldier dwarves were rattling.

Moorthane had finally reached ground level. Standing at the bottom, he was shouting encouragement to those above.

Selquist used admirable restraint and did not throttle the war chief.

"Moorbrain," he said, poking the chief in the back.

"Huh?" Moorthane jumped and turned. He glared when he saw who it was. "The name's Moorthane and what do you want?"

"Auger and I are going to do a little scouting. You and the rest wait for us down this tunnel."

Moorthane frowned, suspicious. "Where are you going? Not thinking of ditching us and running off with the treasure, are you?"

Selquist asked for patience, lest he smash the war chief's teeth down his throat. "No, I'm not. I'm leaving Mortar and Pestle here, as proof I'll return. They have the map. As to where I'm going, I'm going to take a look inside Thorbardin. You're making enough racket to wake the Eighth Kingdom! We should see if the Hylar are up in arms yet."

It was obvious Moorthane didn't like this, but he had to admit that, from a military standpoint, scouting the enemy made good sense. And he remained in possession of Mortar, who was in possession of the map.

"All right," Moorthane growled. "But don't take long. If you're not back in an hour, we're going on without you."

Selquist gave a curt nod. He and Auger left, accompanied by the clatter of a dropped shovel.

"Where are we going?" Auger asked, after a moment. "This is a different direction than we went the last time."

Once out of sight of the expeditionary party, Selquist climbed what appeared to be a sheer wall, but which, Auger discovered by experiment, turned out to have several hand and foot-holds carved into the rock. At the top, Selquist entered another shaft. This one was small; the dwarves were forced to crawl through it on their hands and knees and even then they bumped their heads on the ceiling.

"Like I told Moorthane," said Selquist. "We're going to take a look and see what's going on in Thorbardin."

"Really?" Auger was amazed. "You meant it?"

"Of course," said Selquist in lofty tones. "I don't lie all the time."

"Why didn't we take this way before?" Auger asked. Despite bumping their heads and scraping their hands on the rock, this route seemed easier than the last.

"You'll see," Selquist predicted and, at the end, Auger saw.

The tunnel ended abruptly, opening out into nothing. Auger, peering fearfully over the edge, saw the city of Thorbardin far, far below. The dwarves moving around down there looked like ants in an ant hill he'd once stepped on. He gulped and scooted backward, clinging to the sides of the tunnel with both hands.

"I don't like this," he said in a small voice. "Let's go back!"

"Just a minute." Selquist was hanging perilously over the edge, staring down. Just looking at him made Auger feel queasy. "Something's going on. I've never seen this many people about. I can't see what they're doing, but it looks like . . ."

He fell silent.

"Yes? What? Can we go now?" Auger whimpered, shivering.

"They're at war," said Selquist, finally.

Auger's eyes widened. "With the dark knights? But I thought the Hylar closed the mountain!"

"They did," said Selquist. "They're at war with each other."

He pulled himself back, didn't speak for a long time. He sat so quietly and looked so solemn that Auger was frightened.

"They're not coming after us, are they?"

"No, they're not coming after us." Selquist sighed. "They've got bigger problems. Dwarf fighting dwarf. It just doesn't seem right, somehow."

"Humans fight each other all the time," Auger pointed out.

"That's humans." Selquist was scornful. "We're supposed to be better than that."

"Who's fighting who?" Auger asked.

"I can't tell for sure. My guess would be the Theiwar have finally done what they've threatened to do all these years. They're trying to take over rulership of Thorbardin. The fighting seems to be spreading out from their city—the one we visited the last time we were here."

Auger, remembering the barmaid and her sidewhiskers, expressed a hope that no one would get hurt.

"It's war, Auger," Selquist said. "A lot of people will get hurt." He shook his head, shrugged. "Oh, well. At least that's one threat we don't have to worry about."

He turned and started crawling back down the tunnel.

"Good thing, too," said Auger, coming along behind. "What with those draconians following us."

Selquist bumped his head hard on the ceiling. Twisting around, he glared back at Auger. "What did you say?"

"I said it was a good thing we didn't have to worry about the Hylar."

"I don't mean that! The part about the draconians."

"They're following us. Didn't you know?"

"Well, of course, I knew," Selquist snapped. "It was my idea that they follow us. But no one else is supposed to know. Does anyone else know?" He appeared anxious. "Did you tell anyone?"

"I've told you," said Auger, after a moment's intense thought.

"I don't count! Anyone else? Mortar? Pestle?"

"No," Auger said.

Selquist was relieved, a feeling that evaporated quickly when Auger added, "They were the ones who told me."

Selquist groaned. "Does everyone in the whole bloody party know?"

"I don't think so. Mortar said I wasn't to mention it to Moorthane or the rest of his bunch. Mortar said he figured that it was all part of your plan and that it was pretty damn clever of you."

"Mortar said that?" Selquist was pleased. "Pretty damn clever?"

Auger nodded.

"Well, he's right," Selquist stated. "It was pretty damn clever of me."

He started crawling again, moving along rapidly.

"I don't understand, Selquist," Auger said, scuttling along behind. "Do you want the draconians to be following us?"

"Of course. Otherwise, how will they know how to find the secret entrance?"

Auger assimilated this. It appeared to him to have a flaw. "Do we want them to find the secret entrance?"

"Of course. Otherwise, how are they going to get inside and lead us to the treasure?"

Auger assimilated this, as well. "Why will they lead us to the treasure?"

"Because they have the map!" Selquist was triumphant.

"We have a map."

"Not a very good one. This way is a lot more certain."

Auger crawled along in the darkness, did some more thinking. "But, Selquist, what if the draconians decide to take the treasure for themselves?"

"They won't. They're only interested in one thing—the draconian eggs."

Auger gasped. "The eggs! How do they know about the eggs?"

"I told them." Selquist was smug. "That's why they're following us. And that's why we're going to be following them! Pretty damn clever, huh?"

Auger was overwhelmed at the sheer masterful braininess of this scheme. "Just one thing, though. Won't the draconians be really mad when they find Moorthane squishing the eggs?"

"That," said Selquist lightly, "is Moorbrain's problem."

The two dwarves continued crawling.

*   *   *   *   *

On their arrival, Selquist and Auger found the rest of the dwarves had safely reached the bottom of the air shaft. Moorthane was standing at the bottom, trying to figure out how to recover the ropes.

"Just leave them," Selquist suggested. "The draconians can use them."

"I don't know," Moorthane said solemnly. "It seems—" His eyes bulged. He began to sputter. "What? What? Draconians? What draconians?"

"Don't keep repeating yourself, Moorbrain. It makes you sound even stupider than usual. The draconians who've been following us, of course. The draconians who have the only good map. I can get us and them to the starting point, but, after that, our map's a bit muddled, and we're going to have to rely on them."

Moorthane was rendered speechless.

"Shut your mouth, Moorbrain," Selquist continued. "A rappel will fly into it. You should be thanking me. I'm going to make you a hero! Your name will live in legend and song for centuries to come.

"Now"—he put his arm around the stunned war chief, drew him off to one side—"here's my plan. . . ."

Chapter Thirty-One

The last draconian lowered himself down the rope. Kang waited at the bottom to make certain everyone arrived safely. We could have used our wings after all, he thought. Floated down, not bothered with these ropes.

But he hadn't been able to judge how wide the tunnel was and so he'd insisted that everyone climb. He didn't want anyone breaking a wing in case the shaft suddenly narrowed.

One of the Sivaks, who'd been first down, had been sent out to scout. He came back to report.

"No sign of anyone up ahead, sir," he said. "Although the place reeks of dwarf. They were here, and not long ago. Nice of them to leave the ropes."

Kang grunted. "Yes, wasn't it? Little bastards think they're so clever. Keep your eyes open for ambush." He took out the map. "Slith! Bring that light over here."

The regimental second-in-command brought an oil light that was known among thieves as a dark lantern. Made of iron, the lantern had iron panels that slid open to let out the light of the burning wick. When the panels were shut, the light could not be seen at all. Slith held the lantern over the map.

"The route to the treasure starts in a large chamber. It can't be too far. Look, Southgate's marked down here and Northgate's marked up here. This is where we are, right between the two and off to the west. And that's where the chamber is, just a bit north of us."

"But it's a rat's warren down here, sir," said Slith in disgust. "Tunnels and shafts running off in every direction. How will we find the right one?"

"Simple," said Kang, grinning and shoving the map back in a pouch. "We follow the dwarves. Douse that light. Slith, you go on point."

Draconians, like their dragon ancestors, were at home inside caverns and tunnels. Once their eyes grew accustomed to the darkness, they were able to move along rapidly.

The smell of dwarf was particularly strong in one of the tunnels, a tunnel that had two iron rails embedded in the floor.

Spreading out single file, the draconians entered the tunnel. The walking was easy. The tunnel was large and ran straight into the heart of the mountain. No other tunnels or shafts branched off from it, it neither curved nor bent.

The smell of dwarf led them on, growing stronger and fresher. They walked for what Kang estimated was about an hour and then he saw Slith, who had been out in front, motioning.

"Wait here," Kang ordered and went on ahead.

"What is it?"

Slith opened the lantern's panel. A shaft of yellow light flared out, revealed the dismembered bodies of two dwarves lying huddled in the tunnel. Both wore metal armor and both held swords in their skeletal hands. Both had been brutally ripped apart, the flesh picked from their bones.

"I'm no coward, sir," Slith said, "but I don't mind telling you I wouldn't want to meet the creature that did this."

"I'm no coward, and I agree with you," said Kang. He examined the remains. "They've been dead about twenty years or so. Hopefully, whatever did this has moved on. Still, keep your eyes open."

"Yes, sir. That's what I wanted to tell you, sir. The tunnel curves around a bend up ahead," Slith said, his voice soft. "It'd be a damn good place for an ambush, sir. Dwarves or . . . whatever."

"Right. Go on ahead. We'll keep you covered."

Slith shut the panel, squelched the light, and crept away. Kang brought the troop up, ordered everyone to a halt near the bodies of the dead dwarves.

Slith moved cautiously toward the bend in the tunnel. Almost there, he stopped. The rock face was moist; water was seeping down from somewhere above. The rock glistened faintly.

Slith stood unmoving until his body temperature had cooled to that of the temperature of the caverns. When that happened, he would be invisible to the dwarves, whose night-vision was similar to that of the draconians, allowing them to see objects that radiated heat. He would also be invisible to anything else that might be lurking in the shadows.

When he deemed that he was cooled down, Slith slid around the bend, keeping his body pressed against the wall.

He saw nothing, heard nothing. He drew aside the panel, flashed the light around swiftly. The tunnel continued on ahead, iron rails gleaming in the lantern's light.

He gave a whistle that was the "all clear" signal and continued on. Kang and the troop marched silently behind.

After another hour, the tunnel opened into a small chamber attached to another small chamber. Judging by the pick marks on the walls, the Hylar dwarves had done a lot of digging here, had probably run across a good vein of iron ore. Very little tailings remained, no tools lay scattered about. The dwarves left clean work sites, which practice Kang approved.

The draconians walked through the two chambers, were once again in the tunnel, when Slith returned.

"This smaller chamber opens into a huge chamber," he reported. "Much bigger than the last two. And I've found something. It looks like our guides stopped here and cooked dinner."

"How long?"

"The wood's cold. I'd say five or six hours."

Kang entered the chamber, which was, as Slith had said, massive. Kang guessed that long ago, when this area was in use, the miners must have used the chamber to unload and reload ore cars.

Twenty rusted cars in various states of disrepair stood along the far wall of the chamber. Wheels, axles, and hinges littered the floor. Either the dwarves hadn't bothered to clean up this work site, or they'd fled it in a hurry.

He recalled the bodies they'd discovered, hoped that if anything monstrous was still down in these tunnels, it preferred dwarf to reptile.

"Put out sentries," he ordered Slith. "We'll rest here."

"Sir, do you want torches lit?"

"Might as well. At least we can have a look around. This may be the starting point on the map," Kang said.

The draconians lit torches, but the chamber was so vast the light didn't reach the ceiling. Sentries with torches came to halt when they found a wall.

Soon, the entire chamber was illuminated. Kang saw, with growing excitement, that the chamber was shaped like a kidney bean and that massive blocks formed a wall opposite him, a wall that sealed off one side.

He drew out the map, studied it in the light. The first chamber, the starting point on the map, was shaped like a kidney bean. The blocked-up wall was indicated as well.

"Bless their little hearts," said Kang in satisfaction, looking down at what remained of the dwarves' cooking fire. "They've led us to the right spot."

The draconians rested and ate. Kang and Slith studied the map.

"There should be an exit over there." Kang pointed to his right. "Viss," he called out to one of the sentries. "Take that light over. What do you find?"

The Sivak carried the torch in the direction indicated. "An exit, sir," he reported.

Kang looked back at the map. "Are there iron rails running through it?"

"Yes, sir."

Slith reached out, gripped Kang's forearm. "This is it, sir! This is it!"

"Yes." Kang couldn't say anything more. His elation swelled up inside him, stopped his speech, nearly stopped his breathing. He offered a silent prayer of thanksgiving to his Queen and, again, pledged her his loyalty.

"You should eat something, sir," Slith said, bringing over a hunk of dried meat and a piece of stale bread.

This was the very last of the rations. Kang had left the Baaz back in the village with orders to go hunting—for deer and rabbit, not dwarf. He doubted that they'd find much, however. The drought had forced the deer to seek food and water in areas less harsh than the mountains.

And how were his men going to survive the winter?

Kang put that thought out of his head. One problem at a time. He wasn't hungry, but he forced himself to eat, to keep up his strength. He ordered the sentries changed, so that the rest of his troop could eat, and then looked back at the map. Slith had been inspecting the exit.

"Well?" Kang asked, as Slith returned.

The Sivak scratched his head. "The tunnel's made for dwarves, sir. We'll have to walk bent double. And something else. The stench is gone."

Kang looked up, puzzled. "What stench?"

"Dwarf, sir. I don't smell 'em anywhere."

Kang traced a claw over the first leg of the route described by the map. The route twisted and turned.

He grinned, chuckled. "They don't have the map! They've taken a wrong turn already."

"But they got this far, sir," Slith argued.

"They've been here before, as you said. The route ran straight, with only one bend. This chamber is easy to find. The rest won't be, though. Look at this." He pointed to a fork with four exits, only one of which led to the treasure. "They could be wandering down there for months without a map."

When the last sentry had finished eating, Kang issued orders.

"We'll move on until we're too tired to go any farther. There's no day or night down here, so we go as far as we can, find a safe place to rest, then carry on again when we wake up."

He paused, then added, "Keep your eyes and ears open."

Everyone nodded. They'd all seen the bodies. They repacked their gear, and headed out.

"I'll take the lead, Slith. You stay right behind me. Keep the dark lantern covered while we march. I'll use it to refer to the map when we need to."

The iron rails made the path easy to follow, even in the darkness, which was so thick and heavy that the draconians' night vision had trouble penetrating the endless black. Their pace slowed. The tunnels narrowed, were only dwarf-height. The draconians were forced to walk bent over, their wings scraping the ceiling.

When Kang nearly knocked his head on a sagging beam, he called a halt. He would have given anything to straighten. His back ached from the strain of bending double. Crouching down on the floor, he managed to get some relief.

"Let's see the map," he ordered.

Slith slid the cover of the dark lantern, shone the soft light on the map.

"There's an open area up ahead," Kang said, adding, "Thank the Queen! We can at least stand up and walk like men, not goblins. And keep the light shining. This darkness is slowing us down. If anything sees us, it's welcome to a fight. Better that than knocking myself silly."

They moved on.

After an hour's backbreaking march, the draconians entered another chamber, small in size, but with a ceiling high enough for the draconians to straighten, rub their sore backs, and flex their cramped wings.

"We're at another fork. Which way now, sir?" Slith asked.

Kang brought out the map.

Three times they'd come to forks in the iron rail line. Sometimes the map indicated that they should take the right, sometimes the left. But they were always, Kang noted, following the rails.

He was beginning to understand why. The Daewar had loaded the loot onto rail cars, hauled it to their destination. It was a damn good idea, one he'd already discussed with Slith. The treasure had come in by rail. It would go out by rail.

Gloth came forward, saluted. "Sir, I hear something."

"Yes," Slith said. "I've been hearing it, too. A sort of shuffling and a clanking and then it stops. Sometimes I think it's behind me and sometimes ahead of me."

"I've heard the same. Probably it's the dwarves," Kang said. "They could be anywhere down here, bumbling around in the dark. These tunnels distort the sound, carry it for miles. Let's go."

"I hope it's dwarves and not whatever eats dwarves," said Gloth in a low tone to Slith.

"You and me both," Slith replied.

He drew his sword. The other draconians drew their weapons and, bending over with groans, they entered another tunnel.

The light flashed down the tunnel, stabbing into the heavy darkness, playing off rock and timber and the gleaming iron rails.

Another hour of walking brought them to a three-way fork. Kang was investigating the map when the flame in the lantern started to waver.

"I have to fill it with oil, sir," Slith said.

"Fine. While you're doing that, send scouts down each of these three shafts. Not far. About two hundred paces. See if you can find out what's making those noises."

Slith issued the orders. Three Sivaks split up, each taking one tunnel, and crept into the darkness.

Slith refilled the lantern. He and Kang were, once more, studying the map when they heard a thumping sound. One of the Sivaks was returning on the run.

Kang jumped to his feet. The rest of the draconians formed into battle line behind their commander.

The Sivak ran forward, saluted. "I heard movement down that shaft there, sir." He indicated the left branch.

"How far ahead?" Kang asked.

"I was out around a hundred paces. I stopped for a few moments to listen. I could hear faint scraping sounds off in the distance. I don't know how far. It could be ten feet or ten miles. But it sounded like they were ahead of us."

Kang smiled. "It must be the dwarves. Good. They've taken the wrong fork."

The map indicated the center branch. The draconians relaxed, settled down to rest, wait for the other scouts to return. When they did, neither reported hearing anything.

"We're ahead, now," Kang told his men. "I know you're tired. So am I. But let's press the advantage."

They moved down the center fork. The ceiling was somewhat higher here, they had only to bend head and shoulders. Two more forks took them to their right.

Kang thought how wonderful it would be to walk upright, breathe fresh air, bask in the sunlight. He'd lived out in the open too long. He was beginning to get heartily sick of this tunnel.

Slith's light flared out, illuminated a small chamber off to the right. Kang stopped, motioned for a halt.

"This looks as good a place as any. Let's get some sleep."

Slith agreed. "Is it all right with you, sir, if I send out three scouts? Any forks ahead?"

Kang consulted the map. "They'll come to a fork about a mile and a half down. We cross a bridge over a large chasm, and the fork is on the other side. Tell them to stop there, listen, then come back. Where's Gloth?"

"Here, sir." The Bozak stepped forward.

"You have your magical spells still?"

Gloth cast about in his mind for them. He could only handle the most elementary spell. Anything complicated and he forgot the words or got them tangled up or forgot to draw the symbol or misplaced his spell components. Kang had worked with him patiently, until Gloth was able to retain a few simple spells.

"You go with the scouts. They might need your magic."

Gloth saluted, and moments later he and the three Sivaks disappeared down the tunnel.

Slith entered the chamber, shone the light around.

The chamber was large, filled with tools, including several enormous hammers. Six rail cars stood outside it. Judging by the stacks of rail ties and a couple of bent rails scattered over the floor, Kang decided that this must have been a maintenance shed, used by the dwarves to keep the iron rails in repair.

The draconians set up camp inside the chamber, placing sentries at the entrance.

"I've got to get some rest, Slith, so that I can restore my spells," Kang said. "Áou take the map."

He drew out his holy symbol, held it fast in his hand, and found a darkened corner. No need to gain Her Majesty's attention. He felt her presence almost at once, as if she had been keeping watch over him. The thought was comforting. He smiled and slid into the trance.

*   *   *   *   *

Kang was deeply asleep when sometime later Gloth and his three Sivaks reported back to Slith.

"Keep quiet," Slith ordered, herding them outside the chamber. "Don't wake the commander. What's up? Did you find the dwarves?"

"No, sir." Gloth pointed out his route on the map. "The chasm is there, just like the commander said. The bridge across isn't, though. That is, the bridge is there, but a span's missing in the center. We dumped our gear and glided across the chasm and—"

"Damn!" Slith swore.

Gloth was startled. "What, sir? What's the matter?"

"You say the span from the bridge is missing?"

"Yes, sir, but it's only about twenty feet. We crossed without any trouble—"

"After you dumped all your gear!" Slith gave Gloth a rap on the head. "Use that skull of yours for more than a place to hang your helmet. How are we going to fly back across, carrying dragon eggs and all the rest of the treasure?"

Gloth blinked. Now he looked worried. "I see your point, sir. We'd fall like rocks. What are we going to do?"

"We're engineers, Gloth," Slith said. "It's what we do for a living. Or what we used to do. Everything we need we either brought or we can probably find lying about down here."

"Yes, sir." Gloth still didn't get it. "Need for what, sir?"

"We're bridge builders," Slith explained. "We're going to build a bridge."

Chapter Thirty-Two

Kang woke with a start, after a frightening dream in which he was wandering around lost in a maze of tunnels, carrying a dwarf on his back. The dwarf was heavy, and Kang wanted to get rid of him, but he couldn't, because the dwarf was chained to him and neither of them had the key. He carried the dwarf until he was ready to drop, and the dwarf laughed and laughed . . .

Shaking off the dream, Kang sat up and stared around. The lantern was gone. He couldn't see or hear anyone in the darkness. His men were gone, too.

And somewhere, off in the distance, Kang heard clanging, metal striking metal. He went over the magical spells in his mind, the words to each coming to him like others learn rhymes in childhood. But these rhymes, unfortunately, were very simple.

The spells which he had requested—complex, powerful spells—were not there. His Queen had granted him only rudimentary magical spells, spells that even Gloth could have learned. Kang worried Her Dark Majesty was angry at him for some reason. Hastily he reflected over his time spent in prayer with her, intending to seek her forgiveness if he had said or done anything contrary to her wishes.

But it was not anger he felt, when he approached her throne. It was fear. His Queen was afraid. Her war against Chaos must not be going well. Kang tried to imagine a war raging in heaven, but he failed. Such a thing was beyond his comprehension. Well, he would do the best he could down here on this plane, work with what he had.

The clanging grew louder. It sounded like a pitched battle.

Kang drew his sword, crept out of the chamber and, as he did so, he had the distinct feeling that someone was watching him. He caught sight of a short, squat figure, lurking at the chamber entrance. Kang raised his sword and leapt forward.

"Oh, hullo, sir. You awake?" Viss sprang to his feet, saluted.

Kang lowered his sword, heaved a sigh. "Damn it, Viss, I nearly cut off your fool head! What the devil are you doing out here alone in the dark? Where is everyone? And what's all that noise? Are we under attack?"

"Not that I know of, sir. Slith left me here to keep watch while you slept. The others are off building a bridge, sir."

"They're what?" Kang couldn't believe he'd heard right.

"Building a bridge, sir. You remember that bridge on the map? Well, when we got there, we discovered that the bridge was out. We managed to fly across it, but the chasm's pretty wide and Slith said that flying wouldn't work, carrying dragon eggs, not to mention the rest of the treasure, which he said you wanted to go in the rail cars. So we're building a bridge, sir."

"I'll be damned," Kang said, impressed. "Good for Slith."

Two Sivaks loomed out of the darkness, carrying torches. Seeing Kang, they both saluted.

"We're here for more rail ties, sir," said one. "We're using them as joists for the main span."

"I'll give you a hand," Kang offered.

*　*　*　*　*

The remains of an enormous stone bridge hung over the chasm. The central span was missing, and it looked, to Kang's experienced eye, to have been purposely felled. The dwarven craftsmanship was excellent as always. The bridge—what was left of it—did not appear to be unstable. A quake would have taken down the whole bridge, not just the center.

No, the dwarves had smashed their bridge deliberately. And they must have destroyed it some time after the Daewar had hidden their treasure, because nothing like this was marked on the map.

It was a tantalizing mystery. Kang could picture a beleaguered army, retreating from the foe—whatever foe that happened to be—breaking the bridge after they had crossed. He threw down the rail ties he'd been carrying, spent a few moments studying the bridge.

Slith caught sight of his commander.

"Hello, sir!" The Sivak saluted and grinned. "We're building a bridge, sir!

"I see that. Show me your plans."

Slith and Kang walked across the part of the bridge that remained standing, moved out near the break in the center span. A rough drawing, done in charcoal, adorned the inside part of the bridge's stone railing.

"I had Gloth's second, Drossak, draw this up. He's an understudy to Hornalak, the Plans Officer for the First Squadron. I think he did a good job, considering what we have to work with."

The replacement span was to be a twenty-eight foot drop-in, made of wood, formed in the shape of a triangle. The iron rail tracks would hold it together. The draconians would hoist up one end of the span, keeping the other on the floor. Letting the span teeter, the draconians would then drop the hoisted end down into the gap between the two ends of the part of the bridge still intact. The triangle would wedge itself in between the far and near side, effectively bridging the gap.

It wasn't elegant, but it would do, Kang admitted. Crews would be posted on the other side, ready to align the span when it fell.

The Bozaks were hammering straight the bent rails that would be the mainstay of the bridge, keep it stable. Some of the Sivaks were working to build a network of wooden trestles. Others were scrounging the area for rail ties and tracks.

Gloth coordinated the construction of the triangle support trestles that would be under the rail sections. Wood was nailed and lashed together as best as they could, considering the shortage of materials.

"Squadron Leader Gloth, can I see you for a moment." Kang drew the officer off to one side.

"What is it, sir?"

"You are doing a great job here. Perhaps too great. This bridge only has to get us across and then back again. After we cross, I want to pull it up onto the other side, so that the dwarves won't be able to use it. Don't build me a masterpiece. It only has to be used twice—once on the way over and once on the way back."

Gloth nodded. "I understand, sir. Still, we can't afford to lose anyone, so I thought I'd err on the side of safety. Especially when we're coming back with the eggs, sir."

"That's a big 'if,' Gloth. Don't get your hopes too high," Kang admonished sharply.

"Yes, sir." Gloth looked dejected, puzzled.

Kang was sorry he'd spoken. It was his duty to increase morale, not dampen it. Still, he couldn't help feeling depressed over his lack of magical spells and the feeling that he was being watched, a feeling he couldn't shake off.

Kang sent Gloth back to work, adding a compliment on the fine workmanship that cheered the draconian. His commander went to watch Slith directing the straightening of the rails. They were using four rails to secure the top of the span, to increase its stability and strength.

"What is your estimate of when it will be finished?" Kang asked.

Slith looked around, taking in the work being done. "I'd say we'll be ready to hoist the span in about two hours, then it'll take an hour to drop it into place, sir. That's going to be the tricky part. We don't want to send all this work plummeting down to the bottom of the chasm."

"Three hours." Kang nodded. "Good, that's what I figured, as well. I want two sentries back down the tunnel. We're making noise enough to attract all sorts of attention. I don't want anything sneaking up on us."

The work progressed as planned, but slower than they had hoped. It took them four hours to assemble the span, and then another to secure one end and raise it up, pulling on it with ropes. The hard part was yet to come.

The triangle teetered on the bottom end, the top held suspended in the air by ropes and makeshift pulleys. The draconians now had to shove the bottom end that was balanced on the floor toward the hole.

Eight draconians held the ropes needed to keep the span raised in the air. The rest wrestled the opposite end of the triangle into position, shoving it forward inch by inch, toward the gaping chasm. Twice they were forced to stop when the top began to sway out of control. If the span tumbled over the side, they did not have materials enough to build another.

They inched the span closer to the precipice. Finally, it was about six paces from the edge.

Kang yelled, "Let her down gently, boys!"

Draconians held the end on the floor in place. The rope holders started to lower their side. The span dropped a few inches at a time. As it crossed the halfway point on the descent, however, the draconians had a more difficult time holding it up, keeping it from falling. The span was still five yards above the far side's edge when suddenly the ropes let go.

The bridge span crashed down. The crews who were on the other side, waiting to align it, ran for their lives. The end struck the far side with a thunderous boom, overlapped it by three yards. As it hit, however, the span bent upward slightly, allowing more of the triangle to drop into the chasm. The rails that held the span together groaned under the pressure, then everything went quiet.

The draconians watched, listened.

The span held.

The draconians cheered. Kang felt his depressed mood elevated. Once again, the engineers from the First Engineering Regiment had succeeded in building a bridge.

The yell died down as Kang walked the span, gingerly stepped out onto the rails. Moving forward, he found that the bridge was not only steady, it was also sturdy. He crossed to the other side, turned, and gave his engineers a salute.

The draconians cheered again.

Four Sivaks began pounding stakes into the near side, aligning the rails on the bridge with the existing rails, then bracing the rails together to give them strength. The far side overhung the bridge span by two yards, making it difficult to align. The Sivaks on that side were attempting to wrestle it into place. But, all-in-all, Kang was impressed. The structure would hold.

"Slith!" he yelled back across. "I want a reconnaissance done ahead. All tools and provisions are to be repacked. I want everyone ready to cross this bridge in ten minutes!"

Slith began barking orders, urging everyone to hurry.

Three troopers, one Bozak and two Sivaks, donned their field harnesses and drew their weapons. They crossed the bridge, then trotted off down the tunnel. According to the map, the tunnel forked yet again on the opposite side of the bridge. The iron rails ran to the right, entered another tunnel. The draconians disappeared into the darkness.

Slith had the rest of the troops and all of the kit ready with a minute to spare. Kang returned, recrossing the bridge to pick up his own gear.

"Well done, my friend," he said to Slith.

"What about pulling the bridge back up now?"

Kang shook his head. "It's too damned heavy. We nearly lost it the first time. I don't think we have the sheer muscle-power to—What the devil's that?"

A rumbling sound thrummed around them, bouncing off the chasm walls.

"Quake?" Slith said, looking alarmed.

"The ground's not moving. Where's it coming from?" Kang yelled over the din.

"I can't tell, sir!" Slith shouted. "This damn tunnel! It distorts every sound!"

The rumbling increased. A fearful wail, like the scream of some elf maiden, dying in agony, screeched through the darkness.

"Banshee!" Slith cried and drew his sword.

Every draconian in the troop grabbed his weapons. They faced various directions, keeping sharp watch. Kang was doing his level best to try to remember how to fight a banshee, though he seemed to recall that once you heard their deadly song, it was all over for you.

He was hearing the song all right; the horrible sound pierced his ear drums. He was still standing, was not, as far as he knew, dead yet . . .

And then Kang felt the rails under his feet begin to vibrate.

He looked back down the tunnel.

"There!" Slith gasped.

Riding on the iron rails, one of the ore carts careened into view. Inside were six dwarves, clutching the sides of the cart for dear life. Beards flying, mouths wide open, shouting and laughing in derision, the dwarves hurtled past the draconians at a break-neck speed. The iron cart rolled along the rails, heading for the newly replaced span.

"Look out!" Kang cried and leapt to one side.

Draconians standing on the tracks flung themselves out of the way. The cart rocked violently when it hit the new rails, appeared perilously close to tumbling off into the chasm. The dwarves' derisive jeers changed to terrified screams, several covered their eyes. Rattling and shaking, the cart clung to the rails and sailed across the span.

The Sivaks working on the rails on the opposite side scrambled to safety, leaving their task undone.

At that end of the bridge, the iron rails did not meet. The bridge jutted up about two feet into the air. The cart carrying the dwarves shot off the end of the bridge, flew some distance in the air, crashed, and overturned, spilling out the dwarven rail-riders, who took off down the tunnel at a run.

Kang and his troop just stood there, staring, dumbfounded.

The rumbling sound, that had ceased when the first cart tumped over, started up again. The draconians pushed forward onto the tracks to see what was coming.

Kang yelled "Get back!" just as the second iron cart hurtled out of the tunnel. A third was right behind.

The two carts flew across the new center span. The dwarves' elation changed rapidly to sheer terror when they saw the overturned cart blocking their path. One of the dwarfs attempted to put on the brakes. Sparks flew from the iron wheels. The screeching sound went through Kang's skull, started his teeth vibrating.

The second car shot off the uneven span and lurched into the first. The third careened into both of them. One of the cars remained upright. The other tipped over. Dwarves poured out in all directions, clambering over the sides, crawling out from under the wrecked rail carts. They fled like rats into the darkness.

The sounds of chortles and laughter and insulting catcalls echoed down the tunnel.

Kang snapped out of his dazed state.

"Damn it! Get after them!" he yelled furiously.

Chapter Thirty-Three

"That ride," said Anvil, departing the overturned iron cart, "was the single most wonderful experience of my entire life!"

"Ooh, boy, what a ride," said Mortar, eyes shining. "Where's Auger?"

"Down here," said Selquist.

He bent over a dwarf huddled in the bottom of the car. The dwarf had his head buried in his hands, and he was screaming, "Is it over? Is it over?"

"It's over," said Selquist. He shook Auger. "Hurry up! We've got to get out of here!"

Between him and Mortar, they managed to drag poor Auger to his feet. The sight of the furious draconians pounding across the bridge did a lot to help the dwarf recover after his terrifying experience. He broke into a staggering run. The others dashed along on either side of him. The dwarves from the first two cars had already run on ahead.

Selquist stopped a moment to wave back at the draconians. "Thanks for the nice bridge!" he yelled. "And for showing us the way to the treasure room! It's been a real pleasure doing business with you!"

"Where do we go from here?" Mortar asked, worried. "How will we know the way?"

"The iron rails," said Selquist. "Haven't you noticed that by now? We just keep following the iron rails. And it's not far now, no matter whose map you go by."

Selquist's plan had worked better than even he had anticipated. The dwarves had waited, hidden, in a small shaft branching off from the first main chamber room. They watched the draconians scout the chamber, heard Kang ascertain that this was, indeed the starting point on the map. Allowing the dracos a five- or six-hour head start, the dwarves had then proceeded to follow the draconians through the maze of tunnels.

It became clear to Selquist, as the dwarves trailed along behind, that Mortar's recollections of the map weren't all that accurate. Entire sections had been left out, the wrong forks indicated. Without the draconians to guide them, the dwarves would have been hopelessly lost, would have probably wandered around down here for the rest of their natural lives.

And then the bridge! So kind of the draconians. So thoughtful. That chasm would have been the end of the quest for the dwarves.

Feeling quite friendly toward the draconians, Selquist was a bit saddened to think of Moorthane and his band of cut-throats destroying the dragon eggs. Such very profitable eggs, too. The draconians would be certain to pay big . . .

"To arms!" someone shouted up ahead. "To arms!"

Selquist raised his head. Torchlight flared, glistened off the scales, and shone in the red eyes of three draconians, who were racing frantically back down the tunnel.

The draconians were running straight at the dwarves.

Moorthane lifted his sword, placed himself directly in their path. He crouched in a fighting stance, prepared to sell his life dearly.

The draconians ran around the stout dwarf and kept running. The rest of the dwarves were forced to fall back against the tunnel walls, out of the draconians' path, or they would have been trampled. The three draconians barely spared the dwarves a glance. They ran on down the tunnel, back toward the bridge.

"Cowards!" Moorthane cried, waving his battle-axe in the air.

"Stand and fight!"

"I'll stand and fight you, Moorbrain, you ninny!" Selquist called, struggling to reach the front. "What do you think you're doing? You could have wrecked this entire opera—"

The hair—what there was of it—stood up straight on Selquist's head. He stopped, open-mouthed, and stared, as did the other dwarves in the tunnel.

Auger, grabbing hold of Selquist, began babbling. "What is that? Reorx save us! What is that thing?"

Moorthane sucked in a huge breath and fell back six paces, bumping against Selquist.

"A grell!" he cried, his voice cracking. "It's a grell!"

Selquist had once been extremely sick as a child. His high fever had prompted him to see all sorts of things, from worms crawling out of the woodwork to giant rats dancing on the foot of his bed and, of course, grells.

These monsters are nearly always a part of dwarven bedtime spook stories, their tales having been passed down from the time when the Niedar had once lived in Thorbardin. Legend has it that the grells had been the original inhabitants of the cavern beneath the mountains and that the first dwarves to inhabit the mountain, led by their Thane, Hamish Ironfist, had been responsible for cleaning them out.

Apparently Hamish had missed one.

The grell was a greenish blob, a gigantic brain that floated off the ground about six feet above the heads of the dwarves. It had green tentacles, a beak like a bird's, and, as far as Selquist could judge, a nasty disposition. The grell did not appear inclined to chat or pass the time of day or inquire politely if the dwarves couldn't find some other route through the cavern rather than its living room. The grell swooped down on them, lashing out viciously with its spiny tentacles, gnashing its beak, and obviously intent on killing every one of them.

"No wonder those draconians were running away!" Selquist realized and decided to emulate their excellent example. He turned and ran, pushing and shoving his way back through the crowd.

Moorthane and his soldiers stood their ground, began attacking the grell. They stabbed at the tentacles, which were jabbing out viciously in all directions. Other dwarves thrust their lit torches into the grell's eyes, hoping to blind it. A few of the less daring were huddled back at a safe distance, pelting the grell with rocks.

With the main body of his comrades now between him and the grell,

Selquist stopped running and turned to watch the fight. He wasn't impressed. The dwarves weren't making much headway—three were already down, rolling and writhing in agony from the poison of the grell's paralyzing sting. Selquist was just thinking how smart he had been, bringing along Moorthane to serve as grell-fodder, when Auger, axe in hand, charged straight past Selquist, running headlong for the grell.

"Auger! What are you doing? You're a coward like me! Remember?" Selquist cried. "Let Moorbrain deal with it!"

His friend didn't hear him.

Entering the fray, Auger slashed at one of the grell's tentacles. His sword connected and cut off about a foot of the wriggling arm. Green ooze spurted, splashing over Auger's head, hitting him in the eyes.

Blinded, he staggered about helplessly, wiping ooze from his face. The infuriated grell struck Auger with one of its undamaged tentacles, hitting him in the shoulder.

Auger shrieked, his body convulsed. He pitched forward onto his face and lay unmoving on the ground.

With Auger down, Mortar and Pestle entered the battle, began hacking at the grell with their axes and doing no good at all that Selquist could see. They appeared to be accomplishing little more than irritating it.

The grell hovered above its victim, beak gnashing. Moorthane was attacking it from behind, whacking at the back tentacles, and the grell was whacking absent-mindedly at Moorthane. The grell was plainly more interested in finishing off poor Auger.

Emitting a series of clicking sounds from its beak, the grell lifted a tentacle. An object it held clutched in the tentacle began to glow with an eerie blue light.

Selquist groaned. As if this grell wasn't nasty enough, it had somehow or another managed to come into possession of a wand, a wand that had every appearance of being magical. The wand was a rod about a foot long, black as night and wound round with the bodies of dragons of various colors. The heads of the five dragons formed the top of the wand.

Selquist guessed that this magical wand wasn't the kind likely to cause lovely little flowers to spring up out of snowbanks.

Confirming Selquist's worst foreboding, the grell—having apparently grown tired of Moorthane—whipped about, pointed the wand at Moorthane, and made a loud clicking sound with its beak.

Blue-white light flared from the mouths of the five dragons.

A flash, a bang.

Moorthane made a kind of soggy popping sound, and what was left of him splattered over the walls, the floor, and his fellow dwarves.

Having dealt with this annoyance, the grell turned back to Auger, who still couldn't see and couldn't move. The other dwarves had fallen back in panic, the shocking death of Moorthane having effectively taken the fight of them. The grell raised the wand, pointed it at Auger. The monster started clicking.

Selquist thrust his hand in his belt, drew his knife, and threw it over the heads of the dwarves bunched in front of him.

The grell clicked again, but this time in pain. The knife had imbedded itself in the frontal lobe of the brain-like mass. Green ichor began dribbling down from the wound. The grell faltered in its spellcasting, its tentacles twitched.

Taking advantage of the grell's weakness, Selquist beat and pummeled his way through the crowd. He slipped in beneath the flailing tentacles, grabbed hold of Auger's shoulder, and began dragging his helpless friend back away from the grell. Selquist's feet slipped in the remains of Moorthane, slid out from underneath him.

"It figures!" Selquist thought angrily. "Even dead, Moorthane's out to get me!"

He lay flat on his back, staring up at the grell.

Raising the wand, the grell held it above Selquist. The wand began to glow. The grell began to click.

Selquist knew he was a dead dwarf.

Suddenly, from somewhere behind him, a wave of small crossbow bolts, each one of them outlined in red flame, flew over Selquist and thudded into the grell's brain.

The grell screamed and writhed; its tentacles jerked wildly. Another wave of red-hot bolts streaked over the dwarves, followed by yet another.

The grell seemed to implode. Its brain looked like a sponge wringing out blood and puss. The grell sank to the floor of the cavern, its tentacles twitching and writhing. And then the grell ceased to move at all.

Dazed, Selquist picked himself up and looked over his shoulder. A huge Bozak draconian, carrying a small, hand-held crossbow, pounded down the hallway, hopping over the crouched dwarves as he came. The Bozak was followed by about twenty more draconians, swords and crossbows in their hands.

The dwarves nearly crawled up the walls in terror.

But the draconians were not interested in fighting dwarves this day.

The Bozak jumped over Selquist, narrowly missed stepping on Auger. Reaching the body of the grell, the Bozak swooped down, took hold of the magical wand, and—careful to keep from touching the poisonous tentacles—gingerly slid the wand out of the dead grell's grasp.

His prize safe, the Bozak turned, grinned and snapped his teeth at the dwarves. "Thanks for the nice wand," he said. "And it was really good of you to take on that grell for us. Such a pleasure doing business with you! Keep in touch."

The Bozak bowed to Selquist, then waved his hand and shouted orders. The rest of the draconians surged around the dwarves, leapt over the dwarves, ran past the dwarves, and vanished into the darkness.

"Well," said Selquist, as he picked himself up, "even the best laid plans can go awry, as the kender said right before the griffin bit his head off. And every silver dragon has a cloud. I'm the new leader, it seems."

He wiped Moorthane off his hands and bent down to help rouse poor Auger.

Chapter Thirty-Four

Kang gripped the wand tightly, examined it while he ran. There was no doubt, no doubt at all. This was the wand Huzzad had described to him. It still glowed faintly blue, and he could see by the glow that the wand was a rod made of black onyx, about as long as his forearm, and topped by his Queen's own five dragons.

The dragons' heads were crafted of silver, their bodies encrusted with rubies, emeralds, sapphires, diamonds, and black opals. Their five tails wound down around the rod, twining together to form a handle.

It was the most beautiful, the most awful object Kang had ever seen, much less held. He could feel the fey power in the wand, feel it humming through his body.

Kang began to believe. He began to believe that it all might come true. They might find the dragon eggs, they might be able to cast the spell that would free the female draconians. His village might have a future. Their entire race might have a future.

Of course, there were still these fiends of Chaos he had promised Her Dark Majesty to destroy. He had the feeling that this would require more than just knocking off one slimy grell. But with this wondrous wand in his hand, Kang felt equal to facing anything—including Father Chaos himself.

"Good find, sir," said Slith, running along at Kang's side.

The Sivak held the dark lantern, and now he flashed the wavering light directly on the wand. Slith's eyes glistened. "That looks extremely valuable."

"More than you know, my friend," Kang said, his voice husky with emotion. "More that you know. Here's that crossroad we were looking for." Calling a halt, he reached for the map. The troops bunched up around him.

"What gives, sir?" Slith demanded, his voice harsh and grating.

Kang looked at his second in surprise. This wasn't like Slith.

The Sivak gestured. "You weren't going to attack that grell at all, sir. Not at first. You sure as hell weren't going to risk our lives rescuing those hairy little farts. And then you saw that wand and suddenly went charging forward. You know something, sir? I say you were looking for that wand. You knew it was going to be down here. What's so special about it? And why've you been acting so strangely?"

"You've never lied to us before, sir," Gloth said, joining the discussion. The other draconians gazed at Kang with solemn, grave expressions. "All these years, you've told us straight out what we were up against. We've seen the change in you the last few days, sir. We just wondered what happened, that's all."

"Douse that lantern," Kang ordered. "No use providing the dwarves back-lit targets."

Slith obeyed, slid the panel. The light went out.

Concealed by the darkness, Kang smiled sadly, and he sighed. Never lied to them, they said. Hell, a commander always lied to his troops. That was part of a commander's job.

"I'm sure the general knows what he's doing."

"Those elves aren't as tough as they look!"

"So what if we're outnumbered eleven to one? We've been in tighter spots before."

"What do you mean, dragonfear? There isn't a dragon within a hundred miles of this place."

But Kang knew his men didn't mean that type of lie. He'd been living a lie these past few days or weeks or however long it was that they'd been in these tunnels. It seemed to Kang as if it had been most of his life. He was mindful of time, mindful of the need to hurry. It wouldn't take the dwarves long to recover from their shock and to regroup. But this was very important. His men were losing faith in him.

"I'm sorry, boys," he said, fumbling for words. "It's just . . . Something happened to me. I didn't believe it myself first, and then, when I did, I was afraid no one else would believe me if I spoke about it. Until I knew for certain what had happened was true, I didn't want to raise your hopes. But this"—he held up the wand—"this is proof. Yes, Slith, I knew about the wand. I was looking for it. Do you remember that knight, Huzzad? I met her, back there when we were going through the mountains. She had a message for me from the Dark Queen. She told me I would find this wand down here."

The draconians stared at the wand in the darkness, their red eyes faintly gleaming.

"Our Queen told me where to find it," Kang repeated, his voice clear but hushed. "Huzzad came to me on the mountain. She spoke to me."

He told them all, told them everything. They listened silently, so silently that it seemed some even held their breath. When he was finished, they gazed at the wand in reverence. A few reached out a tentative claw to touch it, for luck.

"Thank you, sir," said Slith. "And, I'm sorry, sir. I didn't mean . . . It's just that . . ."

"I know, Slith," Kang said. "I know."

He sighed again, but now it was a sigh of relief. He hadn't realized until this moment how heavy the burden of his secret had been. It fell from his shoulders, and he felt renewed strength, renewed energy.

"Let's get going. I hear the dwarves behind us. We have to get to the eggs before they do," he added grimly, "or the wand won't matter. There won't be any eggs."

"Why not just kill the little bastards?" Gloth asked. "We'll wait here and jump 'em."

Kang had already thought of this, dismissed it. He knew why he wasn't going to kill the dwarves, but it was hard to put his thought process into words.

"Our enemies can prove useful to us," he said, quoting his Queen. "We would have walked smack into that grell if the dwarves hadn't come along when they did. Plus I don't want to waste the energy needed to kill them. Remember, men, Her Majesty has asked us to do her a favor in return for this wand. I want us to be fighting fit and ready for action. For now, the dwarves live."

"For now," Gloth growled, his tongue flicking over his teeth.

The draconians traveled on through the tunnels. Slith took the lead, shining the lantern light only at intervals. The tunnels were larger here; the draconians could stand straight, for which blessing Kang was most grateful. He had the feeling he'd ruined his back permanently.

They passed a turnoff on their left. Kang paused here, studied the map. The main tunnel went straight on. This turnoff appeared to be a small side shaft which, according to the map, led off from the main tunnel, joined up with it again about a mile farther along.

"This is apparently some sort of siding, used to take the iron carts off the rails, get them out of the way," said Slith, returning from a brief investigation. "There's a bunch of carts shunted off in there."

"And it's marked on the map," said Kang in satisfaction. "We're going the right way."

He was about to motion the troop forward, when Gloth stopped. "Listen, sir!"

Sounds came from the tunnel behind them—a clomping, as of many pairs of heavy boots tromping down the hallway.

The draconians fell back into the shadows, waited.

"Remember," Kang said softly, "no killing unless they start it."

At length, the dwarves came into their view. The draconians' night vision saw them as warm, glowing bodies. Warm, glowing bodies that didn't look nearly as chipper as they had before they ran into the grell.

The dwarves straggled out of line, marched with their shoulders slumped, their heads down, their boots dragging on the floor.

Kang waited until the lead dwarves were within about six paces, then he leapt out of hiding, gave a frightful roar.

Spreading his wings, he bared his teeth and, lifting the glowing wand in his hand, he took to the air. He landed almost on top of the lead dwarf. Shouting a battle cry, Kang stomped his feet and waved his arms. His wings flapped up a gale.

The dwarf stared up at Kang, let out a yelp, turned, and ran head-long back down the tunnel. His yell and his flight spread panic throughout the rest of the party. Unnerved by the attack of the grell and the loss of their leader, the dwarves fled this new, dimly seen terror.

Kang heard one voice at the end of the line expostulating with them, trying to head off the stampede. The one voice wasn't having much luck.

The dwarves dashed out of sight.

"It'll be a long time before they have nerve enough to come down here again," said Slith.

"That's the plan," Kang answered.

*   *   *   *   *

The draconians continued on through the tunnel at a run.

"Sir," said Gloth, "do you notice that it's getting warmer down here?"

Kang had noticed, and he had thought it odd. Underground caverns always maintain the same temperature, winter and summer. But the heat was definitely rising in this one, and it was rising quite rapidly.

He rounded a bend to find that the Slith and his two scouts had halted again, staring into a chamber that opened up in the center of the tunnel. A bright reddish glow spread over them, its source was the chamber.

The path they were supposed to take ran straight into the chamber—a chamber that according to what Kang recalled of the map wasn't supposed to be here.

Kang moved forward to join Slith. The Sivak stood at the entrance to the chamber, peering inside. The heat from the chamber was intense, hit Kang in wave that nearly bowled him over. The heat and the smell—sulfurous and acrid—caused his snout to wrinkle in revulsion.

"What is it?" Kang looked inside, advanced a step or two. That was as far as he could manage.

The chamber walls were not rough-hewn and timber-shored as had been the other walls in all of the other chambers and tunnels built by the dwarves. The stone in this one was smooth and polished and looked as if it had been melted, then hardened again. Waves of rock formed the walls, rivulets of stone cascaded down along the floor.

In the center of the floor was a gigantic pit.

The fiery red light, a thousand times more intense, welled up from the pit. Heat radiated from the pit, beat on the stone walls and continually hammered at Kang. But it was not only heat that assailed him.

Fear—gut-curling, bowel-wrenching terror—writhed inside him.

He knew such fear, he recognized it, though he had never felt it this strongly. Hastily, Kang backed out of the chamber.

"Phew! That's foul!"

Kang paused a moment to clear his head of the fumes. He felt the fear ease when he left the chamber, though it did not vanish completely.

He wondered what to do. His instinct was to run and keep on running, even if he ran into Thorbardin and an army of ten thousand dwarves. Ten thousand dwarves, ten million dwarves, were nothing compared to what might be living inside that pit.

Unfortunately, the treasure room lay on the other side of this chamber.

"There's something in there, isn't there, sir?" Slith said, eyeing his commander. "And whatever it is melts solid rock!"

"I saw a red dragon do that once," offered Viss. "It was when I served under Dragon Highlord Verminaard. His dragon flamed some little village on the Plains. The stone glowed red-hot and made puddles all over the ground."

"I've seen the same thing. But I don't think this is a red dragon." Kang didn't add that he thought this was something much worse. "The rest of you scout around, see what you can find."

Kang needed quiet, to be able to think. Stalling for time, he drew out the map.

"It's not a red, is it, sir?" Slith asked quietly.

Kang shook his head. "I've been around reds before. So have you. I've felt dragonawe, but nothing like what I felt inside that chamber. Did you go in?"

"Yes, sir. Like you, I didn't stay long. So what do we do now? I don't remember this chamber being on the map."

"It isn't." Kang looked over the map. "According to the map, the tunnel runs straight, without a bend or a turn—certainly without a lake of fire and a chamber of melted rock—for at least another two miles. So far, the map has been correct in every detail. I can't imagine the Daewar neglecting to mention this."

"Maybe it's us, sir. Maybe we took a wrong turn."

Kang went back over their route in his mind, compared it to the map. "It wasn't that difficult! We passed the siding." He looked down at the floor. "There are the iron rails. No, this has to be the right way."

Kang studied the map again, had an idea. "Look, the siding circles around this part of the tunnel, comes out down here. That's the route we will take. Move the men out quietly. Whatever is in there, I don't want to disturb it. I—"

"Sir," said a Sivak. "I think you better come see this."

Kang didn't like the sound of that. Whenever someone wanted him to come see something, it always meant trouble. No one ever asked him to come see a marvelous sunset or to come look at a bunch of baby ducks, swimming in a pond.

He walked over to the Sivak, who was peering intently at the wall outside the chamber.

"Look here, sir." The Sivak pointed.

Kang looked. He said nothing. There wasn't much to say.

On the wall, outside the chamber, was carved in the rock a five-headed dragon, the image of Takhisis, Queen of Darkness.

"What does it mean, sir?"

Kang ran his dry tongue over his teeth. "This is the favor. She wants us to face whatever is in there."

"And whatever is in there seems likely to kill us. What good's the wand, sir, if we don't live to use it?" Slith was bitter. "We've got the wand. We'll do her another favor some other day."

Kang recalled his elation when he'd first looked at the wand, first felt its power. He hadn't asked questions of his Queen then. He hadn't doubted her wisdom. He hadn't wavered in his faithfulness.

Was he to back out of his part of the bargain now? Was he to forswear his oath of fealty?

Kang was well aware that those who forsook their promises to his Dread Queen rarely received a chance to forsake any more. But he would not keep his promise out of fear, he said to himself proudly. He would keep his promise because he had made it. A matter of honor.

Kang fumbled at his leather harness, removed the medallion that was a symbol of his rank. He quietly handed the medallion to Slith.

"What's this, sir?" Slith asked. He kept his hands at his side, refused to take it.

"You're in command now, my friend," Kang said. Reaching out, he attached the medallion to Slith's harness. "And high time, too. Take the map, as well." He handed it over. "You and the others continue on to find the dragon eggs. I'll keep the wand and deal with this little matter."

"No, sir," Slith said stubbornly. He plucked the medallion from his armor, tried to hand the medallion back. "I won't go and leave you alone, sir. None of us will."

The Sivaks and the Bozaks gave forceful agreement.

Kang shook his head, crossed his arms over his broad chest.

Seeing that Kang refused to take back the medallion, Slith threw it to the floor. He folded his arms across his chest, planted his feet firmly. "No, sir. I won't go."

Kang found the medallion in the darkness, picked it up. Reaching down, he said steadily, "That's an order, Slith."

Slith glared at him. The Sivak may have acted on his own initiative from time to time, but he had never, in the all years they'd served together, disobeyed a direct order.

"Like the lord knight said, Subcommander," Kang said quietly. "Discipline. Discipline is the one way, the only way, we can win out over chaos."

Slith stood staring at his clawed feet, refusing to look at the medallion, refusing to look at Kang.

Kang waited patiently, confident that his second would come through. Slith had never failed him yet.

Still not looking at his commander, Slith snatched the medallion from Kang. The draconian thrust the pin through his harness. His hand shook, he had to try several times before he succeeded.

"Thank you, Slith," Kang said, breathing out a sigh. "Good luck to you. To all of you." His gaze included the entire troop.

The draconians mumbled something back; they were shocked and numb. Kang had been their commander from almost the very beginning. They couldn't remember a time when Kang hadn't led them.

Slith was a good officer. They'd soon adapt to his leadership.

"You'd best be off now," Kang suggested. He couldn't make it an order.

"Yes, sir," Slith said. He hesitated a moment longer, as if he had something else to say. But, in the end, he didn't say it. Instead, his clawed hand reached out, grasped hold of Kang's hand in the dark, and gave it a squeeze.

Turning, Slith glared at his subordinates. "What in the Abyss are you all staring at? You've had things easy in this outfit, but I'm in charge now. Lively there! March!"

Turning, Slith led his command—his command—back down the tunnel, the way they'd come. He didn't look back.

The other draconians hesitated a moment, then they followed him and soon Kang was alone.

He faced the red-glowing chamber. Before he entered, he placed his hand on the symbol of the five-headed dragon drawn on the wall and asked for his Queen's blessing.

Holding the wand in one hand, his sword in the other, he ran through his catalog of magical spells and began to walk steadily toward the pit.

Chapter Thirty-Five

By much arm-waving, shouts, threats and beard-pulling, Selquist finally managed to stop the dwarves' panicked stampede.

"Stop it! Stop it! Have you all gone mad?" he yelled.

The dwarves straggled to halt, breathing heavily and glancing nervously down the tunnel. They had run almost all the way back to the newly repaired bridge.

"I am thoroughly disgusted with the lot of you." Selquist snapped. "I've never seen such cowards!"

The military dwarves were sullen and defensive. "You didn't see nothing," said one. "'Cause you were way back at the end of the line. Back where it was safe."

"I was guarding the rear," said Selquist, with dignity. "And you wouldn't catch me running from danger. I attacked the grell, after all. And you call yourselves hill dwarves! Gully dwarves is nearer the mark."

The rebuke struck home, gully dwarves being generally acknowledged as the greatest cowards on the face of Krynn. The dwarves glowered at the insult, though some appeared to feel it was deserved. They hung their heads in shame.

Another voice spoke up defiantly. "You weren't there, Daewar. The draconians were. And they've got the wand that sizzled old Moorthane. I'm not going in after them."

Several of the dwarves muttered agreement.

Selquist stood on tiptoe, peered over heads. "Whose that back there? Vellmer?"

"Yeah, it's me." The thick-set, black-bearded brew master, whose face was always flushed, due to the continual need to taste-test his own products, stumped forward. He had a perpetually fierce expression, produced by a pair of bristling black eyebrows that met in the center of his forehead,

"You were Moorbrain's lieutenant, weren't you, Vellmer. I guess that means that you've taken over the troops following poor old Moorbrain's unfortunate demise," Selquist said.

Vellmer gave Selquist a shove that knocked him backward.

"You speak respectfully of the dead," Vellmer snarled.

"That's something I've never understood," Selquist said. "You can bad-mouth a person all you want when he's alive, but the moment he's dead and can't possibly hurt you anymore, you can't say a word against him. Oh, never mind. I don't want to quarrel."

Selquist stepped forward, placed his hands affectionately on Vellmer's shoulders.

"Look, Vellmer. You didn't sign on for this. Moorbr—I mean dear old Moorthane was the one who was all fired up to go smash dragon eggs. Now, if you want to take your boys and head home, you know the way back, I presume?"

The brew master stiffened, regarded Selquist with dark suspicion. "I know the way," he growled. "And I've a mind to do just that. We came down to smash dragon eggs. We didn't know we were going to have to fight grells and draconians with magic wands."

"One grell," said Selquist. "Let's be accurate. And it was pretty puny. But, go if you want."

"We're going," said Vellmer and started off down the tunnel, accompanied by his men.

"That just means more treasure for the rest of us," Selquist called. "You would have been eligible for Moorbrain's share. One two-hundredth."

The dwarves came to a halt.

"What's this?" Vellmer demanded, missing the sound of marching boots behind him. He turned around, clumped back, grumbling all the way. "What good's treasure if we're not alive to spend it?"

"It was sort of a puny grell," said one dwarf.

"And likely that's the only one," added another.

"What about the draconians?" Vellmer demanded.

"Maybe they'll fall into a pit," said yet another dwarf.

Selquist clapped Vellmer on the shoulder. "Too bad you have to rush off. We'll take it from here. It will be a bit of a strain, carrying back all that treasure by ourselves, but we'll manage."

"All that treasure, you say." Vellmer eyed Selquist. "There's a lot of it? Steel and gold and silver and jewels and such?"

"More than you can imagine," Selquist said.

Vellmer thought the matter over. "About those dragon eggs." He frowned, looked extremely grave. "It's our duty to smash 'em. I see that clearly now. And, once that's done, we'll help you carry the treasure."

"You're a true Niedar, Vellmer," said Selquist, shaking the dwarf's hand. "A gentleman and a brewer, as I've always said."

"But how do we get past the draconians?" Auger wondered.

Selquist pulled out his map. "Bring those torches over here. Look, we don't have to go the same way the draconians took. There's a side tunnel that branches off, goes around, and then . . ." He stopped, squinted down at the map.

"Then what?" Vellmer peered over his shoulder. "Ends in an ink blot?"

Selquist glared at Auger.

"I'm sorry," said Auger. "The quill dripped."

"Never mind," Selquist said crossly. "But, as you can see, once we're past the blot, it's straight on to the treasure. We better hurry. The draconians have got a pretty good head start."

The dwarves formed two lines, one led by Vellmer and one by Selquist. The two leaders started off at run, setting the pace. The dwarves swung into step behind. Although these dwarves had been born and raised in the mountains, not beneath them, they had rock-dust in their blood, as the saying went. They traveled fast, making up for lost time, and soon found the siding.

"Listen!" Vellmer said, pausing. "Hear that?"

They all heard it—the sounds of clawed feet scraping against rock.

"The draconians!" Mortar cried. "They're coming back this way!"

"Why are they doing that?" Selquist demanded, irritated. "They've proved a nuisance. I'm really beginning to be sorry I led them down here."

"Quick!" Vellmer urged. "Hurry! Everyone into the tunnel before they see us!"

The dwarves bolted into the siding. They ran past the abandoned ore carts, kept running until they figured they were well out of sight and out of earshot of the draconians. Stopping to listen, the dwarves heard nothing.

"They must have marched on past. Maybe they're giving up and going home," Pestle said hopefully.

"I'm not so sure," said Mortar in a low voice. "I feel sort of crawly inside. Like someone's watching us."

"All I can feel is the heat!" complained Auger, wiping sweat from his face. "It's not supposed to be hot underground, is it?"

"No," said Vellmer. "It's not. It's too hot, and something's watching us. I can feel it. Something's wrong."

"Something's right." Selquist was studying his map. "This siding leads back to the main tunnel. The treasure chamber is right up ahead."

Selquist increased his pace. His excitement was contagious. The other dwarves hastened along after him, faces flushed with heat and exultation. They rounded a bend in the tunnel, came within sight of a vast chamber.

"That has to be it!" Selquist cried.

"If it is, why is the treasure giving off a red light?" Auger asked.

"The luster of gold!" Selquist said. He paused a moment to wipe the sweat from his eyes. "The gleam of rubies. The magical aura of spell-books!"

"And is it supposed to smell that bad?" Mortar held his nose.

"That's probably the dragon eggs," said Selquist. "Likely they're rotten, after all this time. Here! This is it!"

The tunnel in which they were traveling opened into an enormous chamber. The dwarves gathered around the opening, stared inside.

Red light radiated from a pit in the center of the cavern room. The heat was intense and forced the dwarves to shield their faces against it.

"We don't have to worry about the dragon eggs," Vellmer said darkly. "If they're in there, they're hard-boiled by now!"

"Selquist, this isn't the treasure room. It's the wrong shape. This room isn't even on the map," Mortar pointed out. "We must have come the wrong way!"

"Would you look at that!" said Pestle, awed. "The stone walls have melted! Like they were butter or something!"

The dwarves' excitement was melting away, too. They stood outside the chamber, sweating and fingering their weapons nervously.

"This place has an unholy feel to it," said Vellmer in a low voice.

"And it's not supposed to be here," Mortar reiterated.

"Either that or we're not supposed to be here," Pestle said, gulping.

"Bah!" Selquist spoke with considerably more spirit than he actually felt. His stomach was crawling around like it was looking for a way out of his body. "We've come across a lava pit. That's all. The floor probably caved in some time after the treasure was hidden here, which is why this isn't on the map. This chamber is merely a natural phenomenon, caused by . . . by . . . ."

"Seismic tremors," Mortar suggested.

"Thank you." Selquist edged toward the chamber entrance, and looked inside, eyes squinted against the fiery light. "I can see an exit . . . way over there."

The other dwarves crowded back into the entryway.

"You're right." Vellmer gave the exit his official seal of approval. "That's the way out. Unfortunately, to get out, we have to go in."

No one seemed willing to do that.

"Well, now," Selquist said, trying to drum up enthusiasm. "We go in, like Vellmer here says, circle around the lava pit, and go out. That's all there is to it."

"I don't know, Selquist. Something in there doesn't want us in there," Pestle said in a shaky voice, wiping the sweat from his face with the end of his beard.

The dwarves stood, glancing at each other and back into the chamber uncertainly.

"I'll go in," said Selquist finally, and started for the chamber entrance.

Vellmer caught hold of the harness on Selquist's leather armor, jerked him back.

"And stuff your pockets full of treasure while we're not looking?" The brew master snorted. "We all go or none of us go."

"We all go then," said Selquist, relieved. He was not sorry to have the company. He had only taken a single step toward the chamber, and though the room was excessively hot, he experienced a strange and unaccountable chill in the vicinity of his backbone.

Bunched together, weapons drawn, their faces grim and shining wet in the red light, the dwarves shuffled inside the chamber.

Chapter Thirty-Six

The draconians crept silently down the main tunnel, moving each clawed foot with extreme care, wings quivering with the effort of maintaining absolute quiet. Their new commander was in a foul mood, and no one wanted to draw his attention. Two draconians were already nursing bruises, and their only offense had been the involuntarily clicking of their scales, which were spreading apart due to the intensity of the heat.

Fortunately, the heat began to diminish the farther they moved away from the strange, red-lit chamber.

The draconians marched down the tunnel until they reached the siding. Slith halted and glared at the branching shaft, cursed it for being there. If it hadn't been, his commander would have never sent them off. His commander wouldn't now be facing whatever it was he was facing alone.

Slith kicked at a rock wall in passing. Sullenly, morosely he led his troop off into the siding. He came to a halt so suddenly that those behind him had to skip and dance out of the way to keep from running into him. No one wanted to bump him.

"Do you smell that? Dwarf!" Slith whispered, glancing back at his troops. "Douse that light!"

The draconians nodded. The one carrying the dark lantern quickly shut the metal shield.

"They're up ahead of us in the siding. I can hear them breathing. By the Dark Queen," he added vehemently, "I'll get rid of these buggers, at least." He looked back at the others. "Knife work," he ordered. "Quick and quiet."

He drew his knife from his belt. At his motion, the other draconians did the same. Their eyes gleamed red in the sweltering darkness. All felt extremely relieved. Slaughtering a few dwarves was bound to cheer up the commander.

Bending low, to fit into the tunnel, the draconians sidled down the corridor, making sure of every footfall, careful not to let their swords strike against the narrow rock walls or their wings scrape against the ceiling. They opened their mouths, tongues lolling, panting for air. The heat was beginning to build again.

Slith rounded the bend in the tunnel.

The red glow from the chamber washed over him, the stifling heat and the sulfurous smell roiled around him. Slith grinned with the sheer pleasure of it all.

"Thank you, Your Majesty!" he said softly. "And forgive me for doubting you back there. And all those bad things I said about you— I'm sorry about them, too."

He drew out the map, held it to the light radiating from the chamber. "So that's it," he muttered. "The fire pit blocks all the routes to the treasure, which is on the other side. We're up here." He put his finger on the top of the map. "The commander's down here." He moved his finger to the bottom. "We've caught the cursed dwarves right in between both of us."

He turned back to his troops. "Come on, men! We're going—"

His words, his very thoughts, were lost in a boom that shook the cavern. The draconians braced themselves against walls that shivered beneath their hands. The boom subsided, only to be followed by an ominous roar which started low and grew in volume until it seemed to suck the air from the chamber, the courage from the draconians.

Ahead of them, they heard—beneath the roar—the sound of hoarse voices crying out in terror. The red light grew brighter, so bright that it hurt the eyes. With the light came a wave of heat and a foul and stifling odor. Worse than the heat, more painful than the flaring light, awful fear seized the draconians and shook them as a wolf shakes a torn carcass.

They recognized such fear. They'd felt it before, only never this powerful, this strong. Slith's knees went weak, his wings fell limp at his sides, his clawed hands clenched. His mouth was so dry he couldn't move his tongue.

"Dragon!" a draconian behind him croaked.

"It must be the mother of all gold dragons, then," Slith muttered. Up ahead, he could hear curses and shouts coming from the dwarves. Slith turned, motioned his troop to retreat. "We'll just sneak off while the dragon's munching on dwarf meat. Then we'll—"

Slith fell silent. He'd heard another voice, this one shouting loudly and defiantly—in draconian.

"The commander!" Gloth cried. "It's got the commander!"

Kang was battling the dragon alone. Slith took hold of the dragon-fear, formed it into a ball and swallowed it, choked it down. The fear rolled around in the pit of his stomach, but he could deal with that.

Drawing his sword, he ran down the corridor, heading straight into the inferno. The other draconians were right behind him.

Chapter Thirty-Seven

Kang could not move. Terror paralyzed him, wrung him, turned him inside out. He stared at the pit, realized, now that he was close, that due to the angle from which he had entered, he hadn't seen it all. What he'd seen was only a small portion of an enormous pit filled with fire and molten rock, magma that bubbled and churned.

A head emerged. The head of a dragon, but not like any dragon Kang had ever before seen on Krynn.

It was a dragon of fire. Its scales were black, the red of its fiery body glowing hideously beneath. Its mane was fire that crackled in the air. Opening its mouth, it belched forth noxious gases.

He recalled Huzzad's words: "All I see is fire, the heroes withering and dying in the flames. Krynn withering and dying in the flames."

This was the creature of Chaos. This was what would kill the heroes and bring about Krynn's doom.

The dragon's front clawed feet dug into the rock at the rim of the pit.

It was pulling itself up out of the lava pit. Its eyes were dark, empty as a universe drained of all life. The eyes focused on Kang. He saw not only his own death but the death of all living beings. He saw the death of the gods. Fear crushed hope, stomping it out and scattering the ashes.

He couldn't breathe. The dragon's foul breath poisoned the air. The heat radiating from its body was intense, seemed to fuse Kang's feet to the floor. His hands went limp, he nearly dropped the wand and clutched at it in growing panic. As he did so, he felt its power throb in his hand. The wand glowed with a vibrant blue intensity, shone with the same unhallowed light as that given off by the dark moon.

Yet against the living inferno of the fire dragon, the wand was slight and fragile. A whisper from the dragon would incinerate the wand, incinerate Kang. He could not fight this thing! Nothing, no one could fight this thing! Not the dark knights, not the Dark Queen herself. Certainly not one lone draconian.

With a great effort, Kang wrenched his feet from the floor and turned his back, turned to flee. The heat seared his wings; he bit his tongue to keep from crying out with the pain. He broke into a staggering trot. The exit seemed a lifetime away.

Discipline, said a stern voice. Discipline is all that will win over chaos.

Kang recognized that voice, knew it for his own. He looked at the wand, saw its light diminish, felt its pulse wane. The heat was enough to boil his very blood, red-orange flame licked his scales.

"Discipline," Kang said, hissing the word through clenched teeth.

He expected his men to obey his commands. What would they think if they saw him fleeing in terror? What if he did survive? He could never again give another order. He could never again ask his men to believe in him. He could never again ask them to set their lives on the line.

He might as well die as live that kind of life. And he might as well die fighting.

Turning, standing his ground, Kang faced the fire dragon. The wand quickened. Energy, fey and powerful, surged through Kang.

The fiery head loomed over him and, even as he faced this single, dreadful, deadly dragon, without a hope of destroying it, without a hope of surviving, Kang saw a group of dwarves emerge from an opening in the upper part of the chamber.

On the faces of the dwarves was a terror that must mimic his own.

Kang saw them, and then he forgot them. One enemy at a time.

His hand groped instinctively for his sword. He envisioned trying to get close enough to the beast to stab it, and he abandoned the idea. He would be charred before he came within striking range. His Queen had given him the wand. He would use it, even though he wasn't at all sure how it worked. If nothing more, perhaps it would enhance the few spells he already knew.

The dragon's head lowered, drew nearer. Its eyes were focused on Kang. The eyes were empty. They held nothing, not hate, not hunger, not fear. The dragon would kill him, it would watch Kang die without feeling anything. Kang would far rather have fought an enraged elf lord, who would at least feel something at the death of an enemy, even if that feeling were exultation. This dragon's only goal was to destroy any living thing that it found in its path. Fire flickered from its closed jaws; the teeth were black against the glow of the flame. The head drew nearer still, the jaws gaped open.

Fumes filled the air, poisoned it, made it unbreathable. Kang could do nothing but retreat for the moment. Holding his breath, he backed away until he was near the chamber's entrance. He gulped lungfuls of relatively fresh air, then dashed back inside.

The heat was taking its toll. Kang fumbled at the magical spells in his heat-dazed mind. Unlike other races, the draconians could not cope well with extremes in temperature. He was growing limp as a lizard basking in the sun. He had to do something to fight the heat, before he could even begin to battle the dragon. The first spell he cast, therefore, was for himself.

"Water . . ." Kang mumbled the word, through a throat that was burned and parched. His clawed hands traced the requisite symbol on the wall behind him.

He searched around hastily, looked at the stone wall, at the floor.

Nothing, and Kang despaired. He had hoped for a trickle of water, anything to bathe his face, cool his scales that were spreading wide with the heat, forcing his lips to draw back in a rictus grin. His tongue lolled.

The dragon had been watching him. It wasn't toying with him, as one of the petty-minded, vengeful silver dragons would have done. This dragon did not immediately attack because, Kang had the feeling, it didn't see any need to. He couldn't blame it. Why waste the energy? He was going to be dead of the heat before long.

The dragon continued dragging its huge body up from the pit. The stone floor and walls radiated heat. Kang felt as if he were being roasted alive in a slow oven.

269

"Water! Your Majesty! I beg you—"

The wand flared blue in his hand. Power irradiated the wand, startling Kang so much that he almost dropped it.

Water, ice cold and wonderful, splashed down on Kang. Water flowed from the walls, washed over the floor. Water eased the pain of the burns on his feet, cooled his body, revived his mental processes.

The water gushed in a torrent from the ceiling. It ran down the floor, cascaded into the pit. Steam rose in clouds.

Shaking off the lethargy that had almost been lethal, Kang sloshed about in the water, tried desperately to think of his next spell, a spell that would kill the dragon. The water continued to pour down, the chamber was filling with steam. Kang momentarily lost sight of the fiery creature.

But he could hear it roar, and it sounded as if it was in pain. Lurching forward, trying to see, Kang came within sight of the dragon and discovered that his spell was having an unexpected effect.

A torrent of water, flooding down from above, was washing over the dragon. Its scales, constricting from the heat, were cracking. The dragon's red glow was dimming. It roared again in fury.

Water continued to pour down upon the dragon. The fiery light it had brought into the cavern started to diminish. The dragon's roar became an enraged howl. It had managed to pull the upper portion of its body from the flaming pit, but the lower portion remained in the lava below, and the upper part was cooling rapidly.

The dragon snapped at Kang, but its movements were sluggish and slow, and the draconian easily dodged out of the way. The dragon's claws scraped against the rock. The top portion of the body was growing heavy, the bottom could no longer support it. The dragon was retreating, sinking back into the pit.

Kang panted in relief, relief that was short-lived. As far as he knew, the one way out was through this chamber. If he allowed the dragon to escape now, it would probably revive. He would only have to fight it later. He had to prevent it from escaping back into its lair.

The water that had been a blessing now proved a curse. It was over Kang's knees, made movement difficult. Kang floundered through the flood, but it was obvious that by the time he reached the fire dragon, close enough to stick a sword into it, the dragon wouldn't be there anymore.

He would have now traded all this water for a few boulders to come crashing down . . .

"Mud!" Kang said, looking up at the ceiling.

Nothing happened, but this time he was prepared. "I beg Your Majesty . . ."

The wand flared blue. The stone ceiling of the cavern above the dragon transformed, oozed, and liquefied. An avalanche of mud descended upon the dragon, mud rained down into the pit. Soon the mud completely covered the dragon's upper body and head. Kang could no longer see it or hear it. The dragon's tail thrashed up from the pit, flicking molten lava about the walls, but soon the tail went flaccid. Kang could only assume the dragon was dead.

Kang sucked in a shuddering breath. He was about to leave, to go see if he could catch up with Slith and the rest of the command, when the floor and the walls started to shiver.

Looking up, Kang knew immediately what was happening. The shifting mud could no longer hold the weight of the ceiling above it. This part of the chamber was going to come crashing down on top of him.

Kang started running toward the exit, the way he'd entered, only to see it vanish in a sliding wall of mud and rock that would soon overtake him. He was about to suffer the same fate as the dragon.

Turning, Kang ran the only way he could run, the only way left open to him. He ran farther, deeper into the chamber.

He could not see for the steam, but he recalled that he had seen an exit at the chamber's far end. It was a long distance away, and to reach it he had to pass near the fiery pit.

Kang ran, ran faster than he'd ever run in his life, his feet sloshing through the water. The floor sloped uphill, the water was shallower here. And then he was on dry stone, hot stone. He gritted his teeth against the pain of his burned and blistered feet and kept running.

He was circling around the pit, giving it a wide berth, when he caught a glimpse of movement, of the rock within heaving and rolling toward the surface.

Eyes, black and empty, stared from the pit.

Chapter Thirty-Eight

The dwarves took a few tentative steps inside the chamber. The heat was oppressive, the fumes stifling. The pit of molten rock glowed hotter than a smithy's hottest fire. Those daring enough to look at it saw lava bubble and churn. The exit was off to their left, at about a ninety-degree angle. The pit was straight ahead.

The dwarves fell back against the cavern's smooth walls and crept along the edges. Heat boiled out of the pit, a sense of dread wrung the courage from every dwarf as he wrung the sweat from his beard. The dwarves gripped their battle-axes and continued on.

"I saw eyes!" Auger cried, pointing. "Eyes in the pit!"

The other dwarves came to halt. Their faces glistened with sweat, the red of the molten lava gleamed in the axe blades.

Selquist swallowed, tried to find some moisture in his dry mouth. He had never in his life been so scared. He would have never believed he could be this scared. He gave a light and carefree laugh, that was rather spoiled by a gulp in the middle.

"What an imagination you have, Auger!" Selquist said, swallowing again and trying to control a nervous tremor in his hands. He, too, had seen the eyes, but he was trying to ignore them. "You should go to Palanthas and study to be a bard. Those weren't eyes. It was only . . . only shadows. Keep moving."

That order was eagerly obeyed. The dwarves wanted nothing more than to escape this place. They had taken twenty steps and were still some distance from their destination, when a terrible bellow sounded from the opposite side of the chamber.

The dwarves halted again, stared at each other.

"That was a draconian's voice!" cried Pestle.

"First a grell, then eyes with fire for eyebrows, now howling draconians," Selquist muttered. "Those blasted Daewar! There was no need to hide the treasure in such an inconvenient location."

"Look! Off to the right!" Mortar was shouting.

Selquist looked, but an enormous stalactite blocked his view. The draconian bellowed again, shouting words in a tongue that none of them understood. This was followed by a flash of bright, unnatural blue light and the sound of rushing water, coming from off to their right, on the other side of the lava pit.

The dwarves weren't about to hang around and see what came next. They broke into a run. They were almost halfway to their goal, when their goal suddenly vanished in a cloud of hot steam.

The dwarves choked and gasped and blinked. Everything vanished in the thick fog, including each other.

"Stand still!" Selquist yelled. "Keep together!"

Every dwarf who heard this order assumed that it applied to every other dwarf, not him. He was the dwarf who was to run for the exit. Each dwarf consequently stumbled about in the fog, shouting and groping with his hands, endeavoring to find the way out.

Adding to the fear and confusion were the terrible noises coming from out of the fog, noises of a draconian shouting and a frightful hissing and roaring. The fog began to dissipate. Finally able to see, the dwarves discovered that they were scattered all over the chamber— some perilously close to falling in the pit. At that moment, the floor and the walls started to shake.

A sound of an avalanche thundered to their right. The cavern was caving in.

The dwarves headed—once more—for the exit with Selquist in the lead. He was the only dwarf to have taken his own advice. When the fog rolled in, he stopped in his tracks and waited for it to clear. As soon as he could locate the exit, he ran that direction. A shout behind him caused him to turn his head. Involuntarily, he slowed his pace.

A dwarf stood in front of the glowing pit. He appeared to have turned to solid rock, for he wasn't moving, and something inside the pit was. A head of flame and smoke, with eyes as empty as eternity surged upward.

Selquist had never seen a dragon before, much less a dragon made of fire, but he was immediately able to identify this creature as a fire dragon. The one thing he knew about fire dragons was that he should not remain long in the vicinity of one.

The dragon shot a mouthful of flame on the dwarf, who was instantly ablaze. Screaming in agony, the dwarf flailed about, took a misstep, and tumbled with a horrible shriek into the pit of molten rock.

Dread and awe rendered Selquist and all the rest of the dwarves incapable of movement or thought. Another one of their number became a living torch, set ablaze by the dragon's breath. The beast was pulling itself out of the pit, its head swiveling to keep its victims in sight.

Selquist realized suddenly that, unless someone did something, they were all going to die.

"What are we doing? What's come over us?" he asked and struck himself several times on the forehead to bash away the dreadful feeling of helplessness.

This accomplished, he endeavored to rouse his friends.

"Auger! Run! Pestle, you idiot! Get away from there! Mortar, you moron—Oh, Reorx take the fools! What would they ever do without me?"

The empty black eyes focused on Vellmer, who stood shivering in his boots. His battle-axe fell to floor, struck the rock with a dull clang. The dragon drew in a breath.

Selquist hefted his own battle-axe and let fly.

Unfortunately, Selquist had never been much good at axe-tossing. He'd always had better things to do with his time than hang about hurling axes into trees, a favorite amusement of the more militant among the dwarves. Selquist's arms were not particularly muscular, being better suited to climbing nimbly into second-story windows than heaving large and heavy weapons through the air. His aim was not true. He didn't get any lift or height, as is advisable when hurling axes at dragons.

Selquist missed the dragon completely, but he did hit something. He struck Vellmer—fortunately with the dull end of the axe.

Vellmer toppled like a felled tree. The dragon's bubble of flame burst harmlessly over the brew master.

Selquist's attack may have missed the mark, but it kindled the fire of courage in the hearts of the other dwarves.

"Attack!" Mortar shouted. A much better hand at axe-throwing, he hurled his blade at the dragon. It struck the beast in the left eye.

The dragon thrashed about, flinging its head from side-to-side. The eye was a bloody mass, oozing down the dragon's cheek.

Encouraged, taking advantage of the dragon's distraction, the other dwarves threw their axes—and anything else they held—at the fire dragon. Under cover of the fire, Selquist ran forward. Auger and Pestle were bending over Vellmer, trying vainly to revive him.

"Hurry! Drag him out the door!" Selquist grabbed hold of the unconscious brew master by his collar. "I expect free dwarf spirits for a year for this! You two, take his arms."

Pestle and Mortar each caught hold of an arm and they started hauling Vellmer in the direction of the exit.

The dwarves had run out of weapons to throw at the dragon. They kept up the attack however, hurling rocks, waterskins, and even their own hobnailed boots.

Stunned by the barrage, the dragon started to sag to the floor. But it was not finished yet. Shaking its fiery mane, it swiveled its good eye around to find and destroy these annoying pests.

"Retreat!" Selquist shouted when it was apparent that they had nothing more to throw.

The dwarves turned and fled, stopping only to pick up any of their injured along the way.

The dragon made a sudden surge forward, flame erupting from its jaws. The gout of flame caught several of those nearest the pit. Burning embers clung to their clothes and set their hair and beards alight. They stumbled and fell, cried out to their comrades not to abandon them.

A low, warbling chant sounded from somewhere behind the dragon. A draconian ran forward, emerging from out of the red-tinged darkness, chanting his war cry as he ran. He held a gleaming wand in one hand, his sword in the other and his breast and head were protected by a coat of sparkling white frost, that glittered like armor. As the draconian closed on the dragon, the yell increased in volume, grew higher in pitch. The draconian's war cry was picked up and shouted by the other draconians, coming to the aid of their commander.

The dragon tried to find these new foes, but they were attacking at it from seemingly every direction. The first draconian ran in, ducked beneath the teeth that snapped at him. The magical frost armor began to melt in the terrible heat, but it protected the draconian long enough for him to drive his sword straight into the beast's right eye.

The dragon flung its head sideways, attempting to dislodge the sword. The draconian held on, driving the sword deeper, until it seemed he was about to be carried into the burning pit. Letting go at the last possible moment, he fell heavily to the floor. The dragon opened its jaws and was about to devour him when the rest of the draconians arrived and formed a defensive perimeter around their fallen leader. One of them grabbed the big draconian and dragged him away from the pit.

"Now!" Mortar shouted, and with a few of the others he ran back to rescue those dwarves who had fallen, assisting them to safety.

Draconian swords flashed in the red light, stabbing and thrusting. The dragon lurched its head upward and lashed out with its powerful claws. A swipe caught one of the Bozaks in the back, impaling him. The Bozak struggled a moment, then went limp.

"Take cover!" Selquist cried. He had seen a Bozak die once. He knew what was coming. "Duck! Everyone!"

The draconians evidently knew what was coming as well. They began to run, scuttling back for the entrance. The draconian who carried the wand crawled on his hands and knees in the opposite direction.

The Bozak's flesh crumbled, leaving a skeleton. The dragon was endeavoring to shake the skeletal remains from its claw, when the bones exploded. The dragon's head burst asunder, fire erupted from its skull. It tumbled into the pit.

"By Reorx, there's more of them!" Mortar cried in dismay.

The magma in the pit churned. Red waves of fire crashed on the rock shore.

"There must be hundreds!" Pestle gasped.

"Good," said Selquist, rubbing his hands.

"Good?" Auger screeched. "Are you crazy?"

"I am quite sane," Selquist said coolly. "This means we don't have to worry about the draconians any more. Their time is going to be fully occupied."

Standing in the exit, Selquist motioned, yelled, "Down the tunnel. This way! Quickly now! "

A third dragon was crawling up out of the pit. It looked to be the biggest yet, and there were more behind it.

"Have those beasties cleaned out by the time we're ready to come back, will you?" he yelled to the draconians.

The dwarves helped the wounded to their feet. This included Vellmer, who demanded to know what had hit him.

"A draconian," said Selquist promptly. He pointed. "That big guy there, with the crumpled wing."

Vellmer growled, rubbed his head. "I'll fix him," he said savagely.

"You'll have to get in line. The dragon has dibs. And don't you have a job to do?"

Vellmer recalled that he did. Turning, he began to run on wobbly legs, followed the rest of the dwarves down the tunnel—the tunnel that was, finally, going to lead them to the treasure.

Selquist was about to chase after them, when a thought occurred to him.

"Mortar! Pestle! Wait here with me just a minute," he called. "I have an idea."

Chapter Thirty-Nine

Kang lay face down, staring with horror into the bubbling magma. He had once, during a battle near Pax Tharkas, stumbled across a nest of vipers. The snakes had been twined around each other in a writhing knot, so that one could not tell their numbers or even where one snake began and another snake ended.

Dazed from the heat, Kang saw countless eyes, empty eyes, staring back at him, saw incalculable numbers of the fire dragons twisting and turning, crawling over each other, rising full-grown from the molten lava of which they were the magical embodiment.

If these creatures escaped, they would not only overrun Thorbardin, they would decimate Krynn. This, he realized slowly, is the Dark Queen's task for us. Not to kill one or two of the fire dragons. To destroy the viper's nest.

He shifted his eyes that burned with pain inside their sockets to gaze at the wand.

"She never intended for us to survive this mission," Kang realized. "We are her doom brigade, like the fabled knights who rode in the last battle with . . . what's his name . . ." Kang couldn't think clearly. "Huma or some such." It didn't matter anyway.

"Sir! Sir!" A voice was yelling at him. "Commander!"

Kang wished the voice would shut up. Why couldn't they leave him alone for once? What was it now? Expecting him to get them out of trouble again? Expecting him to save their scaly hides this time? They were going to be in for a big disappointment. He was going to go to sleep and sink into the fire . . .

Water splashed over him. It sizzled on his hot scales, but it brought him back to consciousness. A clawed hand had grabbed him by the harness, was dragging him back away from the pit.

The hand dumped him on the floor a few paces away.

"You all right, sir?" Slith asked. He held a dwarven waterskin in his hands.

Kang sat up. He couldn't answer with words, his throat was raw, and his breathing was labored. But he managed to nod his head.

"You just rest here, sir. We'll deal with these wyrms." Slith was off before Kang could reply, returning to the battle.

"We have to kill them," Kang said, talking to himself, stupid from the heat, the fumes and his pain. "Kill them all. Those are my orders."

But it looked as if it was going to be the other way around. The dragon impaled a Bozak on its claw. Kang saw the Bozak die. He had just strength enough left to crawl out of the way before the explosion.

The fire dragon died, but the head of another reared up to take its place. Kang heard a second explosion. Another Bozak dead. How could they fight a creature they couldn't even get close to without sizzling. He sat on the floor, gazing around at nothing, a strange and terrible lethargy affecting him. He was waiting to die.

His aimless gaze lifted to the cavern's enormous domed ceiling. Stalactites, made of rock melted by the heat, looked like enormous teeth. Once black, the stalactites glistened red in the light of the fire. Kang might have been inside a maw of some great creature, whose mouth was filled with fangs. A mouth about to close on them all. . . .

"That's it," said Kang.

He was on his feet, the lethargy gone. He searched for, found Slith, fighting some distance away.

"Retreat!" Kang bellowed, his voice booming through the cavern. "Withdraw!"

Slith looked around, stared at him to see if he'd heard correctly.

Kang waved, pointed to the chamber entrance that was located directly behind the draconians. "Retreat!" he shouted. His throat was raw. He tasted blood. "Go back out the way you came!"

Slith nodded once. His voice snapped orders, and the draconians began an orderly retreat, taking their wounded with them. No panic, like the undisciplined dwarves. It was no rout. The fire dragons swooped and snapped after them, flame flared all around them. Several more draconians fell, but the rest did not break ranks, did not falter.

Kang watched them. Pride for his men swelled in his breast. It was a good feeling, a good feeling to go out on. He waited until the last draconian was clear. Slith turned, and it was only at that moment that he realized his commander had not followed.

Slith appeared on the verge of racing back to the rescue. Thank the Dark Queen, he held his position. He knew Kang had a plan, trusted his judgment.

Kang wished he could feel as certain.

One of the fire dragons, angry at losing its prey, turned and saw Kang. The fire dragon lunged at him, jaws opening wide.

Kang raised the wand and pointed it—not at the dragon—but at the ceiling of the cavern.

"Next time, tell us the truth, Your Majesty," he said quietly. "You don't have to trick us into serving you."

The wand glowed blue. The glow brightened, tendrils of lightning twined across its surface. Kang felt anger, his Queen's anger. It was not directed at him, but at the fate that was crushing her, that would soon drive her from her throne, her world. He did not know or understand it then, but this was Takhisis's last petulant act, her final burst of fury, a hand slap across the face of the Father who had come to avenge himself on his god-children.

Blue-white jagged lightning burst from the wand, struck the ceiling directly above the fire dragons' pit. Stalactites exploded, showering down huge chunks of rock. Boulders crashed into the pit, smashed the bodies of the fire dragons. Some lay crushed near the edge of the pit. Others managed to escape and disappeared rapidly, diving into the pit's molten depths.

Boulders crashed around Kang, as well, but he remained standing, keeping the beam of dazzling light aimed at the ceiling. The beam of light was protecting him from the chunks of ceiling hurtling down on top of him, a benefit he hadn't expected, but for which he was certainly thankful. Striking the halo of light that surrounded him, the rocks bounced harmlessly off, rolled to the floor.

More rock tumbled down. Rock dust rose into the air, lava splashed in great gouts around the cavern room. Kang could no longer see the ceiling, but he kept the light aimed in that direction.

A deep rumbling shook the chamber. A crack appeared at Kang's feet, spread to the rim of the magma pit. The floor was beginning to break apart, shatter.

"Sir!" That was Slith's voice, howling through the chaos.

Kang started to back up, one footstep at a time, feeling his way toward the exit behind him, the exit the dwarves had taken. He kept his gaze and his thoughts concentrated on the destruction of the cavern.

It was much darker in the room now. The fiery light was dying, as the pit filled with debris. Hopefully, this meant that the fire dragons were dying. The only light was the radiant blue light surrounding him and, suddenly, that light went out.

The wand went dead in Kang's hand.

Rocks struck him, small ones, shards flying through the air, lacerating scale and skin. A boulder crashed down beside him, narrowly missing him. A chunk the size of a fist struck his shoulder. Another rock tore one of his wings.

The cavern room was caving in. Kang made a convulsive leap for safety. He landed on his belly, cracked his ribs and knocked the breath from his body. He couldn't breathe, couldn't move. The floor beneath him heaved and shook. Rocks thundered and crashed around him.

Short, dark figures surrounded him. Hands grabbed him, hands with fingers, not claws. Hairy faces bent over him. The dwarves lifted him up by his harness and dragged him toward the exit. There, they dropped him.

Kang raised his head, stared dimly at them. His strength was almost gone.

One of the dwarves leaned down, plucked the wand from Kang's nerveless hand.

"Nice doing business with you," the dwarf said, and dashed off.

And then all was dark around Kang.

All was dark inside him.

Chapter Forty

Coughing from the rock dust that rolled out of the dragon's chamber in great, choking clouds, Selquist slowed his run to a walk. He kept a wary eye on the ceiling, but though it shook and shivered, it did not seem prepared to tumble down on top of him.

"You Hylar dwarves build one hell of a fine, sturdy tunnel," Selquist told any of their dead who happened to be lounging about.

"Where'd everyone go?" Auger asked nervously.

"Probably out of the way of the dust," Pestle said, his voice muffled by his handkerchief, which he tied over his mouth.

"There, I think I see them." Selquist pointed.

The flickering light of a torch was barely visible through the murky dust. Burned and blistered, but otherwise alive, their comrades were gathered together beneath a huge support beam, obviously expecting the whole mountain to come crashing down about their ears. The dwarves were a sorry sight, bereft of their weapons, most of them barefoot.

"Who's that?" cried out a voice, peering through the dust.

Selquist started to reply but at that moment a cloud of dust flew down his throat, making breathing interesting and talking impossible. He choked and spit until he was finally able to gasp, "Me!"

"And Mortar and Pestle and Auger," Auger added.

"It's Selquist. We thought you were dead," said Vellmer in a tone which implied that all his fondest hopes had been dashed. "What's going on back there? Is it the fire dragons?"

"Are they coming after us?" another dwarf asked fearfully.

"The draconians," growled another. "They're coming after us."

Selquist shook his head, coughed a couple of more times, then waved his hands in the air, banishing their fears and getting rid of the dust at the same time.

"No need to worry about fire dragons or draconians. They've killed each other. Brought the whole bloody cave down on top of themselves. We saw it."

He indicated Auger, Mortar and Pestle, who all nodded solemnly.

"That's all very well!" shouted Vellmer, clutching the side of the tunnel to remain standing while the floor shook beneath their feet. "But it's not going to do us much good if they bring the cave down on us, too!"

The rumbling ceased. All was quiet. The rock dust hung in the air, and then began to slowly settle.

The dwarves listened, heard nothing.

"What did I tell you?" Selquist said. "All dead." He hummed a few bars of a dwarven love song, looked extremely pleased with himself. "Now, aren't you glad I brought those draconians along?"

"Not particularly." Vellmer rubbed his sore head. "What's that you're holding?"

Selquist recalled, too late, that the magic wand was in plain view. He quickly shoved it up his sleeve.

"Oh, nothing," he said carelessly.

"It looked like a magic wand. The same wand that grell was carrying," Vellmer said in disapproving tones. "The same wand that killed poor Moorthane."

"Maybe it is. Maybe it isn't." Selquist shrugged. "One magic wand looks a lot like another, at least in my experience. Let's get a move on. The treasure room is really close, as I remember. Where's that map?"

But the dwarves were not to be sidetracked.

Auger looked shocked. "Is that what you stole from that dead draconian?" His face wrinkled. "I don't think it's right to steal from the dead, Selquist."

"It may not be right, but it's safe," Selquist muttered.

"That wand is an artifact of evil," Mortar observed righteously. "I think you should get rid of it and then say a prayer to Reorx, begging his forgiveness."

"I'll say a prayer to Reorx, all right," Selquist said into his beard. "Ask him to pick up the whole lot of you and drop you down in Kendermore."

"You remember what trouble that holy symbol of the Dark Queen was, before you got rid of it," Pestle reminded him.

The wand was cold against Selquist's skin and, at this, he did feel a momentary touch of misgiving. Fortunately logic—which was already calculating the value of the rubies and sapphires, emeralds, diamonds, and what appeared to his experienced eye to be some quite fine black opals—won out over superstition.

"That was a holy symbol," Selquist explained. "Of course the Dark Queen was miffed over my stealing it. She considered it . . . sac . . . sacrilegious." He spoke the large and well-educated-sounding word proudly.

"This wand is nothing to her! Magic. Pooh!" Selquist snapped his fingers. "She wouldn't give two ghouls for it. Her son is the one who's in charge of magic, you see, and from what I've heard Nuitari is relaxed, easy-going, a fun-loving type of guy. He wouldn't go about putting curses on people just because they happened to pick up a magic wand or two that was lying about, unwanted."

The other dwarves did not appear convinced. They cast Selquist dark, sidelong glances and most edged away from him.

"You are so ignorant," Selquist continued in disparaging tones. "None of you think ahead. What happens when the draconians come after us? How are we going to fight them?" He displayed the wand. "With this."

"You said the draconians were dead," Vellmer reminded him.

"They are." Selquist had forgotten his earlier statement. It had been a trying day for him, dealing with grells, fire dragons, and his slow-thinking brethren. "What I meant was grell. There could be more in the treasure room. That's probably where the grell picked up the wand in the first place."

Vellmer considered this point, admitted it might have some merit.

"Do you know how to use that wand?" he demanded.

"Of course," said Selquist.

Vellmer appeared dubious, but he only shrugged and said, "Let's get going, then. We've got eggs to crack. And don't point that thing at me," he added, glowering back at Selquist, who had been waving the wand about experimentally.

"You don't know how to use it, do you?" Auger whispered, marching along beside his friend.

"Not really," Selquist admitted. He tucked the wand back up his sleeve. "But how hard can it be? Draconians used it, after all, and everyone knows they have all the brains of sand lizards. So just keep your mouth shut, Auger. I know what I'm doing."

Auger sighed and shook his head. He was nothing if not loyal, however, and he had faith in Selquist, so he kept quiet. The dwarves started off, Vellmer leading the way. Dwarves are resilient and not strongly imaginative, nor prone to dwell on the past. The terror and horror of the battle with the fire dragons was already starting to fade from their minds.

They were sorry for their fallen comrades, but the thought of chests filled with steel coins, with gold and silver nuggets, with rare and wondrous jewels assuaged their grief. The dead would each receive a fair share, as the dwarven dead have always shared with the living.

Selquist fingered the blue wand in his hand. "I can make it work," he said confidently. "I know I can!"

The dwarves up ahead of him came to a stop.

"What is it?" Selquist asked, pushing his way through to the front. The lead dwarves had rounded a tight bend in the shaft. Before them was a large cavern.

"This must it," Selquist said, his voice tight with excitement. "Shine the light in there!"

The dwarves had only managed to save a single torch, the rest having been tossed at the dragon. The dwarf carrying the light edged into the chamber entrance, shone the torch around. The cavern was long, shallow, and a most distinctive shape.

"Yes," said Selquist. "I'm positive this it. I recognize the shape, like a half moon! The antechamber is back there somewhere."

"Let's make sure there aren't any nasty surprises in this chamber," Mortar said. "Who's going in first?"

"Selquist!" The vote was unanimous.

"You have the wand, after all," Vellmer said in what Selquist considered a nasty tone.

"Oh, all right," Selquist grumbled. Grabbing the torch, holding it in one hand and the wand in the other, he entered the chamber.

The rest of the dwarves gathered outside to watch.

Selquist walked about the entire chamber. It was agreeably empty.

"All clear," called Selquist to his own admitted vast relief.

The dwarves swarmed inside, searched hastily around.

This chamber was very much like the other chambers through which they had passed. Discarded tools littered the floor, mined rock was piled up at one end. The iron rails entered it, but they didn't leave it. They ran straight into a solid rock wall. Not a single steel coin was on the floor, nary a jewel glittered from out the pile of rock.

"Where's the treasure?" Vellmer demanded.

"Behind that wall," said Selquist. "It's false," he added.

The dwarves regarded the wall in consternation. The wall ran the entire length of the chamber. Forty dwarves could have lined up in front of it and still not reached the end. It was built of huge chunks of rock that appeared to have been fused together by some sort of substance which had now become hard as the rock itself. The dwarves had lost all their tools, those having been handed over to the fire dragon along with their boots and weapons.

"We have tools," Selquist said, seeing eighteen pair of glowering eyes turning his direction. "Compliments of the Hylar." He pointed to a pile of discarded digging devices.

Mortar grabbed hold of a pick, only to have the head fall off the handle. "The rest of the tools aren't in much better shape," he reported.

"We don't have to break through the entire wall," Selquist said, "just a portion of it. The antechamber isn't very big. The Daewar opened up a section of this false wall that had been built by the Hylar ages ago."

Selquist recalled the notes left by the scribe. "They hid the treasure and then put a false front over it, making it look like the rest of the wall. If we can find that part, we should be able to knock the false wall in easily."

The dwarves spread out and began rapping on the wall with their knuckles, hoping to find a portion that sounded hollow. Selquist, taking the torch, began to carefully examine the wall, searching for some sort of mark or sign which might indicate that it was false. He walked the entire length of the wall and was forced to admit defeat.

"Where in the Name of Reorx is it?" Pestle demanded, frustrated.

"I don't think it's here at all," said Vellmer grimly. "I think Selquist brought us down here on a kender's errand!"

"I've found it!" called Mortar excitedly.

Selquist wiped the sweat from his brow. He never doubted himself—at least not for long—but he was certainly glad to hear those words.

Mortar knocked against the wall with the head of the broken pick. In one place, the pick thumped. In another, it rang. Their flagging energy revived, the dwarves gathered around to watch. Using the handle of the pick, Mortar scratched out an area on the rock that appeared to be the entrance to the treasure chamber.

Excited, practically able to smell the wealth, the dwarves went to work with a will. Scrounging up tools, they beat on the wall with hammers and picks. In some cases, the more enthusiastic tried to tear through the rock with their fingernails.

Chips flew. Auger knocked a hole in the wall, discovered that it was made of only a single layer of rocks.

"Stop! Wait a moment!" Selquist called. "Let me look."

The dwarves ceased their labors, backed off.

Selquist brought his torch forward. The opening was large enough for him to thrust his fist inside. He bent down, peered inside.

"Keep going! This is it!" he yelled in excitement.

The dwarves continued their work, their efforts redoubled. The hole expanded. A good hit from Mortar knocked another large piece out. The hole was now nearly wide enough for a dwarf to poke his head through.

"Wait! Let me look again!"

The hammers stopped. Selquist thrust the torch inside, peered in. The light flashed on something metallic. The torch light wavered. Selquist's hand was shaking so he nearly dropped it. Hastily, he withdrew from the hole.

"I saw it!" he said, his voice trembling. He was trembling all over. "I saw it, I tell you! Gold, steel, silver, jewels. It's all there!"

The dwarves bashed at the wall with such vigor that it crumbled beneath the blows. Sharp bits of rock flew about the chamber, inflicting minor cuts that no one noticed. Those dwarves who did not have tools hauled the rock off to one side to make room for the others to work.

"We're through!" Mortar shouted, ecstatic. He dropped the hammer. The dwarves surged forward, struggling to enter the small aperture. Selquist managed to squeeze inside first. Behind him, the other dwarves pushed and shoved.

Holding the torch high, Selquist stood still and stared. For once in his life, he was too awed and amazed, charmed and dazzled, to speak. One by one the other dwarves clambered into the room. They, too, looked around and fell silent.

They had found the stolen treasure of Neraka.

Chapter Forty-One

Kang woke to pain and silence and darkness. He could not remember exactly what had happened, but he knew that he should be dead, and he was vaguely surprised that he wasn't. He lay quite still, afraid to move, afraid to find out what was broken. His head throbbed, as did his shoulder, and he was conscious of a crushing weight on one leg. His ribs hurt abominably, every time he took a breath.

The thought came to him of the draconians with the broken backs, how they sat all day, mending leather. Kang gritted his teeth and tried to move his legs. Rock shifted and clattered to the floor. Pain shot through his left leg, but it moved, and so did the right.

Kang spent a quiet moment relaxing in relief. Then he wondered why he should be relieved. He was going to die. What difference did it make if he died a cripple or not?

Lying there, alone and hurting in the darkness, Kang faced the fact that his quest was over. He had no idea how long he'd been unconscious, but the dwarves had undoubtedly reached the treasure room by now. They had reached it and destroyed the dragon eggs.

There was nothing the draconians could have done to stop them anyhow. Not after Kang's decision to bring down part of the mountain on top of the fire dragons. He had obeyed Her Majesty's orders, he had destroyed the fire dragons. In doing so, he had doomed his race to extinction.

But he had obeyed orders, and that was a soldier's first duty.

He could see nothing in the darkness. He could not see walls or a ceiling.

Slowly, carefully, shifting his weight by increments, Kang crawled out from beneath the rock cairn that covered him. Each movement was agony, but he forced himself to go on. Feeling about with his hands, he discovered that, although he had survived the cave-in, he was now trapped in the shaft. There appeared to be no way out. He could not even remember in what direction the exit lay. He was surrounded by fallen rock and wreckage.

Buried alive. Nothing to do but wait for death, wait to die of thirst, starvation . . .

Kang shook off the despair. True, the situation appeared hopeless. He might well die, but he'd do so only after he'd done everything possible to save himself. He sat down again to give the matter logical thought. He sat down to think it over as an engineer.

The cavern's high, domed ceiling had come crashing down on top of the lava pit, which meant that much of the rock would have fallen into the pit itself. The rest of the rock would have formed a mound over the pit, rather like an enormous ant hill. The area where Kang lay—the former exit—was on the edge of the destruction. The rock and debris would not be as deep here. He should be able to find a way out.

Kang used his hands to feel about him, to gain some vague idea of the size of the area in which he was trapped and the extent of the cave-in. He began pushing aside smaller rocks, sniffing, hoping to scent fresh air, which would mean that he had discovered an adjoining tunnel or mine shaft.

Placing his hands on an enormous boulder, he gave it a heave and felt it wobble. He was tempted to shove it out of his way, but forced himself to feel all around the boulder first, to try to find why it was unstable, to capitalize on that instability. The boulder was precariously balanced on top of another. Kang levered his weight against the boulder and eased it forward. It tumbled to one side, forming an opening into a larger area. Kang rolled the boulder out of the way.

Cool air touched his face, made his snout twitch with pleasure. And
there was not only air, but light! Dusty light, dim light, but by it Kan
could now see where he was and what surrounded him.

Kang thrust his arms and shoulders into the aperture created by
removing the boulder. Crawling over crumbling, shifting rock, grunt-
ing from the pain of his damaged ribs, he climbed out of the hole. The
sharp rocks dug into his hands and knees. His left leg burned every
time he moved it. Either he had broken something, or he had a severe
bruise. But the light and the air acted on him like dwarf spirits, intoxi-
cating him and diminishing the pain.

Kang crawled out into the fire dragon's chamber, now vastly changed.

A new mountain had been formed, a mountain of boulders and
debris, a mountain within a mountain. Light filtered in from a crack
somewhere far, far above Kang. So far above him that he couldn't discover the source. He was standing on what one might consider the
new mountain's foothills.

He paused, trying to gain some sense of direction, but the chamber
had changed so dramatically that he had no idea where he was, where
the entrances and the exits had been. He might dig for days without
discovering the way out, and Kang had only days left to him before he
succumbed to thirst.

He might try to climb up the new mountain, to reach the source of
the light. He eyed the enormous jumble of boulders and fallen stalactites, piled precariously on top of each other, and abandoned that idea.
Even as he watched, one boulder fell, came bounding down the mountainside, starting a small avalanche. The mountain was far too unstable and, in his present physical condition—injured, without food or
water—he'd never make it. He was little better off than he had been,
except that at least now he wouldn't die trapped in absolute darkness.

Admitting the futility of his actions, Kang began to dig. He was
scrabbling at the rocks when he became aware that the scraping
sounds he was making couldn't account for all the scraping sounds he
was hearing.

Kang froze, a rock in his hand. The sound continued a moment, then
it stopped. A few moments later, it started again, then stopped again.

Kang grabbed hold of another rock and banged them together. Tap
tap tap, pause. Tap tap, pause. Tap.

He waited, breathless, his heart pounding, for a reply.

Nothing.

He repeated the pattern. Tap tap tap, pause. Tap tap, pause. Tap. Still nothing. His hope waned.

Kang bowed his head, ready to give up. Why fight on? Why not just lay down and die? Despair rushed in to fill hope's void.

Then, he heard a sound like metal on stone ring out from somewhere below him.

Tink tink tink, pause. Tink tink, pause. Tink.

Kang answered, pounding his two rocks together in wild exultation. The answer came back. It was his draconians! It had to be.

Pain vanished. Kang dug rapidly, frantically, dug down through the rubble. He lost track of time, only noticed vaguely that the column of light in the dust-filled chamber had shifted, was lengthening. An hour, maybe two, had passed.

Kang heaved aside a large stone. He was tired, more tired than he could ever remember feeling in his life. The pain returned with the weariness, jarred through him. It seemed he had torn every muscle, his hands were raw and bleeding, his claws broken. He was desperately thirsty and hungry enough to have started eating rock.

He kept digging. The sounds were getting closer. And then, he heard voices. His hands opened a hole.

Slith's face appeared, peering up at him. "Sir! Glad to see you! Are you all right? By the Queen, you look awful. You just rest, sir. We'll have you out in half an hour."

He was gone, but he was back again almost immediately. "It's good to see you alive, sir!"

Kang went limp. He was almost sobbing from fatigue and pain. "I can't dig any more, Slith. I just can't."

Slith barked orders behind him, then looked back worriedly to his commander. "You relax, sir. We'll have you out in no time."

Kang lay in a stupor, sprawled on the rocks. He knew he should be making plans, figuring out what to do next. They weren't out of danger by any means. They might still be buried alive beneath the mountain. He had to think . . . but the stern task master abandoned him, refused to cooperate.

"For once in your life, let someone else take charge," the task master told him.

Kang meekly obeyed, drifted off into exhausted sleep.

A yell woke him. The draconians had broken through. Slith was the first to reach him. With gentle hands, the draconians took hold of Kang, eased him carefully down into the shaft below.

Kang tried to stand, but his knees gave way. Slith helped him to a seated position on a boulder. Twelve draconians stood around him. They were covered in rock dust and blood, their scales were charred and burnt, but every one of them was grinning.

"Water!" Kang croaked.

Slith handed Kang a waterskin. He drank, paused, drank some more, then handed the skin back.

"Any orders, sir?" Slith asked. Reaching out, he attached something to Kang's harness—the commander's medallion.

Kang looked at it, shook his head. He couldn't think of a single thing to do. "No, Slith. No orders."

"Then, sir," Slith said respectfully, "might I suggest that we continue on down the tunnel? We think the treasure room's at the other end."

Kang gazed dazedly, stupidly at his second. "You're saying that . . . the tunnel leading to the treasure is . . ."

"Right here, sir. You're sitting in it. It's marked on the map, but the map shows that it was blocked off. The cave-in must have opened it up."

Kang prodded his dull brain to action. He shook his head gloomily. "Even if it does and we find the treasure, the only way out is blocked off."

"Not so, sir. The side tunnel is still open. That's where we were when the roof fell in. We dug our way through the rubble to where we figured we might find you. The route's clear. It won't be easy, but we can make it."

"You're sure it leads . . . where it's supposed to?" Kang couldn't believe it.

"I sent a couple of scouts down it, sir. They reported back that the tunnel is not only free of debris, but they heard the dwarves, making a big racket, banging and hammering. That was just a short time ago, sir."

"Hammering. That means they haven't found the antechamber yet," Kang said.

"Either that or they've found it and they're trying to break through."

Slith spread out the map. The light from the crack in the mountain above them was waning. He called for the lantern.

"Look here, sir. The treasure is located in this part of the antechamber. By the symbols, the dragon eggs are over in this part. Even if the dwarves do break through, they might be distracted by the treasure long enough—"

Kang was on his feet, hope sparking his weary, aching muscles into action.

"Let's go," he ordered.

Chapter Forty-Two

The dwarves were struck dumb. Speechless, they stared at the treasure, which was more wonderful, more radiant, more beautiful, and more valuable than any—even Selquist—had dared dream.

This was the booty of an empire. A greedy, rapacious empire.

Steel coins spilled out of partially opened chests. Rubies and emeralds, sapphires and diamonds, and myriad other precious gems, sparkling in settings that were lovely and fantastic, lay strewn about the floor, as if some clumsy lady-in-waiting had carelessly overturned her mistress's jewel box.

Armor—still bright, still polished, and obviously magical—was piled in a corner or stood silent sentinel on stands against the wall. Weapons that shone with a fey light were stacked haphazardly against a wall.

Spellbooks of innumerable colors lined another wall. Jumbled among them were magic scrolls, tied in ribbons of black, white, or red. Chests and casks, unopened, ranged about the chamber, tantalizing the dwarves with the possibility of what further treasure lay hidden from their sight.

Selquist's eyes filled with tears. He was forced to cling to Auger for support.

"By Reorx, this is beautiful!" Selquist wept.

His words freed the dwarves from the spellbound trance the sight of the treasure had cast over them.

They surged into the chamber, began rummaging around, opening lids, peering inside, exclaiming in wonder, crying out in joy. They stuffed their pockets with jewels, poured coins down their underwear, and mourned the loss of their boots, which they might have filled with even more loot.

It was at this juncture, at the height of everyone's elation, that Mortar made a devastating discovery.

"Selquist!" he shouted.

It took some time to attract Selquist's attention. He had dug his hands into a vat of steel coins, was happily letting the money trickle through his fingers, dreaming of the palatial home he was planning to build in the city of Palanthas.

"Selquist!" Mortar swatted his friend across the head.

Selquist finally turned to him. "What?" he asked in a voice tinged with dreams of avarice.

"Selquist, the tracks end," Mortar said.

"So?" Selquist didn't see the problem.

"The tracks come to a dead end!" Mortar repeated, his voice rising in panic. "This is a cul-de-sac. There's no way out!"

The last words were a shriek that echoed through the chamber. The other dwarves halted their gloating and counting and turned pale faces toward Mortar. Selquist shrugged and was about to say that they'd just go out the way they had come in, when he remembered that the way they had come in was blocked by a couple hundred tons of rock. He gulped.

A chilling thought brushed cold fingers across the back of his neck. He might well be trapped down here, trapped with no way out, trapped without food or water, trapped for eternity. It didn't take much in the way of imagination for Selquist to envision his skeletal remains draped over this chest of steel pieces.

Hastily he fished out his map. The other dwarves gathered around him, the treasure forgotten. One could not eat jewels, one could not drink gold.

Selquist searched and searched for another exit. He turned the map upside down, sideways, even flipped it over on the back, though he knew well enough there was nothing there.

"Well?" Vellmer demanded, his voice hoarse with anxiety.

Selquist swallowed again. "There . . . uh . . . doesn't seem to be any . . . well . . . any other route . . . that is, that I can find. That doesn't mean that there isn't," he concluded, trying to end on a hopeful note.

The dwarves glared at him. Several, including Vellmer, gnashed their teeth and clenched their fists.

"This isn't my fault!" Selquist protested. "If it hadn't been for those stupid draconians who caused the cave-in, we would have—" He paused. The thought of the draconians had just given him an idea.

"Say," said Auger, who'd been exploring in another part of the chamber and hadn't heard the terrible news, "I've just found a whole chest loaded with eggs. Do you think those are the dragon eggs?"

"Great," Pestle muttered. "At least we can live off those eggs for awhile. That should keep us alive for a week or two."

"They're not very fresh," said Auger.

"Of course not, you idiot!" Pestle glowered at him. "That's why we're all going to die down here!"

"Huh? Die?" Auger looked blank. "What'd I miss?"

"Only that Selquist has led us into a dead end," said Vellmer.

"And Selquist," said Selquist proudly and disdainfully, "will lead you out."

"Yeah? How?" The dwarves regarded him doubtfully.

Selquist pulled the wand out of his sleeve. "This is the very wand which the draconians used to bring down the ceiling. I will use it to tunnel through the rock."

The dwarves looked hopeful, gazed at the wand and at Selquist with new respect.

"Right," he said briskly, forestalling the question of how he was going to make the wand work. "Let's get busy. We have to catalog everything we find down here. Since we can't make use of the iron carts, we won't be able to haul all the treasure out, so we'll just have to take the most valuable objects and leave the rest until we can return with more manpower.

"While I'm busy finding the best spot to tunnel through, the rest of you determine what we take and what we leave behind."

That should keep everyone occupied for a good long while, Selquist thought. Long enough for him to figure out how to use the wand.

Already, the dwarves were practically coming to blows, arguing over whether magical steel bracers were as valuable as ordinary diamond bracelets and whether or not they should haul out the spellbooks now or leave them behind in favor of the arcane weapons.

"Show me those dragon eggs," Selquist said to Auger, and the two started off for a dark and secluded part of the antechamber. Selquist intended to get in a little wand practice.

Pleased to show off his discovery, Auger led his friend to a large chest. The latch had been broken long before the dwarves arrived, probably by the Daewar, who had never bothered to replace it. Auger pried open the lid, proudly exhibited his find. Selquist, interested in spite of himself, peered in.

Nestled in straw were ten dragon eggs, each the size of a large watermelon. The eggs were silver and gold, bronze, brass, and copper. They were smooth and perfectly shaped and would have been exquisitely lovely, if it hadn't been for the faint, sickly, greenish light that began to emanate from them the moment Selquist drew near.

"What's causing that glow?" Auger asked, alarmed.

"Probably the spell that the black-robed mages and dark clerics cast over them," Selquist said. He was equally alarmed but trying not to show it. "I think you should shut the lid."

"I think so, too," Auger said and reached out a tentative hand. His arm appeared to have difficulty obeying, however, for his fingers wouldn't even come close.

"I can't, Selquist," he cried in a strangled voice. "Help! I can't move my arm!"

Selquist grabbed hold of his friend's arm, forced it down, and dragged Auger away from the chest and into a dark corner.

"Forget that," he said. "Let Vellmer deal with it. He's the one who wants to break the eggs. You and I have to figure out how this wand works."

"I thought you said it was going to be easy," Auger pointed out. "Even draconians with lizard brains used it, you said."

"Maybe I should just hand it to you, then, lizard-brain," Selquist retorted. He was beginning to be in a bad mood. "I'm certain I can use it. I just have to practice a bit, that's all."

Selquist thought back to the fire dragon pit, recalled the draconian using the wand, casting the spell. Selquist tried to remember every motion, every gesture, every word. Unfortunately the words had been in draconian, and Selquist hadn't been able to hear them all that clearly, what with the screaming and blasting and shouting. The only words he was certain of had to do with Queen Takhisis

Selquist aimed the wand at a likely looking portion of solid rock wall and intoned, "By the grace of Her Dark Majesty."

"I don't think you should say bad things like that," Auger protested, edging back away from the wand. "Something dreadful might happen to you!"

"Something dreadful has happened to me. I'm trapped in a cave with maybe more wealth than even I'll be able to spend, with no way out," Selquist muttered, but he didn't say it loud enough for Auger to hear.

He stared at the wand expectantly.

Nothing happened. The wand's five dragons, their five tails twined around the bottom, their five mouths gaping open, made no sound, shone with no blue light. They looked—Selquist thought irritably—incredibly stupid.

"Come on, Dark Queen! listen up!" he commanded, and gave the wand a shake.

Auger gasped and covered his eyes so that he might be spared the sight of Selquist being instantly toasted, flayed, skinned, disemboweled, quartered, and changed into a wraith.

This did not happen. Nor did the wand work.

"Well?" came a grating voice.

Selquist turned to discover Vellmer and the rest of the dwarves gathered behind him. They were all, Selquist noticed, now heavily armed, having outfitted themselves with the magical weapons.

"Just give me a moment, will you?" Selquist said coldly. "I'm getting a feel for it."

Vellmer glowered. "Oh, yeah? Well, while you're getting the feel of that wand, I'm going to bust up these eggs." He shook his finger in Selquist's face. "You better be ready to get us out of here by the time I'm done."

"I will be," Selquist said.

Vellmer stalked over to the chest, his sword in hand. He came to an abrupt halt, however; he appeared considerably taken aback at the sight of the eerie green light that was growing brighter, casting a horrid glow over anyone who came near it. The soldier dwarves accompanying him took one look and left hurriedly for the outer part of the chamber. Vellmer held his ground, and he even attempted to bring the sword close to the eggs.

Sweat broke out on his face, his arm wavered in the air. "I . . . can't . . ."

he said through clenched teeth.

Any other time, Selquist must have been entertained by this sight, but now his mind was on higher matters. Such as staying alive.

Selquist turned away from Vellmer, turned from Auger, turned his face away from the light. Facing the deepest, darkest part of the antechamber, Selquist pointed the wand, concentrated all this thoughts, invoked the Dark Queen, promised her his soul and anything else she might like, including a ten percent portion of his take, and cried desperately, "In the name of Her Majesty, Takhisis, Queen of Darkness, I command thee to blast this rock to smithereens!"

Selquist poured every ounce of will and energy and strength and hope and wishing into the wand. His hand shook with the effort of his exertion. The wand trembled, but that was only because his fingers were trembling. It did not respond.

Rage filled Selquist. He had made the discovery of a lifetime, of six lifetimes, he had more wealth than he could have ever hoped to gain in six lifetimes. He had money enough to build a castle in Palanthas, if he wanted, and live like a king, with gully dwarf slaves and dwarf maidens fawning over him and humans bowing respectfully and calling him "Lord Selquist," and he was going to die down here in this stupid chamber and all because this infernal wand wouldn't work.

"Well, what about it?" Vellmer demanded in nasty tones. He had apparently abandoned—at least for the time being—the idea of breaking the eggs. Now he was back to hounding Selquist. "Got that wand of yours working yet?"

"No!" Selquist screamed in fury. "Why don't you give it a try?"

Whipping about, Selquist flung the wand straight at Vellmer's head.

Instinctively, Vellmer ducked. The wand sailed over his head and struck the chest containing the dragon eggs.

Blue light flashed. Green light flared horribly.

An explosion rocked the chamber.

Vellmer flew through the air, crashed into the wall. Auger was blown backward into Selquist, who fell to the floor.

The green light shone brighter and brighter. The dwarves couldn't bare to look at it. They squeezed shut their eyelids, covered their eyes with their hands, and they could still see the terrible light. Tears streamed down into their beards. They roared with the pain.

And then the light was gone, replaced by a darkness that was blessed, at first, and then didn't seem quite so blessed when they discovered that they were all effectively blind. Their torch had gone out.

From the darkness came a strange sound.

Mortar gasped, breathless. "What's that noise?"

"It sounds like eggs cracking," said Auger helpfully.

Chapter Forty-Three

Realizing the implications of what he'd just said, Auger promptly screamed.

"Light, we need light!" Selquist ordered, picking himself up off the floor.

He heard sounds of furious scrabbling and scraping, groping around in the darkness for the torch, then the sounds of nervous hands trying to strike flint and failing. Then a spark, and the single torch sputtered with flame.

The dwarves moved as one toward the chest, saw that their worst fears were being realized.

Every single egg had spidery cracks running through it.

The dwarves watched in shock, unable to move, as the first egg—a gold—split wide open. A tiny lizard-like head thrust up from the shell, struggling to emerge. It opened its mouth and squeaked. Rows of razor-sharp white teeth glistened. Other heads poked up beside it.

305

"Blessed Reorx, save us!" Mortar intoned.

"Reorx nothing," cried Vellmer. He was somewhat singed and considerably bruised from his involuntary flight into the wall, but he was up and moving. "We have to save ourselves. Kill those vermin spawn, men. Kill them now! Quickly! They'll be looking for food, and we're it!"

The dwarves gripped their swords and advanced on the chest.

The eggs hatched. The dwarves couldn't count them all, but there must have been a hundred tiny draconians trying to stand on wobbly legs, their tiny wings, still wet, clinging to their backs. At the sight of the dwarves, the draconians opened their mouths, begging for food. The spell which had protected them all these years was broken. They were helpless, vulnerable as any other newborn.

The dwarves lifted their weapons.

"Freeze!" came a deep, grating voice from the behind them. "Don't move a muscle. The first dwarf who so much as twitches is a dead dwarf."

The dwarves halted, weapons wavering in their hands. They looked back over their shoulders.

Fifteen draconians stood at the entrance to the chamber. Each draconian held a sword in his hand.

"Back off," said the big draconian, who appeared to be their leader.

Vellmer snarled in anger, ready to defy them. He faced around, his sword in his hand, holding the sword above the hatchlings.

"Do your damndest, draco! We're trapped down here, we're dead dwarves anyway! But I'll see you fiends dead at least!"

"You're not trapped," was the unexpected reply. "Throw down your weapons. Back away from the chest. Leave the hatchlings to us, and we'll show you the way out."

"Stop! Vellmer! You fool!" Selquist hurled himself at the dwarf. Grabbing hold of Vellmer's sword arm, Selquist wrestled the weapon out of his hand. "Did you hear what they said? They'll show us the way out!"

Slowly, the other dwarves lowered their weapons. Reluctantly, they turned to face their longtime foes.

"How can we trust you?" Vellmer asked the big draconian.

"Trust them, trust them!" Selquist whispered in his ear.

Vellmer ignored him. "We give up our weapons, and you just kill us all, feed us to your evil spawn."

"My name is Kang," said the draconian. "I command the First

Engineer Regiment. We are tired of killing. We want only to take these, the children of our race, and live in peace. I give you my word."

Vellmer sneered. "You'll live in peace all right. You'll live in peace until these lizard-women grow up and you mate with them, and then there'll be more of you lizard creatures and you'll overrun the valley. And what will happen to us then? What will happen to our people?"

The other dwarves mumbled low-voiced agreement.

"It would be better for our people if we all died down here," Vellmer said grimly. "Every one of us, rather than see that terrible day come about. And, Master Kang, if you're as honest as you claim, you can't tell me it wouldn't."

The big draconian was silent, thoughtful. The dwarves were grimly silent, ready to fulfill their leader's promise and die. The other draconians were silent, ready to kill the dwarves, if ordered. All that could be heard was the squeaking and chirping of the hungry hatchlings.

"You are right, dwarf," said Kang, his voice heavy. "I couldn't guarantee that what you have said will not come to pass. I know my people. By nature we are ruthless and aggressive. We would want to expand and you would be in our way." He lifted his sword, took a step forward.

The other draconians crowded behind him.

Vellmer started to edge near the hatchlings. He could probably kill a great many before the draconians jumped him.

Selquist saw all his hopes, his dreams, his castle in Palanthas, crashing down around him. He made one last desperate attempt.

"You could move!" He blurted out the first thought that occurred to him.

Kang halted, gazed at him. "What did you say?"

"You could move out of the valley!" Selquist repeated. The idea suddenly seemed a good one. Not surprising, since he'd thought of it. "Yes, move! Somewhere. Anywhere. North, maybe?"

Another draconian, standing behind Kang, said, "That's an idea, sir. What with the war going on, amid all the confusion, we could slip away northward through the mountains without anyone finding us."

"There's lots of prime real estate available, especially around Neraka. Abandoned cities, just waiting for some enterprising person— such as yourself—to walk in and lay claim to them. Urban renewal programs. Maybe you could get a grant! You could expand all you liked! Well, is it a deal?" Selquist asked eagerly.

Kang considered, then said, "Yes, it is a deal."

"Vellmer?" Selquist asked.

Vellmer wrestled with the concept a moment, then said grudgingly, "If they'll agree to move out of the valley, it's a deal."

The dwarves lowered their weapons, stepped back away from the chest. The draconians lowered their weapons, stepped away from the dwarves.

Selquist, who had been holding his breath until he had nearly turned blue, was able to breathe again.

Kang walked over, bent to look at the newly born draconians. Cupping his hand, he carefully lifted one from its nest. Bits of eggshell clung to the baby. The little beast squirmed in his hands and opened her mouth to be fed. He gently put the female back into the chest with her sisters.

"The fire dragons are destroyed," Kang said. "Our Queen willing, this means that the heroes will be able to defeat Chaos, and the world will be safe. For the first time in our history, there is hope for our race. When we die, there will be young to take our place. Now that we have a future, we can begin to take joy in the present."

Other draconians came up behind their leader. Reaching down, they picked up the tiny hatchlings. The babies nestled against the adult draconians, seeking their warmth.

"Look, sir," said one. "I think she likes me already!"

The big draconian nodded, too choked with emotion to speak.

Even the dwarves were touched, it seemed. They shuffled their feet and looked askance at each, gruffly pretending that they didn't care, but all the while watching with smiles which they were careful to hide in their beards. The draconians hadn't been bad neighbors. Not really. And they'd be much better neighbors a few hundred miles away.

The draconians, gently and with great fondness, tucked the babies back into their nest of straw.

Kang gave orders for the disposition of the chest. Two of the draconians hefted it.

"Prepare to move out," Kang said. "You dwarves can follow us."

Vellmer stood scratching his beard, looking somewhat embarrassed. He then said, abruptly, "I'm sorry about burning down your village."

"You are?" Kang was surprised.

"Yes," continued the brew master. "And if, in the future, you ever need any dwarf spirits . . . well . . . just let me know, and I'll make you a fair price."

"Thank you for the offer, sir," said Kang gravely, "but we have new responsibilities now. I don't think we'll be needing any more dwarf spirits. If we do, however," he hastened to add, not to be outdone in politeness, "we know that yours are the best, and we'll be sure to trade with you."

Vellmer flushed, pleased with the compliment.

"The secret's in the mushrooms," he told Kang, as they walked together out of the treasure chamber. "You've got to pick them at midnight. And then you . . ."

He continued on down the passageway, accompanying the draconian, enlightening Kang on the fine art of distillation.

The rest of the dwarves packed up, prepared to leave, carrying as much treasure as they could possibly manage and then some. Pestle could barely move; he jingled when he walked. Auger, draped all over in precious gems, was endeavoring to decide which valuable necklace to give to which girlfriend. All of them were nearly bent double with the load, except Selquist.

"Auger?" he began. "Would you give me a hand—"

"No," said Auger. "You can carry your own this time."

"Pestle," Selquist tried his other friend. "It's not much—"

"Absolutely not. I've got all I can manage."

"Mortar. It's my back. I think I wrenched it—"

"Pooh!" Mortar said and walked off.

Selquist stood in deep thought for a moment, then approached a draconian.

"What's your name? Gloth? Well, Gloth, you're a big strapping draco, aren't you? I bet you could pick up that chest of steel coins without any effort whatsoever and probably carry it all the way to Palanthas without ever feeling the strain. Now, I happen to know of this abandoned city that would be perfect for you and your new little brood. It's southwest of Nordmaar. You carry that chest for me and I'll tell you how to get there.

"You see," Selquist continued, "I have this map . . ."